PAUL E. HORSMAN

THE SHADOW OF THE REVENAUNT

VAVAUN

For information contact; www.paulhorsman-author.com

Cover design by Ravven
Edit by: Kira Tregoning

A Red Rune fantasy book

Paul E. Horsman's books:

Zilverspoor Uitgeverij (Dutch Editions):

Rhidauna – De Schaduw van de Revenaunt #1
Zihaen – De Schaduw van de Revenaunt #2
Ordelanden – De Schaduw van de Revenaunt #3

Red Rune Books (Dutch Editions)

De Shardheld Sage

Red Rune Books (English Editions):

Lioness of Kell
The Road to Kalbakar – Wyrms of Pasandir #1 (Fall 2016)

Shardfall – The Shardheld Saga #1
Runemaster – The Shardheld Saga #2
Shardheld – The Shardheld Saga #3
The Shardheld Saga trilogy

Rhidauna – The Shadow of the Revenaunt #1 (Revised 2nd Edition)
Zihaen – The Shadow of the Revenaunt #2 (Revised 2nd Edition)
Ordelanden – The Shadow of the Revenaunt #3 (Rewritten 2nd Edition)
Vavaun – The Shadow of the Revenaunt

CONCERNING VAVAUN

This story is part of the Shadow of the Revenaunt-series.
It tells the story of Damion Luyon-DeAsharte and Uwella
DeGry, the two beastmaster companions of King Ghyll on
his quest in the first two books.
Chronologically, it runs parallel to the events in #3
Ordelanden, starting shortly after the king and his friends
return home triumphant from *Zihaen* at the end of the #2.

CONTENTS

FOUL PLANS

The large estate slumbered in the glow of the late sun. A gentle breeze made the palm trees along the adjacent lakeshore rustle and the pink ibises on their long legs stood motionless in worship of the light.

An old man with curly white hair reclined on an embroidered sofa and stared out over the blue water.

To the side, a servant in a long robe waited patiently for his master's attention.

In the distance, the song of a lyrebird came over the lake. Ten beauty-filled minutes passed until the last note had died away. Only then the old man raised a hand. The servant bowed and whispered, 'The Practicus Syvvan is here, sire.'

The old man gave a vague nod. 'Bring him to me.'

Moments later, a stocky man in the gray robe of a priest of Arikal approached. He, too, bowed and waited.

'Syvvan,' the old man said, and his voice sounded like the whispering of the palm trees. He motioned with his hand to a leather pouf across from him.

'My lord M.' The man bowed again and sat carefully down on the wobbly cushion.

Unobtrusive as a shadow, the servant reappeared with a ceremonial cawah pot and two small porcelain bowls. He poured out and retired without a sound.

'You bring news?' The old man inhaled the spicy scent of the cawah and over the rim of his bowl his quiet eyes inspected the visitor.

'We are ready, my lord. Once you give the order, we can begin.'

'Details?'

The stocky man folded his hands in his lap and spoke of treason and bloody murders.

Across from him, the old man called M. sipped his hot cawah with closed eyes and listened. When Syvvan finished and sat waiting, he nodded. 'Do it.'

His visitor put the cup down and stood up. 'As you command, sire.' As quietly as he had come, he bowed himself from the old man's presence.

The old man turned his gaze back to the lake and his own visions.

CHAPTER 1 – CALLED HOME

'Wella! Help, Adalien... Come quickly!'

A faint voice echoed in Uwella's mind, killing her sleep. She lifted her sleek silvery head and stared at her mate.

'What's that?' Damion said sleepily.

Uwella shook off the cover of dry leaves and rose to her forepaws. Her whole, supple mountain lion's body was tense, on high alert. 'The kerran Adalien called me. There must be something wrong.'

Damion yawned, showing two rows of razor-sharp incisors. 'Your home? Who was it?'

'I don't know.' Uwella felt a wave of angry frustration. 'It was a woman's voice, but I didn't recognize her. She called me Wella. Only my siblings and a few of my oldest friends still use that darned pet name.'

'Strange,' Damion said. 'Someone who has known you from the cradle calls you home, even though we're six hundred miles away?' He rose, his massive black-and-white tiger bulk brushing aside the bushes as he padded into the open. 'You're sure you didn't dream it?'

'Of course I'm sure,' Uwella snarled. 'You caught it too, didn't you? We're going home.'

Damion's whiskers twitched. 'I caught the echo from your mind, love,' he said calmly. 'But I agree it was far too vivid for a dream. Only, what could threaten a whole settlement full of powerful wikken and their high priestess?'

Uwella thought of her home, the kerran Adalien, main center of the Gray Order of Arikal she'd been part of for six years, and a vague fear came over her. She didn't answer, but listened to the forest around them; the talking birds, the smell of the earth, and the great oak rising over them. Here, no danger threatened. Not here.

'They need me,' she said. 'We were going to see Archodea anyhow. We'll go to the kerran and if anything is wrong, she'll tell us.' *Perhaps,* she added mentally. *As the high priestess, Archodea doesn't confide readily. We'll probably have to twist her arm a bit.*

Damion growled; a deep, soul-shattering sound that always delighted her with its strength.

'All right,' he said. 'If we hurry we'll make the temple portal in Jenetrazt before dawn. A teleport to Din-Werdzom and from there you can guide me to Adalien.'

For a moment she thought of the buck they'd killed yesterday. A pity to let all that fresh meat go to waste. Ah well, they could always have a snack rabbit along the way.

'Let's go,' she said.

Without another word, the two beastmasters loped off, mountain lion and tiger. They spurned the main road and ran across country, careful not to stampede the herds of Terekander horses they met.

'All those endless grasslands; it's almost like we're back on the steppes of Zihaen,' Damion said as they swam across another small river.

Uwella grunted. 'Good hunting country. Plenty of deer.'

They skirted a large field of sprouting grains, startling a prowling farm cat.

'Peace, sister,' Damion said politely.

The cat huffed. 'Get off my land. You're scaring my mice away.'

Damion chuckled at the little feline's cheek. 'Just passin' through.'

Then they reached the outskirts of Jenetrazt, a walled collection of stone and half-timbered buildings centered on a massive bell tower. Under cover of a large willow, they changed into their human forms and walked through the unmanned gates into town.

In their own bodies, there was nothing catlike about them. Uwella deGry was a wikke, a member of the Gray Order of Arikal, God of True Chaos and Renewal, and it showed in her attire. Her face was painted white and her somewhat stout

9

body was clad in a voluminous gray dress with lace frills, and a mass of black feathers worked into her hair down to her shoulders. She had the short temper and imperious carriage befitting her birthright as the heir to House Gry and the ducal thrones of Vavaun. Beside her, Damion DeAsharte was a plain young man of average height, dressed in simple leather traveling garb. He, too, was an heir; his House Asharte had for nearly a century been the competitor and mortal enemy of House Gry. Now the two heirs were mates, planning to wed and reunite their country.

Uwella sneezed. As a cat, stench didn't bother her, but the moment she returned in her own form, she was assailed by the many smells of humanity wafting from the town's hearth fires, the privies at the back of the houses, and the tannery near the river.

'Nobody about, while it is way past sunup,' Damion said. 'I'm not familiar with Terekander, but for traders and horse farmers, these folks aren't very active.'

'We're in old Prince Kadory's domain,' Uwella said. 'He's sunk to being a lesser merchant prince because he's a fat slob who would've gone under long ago if he weren't so filthily rich. All his towns reflect his personality. They're somnolent, complacent and narrow-minded. Never buy a horse from them if you want to get anywhere.'

They walked through the hushed town until they came to a square building with a red-shingled roof. The faded mural of a woman amid a field of grain proclaimed it the temple of Asphata Farmgoddess.

Uwella put a hand to the door. 'Locked!' she said. 'Even the priests are still asleep. Probably no one ever uses the portal here. Stand by, I'll try to wake them up.' She pounded the door with the hilt of her hunting knife until a sleep-tousled lad came around the building.

The boy muttered something in a heavy dialect, but then changed into a labored common tongue. 'Temple's not open. Come back at a decent time.'

'It's past six; the sun is up,' Uwella said sternly. 'My lord and I need a port, so be a good fellow and serve us.'

The boy looked them up and down. 'It's a port ya need, mistress? And where-to you wanna go?'

'Din Werdzom. I suppose your portal reaches that far?'

'O-ay,' the boy said doubtfully. 'Guess it does. Ne'er ported thataway, but I got the coords.' He lifted a shoulder in what could be an invitation to follow him and slouched to the back of the temple.

The portal was a big, barnlike structure of which part was used as a hencoop. As they entered, the rooster crowed loudly and the boy chucked a stone at its head. The bird clucked angrily as it ran away.

'There's not much call for your trade?' Uwella said haughtily, looking at the clutter everywhere.

'Nah,' the boy spat into the dirt. 'Who'd wanna go sumwhere? We live 'ere, don' we?'

'We don't,' Uwella said.

The boy showed them his back and muttered something about silly foreigners. 'Make 'aste,' he said. 'Step into the circle; I ain't got all morning.' Then, with a sigh of weariness, he ported them away.

They came out in a building in a field on the edge of a forest. In the distance was a river, and the early morning fog lay low over the land. It was chilly, silent, and desolate.

Uwella stared around at the wild woods, the mountains, the distant river. Din Werdzom was a town on a high mountain plateau, a retreat for several Orders which housed their elderly and sick who benefited from the thin air. This was most definitely someplace else.

'That dolt got it all wrong!' she snapped, stiffening. 'Where did he send us to?'

'Don't worry,' a voice said. A stout priest of Dragos came hurrying, holding up his white robe to his knees as he walked through the wet grass. 'Welcome in Underdin. It's all right;

we recently moved the portal hub from up-there to down-here. There were too many complaints from those elderly souls in the Din about the increase in traffic, you see. At the moment, we're just the portal, the inn, and the river landing, but before long you'll find a real village here.'

'Ah,' Uwella said, relaxing a little. 'We're in a hurry and that bumpkin boy in Terekander didn't impress me.'

'Some of those rascals don't,' the priest said diplomatically. 'But every portal acolyte will have been thoroughly tested; you need not worry.' He smiled. 'Are you passing through?'

'We're for Adalien,' Uwella said.

The priest spread his hands. 'I'm afraid I cannot help you there. At least not yet. I do believe they got themselves a portal acolyte recently, but I haven't received any working coords yet.'

'We'll walk,' Damion said. 'We are beastmasters; the forest isn't an obstacle to us.'

'How exciting.' The man smiled, while his hands fluttered like butterflies. 'Sometimes I envy people like you their roaming lives. As a portal priest I hear of so many wonderful places, but I fear they will always remain a dream. A pity, but my responsibilities are here.'

'Indeed, a pity,' Uwella said politely.

'And he wouldn't leave the security of his portal for a thousand gold crowns,' she said a moment later, as they ran into the forest in their cat-forms.

'Let him dream,' Damion said. 'Reality will never be as beautiful as one's imagination.' His massive black-and-white frame crashed through a tangled mass of flowering creepers without losing speed. 'Take the lead; you know the way. To me all the Gisterwoud looks the same.'

'You're not attuned to the kerran,' she said. 'Follow then; I'll teach you.'

The two cats made good speed. For most of the way they ran along the edges of Nature's plane, the realm of the gods of nature outside the regular world, where all is teeming with life, unchecked. That way, where time flows differently, they turned days of travel into mere hours and it was a little past noon when Uwella slowed down into the human world.

'We're nearly there,' she said. 'I hope...' She broke off as her nose caught the pungent smell of cold fires.

Damion lifted his big head and the hairs on his striped body bristled. 'I smell trouble.'

'Yes.' Uwella put her nails into a centuries-old oak tree and quickly climbed up. 'I can see the top of Adalien's palisade,' she called. Then her human senses translated the cat's vision. 'Smoke! Something's wrong there!' She leaped down without another word and hurried off, with Damion close behind her.

Ten minutes later, they reached the settlement's palisade. Uwella broke through the shrubbery surrounding the wall and came to an abrupt halt. She crouched, tail swishing, her whole body ablaze with anger.

'Curse them all!' Her cat's voice turned into an anguished shriek as she stared at what had been her home.

At her side, Damion stood frozen, his ears laid back, pupils dilated, and his lips curled in a snarl.

CHAPTER 2 – TREASON

Adalien's gates gaped wide open. There was no guard, or anyone else living; only a terrible silence. Inside, the kerran was in chaos. Every building had been wrecked, their contents lay strewn about, among the dead. One cabin was a smoldering ruin and the source of the stench which had first alerted them.

'Arikal!' Uwella said, and her cat's voice changed into a scream. 'My God, where were you when they did this?' Her body shimmered as she changed into her human form. *Not you,* she gestured, as Damion made to do the same. *Cover me.*

With the tiger on her heels, she went from body to body. Every dead face she touched was a friend, to be met with anguish, and a touch of painful relief that the broken and despoiled one was not her brother.

Nothing moved inside the palisade and eventually Damion, too, changed.

'Ten bodies, no more.' Uwella gripped her mate's shoulders, her fingers digging into his muscles. 'Where is Rhydd? Where are the others? How could this happen? This place was so safe.'

'Was it?' Damion said softly. 'Unless the rumors were true.'

Uwella didn't listen. She let go of him and wildly turned around. 'Have they escaped?'

'Archodea's not here either.' Damion stared around narrow-eyed and took in the ravage. 'Ten dead wikken; all of them very old. That should tell us something.' Then he stiffened. 'What's that?'

'What?'

'I thought I saw a flash coming from that hut.'

Uwella frowned. 'There never was a hut; that's where the toolshed stood.' She hurried over.

'Careful!' Damion said, gripping her arm. 'Look at those scorch marks everywhere. Someone's been using fire spells recently.' Then he stopped. 'That hut – It's a pavilion; a teleport-platform. So that priest at Underdin was right, your people *were* starting their own portal.'

'Wait!' Uwella said, shaking off his arm. 'Listen.'

Inside the pavilion, a defiant girl was talking. 'Scared, pig? You'll die. I'll fry you like the others. Why don't you come closer? COME CLOSER, BEAST!'

Damion looked at Uwella. 'Who...?' Then he nearly gasped as the monster stepped from the shadows. It was built like a large human male with a pig's head, heavily muscled under its bristly pelt, and moving swiftly on its hind hooves. Its hands gripped an ax and from its tusked mouth dripped a white thread of spittle. Its small reddish eyes didn't see the beastmasters; the pigman's whole attention was fixed on the one inside the pavilion.

'DeMannau's pig,' Damion whispered, feeling raw fear claw at his innards. He knew it wasn't the same one; Olle had killed that monster just as he had killed its cruel mistress DeMannau herself. Only the fear he felt was the same.

The pigman stood there, swinging its head to and fro as it tried to see its enemy. Then it charged.

The sharp thwack of a bow pierced the beast's raging bellow. A flaming arrow shot from the portal and the pig's challenge turned into a high squeal of agony, then cut off abruptly. The beast stumbled backwards with a tall feather of fire sprouting from its chest, spewing blood and foamy spittle as it died.

'There!' the girl in the pavilion yelled. 'Take that, fool pig!'

'I know that voice,' Uwella said, surprised. She walked toward the pavilion. 'Grisa? It's me, Uwella DeGry.'

'Trickery!' the girl cried. 'Uwella isn't here. You're a traitor, whoever you are. I'll kill you too, you lying coward!'

'It's really me, girl,' Uwella said. Grisa, Marshal DeKramm's daughter. She hadn't seen the girl for several years, but when they were small they'd always been together. Grisa, her twin brother Bartram, and she. Three wild kids; though the DeKramms were several years younger, they'd been the most dauntless playmates a girl could wish for. 'Remember that basket of pears?'

'Pears? I... No, you're lying! It must be a trick. Uwella can't be here. Show me your face,' the girl said sharply. 'Quickly, before I burn you to the ground.'

'Hold your fire, girl; here I am.' Uwella walked to the pavilion. 'See? It is me.'

'Uwella!' A slim girl rushed from the shadows, her face and gray-clad body caked with mud. She had a mass of tangled curls bobbing around a sharp face, full of anger and a hint of fear. In her hand she carried a strangely recurved bow and a handful of flames. As she ran, her fire spell died and her arrows turned back into plain iron.

Uwella held out her arms and as she embraced the girl, said the first thing that came into her mind. 'Grisa, dear, been tomcatting again?'

'Oh gods, it really is you!' The girl hugged Uwella. 'No one else knows about the pears we stole, and how the seneschal used to scold me about my boyish ways. I... We must be quick! That traitor got Bartram. She'll hurt him!'

'Who has got who?' Damion stepped forward

The girl clearly hadn't seen him, for she jumped and cried out.

'Peace! Damion is my mate,' Uwella said quickly. 'Bartram is her brother. Who got him?'

The girl gripped Uwella's shoulders. 'Curly,' she said, and there was so much contempt in her voice that it shocked even Uwella. 'That offal-faced traitoress knocked him out with a spell and dragged him into Archodea's cabin.'

Uwella stared at the girl. Curly was a thickset older woman who worked as a copyist, transcribing old tomes. 'But she is one of us.'

Grisa shook her head vehemently. 'She's not! The lying she-rat betrayed us, just as Syvvan and the others did.'

Syvvan? For a moment, Uwella was speechless.

'So the rumors were true,' Damion said slowly. 'The Dar'khamorth has wormed their way into the Order.'

Uwella let out a piercing scream of rage. 'Syvvan! He's been a wikke for so long. I didn't like him, but I never doubted his loyalty. Traitors; now who can we trust?'

'We'll find out,' Damion said firmly. 'First this Curly. Where is she? Is she alone, or are there any more pigmen around?'

Grisa shook her head. 'She holed up in Archodea's cabin. No pigmen; I just killed the last one.' She looked at her balled fists. 'I was going after her; tear her guts from her fat body.'

'I believe you would,' Damion said. 'But it's my turn now. You will stay here with Uwella. If I remember rightly, Archodea's cabin is the one with the porch?'

'Yes,' Uwella said, cautiously. 'What are you going to do?'

'She'll not expect a tiger in the room,' Damion said grimly.

'But...' Uwella saw him go tiger and lope off. 'Damn, I wanted to go.'

'Bartram is doing that all the time,' Grisa said. 'I hate it!'

The high wikke's home was a small, windowless hut in the center of the residential area, built of the same logs as the other dwellings, yet set apart by its exquisite hand-carved decorations. Its single door was closed, but the destruction of the temple next to it had blown away part of the cabin's roof.

Damion softly meowed in satisfaction. Effortlessly, he leaped up and padded to the hole. He peered over the edge into the shambles of a once neat room and almost grinned. Below him a stout woman of indeterminable age stood over the bound body of a boy stretched out on Archodea's bed. The lad was big for his age, strongly built, with a fine mane of blond curls. His freckled face was red, but he looked defiant, not scared at being bound by throngs and a silver chain. Silver, so the woman was aware of the boy's magic and used the metal's innate ability to block his use of mana.

The woman touched his shoulders, his chest and his muscular arms in a strange, jerky way, muttering in a singsong voice. 'I got ya, I got ya. I'll slit ya gizzard, boil ya feet. I'll enjoin yer ears to meet. Now you'll lie and don't ya stir while I go back to catch the girl.' She grinned and caressed the boy's cheek. 'I know, I know, my rhymes are bad, but I love them, so don't be mad.'

The boy wrestled for a moment, but the ropes were tight and he had to give up. He lifted up his muffled head and suddenly he saw Damion. A look of shock passed over the visible part of his face and the woman chuckled.

'So you're afraid after all, honey?' she said, patting his face. 'Very wise of you.' She stepped back. 'I'll be right back with young Grisa. Then I'll go get some more pigmen and sit back to enjoy them feeding. They so love live meat, you know.' She straightened and her voice became businesslike. 'Soon the Master will return. Then all the world dies and the universe will be born again. In the meantime, I amuse myself a little. Nothing else matters much, now does it?'

Damion growled. *Let's see about that!*

Curly looked up at the sound and her face changed into a mask of pure terror. Her hands started a frantic spell, but then the tiger jumped down, burying his claws into her chest and breaking both the spell and her neck. Curly screamed once, briefly, and went limp. For a moment, Damion remained poised over her dead body and snarled. Then he shook a paw in disgust and turned to stare at the boy on the bed. The boy looked back, without fear, but with a strange mixture of hope and uncertainty.

Quickly Damion changed into his human self. 'Tut, tut; still a-bed at this time of the day? Lazybones.' He pulled out his knife and cut away the cloth gagging the lad.

With his mouth free, the boy inhaled deeply in and out. 'I knew it,' he said hoarsely. 'You couldn't be a real tiger.' Then he looked at Damion sawing away at the thongs around his arms and legs. 'Who are you? You're not a wikke.'

'I'll tell you later,' Damion said. 'You are Bartram DeKramm?'

The boy started. 'How...? Nah; you must have met my sister.' He flexed his freed arms and bit back a groan. 'Thank you. Yes, I am Bartram. Happy to meet you.'

'My pleasure,' Damion said. 'Your sister waits at the portal with my mate. Can you walk?'

Bartram swung his legs over the edge and stood. He gritted his teeth. 'Yes.'

'Excellent. Let's rejoin the ladies.'

The boy looked around. 'My sword. The bitch dropped it here somewhere.' He swayed slightly. 'Oops.'

'Don't turn around too fast.' Damion grinned. 'That pretty poet scrambled your brains with her art.'

'Pretty poet! Those horrible rhymes?'

Steadying himself on the edge of the bed, Bartram peered underneath and pulled forth a plain but serviceable sword. 'Got it,' he said, and checked the edge before sheathing it.

Damion turned to the door. 'Let's go. Your sister sounded a little nervous about you.'

Bartram relaxed. 'She would.' Suddenly he blurted, 'That woman was crazy. I knew her; she always was, well, polite. Not nice, but soft-spoken. Now she had changed! That's horrible. Someone you knew. She must be insane.'

'I'm sure she was,' Damion said.

Bartram looked at him. 'Did you know her?'

'No, but I've met a lot of her brothers and sisters. They're all raving lunatics.'

'She wasn't really a Gray, was she?' the boy said. 'She must've been pretending.'

'I know.' *It's what we were afraid of. All the rumors were true; the Gray Order has been compromised.*

'You do? Then what was she?'

Damion grinned at the boy. *He's got an inquisitive mind. That's good. The world needs warriors with brains.* 'Wait till we've rejoined the girls,' he said. 'That beats telling it twice.'

'All right.' Bartram closed his mouth and in silence they walked back to the portal.

When she saw them coming, Grisa scowled and ran to meet her brother. She gripped his arms and looked him up and down.

'You're back,' she said, taking a deep breath. 'Blockhead!' She still sounded massively angry.

'Yes,' Bartram patted her shoulder. 'It's all right.'

'Did she... hurt you?'

'Nah. She was going to, though. Wanted to feed us to her pigs. She...' Unexpectedly, he began to shake and Grisa put her arms as far around him as she could reach. She peered at Damion past the boy's shoulder. 'Did you kill Curly?'

'So he did,' her brother said, muffled. 'And how! I seen Uwella turn into that mountain lion of hers, but this beast was twice as big! He broke that she-dog's neck just like that.' He stepped from Grisa's embrace and glanced at Damion. 'Now tell me your name.'

Grisa gripped his wrist. 'He's Asharte!'

Bartram froze. 'What!'

Damion bowed. 'She's right. I'm Damion, Valvodjar of Asharte. The war is over, my friend. You and I, we are both Vavauners. The enemy is that woman I killed. And all those others I mentioned.'

The boy's face worked. 'Asharte,' he said. Then he faced Damion squarely. 'I am Bartram DeKramm, son of the Marshal of Vavaun and a loyal follower of Gry. We are foes.'

'He just said you weren't.' Uwella put her hands onto her sides. 'We, the valvodjars of the two Great Houses, declare peace with each other's dynasty,' she intoned. Then she kissed Damion. 'There; done. We have far more dangerous opponents. Look around you. It wasn't Asharte that murdered the wikken. It was the real enemy.'

Bartram seemed to accept her words, for he stared narrow-eyed at Damion. 'If you're no longer an enemy, then who is?' he said bluntly.

Damion looked at him. *These kids are clever. Uninformed, perhaps,* he thought. *But they're already far more mature than I was at their age.* 'Ever heard of the Revenaunt Emperor?'

'The Dead Ages,' the boy said. 'The Revenaunt was some undead bastard who conquered the world and ruled for a thousand years. The good guys beat him and his friends; it's long ago, and all over and done with.'

'That's what we thought,' Damion said grimly. 'But we were wrong. His friends came back; they call themselves the Dar'khamorth now. Uwella and I have been battling them for years, together with King Ghyllander of Rhidauna, Prince Zino of Opit, and many others. Uwella and I no longer fight for a throne, Bartram DeKramm; we fight to survive.'

'We can help,' Grisa said eagerly.

'Perhaps.' Damion didn't take his cool stare off the boy. 'You say you're a loyal Gry. On whose side are you? The duke or Uwella and me?'

'Yours,' Grisa said immediately. 'I followed Uwella even before she and her siblings ran away.'

Bartram growled. 'Father is loyal to the one on the throne.'

'And you?' Damion said.

He reddened. 'The one who gives me honor and glory.'

'That's us,' Uwella said. 'My noble sire spends his days clutching his throne like a broodhen her egg; he doesn't see anything else. With us you'll find honor and glory a-plenty and maybe death, too.'

'And what thinks the Asharte?' Bartram said.

'I don't give a flip for honor and glory,' Damion said harshly. 'They're irrelevant. If you want those things, you'll get them, but I want peace and prosperity for Vavaun.'

Bartram suddenly smiled. 'I'm not an idiot,' he said. 'Peace is nice for afterwards. As long as you promise me action now, I'll follow Uwella.'

'Not good enough,' Damion said. 'You choose DeGry, that's the duke, or you choose Vavaun, that's the valvodjars. Both of us.'

Bartram scowled. 'I meant both of you.'

'Then say so. In matters of loyalty, it's good to be precise.'

The boy flushed hotly. 'Apologies. I follow the valvodjara and if she sees fit to share the throne with you, I will follow you as well. For honor, glory, and peace in Vavaun.'

'I accept that,' Damion said. 'Now tell me how well you can handle that sword.'

'I'm a fire knight,' the boy said stiffly. 'Trained in arms and martial arts.'

'Don't bluff,' his sister said. 'You've been working *with* the fire knights. That's not the same.'

'Fire knights are Mainal's temple guards. They're magic-users; are you?' Damion said.

'We both are,' Bartram said. He raised his sword and immediately the blade burst into flames. 'See? Been three years with them. I liked them better than Rhydd's people.' He sniffed and sheathed his sword. 'Gardians aren't my choice. It's mostly bows and arrows, and knives; that's Grisa's stuff.'

'You want the shiny knight's armor, you vanity cat,' Grisa said. 'Me, I have as much magic as him, but I prefer my bow. But to the Gray Order, I'm their first porter.'

'You're a portal acolyte?' Damion said, surprised.

'No!' Grisa's eyes flashed indignantly. 'I'm not a portaller and I am not an acolyte.' She stuck her nose in the air. 'I said I was a porter, sir.'

Damion grinned. 'All right, I'll bite. What's the difference?'

The girl relaxed. 'A portaller needs a portal. I don't. See?' She cocked an eye at Damion and sighed. 'You don't. What is a portal? Nothing but a barn and a manatap. The tap gathers wild mana from the Intermedium – the multiverse around us – and the only thing a portaller does is connect the mana beam from the tap in his portal to the tap in the destination portal. Then he sends you along that beam and surprise! you're there. It's very fast, cold, and horrible, going through the Intermedium, but it works all the time. Without those two taps, a portaller is as useful as a dead cat. Now I, my dear sir, don't need a real tap. I simply imagine one here,' she tapped her temple, 'and one at your destination; the beam connects the two and off you go.'

She slumped and sighed. 'There is one thing, though. I can't port blindly. To go somewhere, I must have seen the place – or else I need its coordinates. Now I've never been further from home than here in Adalien, and I haven't got any coordinates or images outside Vavaun. I was going on a tour of the main portals on the continent, but then this happened.' Grisa kicked a pillar of the pavilion and cursed. 'I feel so darned useless.'

'But you can port to Vavaun?' Damion said swiftly.

'I can port you to Grymaur – the town, the burg, and the kerran Negardien. And I've got the coordinates of our home at Castle Kramm, and some other places in the neighborhood. That's about it. Not very impressive.'

'Don't feel bad; we'll make sure you get all the coordinates your head can hold,' Damion said. 'For now, Vavaun will suffice.'

The blaring alarm of the portal behind them drowned out his voice.

'Someone's coming,' Grisa shouted, and a flaming arrow appeared on her bowstring as she turned to the shimmering figures inside the pavilion.

'Pigmen,' her brother said. Flames played along the blade of his sword as he assumed a fighting stance.

Six hulking beasts appeared in the portal circle; hairy, grayish boars with wicked tusks and large axes in their hands. In their midst was a blonde woman in a gray robe.

'Orsille!' Uwella said, and her heart froze under her Gray wikke's robe. *But she was a friend!* her mind wailed.

'Beware!' Grisa said grimly, and launched three arrows in quick succession. Two pigmen died before they were aware of it, but the last arrow bounced harmlessly off the woman.

The other beasts shook their heads as the momentary confusion of returning out of a teleport cleared away. They roared and, jumping the fallen bodies of their comrades, ran to the attack.

Orsille, mouth open and eyes popping in fright, yelled a spell, but before she could finish it, the silvery bulk of Uwella's mountain lion had bowled her over. Together, they slammed to the ground. The shock broke Orsille's magical shielding spell and she cried out.

'Uwella! Don't,' she pleaded.

But the cat's claws ripped into the woman's shoulderblades, and her snarling jaws stopped the screaming. Spitting in disgust, Uwella wheeled around, tail lashing. She saw Bartram slashing away at a pigman, with a sword in one hand and a dagger in the other. Both blades burned, turning the boy's young face into a reddish mask of death. His sister had retreated a few paces and shot another beast point-blank. Damion's tiger was battling the last two pigs, and silently Uwella went to assist him.

Moments later, it was all over.

Bartram rested his sword and grinned at his sister. 'We showed them, didn't we?'

'We did.' Grisa gave him a quick smile and then glanced uncertainly at Uwella, who had returned to her own form and stood looking at the woman she'd slain.

Damion put an arm around Uwella's shoulder. 'You knew her?' he said softly.

She nodded. 'For nearly a year I worked with Orsille. She was an herbalist; a good one.'

'Are you sorry you killed her?' Grisa asked softly.

'No!' Uwella snarled, and she felt hot rage pulling at her self-control. 'I'd kill her a hundred times! I liked her, while she... She must've hated me. I...' She rammed Damion's shoulder blade with her fist. 'That damned traitor!' Then she patted the innocent shoulder, gave Damion a quick kiss, and sighed. 'Twins, now tell us what happened from the moment you two arrived here.'

Grisa bit her lip and her brows went down, giving her a savage look. 'At first, nothing much. We did some shooting with Rhydd's people, some odd jobs for Archodea and the seniors, and it was all quite boring. Until that messenger from Negardien arrived – she was pale and sick, a shivering girl with a handportal, vomiting all over the place. They had to carry her to the high wikke, she was that weak. What she told Archodea, I don't know, but that same day I had to bring the whole Order to the Grymaur kerran. Only Rhydd and his people stayed behind, and Syvvan the Traitor was left in command over the elders and the sick.'

'Syvvan.' For a moment, hot rage twisted Uwella's face. 'That innocent old senior who ran Stores. What fools we were.'

'He's a cursed, ugly fiend,' Bartram said bitterly. His nose bled from a stray fist and he wiped it on his sleeve before going on. 'After Archodea left, life went on, more or less as always.' He looked at his sister. 'Yet something had changed.'

'The whisperings,' Grisa said. 'Curly and the other so-called sick were always together, talking in soft voices.

When you came near, they fell silent and smiled at you, waiting for you to go away.'

'That was creepy,' Bartram agreed. 'Then Syvvan,' he spat on the ground as he mentioned the name, 'called Rhydd to him. He said the Drynnath had mindspoken him and she wanted the gardians to join her at the High Pastures retreat. Rhydd didn't like it, but Syvvan was boss and not loath to show it.' Suddenly the boy looked embarrassed. 'They were quite loud and we, I mean Grisa was reading in the next room. I was with her, not... eavesdropping or anything. It's just, we're always together.'

Damion grinned. 'Of course you weren't snooping. Rather awkward, people shouting at each other one door away.'

'Yes!' Bartram said, relieved. 'Well, Grisa did her duty and we ported the gardians as ordered.' His face worked as he wrestled with his anger. 'When we came back here, it was over. The elders were dead, all of them. Those lying sick weren't sick at all! They'd been shamming to stay with Syvvan. The traitors had opened the gates and let in those pigs. We saw the carnage and I...' He turned his head away. 'M'sister had to slap me then.'

Damion lifted an eyebrow. 'She had to slap you?'

Bartram growled. 'I had the flames in my head, I was that angry. If she hadn't knocked me, things would've gotten nasty fast.'

'So she knocked you. What did she use? A pole-ax?'

'Her fist,' Bartram said. 'Grisa is stronger than she looks; no bulk, but she's tough. Anyway, we hid where we could see them. Syvvan was giving orders and he wasn't lame at all. Didn't look that old either, in his black robe. None of the traitors had seen us come back. They all stood round the central fireplace listening to Syvvan's bragging. I couldn't hear what he said, but the others cheered him. Then they ran past our hiding place to the portal and the lot of them left. May the Intermedium swallow them all!'

'Any idea where they went?' Damion said.

Grisa stirred. 'Vavaun. I felt the portal open; it was definitely the burg in Grymaur.'

'We'll be going after them,' Damion said. 'Those five pigs you killed, where did they come from?'

Grisa lifted a hand and a small flame appeared. 'They stayed behind. At first we hadn't noticed them, but then we heard them squeaking and slobbering to each other.'

'Why didn't you go for help?' Uwella said. 'Why kill those pigs yourself? You took a terrible risk, you know.'

'I know.' Grisa stared at the flame on her palm as it tumbled and sprang like an acrobat at a fair. 'I *wanted* to kill them.' She lifted her chin. 'I'm a fighting DeKramm and I'll be darned if I flee from some overgrown piggies. I was going to port us home after killing them all, but then Bartram got himself captured and I was going to save him first.' A sudden smile broke through the strain in her face. The flame on her hand bowed and disappeared. 'Then you came with your brave enemy friend. You are our valvodjara and you will fix it.'

'Of course I will,' Uwella said stoutly. 'Just like I fixed the scrapes we used to be in. But I... Damion and I will need help.'

'You've got us,' Grisa said. 'We...'

'Why?' Damion was following his own train of thoughts. Then he blinked. 'Sorry, not you; those pigmen. Why did they stay behind?'

Grisa stared at the dead monsters. 'Perhaps Syvvan hoped others would come and they could kill them, too?'

'A trap.' Damion stared at Uwella. 'And someone who knew you sent a call bidding you to come here.'

Uwella rocked on her heels. 'Curse it all! Was Syvvan hoping to catch *me*? It was a woman's voice.' She looked at Grisa. 'Did you recognize the other traitors?'

'Apart from Curly and Orsille, there were two others. Mauvine was fawning all over Syvvan and then there was Deldor.'

Uwella hissed. 'Mauvine! She was a friend; I've known her for ages. The voice could've been hers. Why would she betray me?'

'Greed,' Damion said. 'Money, power, politics. What would happen to Vavaun if you were killed?'

'Chaos!' Grisa cried. 'The country would explode.'

'She's right,' Uwella said. 'My sister Gemedda is next in line, but she wouldn't do it. She's very reclusive; even I don't know where she holed up after we ran away to join the Grays. Then Rhydd. He's a good soldier, but no ruler. Too moody, too impetuous, and he ain't ruthless.' She grimaced. 'Not like me. Our father's throne is shaky enough of its own; with the succession in doubt, he could very well fall. Besides, if their trap got me, they'd get you as well. Your grandfather would accuse my father of having you killed and there'd be civil war.'

'Creating chaos,' Damion said. 'It's what the Dar'khamorth tried to do in Rhidauna when they murdered Ghyll's family. Anyway, I'd say you two saved our lives.'

'I'm glad,' the girl said.

Uwella nodded absently. She looked round the ruined kerran at the blackened huts, the broken palisade and the dead, and pressed her lips to a thin line.

Damion watched her face. He put a hand on her arm and felt the rigidity of her muscles under the gray cloth of her dress. He had no words of solace and he knew she didn't want any.

'We'll kill the bastards,' he said simply.

After a moment she nodded. 'Of course.' She turned away. 'We're done here.'

'We'll go to Vavaun. Grisa...' Damion broke off when somewhere over their heads, a shriek rent the air; a demented cry of anguish that sent shivers down his back. He opened his mind to discover what it was, and immediately hot needles of agony stabbed his brain. He gasped and staggered.

'What's wrong?' Uwella cried. She drew her arm around him. 'Steady!'

Grisa pointed upward. 'It's come back! Cursed beast; I thought I'd chased it away.'

Damion pressed his hands to his temples and looked up. It was a bird. A flying monstrosity as large as a horse, with a curved beak and covered in wickedly hooked feathers. It circled around over the kerran in a slow downward spiral.

'Impossible,' Uwella said and her eyes narrowed to slits. 'The ballads say they're extinct. I never heard of any hookfeathers still living in Rhidauna.'

Damion fought against the pain. 'It's... wounded. Waves of hurt, rage, and hunger.'

'Dar'khamorth!' Uwella said sharply, drawing an arm around his waist.

Damion, still on the outer edges of the bird's mind, gripped her shoulder and nodded. 'I caught the image. A cave or some underground place, and a figure in black bringing food.' He tried to make contact with the bird, as he would with any wild beast. But the hookfeather screamed at his touch, a high cry of rage so immense it was terrifying. The beast plummeted down, its claws stretched out and its beak open in that bone-shaking screech.

Grisa's flaming arrows met it halfway, and the bird bucked as fire blazoned on its chest. Miraculously it didn't die immediately, though it smoked through several wounds.

Damion, caught in the bird's mind, nearly buckled under its agony, but Uwella's arm held him upright. On his other side, Bartram stood holding a flaming sword, watching his sister intently.

The hookfeather flapped its wings in an attempt to get away. Grisa sent a second volley after it and myriads of tiny flames appeared from under its scaly feathers. It fell, landing heavily amid the dead wikken, and burst into flames.

'Gods,' Damion said faintly. 'Dear gods.' Then he sagged in Uwella's arms and began to shake.

Grisa looked surprised. 'Why are you upset? It's only a beast.'

'Damion was in contact with its mind,' Uwella said. 'That made its death kind of personal, you know.'

'Oh,' the girl said, looking shocked. 'I'm sorry.'

'Don't be,' Damion said, wiping his mouth. 'You did the right thing. It would've killed me if you hadn't shot it. Shatter me, but that bird was beautiful! Insane, and very beautiful.'

'You think so?' Grisa said doubtfully. 'I thought it horrible.'

Damion caught Bartram's puzzled frown and forced a smile. 'You're right, it was horrible. But its power... I bet it would be very fast in the air. I must try its form.' He shook himself and straightened. 'Damn; the beast broadcasted its pain. It must've been used to communicate with humans.'

'If it's a Dar'khamorth creature, they'll have trained its mind,' Uwella said.

'And taught it to recognize friend from enemy. It attacked me the moment I thought at it.' Damion swallowed against the taste of bile in his mouth. 'Let's go; we must find Archodea and Rhydd. Grisa, could you port us to Vavaun?'

The girl cocked her head. 'Of course. Negardien? Burg Grymaur?'

Damion considered for a moment. 'Better not there; we should know what's going on first.'

'I can port us home, to Castle Kramm.' Grisa plucked at her tunic. 'I could use some clean clothes.'

'Me too,' her brother said and he perked up. 'A hot bath!'

Damion grinned at their sudden eagerness. He wouldn't be averse to a hot bath himself. 'Kramm will be fine.'

'Give me your hands,' the girl said. For a moment, her fingers were warm; then her firm grip dissolved into the familiar sensation of impossible shapes and distorted perspectives of the Intermedium. Hostile, airless – a place of infinite dimensions; timeless, limitless, and utterly inhuman.

It took a second, then there was a sudden wrench, a moment of unbearable pain, and they came out at night in the open air on a bald mountain. It rained, and it was dark and bitterly cold.

CHAPTER 3 – DETOUR

'You goofed up, girl,' Bartram said, staring at the unexpected surroundings. 'This is High Pastures, where we put Rhydd's people down.'

They stood in a sloping field high up a mountain. Overhead loomed the black shape of the mountain's peak and below the only visible thing was a low stone building with blank walls oozing dreariness.

'I didn't... Something happened.' Grisa gripped her temples. 'My head hurts. What went wrong? It wasn't me.' She was silent for a moment. 'I have the coordinate,' she said in a scared voice. 'But it's blurry; I can't read it.'

'Coordinates?' Damion said quickly. 'You didn't use an image?'

'I prefer coordinates,' she said, and massaged the sides of her head.

Damion avoided looking at her. *It felt familiar,* he thought. *A bit like that time the Dar'khamorth sabotaged our port to Rhidaun-Lorn and we were lost in the Gisterwoud. But this time we arrived somewhere. That could mean it's something else. Perhaps there's something wrong at Kramm.* He glanced at Uwella and saw her shiver.

'I don't know,' he said aloud. 'But it's dark and cold, so we can shelter inside that building until tomorrow.'

Uwella nodded. 'Right now I'm not going anywhere.'

'Damn,' Grisa whispered. 'I so wanted to go home.' Her voice trailed away.

'We must get in somehow,' Damion said as cheerfully as he could manage. 'There should be beds at least. Shall we break down the door?'

Uwella walked to the building. She tried the handle and shook her head. 'Locked. No, you won't get inside that way. I've heard of this place.' She grimaced. 'It's not a fun spot.'

Damion looked around at the dripping grass and the unrelieved night. 'You can say that again. Who would want to retreat here?'

Uwella's smile was grim. 'No one, at least not voluntarily. It's a place of penance for those who transgress against the rules.'

Damion looked up. 'Seriously? I always thought you Grays were the only Order free of that nonsense.'

'We're not. Anyway, that door can't be opened unlawfully.' She put her hands to the lock and closed her eyes. Inside the mechanism something clicked a few times, and the door swung open.

Damion lifted an eyebrow. 'Unlawfully? Are you supposed to know how to do that?'

Uwella grinned. 'Of course not. But using the spell itself is lawful, however you came by it. I like to be prepared, just in case I irritate someone too much. So I cozened someone into teaching me the words.' She went inside. 'A light would be welcome.'

Without a sound, all the candles on the walls burst into flame. Surprised, Uwella turned to Grisa. 'Thank you!'

Grisa gave a tired grin and pointed a thumb at her brother. 'Not me; 't was him.'

'Then I thank you, kind sir,' Uwella said and the boy blushed slightly.

The central room was cold and immaculately clean. To the left was a kitchen area and to the right were five bunks, and there was no fireplace anywhere. The room smelled vaguely after soap and cabbage and it was easily the most depressing place Damion had ever seen.

'It doesn't reflect the hospitality of the Order,' Uwella admitted. 'But it will have to do.' She rummaged in the kitchen's small pantry. 'Let's see about rations. I'm not going to catch a mountain goat in the dark.'

'I wouldn't mind steaming, raw goat,' Damion said, 'but our friends here haven't got the teeth for it.'

Bartram dropped down on the nearest bed and groaned. 'What's this? A stone pallet?'

'The beds are not supposed to be comfortable,' Uwella said from the kitchen. 'They're meant to make you reflect on disobedience and the loss of privileges.'

Bartram sighed. 'Yeah; that's what I needed.'

'Food!' Uwella returned triumphantly. 'A whole box of nibble cakes. Two each should do it.'

'What's those?' Grisa said, eying the dark-brown biscuits warily.

'Cookies, girl,' Damion said. 'Travelers' cookies. They've saved a lot of lives already.'

'Cookies?' Bartram's face brightened and he sat up.

Grisa bit off a small corner and chewed cautiously. Then she relaxed. 'Good,' she mumbled. Halfway through the second nibble cake, she sighed, lay down, and slept.

'Sleep before food?' Damion grinned. 'She really is tired.'

'She must've spent a lot of energy; the gods know how she did it. Five hulking pigmen.' Uwella finished her last cake. 'Bo could have done it, but a fifteen-year-old acolyte?' She shook her head in mock wonder. 'What's the world coming to?'

'Amazing, isn't it, grandma?' Damion said. 'The girl's at least five years your junior.'

'Hush,' she said. 'I'm feeling old already.' She closed her eyes. 'You know what? We haven't slept for two nights either.'

'We're cats,' Damion protested. 'We don't need much sleep.'

But Uwella's only answer was a soft snore.

Damion and Bartram exchanged glances.

'It's all a mess, isn't it?' the boy said drowsily. 'I've never known Grisa to botch a port before.'

'She was tired.' Damion grinned. 'And so are you. Sleep and try not to reflect too much. Good night, Master DeKramm.'

The boy snorted. 'G'night, Asharte.'

Silently, Damion slipped outside. He changed into his tiger-form and lay down for a snooze, all his senses alert.

The next morning Damion woke with the break of dawn. He rose, stretched, and yawned. Then he changed into his human form and for the first time gazed around at his mother's country. Vavaun didn't show its best; it looked bleak and chilly in the early light. Overhead, the sky was a dreary, rain-laden gray, while below him a herd of clouds like sheep drifted across the misty valley.

In the distance was a patch of smoke on the horizon. For a moment Damion wondered if the sun played tricks, but it really was smoke. That meant something large burned – only what or where, he had no idea. Uwella or the twins would know; he was a stranger in his own country.

Softly he stepped inside to find the others were already up and about.

'Where have you been?' Uwella said.

'Outside, keeping watch,' Damion said. 'Catnap watch.' He looked at her hunched stance. 'Stiff?'

'Those beds are terrible.' She looked at him. 'What's wrong?'

'There's a fire in the distance. It must be large, to be visible over here.'

'Where?' Uwella followed him out, her fingers busy on the tangles in her hair. 'A forest fire? Would be bad.'

'That must be Grymaur,' Grisa said from inside the door.

'Ah!' Uwella cried out as she inadvertently tore at a snarl. 'Curse it, there's a fire in the city! We must hurry. Crows? Too slow. Hawks!'

'We can't,' Damion said calmly. 'We're not alone, remember?'

35

Uwella sagged. 'Yes, of course.'

'Whatever is happening there is out of our hands. They've got soldiers in the city, haven't they?'

'Naturally; the Burg Grymaur garrison.'

'Then any fire is their job.' *Unless they, too, were overwhelmed by the enemy.* But he kept those thoughts to himself. 'How far is it on foot?'

'Fifteen hours.' Grisa pointed to the valley visible between the clouds. 'Grymaur is on the next mountain. To get there, we must walk down to the valley. That's two thousand feet. At the bottom is the bridge across the river and the village of Kastelmaur. Then another long trek to Grymaur.'

'You know the area well,' Damion said.

'Of course she does,' Bartram said behind them. 'Everything down to the bridge is our land. Our father is the baron of Kramm and we've traveled to Grymaur many times. On horseback, but that doesn't make it any faster.'

'I see.' Damion looked the twins up and down. 'Before we go, there's soap and scrub sand in the kitchen. Why don't you go wash your faces and your hands?' He pointed at the mountain stream beside the building. 'You're not mud goblins, after all.'

The girl opened her mouth to protest, but then she looked at her grimy and bloodstained hands. She swallowed. 'I'd better. Come, let's get a pail.' She dragged her brother inside.

'I'm worried about that bump we made with that last port,' Damion said softly, when the twins were out of earshot. 'It felt too much like the hiccup that stranded us in the Gisterwoud.'

Uwella stilled. 'That was the Dar'khamorth's doing. But they can't have tampered with something in Grisa's mind.'

'Probably not. But Grisa said she used Kramm's coordinate instead of her memory of her home. That's probably her schooling speaking; I know Bo Lusindral, who once explained all this to me, prefers images.'

'What's the difference?' Uwella said. 'Damn, I should have paid more notice, but wikken aren't good at portaling.'

'Porting to a coordinate is exact. It brings you to a doorway, a tree or a portal circle; whatever. A memory is flexible; you can come out anywhere within the borders of the image.'

'Yeah, I see that. So Grisa used a coordinate. And?'

'You cannot come out inside an object,' Damion said patiently. 'The genius who wrote that spell was clever enough to think of that. Should someone place a chair on your coordinate, or a stray dog chose it for its nap, you will come out next to it.'

'I know *that*. But?'

'But. If someone blows up the whole place around your coordinate, the spell is stumped. Then it reroutes you to the nearest other coordinate the porter knows. For Kramm, that could well be this place.' Damion pulled a face. 'That last bit of the port did feel like we were kicked aside.'

For a moment the snarling face of a mountain lion passed over Uwella's painted countenance and she growled softly.

'If you're right, we must be careful.'

'I hope those two youngsters are strong enough,' Damion said. 'If I *am* right...'

'They're fighters, like their father. The marshal often said how tough and independent they were.'

Then the twins returned, more or less cleaned up.

'Much better,' Uwella said with a fine show of cheerfulness. 'Now we are ready to go.'

'Are we?' Damion said, looking around. 'Where's the way down?'

'Follow me.' Grisa walked through the rain-drenched field and there was the path. 'It will get wider farther down, but this trail leads all the way to the Kastelmaur bridge.'

On the way down, there was no sign of an enemy, only that thinning cloud in the distant sky. There wasn't a trace of Rhydd and his gardians either. A small group of black mountain goats with long, curved horns crossed their path, but when the animals got wind of them they fled, jumping down the slope in a harrowing display of agility.

Their own descent was far slower. The path was narrow and in places so steep they had to be careful not to slip.

After an hour, they reached the edge of the forest. Old, mossy larches in winter-bare branches clung to the mountain walls and hid the smoke over Grymaur from their view.

Sometime later, the road became less steep and they came to a large plateau. The bitter stink of burning hung between the trees and Damion's uneasiness grew. Grymaur was still too far away; this was a local smell.

'We are close to Kramm.' Grisa's face and body were tense, as if she braced herself for the worst. Beside her, Bartram's hand hovered over the hilt of his sword and small flames danced along his fingers.

It's quiet here. Too quiet, Damion thought, letting his mind roam around. There wasn't an animal nearby, not even the always-present birds.

Then the castle came into view and he immediately knew what had scared away the wildlife. It was Adalien all over.

Grisa froze. She didn't utter a sound, just stood there with her balled fists to her mouth as she stared wide-eyed at the blackened ruins of their home.

Two steps behind her, Bartram stood crying and cursing, holding his sword in his shakings hands. 'Sliver them,' he said endlessly. 'Sliver the rotten beasts!'

'Stay here, you three,' Damion said. 'I'm going in.' He changed into his tiger form and crept like a shadow toward the ruined keep and the overpowering smell of no-longer-fresh kills.

Nothing moved. The ashes looked several days old and drenched by yesterday's rain. Damion growled deep in his throat at the sight of the still bodies of soldiers and pigmen. He studied the dead beasts and his lips curled in disgust. They were like the ones at Adalien – nearly nude, covered in dark, bristly hair, and wearing nothing but leather thongs and straps, with copper bands around their arms and ankles. Some had carried swords, others an ax or halberd, but all arms were crude and of cheap quality.

Damion slipped into the inner court. Here, too, were bodies, but not as many as outside. The roof of the central hall had collapsed, leaving only burned walls standing. Damion halted and looked around. He saw only soldiers, no civilians anywhere, and he wondered if the servants had managed to escape, with the soldiers covering their flight. But where could they have gone? Quickly he returned to his human form and hurried back.

'Rhydd was here,' he said as he rejoined them. 'I counted one dead Gray gardian and twelve soldiers in red-and-green. The other bodies were all pigmen. The family and the servants must have escaped.'

'Rhydd will have taken them to some safe place,' Uwella said. 'They'll be all right.'

Bartram only nodded, his face a rage-filled mask. He'd drawn an arm around his sister's shoulder and didn't pay attention to the little flames running from her hands to his sword arm and back. 'We'll kill them,' he said harshly. 'We'll kill all of them.'

Damion looked at them. 'We will, but try to relax. Now is a time to think, to plan. This is your land; where could your people have gone to?'

The boy visibly forced his muscles to obey. 'Andauz. It's the ruin of an old castle lower down in the forest. There is water and a hunting lodge.'

'I've heard of it,' Uwella said. 'But that's all. Is it far from here?'

'Several hours on foot.'

'We've never been there,' Grisa added. 'Too young to hunt, Daddy said. So no porting.' Her face was a tear-streaked mess, but she had herself under control.

Damion looked at Uwella. 'We can have a look.' He turned and inspected Grisa from head to toe. 'You're not very big, are you?' he said thoughtfully.

The girl turned around, snarling. 'Why?'

'I wasn't belittling you,' Damion said calmly. 'I was thinking of your weight. I believe you rode a horse?'

She rubbed her face. 'Sorry. Yes. I had a pony.'

'And Bartram? You're the heavier one.'

'I had a tsenevazer. Why? Do you have a magic horse up your sleeve?'

'I'm a beastmaster,' Damion said. 'So the answer is yes, I have. Though the horse ain't my favorite animal.'

The boy shuddered as the anger flowed from him. 'I didn't think of that.'

Damion smiled at him. 'No matter; you two are going great.'

'Have you ever done a horse?' Uwella said.

'No, but I've seen that big courser of Ghyll's so many times I could imagine him from memory alone. He can carry two easily.'

'I'm not a lightweight,' Bartram said.

'Wait till you see the horse.' Damion closed his eyes and imagined Ulanth from his proud head to his massive feet, and swiftly changed. He didn't feel anything; the whole process was almost instant and devoid of sensation.

When he opened his eyes again, he stood taller than even his tiger, taller than his human form, and felt far heavier. The warhorse's extreme masculinity made him feel uncomfortable, as did the animal's air of superiority. Instinctively, he threw his head back and whinnied.

'By the Fire,' Bartram said reverently. 'He's magnificent.'

Damion found his horse's ears were well enough attuned to the human voice to understand the gist of the boy's words. He grinned as the horse's ego, so different to his own, took the comment as a matter of course.

'He's big,' Grisa said with some hesitation. 'Really, really big.'

'You're too old for a little pony,' Uwella said encouragingly. 'Mount up, folks.'

Carefully, Grisa climbed onto the massive back and sat straight.

'Bartram, behind me,' she said, patting her sheathed bow. 'I want to keep my hands free in case we meet a pig.'

Her brother sighed but did what she told him.

Damion walked some paces and both riders swayed to keep their balance.

'You'll do,' Uwella said after a while. 'I'm going cat now. If there is anything, wave your arms and holler.'

Gradually, Damion increased his speed to a trot, trusting his reflexes to help keep the two on his back.

After a while they came to a fork in the road. The main path went down the mountain, winding towards the valley and the bridge, while a woodcutters' trail led them to a heavily forested ridge. Grisa leaned over the proud head and pointed to the smaller path. Obediently, Damion followed her directions.

It had started to rain and the woods around them appeared gray and dreary. After another hour, Grisa slapped the stallion's side with her open hand.

'Whoa!' she shouted in the large ear and Damion came to a halt. Groaning, the twins slid to the ground and both beastmasters changed into their human bodies.

'Gods, I feel like my bones are all adrift,' Grisa said, as she jumped up and down. Then she stretched. 'We're getting close to Andauz.'

'Then we'll walk the rest,' Damion said. 'If there's anyone there, we'd better not startle them with our beast forms.'

The path was narrow and led them through a densely overgrown area of hawthorns and birches.

'We're not the first who went this way,' Uwella said.

'No, and not all those who passed were woodsmen,' Damion said, waving at the broken twigs and flattened shrubs. 'They left a trail a mile wide.'

Away from the path, a branch snapped.

'Stop!' a cool voice said from the shadows. Two sentinels in battle-torn red-and-green uniforms barred the way, bows at the ready. 'Identify yourselves, and quickly, or we'll shoot.'

'It's us, Lobarth,' Bartram said, stepping forward.

'Master Bartram!' The first soldier was a tall corporal with a slight squint and a long, unshaven chin. Dark hair peeked from under the rim of his helm. His mate was younger, with a bloodstained cloth around his head.

The corporal lowered his bow. 'You two are a surprise, Master and Miss,' he said, and there was a hint of dismay in his voice. 'I didn't expect you at Andauz, of all places.'

'We went home first,' the boy said, visibly wrestling against his rage. 'We guessed any survivors would gather at the lodge. Are our parents here?'

Lobarth shook his head. 'No, Master. Your mother will be safe; she's staying with your aunt in Opit. Your father was in Grymaur; I'm afraid we have no news of him.'

'I understand,' Bartram said and his voice shook a little.

'I'm sure he is all right, Master,' the corporal said. 'Who are your two companions?'

Grisa frowned at him. 'You don't recognize her? She's the valvodjara.'

Corporal Lobarth gave Uwella a surprised look and then came to attention. 'Highness! Forgive me. Are you here with the Order?'

'I'm not,' Uwella said. 'My companion and I are here to save our country. Have you seen my brother?'

'Prince Rhydd is in the camp, with Captain Mannar, Highness. Please follow the path. It will lead you to them. We're not supposed to leave our post, so we can't guide you.'

Uwella smiled grimly. 'Certainly not! Stay where you are and be vigilant. We'll find Prince Rhydd.'

The two soldiers saluted quickly and disappeared back into the shadows.

'Rhydd is here,' Uwella said. 'Good.'

Damion glanced at her face. She looked completely controlled, but he had caught the echo of relief in her voice.

After a hundred yards, they came to the weathered walls of a ruin, partly hidden by shrubbery. Beyond was a low cabin built of squared logs with a porch along the front. On the steps sat a soldier in the colors of Kramm, and beside him was a young man Damion recognized immediately. He was the same fellow who'd come with Olle that day in the Gisterwoud, Gardian Commander Rhydd DeGry.

As they walked toward him, Rhydd rose, a look almost of shock on his white-painted face.

'Wella? I thought you safe in Rhidauna,' he said and held out his hands to her.

Uwella stopped a few paces away from him, legs apart and her hands to her back, in what Damion called her "imperious pose". Apparently Rhydd knew it, too, for he dropped his arms and straightened. *No family gathering today,* Damion thought. *She's all valvodjara.*

'Rhidauna isn't all that safe these days,' Uwella said harshly. 'The Dar'khamorth has destroyed the kerran.'

The blood drained from the gardian's face. 'Adalien?' he said blankly. 'What? When?'

'While Grisa ported you to the High Pasture, a horde of beastmen attacked. She and Bartram returned there to find themselves the only survivors.'

Rhydd surged forward. 'I knew I shouldn't have left! I knew it! I've failed my duty. I must go back; I...'

She called her brother too impetuous, Damion thought. *That's a bad habit for a commander.*

'You will not,' Uwella snapped. Then she softened a little. 'It's no use; all is gone. I need you here, Rhydd.'

With clenched fists, the gardian seemed poised to attack. Then Damion saw all anger leak out of him and with a sigh like a sob, he stepped back.

'You're right,' he said. 'Vavaun comes first.' He stared at the sword in his hand as if puzzled how it came there. With a grunt, he sheathed the blade and nodded to the twins.

'Glad to see you safe. You must've had a harrowing time back there.' He looked at Damion with furrowed eyebrows. 'You're no Gray. Who are you?' Then a look of recognition dawned in his eyes. 'I've seen you before. You were with King Ghyllander that day we killed the blackrobe sorceress. Don't know your name, though.'

'I was there,' Damion said. 'I'm still grateful for your saving our skins.'

Uwella stared at her brother. 'You will leave all your weapons where they are. You won't get mad, or behave aggressively, is that clear?'

Rhydd nodded, surprised. 'Why?'

'This is Prince Damion DeAsharte. My mate.'

Rhydd's hand clutched his sword, and his face was tight, but he did control himself.

'The secret heir, is he? Damn it, Wella!' He gave Damion a jerky nod. 'Welcome, Prince,' he said between gritted teeth. 'I didn't know it was *you* we rescued.' Then he turned to his sister. 'Mate?'

She waved impatiently. 'Later. First you will fill me in on the situation.'

Trying not to glare at Damion, the gardian obeyed. 'Six days ago, the Drynnath received a distress call from the Grymaur kerran. Someone had poisoned the evening meal and all were dead or dying. Archodea went to their aid and took most of the wikken with her. She left old Syvvan in command and me to defend the kerran.' He paused. 'The third day, Syvvan told me he had received a mind-call from Archodea to send me and my gardians to her at the High

Pastures. I didn't want to go and leave the kerran undefended and we had a discussion.'

'So we were told,' Uwella said. 'The twins were next door to the office and you were rather loud.'

'I daresay; I was very angry, but I couldn't refuse. Gods, I never could stand the old guy, but he was in charge, so we left. Had I but known... Curse it, Adalien was the safest place in the world.'

'Finish your report,' Uwella said impatiently.

Damion stared at her. *She really is boss and he knows it.*

Rhydd swallowed. 'The situation here in the south is still unclear. From the High Pastures, we saw fires in Grymaur and left for the city. At Kramm, we arrived in the middle of a battle.'

'Pigmen,' Uwella said shortly. 'We passed the same way.'

Rhydd nodded. 'Together, Mannar's men and my gardians managed to kill them all. That was three days ago. With Castle Kramm lost, there was nothing more we could do there. I decided to join forces with Mannar's men and that's why you find us here. I was about to send scouts to Grymaur, to check out the situation there. Tell them about your side, Mannar.'

The captain stood at attention. His rugged face twitched and he seemed to avoid the twins' eyes.

'We had nary a hint of anything amiss, Highness,' he said heavily. 'Those beasts jumped us before we knew they were there. I'd never heard of nor seen such half-beast, half-man creatures before, let alone what they can do. They came through the woods, up the slope where no man could go. We barely repulsed the first attack and we would all be dead if the prince and his gardians hadn't joined in then. We sent the servants into the woods to Andauz and rallied back on Kramm. It was already burning then! Together, we defeated the pigs, but we lost the castle. We lost the blasted castle!'

The boy swallowed. 'I... we saw. Captain, we can rebuild Kramm. You got most of our people out. That's the important thing and I'm sure my father will say so, too.'

'I agree with Master Bartram,' Uwella said. 'Those pigmen are creatures of the Dar'khamorth. Somehow we thought the minions of the Revenaunt Emperor would overlook Vavaun. They attacked Rhidauna, the Nhael, Opit, but they would pass us by. We were wrong.'

We, Damion thought. *She means her father. We warned him, that day of Ghyll's coronation. That day the Dar'khamorth sank the fleet at Yanthemonde. Ghyll warned him to look to his defenses. But apparently he didn't.*

'We'll hit back and we will get them, Captain Mannar. We'll get them all, those murderers,' he said aloud. 'For the moment, I want the gardians and the men of Kramm to stay here. This place is well hidden and looks defensible. Uwella and I will scout the city.'

'You think you're better trained than my gardians, Prince?' Rhydd said and he didn't attempt to hide the scorn in his voice.

'Rhydd,' Uwella said softly. 'When I first met Damion, I thought like you – DeAsharte, enemy, hand me a rope. I even said something like that once, I believe.'

Damion nodded. 'It came close.'

'But he and I got to know each other and now I've radically altered my plans for Vavaun. I have come to realize how bad the eternal struggle between our two families is for our country. You've never been beyond the kerran Adalien. Damion and I have seen a lot of the continent, first with King Ghyll and later when we went to visit our countrymen abroad. Let me tell you this; compared to Rhidauna or Opit, we're a bunch of ignorant peasants. Why? Because we spend all of our energy on that stupid catfight between Gry and Asharte. I'm done with it. Forget father and old Duke Cymric; I'm going to stop that silliness.'

Rhydd still stared at Damion. 'Brave words, Wella. But how do you think to do that?' Then his face twisted and he pulled his sister roughly towards him. 'Mate! You mean you and that spineless...'

Uwella nodded. 'Damion and I are getting married. Together, we ascend the throne of Vavaun and then there is no more reason to fight.'

'But, but,' Rhydd's face grew red. He let go of his sister and pointed accusingly at Damion. 'Him? That scrawny Asharte's not a man! What good is he in battle? I bet he can't even hold a sword.'

Uwella opened her mouth, but Damion raised his hand and she pressed her lips together.

The beastmaster grinned. 'You know, Rhydd,' he said in a tone as if they were talking about the weather. 'My grandfather said the same. But looks can be deceiving, gardian. I'll give you the same answer I gave him.'

He shimmered, and suddenly Rhydd saw himself faced by a huge black-and-white tiger. He scrambled back wide-eyed, but ended up against the lodge wall. Damion put his front paws on Rhydd's shoulders. Gently, he pushed him down and licked his face. When he thought the message clear, he rose and turned back into his human form.

'Bah,' he said, spitting on the ground. 'That face-paint of yours tastes horrible.' He grinned at Captain Mannar, who stood staring with his sword in his hand. 'We're beastmasters, Uwella and I. Neither has need of blades or armor. We have our teeth and claws. Sort of cheating, isn't it?'

Despite himself and the situation, Rhydd began to giggle, and then to laugh. 'Curse it, Wella,' he roared as he stood up. 'You found a bigger cat than yourself?'

Uwella nodded. 'He's a better beastmaster than me,' she said seriously. 'And he does everything with his mind, while I need my amulet to strengthen my will. Besides that, he is a war tactician. He has a natural talent for those things.'

Her brother sobered. 'All right, I'm not fully convinced, but you're the valvodjara. I've always followed your lead and I won't stop now.' Rhydd gave a lopsided grin. 'Father will be furious.'

'Isn't he always?' Uwella sniffed. 'Our loving daddy.'

'Now that we are agreed,' Damion said quietly, 'I want to return once more to my earlier comment. Uwella and I go to Grymaur, and the gardians with the soldiers of Kramm will stay here.' He looked at Rhydd, who nodded.

Damion lowered his voice even more. 'There are things you won't be aware of. We went to Adalien because we had heard rumors about traitors in the Order. We spoke with too many compatriots who told the same stories and we wanted a word with Archodea about it.'

'Traitors in the Order? That's impossible,' Rhydd said stubbornly. 'Wikken are loyal to Arikal.'

'Not all of them,' Uwella said. She turned to the twins. 'It's your tale; tell him about the attack.'

In turns, they gave a clear account of all that had happened, and when they were done, Rhydd sat frozen.

'I didn't want to go,' he said quietly. 'But Syvvan outranked me. I should have followed my instincts. I should have left half my force behind.'

'It doesn't work that way in the army,' Damion said. 'In the end, the fault is Archodea's, not yours. She's the Drynnath; she made the guy a senior, and she put him in command of the kerran. You could only obey.' *What a mess* he thought. *The defender of the kerran should have been independent of anyone but the high wikke. Those Grays were far too trusting.*

Rhydd started pacing the porch. 'Syvvan. Why did he suddenly betray us?'

'Not suddenly,' Damion said. 'I think he was an infiltrator, a long-time Dar'khamorth agent. Archodea once told me that the Gray Order took in everyone who walked away from another temple. Did anyone ever look into those people's past?'

Dumbly, Rhydd shook his head. 'We checked whether the newcomer had sufficient knowledge of their original Order, such as names, ceremonies, and liturgy. And of course we tested their magical knowledge.'

'All things an impostor would find out beforehand; buyable information.'

'Buyable!' The gardian looked shocked at the thought.

'Everything is for sale,' Damion said. 'Like Syvvan and his ilk had a price.' He gave Rhydd a hard look. 'How sure are you of your gardians?'

Rhydd froze. 'My people are true. Every one of them is a follower of Gry. A true follower.'

'That's what I thought of Mauvine,' Uwella said bitterly. 'I've known her forever, but apparently I didn't know her at all.'

Rhydd's face turned desperate. 'How can I trust anyone if not by years of service?'

Damion shrugged. 'You can't. We'll all have to be very watchful. But now...'

'Food!' Uwella said firmly. 'I'm not going anywhere on an empty stomach.'

Rhydd shook himself, his face taut as he rubbed his eyes. 'Come, I will see you fed.'

Damion wiped his bowl with his last bit of bread. 'That went down well,' he said. 'Uwella and I will go see what's happening in the city. Grisa...'

'We're coming with you.'

Damion shook his head. 'Too dangerous. We're just going in quickly and...'

'I can take you there much faster,' the girl said stubbornly.

'She's right,' Uwella snapped. 'We need to know the situation now, not tomorrow. Besides, they've shown they can defend themselves.'

Damion threw up his hands. 'All *right*. What would be a good place to jump to?'

'The old graveyard?' Bartram said. 'No one in his right mind goes there after dark.'

Damion thought of the undead armies they'd fought in Zihaen. 'Unless you're a necromancer.' He shrugged. 'No place is safe. We'll risk the undead. Do you have the coordinates?'

'Of course,' Grisa said.

'Let's take a look then. Are we ready?'

'We've been for hours, chatterbox,' Uwella said.

Damion pulled her head towards him and kissed her. 'See you later,' he told Rhydd. 'Take us to Grymaur, Grisa.'

CHAPTER 4 – RECONNAISSANCE

The old graveyard was quiet and desolate in the rain. Gray triangular gravestones sprouted haphazardly from the earth. Gnarled willows weeped over them, dripping water into the many puddles. To one side, the sky was orange-red, like a dying hearth, and even the rain couldn't mask the smell of burning.

'It's a big place, this,' Damion said.

Grisa stirred. 'It's only the western part. On the other side of Duke's Road lay the dead of Grymaur's eastern half.'

'The city is divided?'

Bartram gave a snort. 'You can say that. The Eststaul is mostly artisans, and where we stand, the Veststaul, live the merchants. They're not fond of each other.'

'Why not?'

'Jealousy. The merchants have a charter to trade but not make; the artisans make but aren't allowed to trade.'

Damion shook his head. 'How's that?'

'The Grymaur Guilds,' Grisa said, brushing the wet hair back from her face. 'Long ago, the Merchants Guild and the Artisans Association divided the town between them. Veststaul sells ore, textiles, and whatever more to Eststaul, and buy tools, clothes, and stuff in return. The guildmasters get a percentage of every deal.'

'I see,' Damion said. 'Those guild leeches are in for a surprise. When the temples come to Vavaun, they'll bring their own guilds with them. That will shake up things.'

Uwella had barely heard their exchange; most of her mind was listening to the thoughts of Grymaur's animal life. Things seemed calm around here and she relaxed slightly.

'I must know what's burning,' she said in a hard voice. 'You three will wait for me.'

She glanced at Damion, but he only nodded. She loved him for it; he understood her need to see for herself what was happening. Quickly, she changed into a hawk and winged silently away into the darkness.

From the air, the city looked eerily dead. Normally there was plenty going on after dark. Peddlers, carousers, lamplighters, whores... Her Grymaur was never silent. Now the streets were empty, no bobbing torches of the watch, no light anywhere – even the burg was a pitch-black shape against the racing clouds.

Uwella flew low over the houses, her senses alert. At the town gates, she noticed the doors were closed and beastmen posted on the towers. Beyond that...

She let out a raucous scream of rage. Outside the wall was the Kyrstaul, the unguilded quarter. Here lived the laborers and woodsmen who worked the surrounding farms, mines, and forests. Uwella remembered the district as a mass of wooden dwellings, crooked cottages all sagging and leaning into each other on both sides of Kyr Gap, a narrow chasm with a river at the bottom. Now, the whole, teeming area was a field of burned-out ruins, still steaming in the rain.

Numb with shock, she flew over the wreckage. One round was enough to know nothing lived there, not even the rats. She stretched her wings and hurried back to the others.

Uwella gave a harsh caw as she saw them waiting and shimmered into her human form even before her feet touched the ground. Damion grabbed her waist as she stumbled.

'It's the Kyrstaul,' she stammered, overcome by shock and anger. 'Burned; all burned. Gods, the people!'

Damion tightened his grip on her arms. 'What's the Kyrstaul?'

'The workmen's quarter,' Bartram said in a strained voice. 'It's outside the walls.'

Damion put a hand to Uwella's cheek. 'You all right?'

She shook her head angrily. 'No, I'm not!' She closed her eyes and for a moment just stood there, feeling Damion's hands holding her. Then she gave a shuddering sigh. 'Let's go.'

Without another word, they crossed the graveyard into the street. Damion watched Uwella's face, seeing the rage underneath her calm as she took the lead and marched them briskly through a maze of alleys to some place only she knew.

Everywhere they went, the city was buried in darkness. No torches burned in the streets, the houses had their shutters closed, and even the massive keep to the north was a silent and lightless mass against the sky.

This town is... old-fashioned, Damion thought, seeing the open sewers running through the middle of the streets, smelling of disease and worse. He was used to Rhidauna's clean cities and underground drainage, and this more than anything brought home to him how backwards his new country was.

His companions didn't seem to notice the stinking drains, the many unpaved streets, and the refuse everywhere. To them, even to Uwella, it was the normal state of things. *We'll discuss it later,* he thought. 'Where are we going?'

They walked down a cobbled lane with tall, narrow houses of run-down respectability.

'Someone I know,' Uwella said curtly. 'He may have information.'

At the end of the lane was a small square of two-story houses. Here stood a statue of a gaunt man in a long mantle, his hair tied into a ponytail under his floppy hat. In his hand he held a staff with a swirling gray light on top.

'Arikal, bless us,' Uwella said softly as they walked past.

Your god hasn't done much blessing lately, Damion thought. *If I were the Grays, I'd be looking for a more considerate patron.* He'd never had much to do with the gods. His father was a follower of Mainal Wargod, his mother a disciple of Iodraune Beastgod, and no other deity had ever come his way, least of all this God of Chaos and Renewal. Just as his Gray Order, Arikal was almost an outsider, not well known and not fully trusted by others than a Vavauner.

'Watch out!' Uwella's harsh whisper shocked him back into the sphere of men. They were in a short alleyway with a blind wall on one side and a costermonger's vegetable stall on the other. Uwella motioned them into the shadows of the empty stall.

Again fully alert, Damion peered over the counter into the darkness. A little further on was a crossroads and there he saw a squad of monstrous forms walking toward them. They were pigmen, like the slain ones they'd seen at Castle Kramm. Only these were very much alive; aggressive and frightening. At the alley's entrance, the beasts halted. Their low-pitched voices were unintelligible, but their excited squeals and wild arm-waving indicated they had been quarreling over which way to go. For a second Damion thought the beasts would fight it out, but then the biggest of the pigs cuffed a few heads and the others backed down. Grumbling, they walked away down the main road and disappeared into the dark.

Damion relaxed. 'That's bad. They're walking around as if they own the place.'

Uwella looked at him without saying anything, and they hurried on into the next street, now keeping to the shadow of the houses.

Several streets on, they came to a half-timbered building with a painted sign squeaking softly in the wind.

Uwella looked around before knocking on the shutters. Nothing happened. Nothing moved as they waited.

She knocked again, and now they heard a soft shuffling inside. Near the door it halted.

At the third knock, the door opened slightly.

'Beredt?' Uwella whispered.

'Who is there?'

'Four for the Three of DeGry.'

The door swung open. 'Come inside. Quickly!'

Hardly had they entered the small living room when the door closed behind them. A small light sprang into being and a thin hand held the candlestick close to their faces.

'Highness!' a man said. 'It's you yourself! Come on in. And who are these? A strange gentleman and... The marshal's children, aren't you? Come in, come in!'

They followed the floating light to the back and Damion heard the groan of a wooden hatch. After Uwella, he went down into a low basement. Here a few candles burned and he saw their host was a stocky old man in a long buttoned robe.

Suddenly Bartram stepped forward. 'You're Beredt! The old pantryman at Grymaur.'

Their host smiled. 'Ah, Master Bartram. You have not forgotten!'

'How could we forget you; you always had something when we came down hungry.' Grisa held out her hand. 'We missed you when you were gone; the new man was very strict.'

'It is good to be remembered, Miss Grisa,' Beredt said gravely. He turned to Uwella and bowed. 'Welcome in my house, Highness. And you, of course, lord.'

He gestured to a table where two others sat, a small, skinny male and a lush woman in a slightly too tight dress.

'You will know Jupold, Highness. The lady is Levianne.'

The woman laughed, a hoarse sound that ended in a cough. 'Beredt really should start wearing glasses, if he calls me a lady.'

Uwella nodded at her and smiled at the little man. 'Jupold, I haven't seen you for ages. How are the horses?'

Jupold was drunk, so much was obvious. His eyes were bloodshot and he could hardly focus on Uwella's face. 'Not well, 'ighness,' he said thickly. 'Them monsters have eaten them.'

'I'm sorry,' Uwella said softly. 'You had poured so much effort into them.' And to Damion she added, 'Jupold was once a groomsman at Burg Grymaur. He started for himself as a horse trader.'

The man shrugged. 'There are more horses in the world, 'ighness. But first we have to get rid of them monsters.' He put his mug to his mouth and drank deeply.

'I forget my manners,' Beredt said. 'Can I get you anything, Highness? And you, lord?'

'Another time. We need to keep our heads tonight,' Uwella said.

'They're easily lost, these days.' Their host spread his hands. 'These are dark times. Trade has come to a standstill.'

Uwella turned to Damion. 'Beredt retired from our service to become an honorable merchant.'

'Honorable! That's a good one.' The blonde woman gave a laugh like a smithy's bellow.

'Hush, Vianne,' Beredt said over his shoulder. 'Don't mind her, Highness. The lady is a hostess at the inn down the road. But there is little patronage at the moment.'

'We saw some monsters in the city,' Damion said politely. 'We will rid you of their presence.'

The blonde barmaid looked at him quizzically. 'You're just a boy,' she said. 'How do you plan to do this?'

'Hush, Vianne,' Beredt said again. 'The lord is a friend of the valvodjara's.'

'I can't tell you everything,' Damion said with a smile. 'Let me say that the valvodjara and I have the power and the people to defeat the monsters. But first we need information.'

The barmaid studied his face. Finally she nodded. 'I think I believe you. Don't let me down, will you?'

Damion bowed. 'I will do my best, lady.'

Again she bellowed her loud laugh. 'Now the great lord calls me so. I'd almost believe it.'

Damion turned as Uwella touched his arm. He saw the impatience in her face and the massive anger behind it. To him, the enemy in Vavaun was a tactical problem; an obstacle keeping him from his purpose. But to Uwella, it was a personal matter. Like burglars in the house, it both offended and scared her, so he accepted her abruptness and merely nodded.

'Beredt,' Uwella said. 'What's the situation?'

The old man ran a hand through his thinning hair. 'We are occupied, Highness. Conquered by the vilest monsters imaginable. People with the head of a pig, a dog, or a cat with spots.'

'And don't forget the renegades,' the horse trader added, raising his nose from his tankard.

Beredt looked at him. 'The renegade wikken. No, I won't forget them.'

'I heard rumors,' Uwella said carefully. 'There are sorcerers posing as members of our Order?'

Beredt shook his head. 'Not posing; they really were members of the Gray Order, Highness. They knew all the passwords, all the rituals, and some of them I've known by name and face for years.'

'So they are infiltrators,' Damion said. 'This must be a long-term plan.'

'Sleepers.' Beredt sighed. 'A known merchants' trick, to put a man of your own in the house of a competitor. Disgusting, of course, but clever. This won't be an Asharte operation – not against the Gray Order. So whom do they serve?'

'It is not Asharte. Does the name "Dar'khamorth" mean something to you?' Damion looked sharply at the three Vavauners, but it was clear from their faces it rang no bell.

'The Dar'khamorth are people who want to bring back the Revenaunt and his Dead Ages,' he said. 'Rhidauna is at war with them, and so is Opit. Now Vavaun is too. Tell me from the beginning what happened, please.'

For a moment, nobody spoke, and from somewhere in the room came the rustling of a mouse. Damion watched the old man, waiting for him to speak.

'Well, lord, it all started with the murder of the castle guards and the wikken,' Beredt said. 'The real wikken, I mean. There must have been a lot of them infiltrators in the kitchens of both the burg and the kerran, because they poisoned the food for both meals at the same hour and something like that requires a tight organization.'

'Do you know of any survivors?' Uwella asked.

The man spread his hands. 'I did hear a few wikken lived, but I have no names. The whole city is silent, Highness. There are many things going on, yet no one knows what. It went so fast. With the watch out of the way, Grymaur was defenseless, and the beastmen walked right in. They are perhaps a hundred, no more, but very strong and ruthless. Before anyone realized what was going on, the bastards had taken the burg and the watchtowers.' He hesitated. 'You've heard of the Kyrstaul?'

Uwella inhaled sharply. 'I've seen it.'

'Those beasts put it to the torch to demonstrate what would happen to any resistance. Most of the folks there have fled. Those who had family in the Old Town were lucky. The others must have gone into the country, for the streets aren't safe anymore. Anyone who shows his nose outside is likely to be killed, so the people hide in their houses. That's the situation right now. As long as people have food and water, they'll manage, but then? Will those beasts butcher the entire town? Why would they do such a thing?'

Uwella didn't answer. 'My father and Marshal DeKramm?'

Beredt shrugged deprecatingly. 'I don't know either. Only that they must've been at the burg when the beastmen came.'

Damion looked at Uwella. 'We'll go to the kerran.'

'Negardien is taken, lord!' Beredt said hastily. 'After the poisoning, those infiltrators moved right inside. You can't go there.'

Damn. Whoever thought this up planned well. 'Taken? So Archodea and her wikken walked straight into their claws.'

Behind him, Grisa gasped.

'Oh, and I brought them there!' she said, shocked. 'I didn't know; all looked as usual, so calm. Oh, this is terrible.'

Damion took her hands. 'It's not your fault, girl,' he said gently. 'Archodea told you to bring them there, didn't she? So you did. It would've been wiser had she been more careful, but that's her mistake, not yours.' He grinned a little. 'Cheer up. We're going to get them out again.'

It was clear there wasn't any more information to be had here. Damion looked at Uwella and she sighed.

'Let's go to Negardien,' she said.

'Tilia's Luck to you both,' the barmaid called as they followed Beredt out of the cellar. 'And remember your promise, lord.'

'It will be all right,' Uwella whispered as the old man opened the front door to let them slip out.

'Arikal is with us, Highness.' Beredt didn't sound as if he believed it. Then the door clicked shut behind them and they were back in the dark street.

'Follow me.' Swiftly, Uwella led them away.

They hurried through deserted streets, all their senses alert. Twice they saw roaming beastmen, but both times they managed to evade detection.

'I hate running away,' Bartram muttered after the second patrol had disappeared into the dark.

'Preserve your energy; there will be fighting at the kerran,' Damion said.

Bartram grunted. 'It'll be about time.'

The kerran was as dark and silent as the rest of the city. Its walls loomed before them, hiding whatever waited inside.

'Stay here,' Damion whispered to the twins.

'More delays,' Bartram muttered.

'As soon as you learn to fly, you can come along,' Damion said. 'We'll be as quick as we can and open the gates for you. Listen for the crow's caw.'

'Go, go,' Grisa said. 'Hurry! We'll wait.' She pulled her brother back into the shadows. The two beastmasters changed into crows and soft-winged away into the night.

From the air, the kerran appeared a village within the city, with its own ramparts protecting a collection of larger and smaller houses. In the center stood a building with three floors that, unlike Adalien, looked like a temple.

Probably done for the locals, Damion thought. He remembered Archodea telling him her people didn't care for formal temples.

Within the kerran, all buildings were as lightless as the rest of Grymaur. The gates were closed and on the towers they saw dark shapes standing guard. Damion dove low over the head of one of the watchers. It was a human being, not a beastman. Only, was it a real wikke or an infiltrator?

Damion landed on the wall and shifted from crow into tiger in one bewildering changeover. He paused to get his bearings for a moment, but then he saw the watcher coming his way. He grinned as he recognized the familiar black robe of the Dar'khamorth. *No disguise, no subterfuge. Thinking yourself safe, are you?*

Without a sound, he crouched down and waited. When the man was within thirty feet, the tiger jumped and the watcher died.

From the opposite site of the gate came a cry. 'Alarm!' But then the shout broke off and the night was silent again.

'Curse it,' Uwella spat as she met him in the kerran's courtyard. 'I was slow.'

Damion gave her a quick kiss. 'Nobody heard him. Let's get that wicker gate open, before those eager twins decide to burn it down.'

Built into the main doors was a smaller one, the wicker, locked with a single, well-oiled bolt that slipped aside easily. Damion looked outside and pursed his lips around the crow's raucous laughter.

Moments later, the twins came running.

Grisa grinned. 'Took you long enough! We were about ready to go kill the first pig band we could find.'

'Patience is a warrior's virtue,' Damion said as he closed the door behind them. He looked around. 'Uwella?'

From the side of the building came another caw and they hurried over to an open window.

'In here,' Uwella said softly.

Damion hid a smile. *The twins aren't the only impatient ones.*

The windowsill was inconveniently high, but one after another they scrambled inside.

They found themselves in a small closet with a collection of brooms and pails. Damion opened the door a crack and looked out. There was no one in sight, so he stepped into the small hallway. To the left was a narrow staircase leading up. His tiger-trained ears caught the faint sound of voices coming from the first floor. One of the voices was familiar. He looked around at Uwella and pointed up. 'Archodea,' he mouthed.

Uwella nodded. At her side, Grisa's face was puzzled. 'What's she doing there?' she whispered.

Damion didn't know either. He couldn't imagine the high wikke being unfaithful to Arikal, so he supposed she was a prisoner. Still, it wouldn't hurt to be careful; there had been too much betrayal in the air already. He put a finger to his lips and motioned for the others to follow him up the back stairs.

The first floor door was open and they came to a carpeted corridor. Halfway down was the main staircase to the entrance hall. Across from the stairs was a pair of double doors and Damion nodded grimly. That's where the voices came from.

As they crept along the corridor, a door slamming below froze them. A black-clad woman walked briskly through the hall, carrying a tray of glasses.

Damion held his breath, afraid the sound of his heart beating in his throat would alert the sorceress. But her attention was focused on the tinkling glasses and she disappeared into a room without noticing.

'Phew.' Damion grinned at the others. 'We're going in.' He waited for Uwella to finish her metamorphosis and threw open the two doors.

Beyond was a comfortable room with a fire burning brightly. To the right was a long table surrounded by high-backed chairs, and to the left, rows of shelves laden with books and spell scrolls.

In front of the fireplace, Archodea sat upright in a wooden chair. Thin chains tied her wrists to the armrests, but her face was as impassive as ever. A spare woman with a graying bun stood facing her. She had a pleasant face, the sort that inspired confidence, but the sneer on her lips betrayed its falseness.

'Uwella,' the high wikke said calmly. 'Get her!'

The woman half-turned to the newcomers and her sneer became a feral grimace. She lifted her hands, but before she could finish whatever spell she planned, the full weight of an angry mountain lion slammed her down.

'Be very quiet,' Damion warned her. 'Maybe Uwella won't bite your throat immediately.'

He leaned over the Drynnath and put his knife to the fine bonds around her wrists.

'Silver-threaded rope, Archodea?' he said. 'They do fear your magic.'

The high priestess smiled. 'They're no heroes, Damion. Most traitors aren't.'

'No,' Damion said. 'I believe you.' With the rope in his hand, he looked at the woman on the ground and smiled without a hint of mirth. He leaned over her, while Uwella moved aside. The woman looked at him and there was no longer anything pleasant to her face. Her breath hissed between her bared teeth, but she said nothing. Roughly,

Damion turned her around and tied her arms, while Uwella went back into her own form.

'Done,' he said finally. 'Are there many of these jokers here, Archodea?'

'I don't know exactly,' the wikke said. 'A dozen, I think. Most traitors are in the burg, with the beastmen.'

'Traitors!' the woman tried to spit into Damion's face. 'We are no traitors, wretch.'

Uwella bent over the woman and slapped her face hard with the back of her hand. 'Take that, filthy murderess!'

'No traitors?' Damion said. 'You are Dar'khamorth; so what else would you want to call yourself?'

The woman turned livid. 'How...'

'I can smell Her slaves from afar,' Damion said carelessly.

'Don't tell her too much,' Archodea warned, but Damion showed his teeth in a tigrish smile.

'Don't worry. This Hamorthian she-dog won't leave here alive.'

'Are you going to kill me, boy?' the woman said mockingly. 'Can you do that?'

'I'm Asharte,' Damion said and for the first time in his life, he felt that way. 'I have no problem with your death, she-dog.'

Uwella looked at him and nodded in approval. 'Well said.'

'And now you will talk, dog,' Damion said, as he placed his long hunting knife to her throat. The woman stared at him, her eyes calculating.

'I think not,' she said and raised her head. Damion's knife slid through her jugular and the blood gushed forth, staining her dress and forming a pool on the polished floor. All the while her eyes shone with triumph. Then the light in them died and she collapsed.

'Curse the bitch,' Damion said, and he rose, staring at the blood forming a puddle under the dead woman's head.

Uwella put her arm around his shoulders. 'You're a real prince of Vavaun,' she said. 'Hard and ruthless.'

Damion felt a shiver run down his spine. Absently, he sheathed his knife. He didn't feel particularly ruthless, just tired. He glanced at Archodea. 'Where are your other wikken?'

'All the able ones are in the next room. I left the elders and Rhydd's gardians in the mother kerran.'

Damion heard Uwella's sharp intake of breath. 'I'm sorry,' he said softly. 'Rhydd was tricked into leaving and the Dar'khamorth destroyed Adalien.'

The Drynnath stilled as if his words had turned her into stone. Not a breath, not a blink, her eyes fixed unseeing on his face, as she took in the enormity of her loss.

Finally she stirred. 'Tell me.'

Uwella moved forward, gripping Damion's shoulder as if she took comfort in his nearness. Quietly she spoke of the call she had received, of their arrival in the kerran Adalien and the twins' tale of woe and bravery.

When she had finished, the high wikke slowly came to life again. She took a deep breath.

'Thank you.' She turned to the fire on the hearth and all was quiet. Then she whispered, 'You too, Syvvan? How is the Order ever going to survive this treachery?'

'We will fight,' Uwella said in a hard voice. 'We'll weed them out and when we've won, new wikken will come fast enough. But first we must recapture the kerran here.'

'You are right. Other thoughts are for later.' Archodea turned and smiled grimly. 'Let us first liberate our true brothers and sisters.'

'Where are they? Any guards?' Damion asked.

'They are next door, watched by two or three traitors, no more.'

'That should be no problem. How do we get in?'

'They used a special signal.' Archodea walked to the door, while the two beastmasters assumed their cat forms.

The high priestess knocked and the door opened. With a deep roar, Damion the tiger jumped and slammed the nearest false wikke to the ground. His reflexes saved him then, because he immediately jumped again and escaped the deadly energy beam that knocked away a piece of the wall. The sorcerer who had fired died immediately after, as flaming arrows pierced his black robe and set his innards to burning. Meanwhile, Bartram's burning sword tore the third infiltrator's chest to ribbons and the battle was done.

'Very efficient,' Archodea said approvingly, while she opened the door to the last room. Ten wikken sat or lay on the ground and were quickly freed from their chains.

'Uwella?' A young girl gripped the valvodjara's hand. 'How'd you get in here? They were going to kill us, Wella.'

'Try to keep me out.' Uwella grinned, embracing the girl. 'We won't let you down.'

When everyone was freed, Damion said, 'Spread out through the house, all of you. Gather your magic and sweep every floor, while we do the same with the grounds and the workplaces. Quickly now, before someone comes up with the idea to alarm the burg.'

Grimfaced, the wikken ran down the stairs. As a rule, the Grays weren't a fighting Order; they had the gardians for that. But they were fueled by fury and by no means helpless, so within the space of thirty minutes, the kerran was back in their hands.

'That was that,' Damion said as they came together in the downstairs hall. 'We got all that were inside the walls.'

'Syvvan?' Grisa said tersely.

'He wasn't here, nor the others from Adalien.'

The girl smiled thinly. 'I want him, the creepy toad.'

Damion turned to Archodea. 'Should the beastmen in the city try to retake the kerran, can you resist them?'

For a moment, the Drynnath lost her air of confidence. 'I am afraid not; we are too few. If my gardians were here, it would be different, but where have they gone?'

Damion smiled. 'We have located them. Drynnath, I will be completely honest with you. Vavaun is at war. We will protect the Gray Order, but I need Rhydd's people elsewhere.'

Archodea stiffened. 'Impossible! The gardians are servants of the Order! If you know where they are, I demand they be returned to me.'

Damion blinked at her unexpected vehemence. 'Demand?' he said, and he couldn't stop the burst of hot anger flaming up in his chest. 'After we just saved your lives? The gardians have been commandeered into the ducal service. Until we have retaken Grymaur burg and town, we will station the men of Kramm at Negardien. They will offer you protection, but remember they answer to us, not to the Gray Order.'

'If you steal our gardians, the Order will withdraw its support of Vavaun,' Archodea said sharply.

Damion growled. 'In that case, Grisa will port your people back to Adalien. This kerran will be confiscated. And be sure the other Orders will be more than pleased to take your place here.'

For a moment, Archodea stood glaring at Damion. Then she sighed. 'You win. I accept your *protection*, Valvodjar DeAsharte. Uwella, you know you are no longer a wikke, don't you?'

'Kicking me out, Archodea?' Uwella looked coolly at the Drynnath. 'I had decided to leave already. As the ruler of Vavaun, I cannot belong to any Temple Order, so the oaths I swore would have become void on my succession anyhow. But you must realize one thing. The losses you suffered and the position you find yourself in are your own fault, not of me or Vavaun. We trusted the Gray Order to keep the Dar'khamorth out of our country and you have failed us. So do not come to us with demands, Drynnath. You have lost the right.'

The high wikke looked about to explode, but then the rigidity leaked away and she smiled wanly. 'You are, of course, correct; both of you. I apologize. After the way you freed us, I should have been more gracious. I will be pleased with the presence of the brave men of Kramm and I will leave you the services of the gardians with my good will.'

Damion bowed. 'Thank you, Archodea. Vavaun and the Gray Order have long had a strong relationship and I hope this will always remain so.'

As they walked from the hall, he glanced at Uwella's closed face. 'Don't take it too hard. I shouldn't have lost my patience. She's old and upset, and her whole world lies in tatters.'

'She's spoiled,' Uwella said angrily. 'Father never said no to her, and as sole high priestess in Vavaun, she's used getting her way.'

'She won't be sole anything for long. As soon as we've licked those traitors, we'll invite all her peers to open up temples here. A bit of competition will be good for her.' Damion took her hand. 'Do you think you can work with Archodea, or would you rather fetch Kramm's soldiers?'

'Don't be daft,' Uwella snapped. 'Of course I'll work with her. I'll even smile while I'm doing it. Now hurry up and go get them.'

Damion kissed her fingers. 'As you command, m'dear.' He turned. 'Ready, Grisa?'

The girl stuck her nose in the air. 'What a stupid question; I'm always ready. Give me your hands.'

Seconds later, an arrow missed Grisa's head by a hairsbreadth and stood trembling in a tree only a dozen feet away.

'Miss Grisa!' a deadly pale archer cried. 'Don't do that again, arriving so close by the camp's entrance. I had almost killed you!'

'Good shot, soldier,' Damion said. 'Your alertness is commendable.' He looked at Grisa. 'Try counting to ten before you act,' he said sternly. 'A porter should keep their impulses under control.'

'Sorry.' Grisa looked a little pale at her near escape. 'I know. I never could. I *am* trying to be good, I really am. But it doesn't always work.' She nodded to the soldier. 'The next time I'll come out farther away.'

Damion pointed at a big oak some yards away. 'Over there. Pass the world, soldier; that dead oak is a temporary portal.' He glanced at the rain-drenched woods. 'Dismal weather.'

They found the officers standing in the mud, overseeing some joint exercises. Both were pleased to hear of Negardien's liberation, but when Damion gave him his orders, Captain Mannar frowned.

'I'm a Kramm man,' he said hesitantly. 'Of course I don't mind defending the kerran instead.' He glanced at Rhydd.

'It's all right,' the commander said. 'Go prepare your men, Captain.'

When Mannar was out of earshot, Rhydd turned to Damion. 'Why him? Defending the kerran is my duty.'

Damion grunted. 'As a prince of Gry, your prime duty is to Vavaun, and so I told Archodea. We will protect her precious Order, but it won't be by you. Mannar's people are grunts; your gardians are far more versatile. I want you on hand for other things than simple guard duty.'

'She didn't like it,' Rhydd said with a straight face.

'No, but I'm not terribly impressed by the high wikke. As your sister informed her, this whole mess is her fault. Had she been less trusting, those infiltrators wouldn't be here with their monsters.'

'You're beginning to sound like your grandfather,' Rhydd said, grinning.

Damion rubbed his eyes. 'I know. Be glad I'm not like my father. He'd have you cleaning boots for questioning your orders. Ironbiter, his men call him, and even as a sergeant, the whole army of Rhidauna feared his anger. But I'm tired, hungry, and pissed at the whole idiotic situation – Archodea, your father, my grandfather, the whole pack of fools who cared more for their petty squabbles than for the country. Now, let's go get those Kramms.'

'I know,' Grisa said. 'You're crabby. It must be the army that does it. My father can be a terrible grouch when maneuvers don't go well, or an officer misunderstands an order. Bartram has it, too.'

'And you don't?' Damion said.

'Never.' Grisa smiled brightly, looking like a just-surfaced mermaid with her hair plastered to her wet face. 'I get mean; real mean. But not crabby.'

When they returned and Bartram came hurrying to show the men their quarters, Damion joined Uwella in the hall.

'Jupold is here,' she said immediately. 'He wants to talk to you and you alone.'

Damion hung his dripping cloak across a chair. 'That horse trader? Funny, I only just met the man. Where is he?'

'In the common room. He isn't sober yet.'

'No. The loss of his horses must've hit him hard.'

The small man stood with his hands in his pockets, inspecting the painting of a famous Vavaunan nobleman from a bygone era.

'A miserable 'orse,' he said as Damion walked into the room. 'Nervy.'

Damion looked at the rider and his mount and somehow the scene reminded him of a horse a coper had once tried to sell him. The painter was good; he'd portrayed the horse's expression well.

'That beast is scared,' he said. 'His rider seems an angry type.'

'That's often so,' Jupold said. He turned around, a little unsteadily. 'You know 'orses, lord?'

Damion smiled. 'Not in particular; I know animals. I'm a beastmaster, so I can read their thoughts.'

'Oo-aah, is that so?' The horse breeder looked wistful. 'Would be wonnerful, that.'

Damion inspected the man, with his bleary eyes, filthy clothes, and the unmistakable horsiness of the born stabler. He was really very drunk. 'You had something to tell me, Jupold?'

'What?' Jupold tried to focus his eyes. 'Oh, yes, lord. I talked to a buddy of mine. He passed a farm with many 'orses.' The man fell silent and stared into the distance; to a farm full of horses perhaps, or maybe just into nothingness.

'Go on,' Damion said softly.

Jupold steadied himself, leaving a smudge on the wall where his hand touched the plasterwork. 'Eh? Oh, what I wanted to say. He saw *him* there.'

Damion looked expectantly at Jupold. 'Him?'

'Him,' Jupold said impatiently. 'Their father.'

'Whose father?'

Jupold burped. 'The little porter and that bruising brother of 'ers.'

'Grisa and Bartram's father? DeKramm?'

'Yes, him. The Marshal of Waw...Vavaun.'

'Where is that farm, Jupold?'

'Over there,' the drunken little man waved vaguely to the northeast. 'In the woods. Smelaz.'

Suddenly the horse breeder's lights went out and he slid to the ground before Damion could catch him.

Uwella came in with two cups of hot cawah. 'I think Jupold could use this. Where is he?'

Damion nodded toward the snoring man on the floor. 'Too late, our hero has lost the battle.'

'Then I'll drink it myself,' she said. 'Did he have something useful to tell?'

'Does the name Smelaz tell you anything?'

Uwella looked at him over the rim of her cup. 'Do you mean the glover, the miller, or Smelaz-in-the-Forest?'

'Oh, it's a person, too? The latter, I think. Jupold spoke of a farm with lots of horses.'

'That's Smelaz-in-the-Forest. They're the biggest horse breeders in the duchy. Why?'

Damion stepped closer to the roaring hearth and watched his clothing steam. 'I'm evaporating,' he said inconsequentially.

Uwella snorted. 'You should turn tiger; you'll dry much faster without clothes.'

'No need; we'll be going out again.' He looked at Uwella. 'Jupold told me a friend of his had seen the twins' father at this Smelaz place.'

'The marshal!' Uwella cried. 'Has he escaped? That's great news. He's a good soldier, Baron DeKramm. We must get to him.'

Damion turned and shouted. 'Grisa!'

'Coming!' A moment later the twins ported almost into his arms.

'Darn; use your feet,' Damion growled.

'Now you sound like my mother,' Grisa said.

'Then she is right. Listen, do you know the farm of a man called Smelaz?'

'The horse breeder? Sure.'

'Can you port the four of us there?'

Flash.

'Not so fast!' Damion shouted, stumbling as he found himself in the grass beside a muddy path. All around them was a forest of tall firs, and a pale sun tried to brighten the gloomy scene.

Uwella hid a grin behind her hand. Even as children, Grisa had always been the one to act first and think later. She'd ported the three of them into trouble often enough. Out of it as well.

Grisa lifted her chin. 'You wanted a port to Smelaz? Well, you're here.'

'Dammit, think first, girl,' Damion said. 'Before you port us all into a mass of beastmen.'

'If you can do it better?' the girl huffed.

'We can,' Damion snapped. 'Our hawks aren't all that much slower. But then we'll leave you and your brother with Archodea and you will miss all the fun.'

The girl blanched. 'No! I'll be nice.'

'She will behave,' Bartram growled. 'If she knows what's good for her.'

Grisa gave her brother a dark look but kept her mouth shut.

Uwella winked at Bartram and his face relaxed into a grin.

In silence, the four of them walked down the dirt path. Once through the next bend, they saw the farm – a low stone building with a sagging thatched roof. Beside the house was a pasture with a small herd of horses. In the farmyard stood a man watching them graze.

'Daddy!' Grisa cried. Without thought, she ported directly into the man's arms.

'Hey!' Bartram said and started running.

Uwella gripped Damion's arm and hurried after them. They were just in time to see father and son hugging each other.

The marshal was a tall man with a moustache and the long hair of a swordsman, without the curls that characterized his children. His uniform was immaculate, with no hint of having been in a battle.

'What are you two doing here?' he said gruffly. 'I thought you were in Rhidauna?'

'Oh, Dad,' Grisa cried. 'The castle! They have destroyed our home!'

DeKramm nodded. 'I know, girl. But how...'

Damion took a step forward. 'Grisa and Bartram are here because those beastmen raided the kerran Adalien as well.'

The man turned away from his children and inspected Damion sternly. 'Who are you, sir?'

'Marshal DeKramm,' Uwella said in a commanding tone she rarely used.

The marshal looked at her and his face tautened as he recognized her.

72

'Highness,' he said, his eyes suddenly watchful. 'I did not expect you here.'

His reaction surprised Uwella. DeKramm was House Gry's staunchest supporter, besides being the father of her best friends, and his unexpected stiffness bothered her.

'I'm the Valvodjara,' she said, instinctively falling back on her imperial pose. 'When my land is in danger, I will come to its defense.'

'We are all grateful for your presence.' The marshal said. He hesitated. 'I have bad news for you.'

Uwella's heart skipped a beat, but she only lifted an eyebrow. 'More bad news?'

DeKramm straightened. 'The monsters have captured your father.'

'My father?' For a moment, Uwella was at a loss for words. Damion drew his arm around her, but she brushed him off. *I can handle this!* She swallowed against a strange lump in her throat. 'The fool!' she said. 'Even that...' But the usual anger wouldn't come. She took a deep breath and lifted her chin. *Father is captured. I must act now, may the Gods help me.*

'Marshal,' she said, and her voice was hard and steady. 'In my father's absence, I rule Vavaun.'

DeKramm stepped back as if she'd slapped him. 'You have no experience, Highness. Your youth, your gentle sex...'

Gentle sex? You blithering idiot! she wanted to scream, but she knew she had to stay in control. She made a chopping motion with her right hand.

'I have reached my majority, Marshal. And what the heck have those men of experience brought Vavaun? Endless bickering that sapped our country's strength and when the real enemy came, they failed us.'

She stared at the marshal as if she saw him for the first time. *I thought him stronger. Is he another of my father's yes-men?* A massive anger welled up inside her and it must have shown, for she saw the marshal stiffen.

'I'm the Valvodjara,' she said in an iron voice. 'I am my father's rightful successor. Are you loyal, Marshal DeKramm? Are you?'

Without taking her eyes off the marshal, Uwella noted the twins' stiff postures and knew what they must feel right now. Her own father's pedestal had shattered years ago, long before she and her siblings ran away from home to join the Gray Order. It is painful to discover your parents are only human.

DeKramm capitulated. 'Always, Highness.'

Grisa relaxed slightly, but Bartram looked at his father with narrowed eyes and Uwella wondered what the boy was thinking. Grisa gripped her brother's arm as if she wanted to keep a rein on him, and her eyes went from Bartram to their father and back.

The boy opened his mouth, but Damion was quicker.

'Are you here alone, Marshal?' he asked.

Bartram closed his mouth again and nodded.

DeKramm turned his head. 'Certainly not, sir. I have the full nightwatch of Burg Grymaur with me; fifty men.'

Again, Bartram seemed about to say something, but then he watched Damion instead.

Damion nodded. 'Fifty men. How come you all managed to escape the city?'

DeKramm looked as if the question affronted him. He turned to Uwella. 'Highness?'

'Marshal,' Uwella formulated her words clearly. 'In this time of war, the Great Houses of Vavaun have shed their differences. This is Damion, the Valvodjar of Asharte. Please answer his questions.'

'Asharte!' For a moment, the marshal looked taken aback. Then he saluted. 'Welcome, Highness. DeGry and DeAsharte working together. That will make my job much easier.'

'I am glad you approve, Marshal DeKramm,' Uwella said curtly. 'This is the new fashion in Vavaun. I expect all our liegemen to make peace with each other will they, nill they.

There are dangerous forces trying to destroy our country and we must stand together to survive. The Valvodjar Damion is my co-ruler and in overall military command.' *There, let's see how you take that.*

DeKramm's thin cheeks turned slightly purple. 'You have martial experience, Prince DeAsharte?'

At least he doesn't start screaming, Uwella thought. *That's positive.*

Damion stood as tall as his stature let him. 'I've fought the Dar'khamorth actively for the last two years at the side of King Ghyllander. Golems, beastmen, firebirds, daghuur – we've beaten them all. And I have been trained in the tactics of war since I was old enough to climb onto the map table at home. My father is without doubt the best instructor at the Rhidaunan military academy and he force-fed me on the stuff. I know what I'm doing, Marshal. Now kindly answer my question.'

'Thank you, Highness,' DeKramm said, surrendering a second time. 'It wasn't a matter of escaping, as we weren't in the burg when the enemy came. You see, that day was the second of Gramatte, the day of the yearly Veststaul Hunt.'

The poison attack was on a Hunt Day? I hadn't realized that.

'Would you care to explain that?' Damion said.

'The Veststaul quarter of Grymaur supplies the nightwatch, both men and materiel,' DeKramm said stiffly. 'The Eststaul quarter provides the daywatch. The Veststaul men have their hunt in the month of Gramatte, the Eststaul men in Ogstall. It's an old tradition.'

Damion nodded slowly. 'I see. So twice a year Grymaur has only half its number of soldiers. The enemy must have liked that.'

'Highness!' The marshal looked outraged. 'How could I know there *was* an enemy?'

You should have, Marshall, Uwella thought. *That is your job, even if my father didn't encourage independent thought.*

It was clear Damion thought the same, for his face was politely critical.

'The Dar'khamorth has attacked Rhidauna, Opit, and the Nhael,' he said. 'Was there any reason to suppose Vavaun would be spared?'

DeKramm frowned. 'Is it indeed the Hamorth we are up against? I remember when Duke Venric returned from King Ghyllander's coronation, he informed me of the sorcerers attacking Rhidauna's fleet. He told me to prepare, strengthen the garrisons and all that.' The marshal fell silent, as if unsure how to go on.

'But?' Damion prompted.

DeKramm sighed. 'No extra budget. Soldiers like to be paid; if not, they leave. Present funding is barely enough to keep Grymaur and Gry manned. The other garrisons are privately financed. And though I am commander of all Vavaun's forces, the troops of Asharte follow only their own leaders. I sent a messenger to Duke Cymric. His highness told me he would defend his part of the country and advised me to take care of mine. That ended the preparations.'

'I'll square Asharte,' Damion said. 'As soon as we're done here, we'll go north.'

Uwella looked at the marshal. *That hunt business – it must be an unhappy coincidence... He can't be an infiltrator; he's too much the Vavaunan baron to betray his country. Damn, I'm going out of my mind. Not DeKramm; I've known him all my life.*

'You know what happened in Burg Grymaur?' she said suddenly.

All stiffness left DeKramm and he looked both shocked and worried. 'Yes, Highness. I had an agent in the burg who sent me a report. To poison the daywatch... What monsters would do a thing like that?'

'The Dar'khamorth isn't concerned with lives,' Damion said. 'Who prepared the soldiers' meals?'

'Our kitchen staff is supplied by the kerran,' DeKramm said. 'That relieved my budget, you see.'

So that's how they did it, Uwella thought. *Those homicidal scums cooked for kerran and watch both.* 'Was that arranged with the Drynnath?' she said.

'No, it was a suggestion of the Negardien wikken. I saw no harm in it.' The marshal looked agonized now. 'Apparently I was wrong.'

'Yes,' Damion said. 'But I accept you weren't to expect treason from inside the Gray Order.' He gave a grim smile. 'Probably their yearly hunt saved the nightwatch being poisoned as well.' He slapped his thigh. 'Let me fill you in on the situation. Grymaur and the burg are in enemy hands, but we have retaken Negardien. The Drynnath leads the wikken. I left your captain in command of the garrison.'

'Mannar?' The marshal brightened a little. 'That is fortunate. I thought all had fallen. How many men has he got?'

'Twenty-eight. Prince Rhydd arrived at Kramm during the battle. Together, they defeated the attackers and pulled back on Andauz. I took the gardians away from their Order and made Rhydd general of Vavaun for the duration. I want to concentrate our forces in one spot, ready to leave at a moment's notice.'

DeKramm straightened. 'Prince Rhydd is at Andauz? Then I will gather my men and join him there. Bartram, Grisa, I want you to come with me.'

'No, sir,' Bartram said, his face hard. 'I can't.'

'Nor I.' Grisa still gripped her brother's arm, and the look she gave her father was filled with defiance.

'You children have your duty. You will come with me,' DeKramm said.

Bartram crossed his arms over his chest. 'I've sworn an oath to serve Vavaun. The valvodjars need every sword they can get.'

'And I'm the only porter in the country. Besides,' Grisa said, 'we're no longer children. Both of us are bloodied warriors.'

Damion took DeKramm's arm. 'I understand your concern, Marshal. But the twins have proved themselves as soldiers. At Adalien, the two of them killed many pigmen. I don't know when you saw the twins last, but between them, the fire knights and the gardians turned those two and their magic into young warriors any general would be proud to have under his command.'

'They're only fifteen, Highness,' the marshal said stiffly.

'We are DeKramm,' Grisa said. 'No DeKramm runs away from their responsibilities. How often have you told us that?'

For a moment, the marshal looked at his children's unyielding faces, and then he nodded. 'So I eat my own words. If that is where your duty lies... Go with the valvodjars.' His face smoothed out, as if he wiped his parental worries from his mind. He turned to Uwella. 'Highness, would you inspect the troops? I think it is important they see you and know you have taken over.'

Uwella looked at him, her eyes narrowing. *I have taken over. I'm the Valvoda now. Damn, I've been waiting for this for years, but not in the middle of a war, nor with father in the dungeons. Buck up, girl; you must show them you can do it.* 'Of course, Marshal,' she said coolly, feeling a little bit guilty as she saw him start breathing again after her stare. 'Give them time to get ready, I'll be there.' *And I need time as well. Time to change.*

DeKramm saluted and strode away.

Damion had followed the whole scene with mixed feelings. He understood Uwella's excitement at being ruler, her apprehension, and her worry. At the same time, he could imagine DeKramm's dilemma. Duke Venric wasn't dead, only imprisoned. The marshal of all people must know Uwella left court to join the Grays because she strongly disagreed with her father's rule. For six years she had stayed away from Vavaun, certain her father wouldn't let her escape a second time if he caught her.

DeKramm as commander-in-chief was enough of a politician to realize Uwella, with her two siblings' aid, had enough of a following within House Gry to keep the throne for herself even when Venric would return. That he acquiesced in her accession meant he chose her side.

Damion couldn't help smiling a little. To all effects, he'd just witnessed a coup d'état, whether his love realized it or not. He turned to Uwella. 'It is done. What now?'

'I must have water and towels,' Uwella said hurriedly. 'Grisa, help me. Is anyone of the locals here?'

They walked over to the house, but the farm was abandoned. Damion followed her and Grisa into the kitchen. 'Away with you!' she said, pushing him back to the door. 'Go play outside with Bartram. Pick some flowers, speak with the horses, whatever. Leave us women alone.'

Damion had no idea what she intended, but he knew her well enough to do what she said. He put a hand on Bartram's shoulder and steered him back out. At the pasture, they leaned on the gate and stared at the horses.

'All right?' Damion said after a moment's silence.

'I'm pretty mad,' Bartram said. 'I never saw father like that. He didn't trust you and Uwella. Or us. It made me feel ashamed.'

Damion looked aside at the boy's angry face. 'Don't. Try to see it from his side. Your father lost half his force to treason while he was out hunting. Even if he couldn't help it – and I'm sure he couldn't – it must hurt him terribly. He has lost his ruler and now he gets a new one who is both a girl – did Vavaun ever have a female ruler? I guess not – and one not all that much older than his own daughter. To top it all, a whippersnapper enemy – me – supersedes him as top commander. Give him time to adjust. You and your sister got what you wanted; she's transport officer and you are aide to the valvodjars. Let that be enough.'

Bartram's hands gripped the old wooden post of the fence. 'It must, I suppose. Still, Dad was always so, well, in command. Untouchable. You see what I mean? Nothing like he was just now. For a moment...' He lowered his voice. 'For a moment, I thought he would deny Uwella. Break his oath.'

And he did, Damion thought. *He broke his oath to Venric in favor of Uwella. But I'm not going to tell that to his children.* 'A moment of doubt is normal; your father is only human,' he said. 'All parents are. I thought my father a tyrant, a fearful monster. I was terribly glad when our liege lord took me away from him. Now I wonder if he wasn't simply frustrated because I refused to become a soldier like him.'

Bartram stared at him. 'You *what*? But you are a soldier.'

'I'm not,' Damion said. 'My tiger is a fighter; not me. I'm a general and that's not at all the same. It is why I don't wear a sword. I don't *want* to wear a sword; I fight with my mind.'

Bartram shook his head. 'I don't understand.'

'Don't worry.' Damion slapped the boy's shoulder. 'It's just my way of coping with a bully of a father.'

From the corner of his eye, he saw the kitchen door open and Uwella came out. All thoughts of soldiers and generals vanished as he took in the change. Gone was the white face paint, the feathers, the lace, and all the other frills. Gone was the wikke and in her stead came a young woman, one not too tall and somewhat chubby. She wasn't pretty. No one would stop and stare after her in the street. But her skin was clear, her lips were pleasantly full, and the funny dimple was unchanged. Overall, Damion liked the difference; she was still Uwella. His Uwella. He reached out to her and shyly she stepped into his embrace. He kissed her and she sighed.

'Why?' he asked softly.

'Archodea said it; I'm no longer a Gray Wikke.' She looked at him. 'For years I thought the Order infallible, superior to the other temples. Now I know they're not. They are nice, well-meaning, and very silly. I'm done with them.' She lifted her chin. 'I'm the Valvodjara-regent.'

He hugged her without speaking. Behind her brave words lay a world of hurt. That her own Order had been the Dar'khamorth's instrument to occupy her beloved country must feel like betrayal. They stood holding each other for a moment; then she pulled away.

'We should go; the troops are waiting.' She whistled like a street urchin and Grisa came running from the kitchens.

'Do you like the change?' the girl said breathlessly. 'She's back being Uwella again. I love it.'

'I love her too,' Damion said with a straight face.

Grisa laughed. 'You see,' she said to Uwella. 'I told you he'd like it.'

As they walked to the camp, Bartram gripped his sister's arm. 'What happened?' he said softly, with a surreptitious glance at Uwella.

Grisa shook her head. 'Nothing you'd understand.'

Her brother closed his mouth and shook his head. 'Girls,' he muttered.

DeKramm's base was set up on a large paddock just inside the forest. Where Rhydd's gardians had come to Andauz fully kitted-out, the nightwatch had been on a festive day's hunting and the men carried only their personal gear. In spite of that, Uwella thought they built a neat camp.

For want of tents, the soldiers had made five-man huts of leafy branches. They had dug small earthen fire troughs on which each man cooked his own meal in his mess bowl and there were none of the usual large fires for roasting deer, which produced a lot of smoke to betray their presence.

The fifty men of the nightwatch of Vavaun lined up at the forest edge. Their uniforms were polished to a shine; the black tabards with their silver wolfshead badges immaculate and their weapons sharp and shiny.

As the two valvodjars approached, the marshal saluted and led them past the waiting lines. Solemnly Uwella inspected each soldier, touching a slightly crooked strap here, testing the sharpness of a blade there, all with sternness as if it was the Duke's Day Parade.

When she had complimented the last man, a nervous and very pimply young drummer, Uwella turned to face the troops.

'Men,' she said, and her voice rang out over the camp. 'Vavaun is depending on you. Our country goes through difficult times, but we will overcome together. Together, just as the Valvodjar Damion DeAsharte and I fight together against the enemies threatening our homeland. For know this, soldiers of Grymaur, as of today there is no more conflict between Gry and Asharte. We are one people. We are Vavaun. As Vavaun, we stand strong. As Vavaun, we will overcome. We recaptured the kerran Negardien; now the men of Kramm stand guard there. Soldiers of the Nightwatch, my brother Prince Rhydd and his gardians await your arrival in their camp at Andauz. Our porter Grisa will bring you to them. Valvodjar Damion and I will go to collect more troops, and when we are enough, we will retake Grymaur burg and town. We will avenge our murdered people. Vavaun will overcome!'

'Three cheers for our rulers!' the marshal shouted and the men yelled their throats hoarse. This was the language they understood, the words they wanted to hear. They had leaders, a plan, and a purpose.

On the marshal's command, the ranks changed into the close formation for porting, and Grisa flashed them away.

Uwella turned to Damion and cursed softly. 'There's so few of them.'

'That means they have to be smarter,' Damion said. 'It's not the numbers, it's the quality. Our men can beat those stupid pigs any time.' He touched her cheek with his fingers. 'You did beautiful, love. Just the right words.'

'Love?' she said, surprised. 'That's what Ghyll says to Kerianna.'

'I know. He's serious and so am I.'

'Well,' Uwella said, feeling suddenly better. Then she grinned. 'You're our warleader now, so I should leave the planning to you. What's next?'

'Grandfather,' Damon said immediately. 'We need him on our side, one way or another.'

'So we'll go to Asharte; it's a long walk away.'

'Asharte?' Bartram swallowed. 'No man of Gry ever goes there. Will they let us pass? It's not like Grymaur; the people of the north are very distrustful of strangers.'

Damion patted his jacket's inner pocket. 'I have a letter. Last year, I met the old man, ah, Duke Cymric that is, at King Ghyll's marriage to Kerianna of Opit. I didn't know him, and he didn't know I existed. Nor did we see eye to eye, and as I had my obligations to Ghyll, I only promised to seek him out when I was free. Before he left Rhidauna, he sent me a letter acknowledging me Damion, Valvodjar of Asharte. Even illiterates will recognize that fat bear seal of his.'

Uwella patted his cheek. 'Brilliant. Now, why don't you boys surprise our porter and get us some horses? There's a meadow full of them and the owner has fled. I'm sure you'll find tack for them in the stables.'

'Ooh,' Grisa said when she came back and found four mounts waiting. She clapped her hands. 'We'll ride a real horse? With a saddle? Better and better. But why four?'

'Because horses and big cats are a bad mix,' Uwella said. 'Horses aren't very clever, and they scare easily. So we'll all ride.' She grinned at Damion. 'Like in the good old times with Ghyll. And this time I am better prepared.' She hopped in the saddle and pulled up her skirt, displaying a pair of tight leather breeches underneath. 'Horsebreeder Smelaz must be about my size. These fit quite well.'

'They suit you,' Damion said admiringly. 'An elegant leg, love.'

Uwella bowed. 'Thank you, kind sir.'

As they rode away from the farm, she listened with a small part of her mind to the sounds of the beasts in the fields. They left the forest and followed a narrow trail through a mountain pass into the next valley. The birds sang, wild goats leaped across their path and disappeared, a fox, a far-away bear – all the normal sounds and sights of the countryside. *No beastmen yet.* Uwella thought. *I wonder how many are there?* Then, just as they rode through a small brook, she caught a thought and reined in to listen.

Damion stopped beside her and grimaced in disgust. 'Vile beasts!'

'What's wrong?' Grisa said. As she looked around, her hand went automatically to the bow sheath at her hip. 'Danger?'

'Beastmen,' Uwella said. 'About a mile away.'

The girl growled softly. 'Many of them? We should have a look.'

Uwella hesitated, and then nodded. 'A handful, at most.'

After ten minutes, they came to the edge of a stony field with a few buildings and what looked like a small chapel, all built of local stone.

'I thought their minds felt different,' Uwella whispered, when she saw the lanky shapes. 'They're some sort of dogs.'

'There's only four of them,' Grisa said in a low voice.

They left the horses bound to a fence and crept closer. The dogmen were watching the chapel door. One of them, a broad-shouldered monster with a black stripe down its spotted back, gripped the door handle and gave a mighty pull. The door groaned, but held. From inside the chapel came the screams of terrified villagers and the monster bayed in excitement.

Uwella went mountain lion. Her cat's screaming rage was a bone-chilling sound and the dogmen wheeled around. The black-striped one barked and went for his sword, but it hadn't counted on the mountain lion's reach. Uwella jumped across the forty feet dividing them. Her claws tore into the monster's bare chest and her sharp teeth went for its jugular. With an audible sound of ripping muscle, she tore open its throat and the monster fell down dead.

Blazing, the cat turned. The second dogman yowled and fled.

'Mine!' Grisa screeched, and Uwella slithered to a full stop as a fiery arrow tore past in pursuit of the fleeing beast. It caught the dogman between the shoulderblades and with a high-pitched scream, the monster tumbled onto the grass. Flames sprang up around the wound and erupted from its nose and mouth.

Meanwhile, Bartram engaged a yellow-stained dogman. With his sword blazing in one hand and his flaming dagger in the other, he looked nothing like a fifteen-year-old boy and the monster yelped in fear.

'Die!' Bartram cried, slashing at the beast. The dogman leaped aside, but the flaming sword caught him in the shoulder, and the dagger followed into the flank. The wounds burned and the dogman fell down, writhing and howling. Then Bartram stooped and cut its throat. Blood gushed out, carrying flames with it, and the dogman died.

Damion had killed the fourth dogman and stood watching the others, lashing his tail and growling noisily.

Bartram looked around. 'We got them all? Good.' The flames on his blades died and he sheathed his weapons. 'Father should have seen this,' he said softly. 'I don't think he really believes we can do it.'

'He will,' Grisa said confidently.

Uwella uttered a piercing yell of triumph. Then she took her human form and walked to the chapel door.

'Hello in there,' she called. 'It is safe. The monsters are dead and you can come out.'

'No!' a voice cried. 'Don't believe them; it's a trap!'

'All right,' Uwella said. 'If you don't want to believe me, then you won't. As you wish; we're not going to wait on a bunch of whiny cowards.'

'We're no cowards!' a deep voice said. 'Those monsters are terribly dangerous!'

'They're dead, friend. But if you think I'm lying, then stay inside, by all means. By Tilia, let's go. I've had enough of this.'

'She calls on Tilia, so she can't be a monster,' a woman said hopefully.

'I'll open the door,' the deep voice said. 'I think she speaks the truth.'

Chains rattled and twenty men, women, and children appeared, blinking their eyes against the light.

'They're truly dead!' the man with the deep voice said.

Damion nodded gravely, trying not to laugh. The deep voice belonged to a scrawny little person whose face had turned sickly green at the sight of the fallen dogmen.

'These are dead, but are they the only ones? Who protects us if there are more of these beasts?' a young man with long blond hair cried, his face contorted. 'Where is the army? The duke?'

Uwella raised her hand. 'Calm down, friend. These aren't the only monsters in the land. They got Grymaur and captured the duke. The valvodjara is back and she has taken command.'

'You bring bad news,' the man with the deep voice said. 'The valvodjara is only a girl!'

Uwella stiffened. 'She is not "only a girl", fellow. I... The valvodjara is a trained fighter. Besides, she is not alone. Gry and Asharte have put aside their quarrels and stand hand in hand in defense of our country.'

'It's about time,' the blond man said. 'We farmers are fed up with those eternal battles. But who will defend us now?'

Uwella looked at him intently. 'Do you want an honest answer? Nobody. You have two choices – Prince Rhydd and the Marshal of Vavaun are gathering an army to fight the enemy. You can join them; their camp is near Kramm.'

'But... But...' The blond man was at a loss for words.

'All our possessions are here,' a woman wailed. 'Who says the monsters won't destroy the farms if we leave?'

'Not me,' Uwella said calmly. 'Your second choice is to stay here and defend yourself.'

'We are not soldiers, lady.' The man with the deep voice stared with a hopeless look at the dead monster. 'Against beings like those, we are helpless.' Then he gestured at the women and children. 'I must think of my family. I'm going to the prince.'

The blond man clenched his fists. 'Then so must I,' he said dully. He turned and shouted, 'Get our things together. Anything you can bear. Quickly, we're leaving.'

'The cow,' the man with the deep voice said. 'What do I do with the cow?'

Grisa looked at Uwella. 'I can take them to Rhydd. Cattle and all.'

Uwella nodded. 'Good idea. You hear it, folks. Our porter will bring you to the prince's camp. You can take the cow.'

'Is she that strong?' the man said doubtfully.

'She's the valvodjara's transport officer,' Uwella said.

'Then I thank you very much, lady porter.' And to his wife, 'You hear it; now be quick about it.'

The locals ran to their houses to collect what they could carry and within twenty minutes they were back, laden and ready.

'You saved our lives,' the man with the deep voice said, bent low under an assortment of farming tools. 'I can't thank you enough.'

'There's no need,' Uwella said. 'We are all Vavauners.'

Then the group flashed away.

Uwella sighed as she turned to Damion. 'May the gods help our poor farmers if there are many such beasts on the loose.'

She walked over to the nearest dead body. 'They're less bulky than pigmen.'

'They look like those jackals we saw in Opit,' Damion said. 'They have that same lean, starved look.'

'But why the beastly cruelty?'

'To put fear into the people,' Damion said. 'They're a terror weapon, no more.' He sat down in the grass and closed his eyes.

Uwella grinned and sat down across from him. Around her the birds whistled and all was back to normal.

Damion woke up when she shook his shoulder.

'The twins are back.'

Damion blinked and grew red-faced. 'I fell asleep? Sorry, love; how rude of me. You should've kicked me.'

'No,' Uwella said contentedly. 'I spent the time watching you. You look cute when you sleep, boy.'

Damion grinned a little sheepishly. 'Thank you.' He glanced at Grisa, who couldn't suppress a huge grin. 'Don't laugh, girl!'

'I think it's sweet!' Grisa said. 'Oh, he's sooo cuuute....'

Damion grabbed her around the waist and held her upside down. With long strides, he walked to the rain barrel at the front of the nearest house and held her head just above the water.

'Are you done laughing, or shall I teach you to swim?' he asked menacingly.

'That's not... cute,' she snorted. 'Let me go! I'm done already. Would you like to know what my father said?'

Damion set her back onto her feet. 'What did he say?'

'He thanks you for the milk, and he thinks it a good idea you sent those people. He's already sent out scouts to collect as many refugees as possible. He'll teach all able folk some fighting techniques, and enlist them as aux... aux...'

'Auxiliaries,' Damion said. 'Reserve troops. Very good; we need every sword we can get.'

'Yes,' Grisa said. 'And I brought some more provisions.'

'You did? For that, I forgive you your transgressions,' Damion said grandiosely. 'Let's eat.'

The girl bowed. 'You are too good, Highness.'

They sat down in the grass and shared the bread and cheese. After a few minutes of silence, Bartram coughed. 'Asharte?'

'Hmm?' Damion said with his mouth full.

'Do you know about the gods?'

Damion swallowed the bite. 'The gods. What's with them?'

The boy seemed unsure, uncommonly shy about something. 'Do they, well, *talk* to people?' Bartram said. 'Ordinary people, not priests or kings?'

'It happens,' Damion said carefully. 'Not often, but sometimes they do. Why? Did you hear one?'

Bartram nodded. 'I think so. When I fought that dog. He said how to do it and when I did, it worked.'

'He?' Damion said. 'Which god was it?'

The boy frowned. 'Fantus. He was in my head and spoke to me. He laughed, you know. In a nice way. He said his father wasn't the only one who could inspire warriors. Only he used twins, he said. Igniter twins, whatever that may be.'

'Fire-lighters. Is that what you did with that dogman?'

'The beast burned, didn't it? Inside, I mean.'

Grisa stared at her brother. 'Like my pigmen did. You mean that's *Fantus'* doing? But he's a smith. I know nothing about smithing.'

'He's the god of fire, as well,' Damion said slowly. 'Not fire as an elemental, that's Wimaun. But fire as a raw force, a tool. You should ask Bo Lusindral if you want to know more. He's Rhidauna's court mage and a good friend. But this is something... If Fantus claims you two, that's new. And his father did the same to someone else? Mainal isn't my idea of the ideal patron.' He stared at Uwella, but she could only shrug.

'No idea what it's all about,' she admitted. 'I've never heard of gods claiming people.' She frowned at Bartram. 'I must think on this. Tell us the next time he visits you.'

CHAPTER 5 – WEDERGANGERS

After the meal, they left the hamlet with the dead beastmen and continued their journey northward. A winding trail led them around the mountain and through a pass to the next valley.

The view from up here was breathtaking and under other circumstances, Damion would have enjoyed the hues of the wooded mountain ridges disappearing into the cloudy horizon. But his mind was on Asharte, and each new ridge was just one more obstacle on their journey.

Late that afternoon they saw the square shape of a small keep in the distance.

'Erpenstaun,' Uwella said. 'The lord is one of your grandfather's vassals. I've seen him at my father's court once or twice. A bit of a plodder, I thought – but I was a lot younger then, and prejudiced against Ashartes.'

Damion grinned. 'Were you now? Let's forget him. I want my grandfather; we can meet his liegemen another day.'

The road let them through a landscape of rocky, still winter-bare fields and passed Erpenstaun within a mile. Automatically, Damion sent his thoughts round the area. 'No beastmen. I hear nothing.'

'I do.' Grisa sat with her head tilted and her eyes closed. She shivered. 'It's creepy.'

'Moaning,' Bartram added. 'Like...unhappy cows.'

Now Damion's ears caught it as well; a low-pitched sobbing, frightening and full of a brainless longing. In his mind he saw the mighty undead armies that sick bastard Vasthul had gathered that day at the Owan Abai. Those had sounded the same; the hungering voices of the undead.

'This changes things,' he said. 'If there is trouble, we'll have to aid those people.'

Uwella sighed. 'I hate those stinking corpses. But you're right.'

Damion touched Bartram's shoulder. 'Ever seen wedergangers? I'll show you.'

They came to a small river on the other side of the keep. It stood on a small hill, surrounded by a wall and a moat; a tall, square structure of gray stone, about three stories high, with a single garret serving as lookout tower. Around it were several buildings, probably barns and workplaces. From the garret roof, a proud banner displayed a red cock prancing on a green field. To the left was a palisaded village of small stone cottages.

'A nice property,' Damion said. 'Not over-large, but easy to defend. The village seems empty; perhaps the folks didn't trust their stockade and ran to the keep.' He pointed at the figures shambling up and down the banks of the moat. 'Can't blame them. See those wedergangers – they're undead, but no soldiers. The one who raised them must've used the local cemetery. Somehow that makes it even worse.'

'By the Fire,' Bartram whispered, fingering his sword hilt. His face was a mixture of loathing and horror at the sight of the decaying bodies. 'What did you call them?'

'They're wedergangers; walking corpses.' Damion's face was grim. 'Look around the fields; there must be a necromancer somewhere. That's the one we have to eliminate.'

'What are they doing here?' Grisa said. 'They can't hurt the castle, can they?' She had taken her bow from its case and was readying it.

'Not the castle.' Damion stared at the top of the keep, where he saw tiny figures walking back and forth. Occasionally, an arrow came down without doing any damage to the lumbering corpses. He looked at Grisa. 'Can you bring us inside?'

The girl shook her head. 'I need a place to port to...' Then her eyes narrowed as she stared at the keep. 'Wait here,' she said absently. 'You too, brother,' and flashed away.

'Hey!' Bartram began, but before he had finished, she was back.

'I can port you,' she said, beaming. 'I just went to that bit of roof I saw up there. It has a stairwell beneath it. I could see most of the courtyard; easy as pie.' She grabbed Damion's hand and Uwella's arm, and moments later they and their horses were in the courtyard of the keep, in full view of various nervous archers.

'Asharte!' Damion roared. 'Asharte!'

Bartram waved an arm and several arrows dropped from the sky, burning.

'Sis, you're a fool,' he said scathingly. 'Start using your brain, before you get us all killed!'

'Your reflexes are perfect, laddie,' Damion said, but that was as far as he got. Several soldiers pressed forward, their eyes wild as they waved their weapons. A gaunt man in old-fashioned armor forced his way past them and pointed the tip of his sword at Damion's chest.

'Speak up before I have you all executed! Who are you and how did you get inside?'

'Put up your blade, man; I'm Asharte,' Damion barked.

The man lifted his chin, waggling a pointy, reddish goatee. 'Are you now? I've spent many a day at Duke Cymric's court an' I never seen your beardless face before.'

Then he looked at Uwella. His face turned dark and he snorted like an angry bull. 'I know her, though. She's not Asharte! She is the false valvodjara, that traitoress of Gry.'

Damion growled. 'I am Asharte,' he said harshly. 'The Princess Caerch's son.' He put his thumb and forefinger on the threatening sword point. 'Hold still while I get my proof.' Slowly, he took his grandfather's letter from inside his tunic. 'Recognize the seal?' he said. 'Look at my grandfather's signature.'

The lord stared at the seal rather than the text, and for a moment Damion wondered if he could read.

'You're the awaited heir,' the man said finally. He lowered his blade and waved his men away. 'The duke mentioned you were expected.'

'I'm Asharte's heir,' Damion said. 'The Valvodjara Uwella and I were on our way to Asharte to meet with my grandfather when we saw your undead trouble. So we had our porter bring us in to help. You are Lord Erpenstaun?'

The man nodded. 'I am, but Asharte...' He looked away without finishing what he was going to say.

Damion watched him for a moment. As the lord kept silent, he shrugged. 'Those wedergangers – how long have they been out there?'

'Two days,' Erpenstaun said. 'They don't do anything. As long as we stay within the walls, we are safe.'

'That's what you think,' Damion said. 'Their danger is more subtle than that. They bring creeping anxiety, panic, and finally madness. In addition, they poison your water with their body fluids. They can't get in, but you can't get out either. I don't know the state of your provisions, but remember those undead don't need any. They have infinite time and infinite patience. You will run out of food and when the poison they excrete reaches the groundwater, you'll get very thirsty quickly.'

The lord's face turned sickly pale. 'I know, but what can I do? I sent my pigeon to Asharte, asking for help, but I got no reply. I can't fight them alone; I have only two score men under arms, and there are over a hundred undead.'

'There must be a sorcerer nearby; someone who drives them. Has anyone seen a living person? A magician in a black or gray coat, or someone like that?'

'I haven't heard of any strangers, but I'll have my squire ask around.' Erpenstaun beckoned to a pimply fellow at his shoulder and repeated Damion's question. 'Go around and ask; bring me anyone who has seen such a person.'

The squire hurried away, to return with a small, thin boy and a small, thin dog.

'Heere naw,' he said in a thick local accent, and shook the boy's shoulder. 'Tell the Hoighness whaat you saw.'

'Thank you,' Damion said politely but dismissively, and the squire's face colored hotly. He bowed awkwardly and fled to the obscurity of his lord's back.

Damion grinned at the boy. 'Sheep- or goatherd?'

'Goat, lord,' the boy said without looking up. 'Twelve big beasts; ne'er a sick one among them.'

'You seem a clever lad with a stout dog, so they'll be in good hands,' Damion said. 'As a goatherd, you must be a watchful type, too. Are there wild beasts around? Any wolves or bears?'

The boy scratched his thin hair. 'Not 'ere, lord. Way north be bears, they say, but I haven't seen one. Wolves sometimes, but me goats are too fierce for the likes of them.'

'Of course; no wolf would want to cross swords with a big bad goat. And strangers? You did see those?'

The goatherd nodded, still staring at the noses of his scruffy shoes. 'That I did. At Hallow Cave they were. Strange folk in black robes, doin' mischief, lord. They musta been wakin' them!'

Now he looked up for the first time, gazing anxiously at Damion.

'They shouldn't be doin' that, should they? Me dad lies there; they can't go an' awaken him!'

'Certainly not!' Damion said. 'We're going to stop them. How many strangers did you see?'

The boy held up a hand, with four fingers spread. 'A fat one, a bald one, a blonde woman, an old one with a beard,' he said, ticking off each finger. 'That many, lord.'

'Thank you,' Damion said gravely. He dug into his pockets and produced a bronze penny. 'Good service must be rewarded.'

The boy gaped at the largesse. 'Thankee, lord!' he said breathlessly. Then he turned on his heels, clutching the coin in a dirty fist, and spurted away with his dog.

'Hallow Cave,' Damion said. 'Where would that be?'

'It's not far from here,' Erpenstaun said. 'Follow the river road to the left, and it's about half a mile past the castle field. The cave system is large, but only the first chambers are in use.'

'Used for what?' Damion said.

Erpenstaun grimaced. 'Hallow has been the village burial place since the old Revenaunt's time.'

So those corpses are *the local dead,* Damion thought. *What a vile business!* He looked around at Uwella. 'We must stop them. We don't want an army of undead on the loose.'

'Of course we must,' she said. 'The villagers don't deserve their dead disturbed.'

'We will see to the matter,' Damion said to Erpenstaun. 'Have someone care for the horses, please. Grisa, can you port us back to the spot from where we first saw the undead?'

'Of course. Do you want to go now, or would you rather wait and think a while?' she said, giving him a challenging look.

Damion grinned. 'Now, please.'

They emerged on the road, about half a mile from the keep. It rained again, making the naked fields and the shambling corpses even more awful in their dreariness.

Grisa shivered, her earlier defiance evaporated. 'Those necromancers. Why do they do this?'

'Raising undead?' Uwella looked over her shoulder. 'Or waging war?'

'Both.'

'They're twisted. The Revenaunt Emperor touched them and few human minds can resist his whispering. So they fell. Now they do his bidding, preparing the world for his return.' Uwella thought for a moment. 'Wikken know more of the Hamorth than most Orders; the Grays have studied the Revenaunt for as long as they exist.' She looked at Damion. 'Perhaps that's in part why those traitors never betrayed themselves. Most of the wikken are interested in the Hamorth's doings and everybody talks about them.'

'Even better reason Archodea should've been more careful in her recruiting,' Damion said.

Uwella hunched her shoulders as she stared at the undead across the river.

'I know,' she said bitterly. 'Enough; this isn't the time or the place for those conversations.'

Without speaking, they walked on past the keep, through a landscape of rippling hills dotted with gorse and coarse grasses. They didn't see anyone, alive or dead, and the silence was immense.

Damion sent his mind roaming, but there wasn't a beastman anywhere; just the normal wildlife.

'Over there,' Bartram said after a while. 'Is that the Hallow?'

Damion pulled his mind back. 'Where?' Then he saw to the left a large outcrop of rock with the dark jaws of a cave.

'Someone wanted in,' Grisa said, with an almost believable attempt at cheerfulness.

The cave had been closed by a wooden gate, but some great force had shattered it.

'I believe you're right,' Damion said. 'Time to change.' He looked at the twins. 'I want you to stay here.'

'We're going in,' Bartram said firmly.

'It's no fun outside in the rain,' his sister added. 'And you know you'll need us.'

Damion closed his mouth. *They're warriors. Fantus will look after his own.* 'We'll stay together,' he said. 'Watch out for any undead and for those blackrobes' spells.'

Bartram gave him a silent stare.

'I know you know,' Damion said. 'Just be careful, will you?'

Both twins sniffed.

Moments later, the black-and-white-striped tiger slipped into the cave. The first room was a vestibule, with hangers for cloaks and some crude benches. A corridor led deeper into the rocks. There came a musty smell from it that reminded Damion of the caves under Nadril; a smell of earth and old death.

Bartram held up his knife and suddenly it sparked into light. He muttered something and the brightness dimmed to a glow just enough to see where they were going.

The tiger moved away from its light; to him the corridor was filled with a gray gloaming in which he could see well enough.

To the right was a room partly filled with simple pinewood coffins stashed in plots, like family to family. Whole stacks of them were forcibly opened from the inside, their occupiers walking outside.

'That's creepy,' Grisa whispered. 'I'll never dare visit our family vault again.'

They hurried on, past a second room, its coffins undisturbed, and a third with stacks of empty caskets. The few rooms after that were bare, and then the corridor ended at a blank wall.

Damion changed back and tapped the stone with his knuckles. 'It sounds like solid rock,' he said. 'If this is all...'

'It's not,' Grisa said brightly. 'You bigger ones always look down, never up.'

'You're right,' Bartram said excitedly, pointing. 'There's an opening between the top of the wall and the ceiling.'

'Yep. Help me up, will you?' his sister said, turning her back to him.

Bartram put his hands to her waist and almost threw her upward. Grisa scrambled into the opening.

'It's just a hole,' she said. 'Not too big; about three manlengths deep. On the other side's a room with a second corridor beyond it.'

Uwella jumped up and joined her, tail swinging.

Bartram grimaced. 'Grisa always was the athletic one. I'm too heavy.'

Damion laughed and put his back to the wall. 'I'll give you a hands-up.'

Bartram clambered onto his shoulders and heaved himself up beside his sister.

'Your tiger won't fit,' Grisa called down.

'Hush! Don't shout,' Bartram said. 'There may be enemies within, remember?'

Moments later, a large crow hopped across their legs onto the floor of the next corridor and changed into Damion.

'Looks like a hallway of sorts,' he said, looking around him. 'But that hole we came through can't have been the regular entrance.'

Uwella jumped down and padded to a heap of stones. Here she stopped, growling softly.

'Here was a door,' Grisa said, joining her. 'It's partly hidden behind that rockslide she's standing on.'

'Hamorth!' Damion said, staring at the broken arch of the doorway. 'That's their firebird emblem in the stone.' He balled his fists. 'Even in Vavaun they built their cursed temples.' He turned and looked down the corridor. Ever since he had been touched by that Annan-at-Aghraim temple at the very beginning of Ghyll's quest, he'd remained sensitive to the darkness that was Her, the Dar'khamorth goddess. The horror, the alienness of it all had been etched into his soul. Now he stood still, letting the silence envelop him, and searched for traces of Her. She wasn't here. Not anymore. Yet there was something...

He didn't change; in tiger form, he wouldn't sense the dark magic. Carefully he went down the corridor to an inner door opening. One of the others said something, but he gestured impatiently for them to be quiet. He needed his concentration.

The door was open. Inside was an enormous space; an underground cave of massive proportions. The first part was empty of anything; just rough walls and a bare stone floor that abruptly ended halfway. At the other end was darkness impregnable. He motioned to the others to stay where they were and edged along the wall deeper into the hall. Then he froze.

The second part of the hall lay thirty feet lower, with a grand stone staircase leading down. Shrouded by the darkness was a towering statue of Her, the four-armed goddess of the Dar'khamorth.

The statue was lifeless, but what made Damion hiss softly were the four necromancers below, kneeling at the feet of a stone sarcophagus. Candles burned around them, spreading a dull black light, and the air was heavy with the reek of falmagic. The sarcophagus hummed, a barely audible noise that set his teeth on edge and his heart racing. He backed away and hurriedly rejoined the others.

'Trouble,' he said, and told them what he had seen.

'Black light?' Grisa said. 'I never heard of that.'

'It's falmagic,' Damion said. 'The anti-magic the Dar'khamorth receive from their goddess. Like antimatter to matter is anti-magic deadly to us; you can't use it without being corrupted. Never ever try, not even once.' His tone was hard enough to shock the girl.

'I won't; I just wanted to know what it was.'

Damion touched her arm. 'It's all right. I'm angry at those bastards trying to raise the gods know what, not at you.'

'I don't know much about that Her goddess,' the girl said. 'Who is she?'

'No one knows much about her,' Damion said. 'The gods won't speak about her. We *think* she is from the Intermedium, not a goddess of our world. The only things we know is that she wants us destroyed and that the Revenaunt Emperor was her instrument.'

'Let's go kill those guys first, shall we?' Bartram said, impatiently. Then he stooped and grabbed a few hands of pebbles from the floor. 'I'm not ranged, like Grisa,' he said, filling his pockets with the rocks. 'But that doesn't mean I can't throw stones.'

'What good will they do?' Uwella said.

The boy grinned. 'You'll see.'

Damion looked at him. 'Don't do anything stupid, will you?' he said. He caught the boy's glance and shook his head. 'You won't; sorry. You know your own magic best. Let's go.'

At the edge of the unholy sanctum, they stopped.

Grisa had readied her bow and Bartram produced a handful of stones.

'Shall we?' he said, his eyes brimming with anticipation.

Damion breathed deeply. Then he nodded. 'Go!'

Immediately, Grisa loosed her first arrow. In mid-flight it changed into a straight flame that buried itself between the nearest sorcerer's shoulder blades. At the same time, her brother threw the first pebble at another blackrobe. The kneeling sorcerers made good targets and the stone hit the unsuspecting Hamorthman squarely in the back. On impact, the pebble burst into small flaming shards that dug deep into the man's ribs. While he screamed and burned, Grisa shot the sorceress as she turned around. She opened her mouth, threw her arms back, and slammed against the coffin's pedestal while the flames turned her robe into a mass of fire.

The fourth man, the old one with the beard, as the goat boy had named him, jumped to his feet. His mouth moved as he faced them. Then his form shimmered and Bartram's stone slipped harmlessly to the ground without hitting him. Grisa sent an arrow down, but like the stone, it bounced.

'He's got some sort of shielding,' Damion said. His eyes narrowed as he stared at the sorcerer. The man was frantically shouting a spell at the sarcophagus.

Grisa pounded Damion's arm and screeched. 'Look at that coffin! It's smoking.'

And indeed, tiny tendrils of dark flowed from under the lid, writhing and dancing toward the roof of the hall.

'He's raising another undead,' Damion said. 'But this won't be a simple villager; not at the feet of Her. It must be a high Hamorth priest or sorcerer buried here.'

Beside him, Uwella's cat-form growled, crouching, her tail swishing angrily.

'Wait!' Damion shouted, but the mountain lion launched herself from the ledge straight into the sorcerer.

It was as if she ran into a wall. She bounded away, dropped to the ground, and lay still. The blackrobe swayed and gripped the sarcophagus to steady himself, still mouthing his incantation.

Damion's roar of anguish was drowned by the clang of the lid falling away from the coffin. Amid the smoke, a bony undead in a magnificent robe rose to his feet, leaning on a crooked staff.

'Uwella! Bartram and Grisa shouted almost with one mouth. The boy stretched his arm back and threw a full hand of stones. Like a shower of fiery comets, they shot toward the undead, but a flick of the fleshless hand waved them from the air. As they fell down harmlessly yards away from the sarcophagus, the undead pointed his staff and a thin burst of energy hit the ledge just below their feet.

'Curse you!' Bartram gripped a new hand of stones, but before he could throw them, the bearded sorcerer sprang, and both blackrobe and undead disappeared.

Grisa yelled a string of curses that would've blistered the soul of a dockworker. 'He ported! Blast him, he ported!' Then she burst into tears of shock.

Blind to anything else, Damion ran down the stairs to Uwella. He dropped to his knees beside her and touched her cheek with her fingers.

'Love?' he said, his heart in his mouth.

She opened her eyes. 'Present. Is he...?'

Damion sighed. 'Escaped. That sorcerer ported away with the undead he'd called.'

'Rats!' A bit wobbly, she came to her feet.

Damion hastily drew an arm around her waist.

'I can stand,' she said testily.

'I know, but I like holding you,' he said, and kissed her.

She leaned her head on his shoulder. 'Then it's fine.'

'You had me scared,' he said, pulling her close.

'That shield of his was strong,' she said dreamily. 'We need something like that.' She turned her head and nuzzled his neck. 'Sorry. I hoped to spoil his spell. He did call an undead then?'

'A daghuur, a big mage that threw beams with his staff. Gods, if it's as powerful as our Archmage Neferestan, we have a problem.'

'Any idea where they went?' Uwella looked at Grisa. 'Did you notice anything?'

The girl shook her head. 'Nothing. I saw him port, but I didn't feel a thing.'

'It probably was falmagic,' Uwella said. 'The whole place stinks with it.'

'You two did well,' Damion said. 'More than just well.'

Grisa giggled. 'Tell Daddy how awesome we are. He doesn't believe it yet.'

'We believe it,' Damion said. 'The gods know whether you are warriors, mages, or whatever, but you two are very useful.'

'I'm a soldier,' Bartram said quickly. 'Never a mage! I want to be a general one day.'

'At least he knows,' Grisa said. 'I don't. For the moment, I want to be a good porter, as long as I don't have to run a portal; that's too dull for words. And be a good archer, too. What does that make me?'

'An army porter,' Damion said. 'The first porter who is not a mage or a temple priest.'

'I won't be a priest!' she said. 'I just ain't the type for it.'

'No,' Damion said. 'I didn't think you were.' He looked at the twins, weighing their qualities – Bartram's strength and Grisa's sometimes impulsive quickness – against their youth.

'If I followed custom, I'd make you both squires and be done with it. Or enlist you with Mainal's temple.' He saw Bartram's frown and he had to laugh. 'I know; squires rarely become generals and you don't want to join the temple. Don't worry; I won't. From now on, you are both sublieutenants in the army of Vavaun. That gives Grisa enough rank to be transport officer and Bartram as aide to the valvodjars.' He grinned. 'You're a bit young for the honor, but so are Uwella and I.'

'Sublieutenant!' Bartram breathed, suddenly beet red. 'I never thought...'

'You've both earned it,' Uwella said. She gave Damion a hug. 'I love that devious mind of yours. You piss off the temples and the soldiery in one fell stroke.'

'Shake them up; they will learn times have changed.' Damion gave her a quick kiss. 'I think we're done here. Let's see how things are at the keep.'

As they reached the exit, it was fully dark outside. The rain had stopped and a sliver of moon peered through the clouds.

'What's going on there?' Bartram said, as they saw the bobbing torches in the field where the undead had been.

A burly villager with strips of cloth wound round his hands and over his mouth and nose saw them coming. He lowered the rickety pushcart and came up to them. He touched his cap.

'Yer pardon, Highness. You been to the Hallow, our lord said. Is it safe again?'

Damion nodded. 'The ones who called the undead are done for. One escaped, but I don't expect he'll come back here. What are you people doing?'

'We gonna put them back,' the peasant said hoarsely. 'It's not fitting our dead be treated this way. They must be laid a-resting again.'

'Of course, and rightly so. You can return them to the burial caves, up to the end of the corridor.'

'We never go beyond them caves, Highness,' the villager said. 'What lies beyond we don't know, but it brings bad luck.'

'And so it will. As soon as possible, I will send people to cleanse the space beyond and close it up, but it will forever be taboo. Death lurks inside; a messy, painful, walking death.'

Damion saw the man pale under the dirt on his skin.

'I'll pass the word, Highness.' He gestured to the field. 'But after this, not even the boldest will want to go to the forbidden part.' The man touched his greasy cap again and went back to his grisly work.

Damion turned away. 'To the castle.'

'Erpenstaun will have to put us up for the night,' Uwella said. 'We're not going anywhere without some sleep.'

The lord received them with relief. 'I was about to send someone after you, Highness. Then the undead suddenly dropped – well, dead, and I gathered that must've been your doing. Were there really necromancers stirring them up?'

'There were.' In a few words, Damion described the temple and the four sorcerers. He left out the statue and the undead revenant; that would only worry Erpenstaun. 'Now all is well again. Now we are counting on your hospitality, Lord Erpenstaun. We'll continue our journey tomorrow, but we must have some sleep first.'

'You honor me,' the lord said. 'I'll have my own chambers prepared for you and the valvodjara. Your squire and the young lady?'

'My aide and my teleporter. They're both army officers. Perhaps you can whip up two pellets in our room?'

'Of course.' For a second, Erpenstaun looked at the twins, as if trying to guess their age, but he didn't say anything.

Erpenstaun's private room was just large enough to accommodate the four of them.

The hearth was dead, and had been for a long time. 'Chilly place,' Damion said.

'You're spoiled with all those rich Rhidaunan castles,' Uwella said. 'We Vavauners are a sober people.'

'Not rich,' Damion said. 'Modern. The castles in Vavaun are hopelessly antiquated. That's not sober, love; that's provincial.'

'We never had a fire in our rooms,' Bartram said. 'Our father doesn't hold with pampering his children. Of course, Mother insists on a blaze in their rooms.' He pulled off his boots and sighed with relief. 'They're getting a bit small,' he said, wriggling his toes.

'As soon as we've time, we'll provide uniforms for both of you. New boots included,' Damion said.

Bartram stretched himself out on his pellet and pulled the sheepskin cover up to his chin. 'That would be great,' he said.

'I'm not growing,' Grisa said. 'He's already a head taller than me. We're twins; it's not fair.'

'Your time will come.' Uwella slipped from her gray dress and stared ruefully at the tiny rents and creases in the skirt. 'I'm beginning to look like a beggar girl.'

'Are you?' Damion said suddenly. 'I mean, I've no idea about our financial position. Neither as rulers nor as country. Are we rich or poor?'

'No idea.' Uwella pulled a face. 'Father is a terrible skinflint. He never spends money and refuses even to talk about it. I always pictured our cellars filled with coins. Probably not, though. We'll ask Costare, our seneschal at Gry. He'll know; he rules my father's household, including the finances.'

'There's no government?' Damion said, surprised.

'None. Father makes all the decisions. He doesn't trust anybody; 'course, he's always afraid of Asharte spies.'

'That is nonsense,' Damion said. 'I think we'll hire some of Ghyll's people and have them train our own bureaucracy.'

'Good idea,' Uwella said, yawning. 'Are we done now? The twins and I want to sleep.'

'Sorry,' Damion said. 'I'll shut up. G'night, all.'

The next morning they rose in time to join their host in his devotions. Erpenstaun's clerk was a chaplain of Arikal, one of those half-educated laymen the Gray Order taught enough of the holy rites to serve a small community like the castle. Damion sat through the service watching Uwella's critical face as she joined in the ceremony. He didn't particularly connect with Arikal, but she did and it was clear to him his love wasn't impressed with the chaplain's efforts. But she was good and kept her opinions to herself. She even thanked the man afterwards.

As they walked to the great hall for the morning meal, he took her hand and as she looked at him, he kissed her fingers. With Erpenstaun present, he didn't say anything, but still she blushed.

Their host wasn't a rich man, but his servants had done their best to feed their high visitors well. A rich stew, with freshly baked bread; a cured ham, roast capons with steamed apples, and both wine and ale to slake their thirst. As they ate, Damion told of their earlier adventures against the Dar'khamorth; of Rhidauna, Opit, and Zihaen, places Erpenstaun clearly knew by name only.

In return, their host spoke of the woes that beset a small lordship; of harvests and his men's state of readiness. Strangely enough, he never mentioned Asharte, and Damion wondered why.

After breakfast, they made ready to depart. As they stepped into the courtyard, the soldiers cheered.

'Long live Asharte!' an archer shouted, waving his bow in the air. 'May our side rule again!' Then, with a glance at Uwella, the man paled and stepped back.

Damion shook his head. 'Times change, friends,' he called out. 'Today we are one nation, Asharte and Gry together. Those endless wars will stop. Remember those undead – we have far more dangerous opponents to worry about.' He raised his fist in the air. 'For our homeland! For Vavaun!'

The men looked at him and hesitated, unsure what this meant. Then Erpenstaun raised his voice. 'I follow the Valvodjars! Asharte for Vavaun!'

Immediately, the men joined him.

'Folks!' Damion spread his arms out and everyone fell silent. 'Countrymen! Our enemies are many and strong. Grymaur has fallen. They have captured Duke Venric, our Valvode, and their monsters roam our forests. We have work to do! We're going to kick them out of our country. Together we will win! Together Asharte and Gry will win; the Valvodjara and I will win. You and we will win. Together! For we are Vavaun! Together we are Vavaun!'

The men cheered and raised their arms in the air. 'Vavaun!'

Damion raised a fist. 'We must depart; we still have a way to travel. Men and women of Erpenstaun, do your duty and Vavaun shall overcome!'

As he stepped back, Erpenstaun spoke softly in his ear. 'There is something you must know, Highness. Walk with me, please.'

Damion frowned, but followed the lord.

'There is news,' Erpenstaun said. 'Bad news. I haven't told the men yet; no sense in worrying them. But...'

His face was screwed up in worry.

'What is it?' Damion said.

'I said I sent the duke my pigeon to ask for help but didn't get a reply? Well, I did; I got a message from the duke's constable. No help would come; Asharte itself has fallen.'

Damion felt his heart skip a beat. *Damn,* he thought. *I'm too late! Those bastards move quickly.* 'Any news of my grandfather?'

'The duke got out with most of his men. That's all I know, but it's bad enough. I... My keep is a hovel compared to Asharte. If they fall, what chance do I stand?'

Erpenstaun's face was creased in worry as he stared at Damion.

'I don't think the enemy will come for you as yet; they'll be occupied with the major spots. Asharte, Gry, the capital, and we'll lead them a pretty dance there. In the meantime, keep a good look-out and be prepared,' Damion said. 'How are your provisions?'

Erpenstaun wrung his hands. 'Not overly large. With the extra mouths from the village, I can hold out for two weeks, three at most.'

'By that time all will be over,' Damion said calmly. He felt like an awful liar, but he knew that if they hadn't kicked the bastards out in three weeks' time, they'd all be done for. The Dar'khamorth wasn't here to conquer, but to destroy their world. 'Any idea where I could find my grandfather?'

'Knowing the duke, he won't be far from the castle,' Erpenstaun said. 'He'll have a camp somewhere in the surrounding forest.'

'We'll find him. You will hear from me, Lord Erpenstaun.'

They shook hands. 'I am glad you are with us, Highness,' the lord said earnestly. 'The duke can use some stout back-up at his age.'

Damion nodded but he wasn't going to criticize his grandfather to one of his vassals.

He rejoined the others. 'We must hurry,' he said tersely.

Uwella gave him a searching look. 'Something wrong?'

'When we're outside.' Damion mounted and waited impatiently for the others to join him.

Amid loud cheers from the castle folks they rode off into the fields. Once they were out of sight, Damion slowed down. 'Erpenstaun just told me. Asharte has fallen.'

'Gods,' Uwella said, shocked. 'It was to be expected, but still... Damn. Now what?'

'We'll go on. I want to know the situation. Grandfather must have a camp in the woods surrounding the castle. The only problem is how to find him.'

CHAPTER 6 – COUP

The old man with the curly white hair walked down a path in his extensive gardens. With pleasure, he contemplated the blossoms of the oleander shrubs along the path, so innocently beautiful and so toxic.

'They are doing well,' he said. 'Quite well.' He turned to the stocky man beside him. 'And you, Syvvan? How are you doing?'

'The plan goes well, too, my lord M,' Syvvan said. 'I am happy to report we took Burg Asharte. The old duke must have had a handportal, for he and his surviving men fled. We know where he is hiding and my pigmen will flush him out shortly.'

'Do that,' the urbane old man said gently. 'His is one head that must roll for our master's plans to succeed.'

'I hear, my lord. The Asharte will die before the week is done. Do you want his head?'

The old man thought for a moment. 'No,' he said finally. 'I will accept your assurance, Syvvan. You will not fail me, will you?'

The stocky man shook his head. 'No, my lord! I will not fail you. The old duke will die, as will the valvodjara, and we'll raze their settlements to the ground. You have my word, my lord.'

'Make it so, Syvvan,' the old man murmured. 'The master demands it of you, Practicus.'

'I hear and obey, my lord! Bowing, Syvvan backed out of the old man's presence.

M turned around and resumed his study of the white blossoms, savoring their fragrance. Success waited around the corner, and that, too, filled him with satisfaction.

As Damion and Uwella rode north, weather and landscape changed around them. The oaks and birches gave way to pines, each new valley was higher than the one before, and it grew colder.

On a stone bridge across a fast flowing river, Uwella reined in. 'That's the Dana,' she said. 'Beyond lies Asharte's heartland.' She touched Damion's knee and grimaced. 'It feels strange, you know. No DeGry has been here for fifty years or more.'

Damion looked curiously around at the dark pine forests. So this was his ancestral domain. It didn't look very hospitable, or as fertile as the soil around Grymaur was.

He gripped Uwella's hand. 'We'll have to be careful,' he said. 'I don't want to be shot by my own retainers.' He flashed her and the twins a grin. 'Welcome in Asharte.'

They rode on, following a stony path through a rough forest. Several times they saw deer, and Damion heard the voices of many other animals, from foxes to wolves, and a pair of eagles nesting some goodly distance away.

Suddenly, he straightened in the saddle, as his instincts said they were being watched. A glance at Uwella showed she had felt it as well, but she said nothing.

The trail made a sharp turn to the right and two men stepped from the shadows to bar their way.

'Stop,' the older of the two said. 'Right there.'

'Good day, friends,' Damion said. Behind them, three other men appeared; they were surrounded.

'Is it a *good* day?' The man, a gray soldier well past retirement age, looked at them with raised eyebrows. 'Maybe. Maybe not. That depends on you. A man, a woman, and two youngsters. Here, in Asharte, but not of Asharte.'

'Those are your words, my friend,' Damion said. 'Do not judge too quickly, man of Asharte.'

'The woman and the youngsters are of the south, and that is Gry.' The man spat on the ground. 'You are a stranger. Who are you and what are you doing here?'

'I seek the duke, friend.'

The man stilled and Damion heard a few swords leave their scabbards.

'You seek His Highness? Well, well, you're not the only one.' His dark eyes stared at Damion. 'Why?'

'That's between His Highness and me, friend.'

'Kill them,' one of the men behind him said. 'They're assassins from Gry come to take advantage.'

'Quiet, Marl,' the gray man said.

'Don't we have more important enemies, Marl?' Damion said without looking. 'Have Asharte and Gry nothing better to do these days than chase each other?' He kept his voice friendly, but with a sharp undertone.

'Maybe those other enemies are friends of Gry?' The old warrior grinned joylessly and showed a row of brown teeth.

'With half of Grymaur gone up in smoke and the burg taken, with Castle Kramm destroyed and the marshal put to flight? I don't think so, friend.'

The old warrior stiffened. 'What? We haven't heard from the south for a while, but... Tie them up and blindfold them. Their fate is for the highness to decide.'

Uwella wanted to say something, but Damion raised his hand and she closed her mouth. He dismounted and turned to the man in front of him. 'Blindfold us, if you must, but let's hurry. The situation is dire and I need to see the duke urgently.'

Rough hands tied their arms behind their backs and tied strips of cloth over their eyes. Then they were led along a narrow dirt road deeper into the woods. Damion's sharp nose smelled the pines around him, their captors' sweat, and before long, the pungent odor of campfires. Voices called greetings and questions till their leader commanded them to be silent. Then Damion felt the warmth of a fire and the intimacy of a tent.

'Highness,' the first man said. 'These four were looking for you.'

'Untie the man,' a gruff voice Damion recognized said. 'Quickly, fool.' There were many undertones in that voice. Surprise, exultation, and something darker. Anger?

Hurried hands removed ropes and blindfold, and Damion looked into the face of the duke.

'Well, Grandfather?' he said coolly.

The warrior behind him inhaled sharply and Damion smiled.

'Free the others too, friend,' he said quietly over his shoulder.

The man glanced at the duke, who gestured impatiently. 'Take off their bonds and get out.'

Moments later, the four of them were alone with the duke. The tent they found themselves in was old and stank of damp and rot, as if it'd stood here for a long time. *A hunters' camp perhaps*, he thought.

The old man, with one arm in a dirty sling, looked at Uwella. 'So you brought her anyway,' he growled.

'The valvodjara and I are together, Grandfather,' Damion said. 'You have us both or neither.'

The duke's eyes flashed dangerously. 'Asharte and Gry do not go together.'

'Asharte and Gry go well together.' The old man was nearly a head taller, so Damion had to look up. He crossed his arms over his chest. 'Grandfather, Vavaun can no longer afford a conflict between our Houses. The enemy is everywhere, all bastions have fallen. Asharte and Grymaur are in the hands of the enemy.'

'More treacherous Gray wikken,' the duke snapped, and his face contorted in pain as he moved.

'Treacherous Dar'khamorth,' Uwella said softly. 'Let me look at that arm.'

'What? What?' The old man looked from one to the other. 'Dar'khamorth? Here in Vavaun?'

'It's what King Ghyll warned us for, remember. The Dar'khamorth wants to take over the world. They have been at it for a long time and seeded their infiltrators into the Gray Order.' Uwella undid the dirty bandage around Asharte's arm and looked at the swollen limb. 'Tsk; that must hurt. Grisa, be kind and give me my bag, will you. Last week, the infiltrators awoke. They killed the kerran in Grymaur and the burg's daywatch. When the Drynnath came to her people's aid, the Dar'khamorth destroyed the kerran Adalien as well. Grisa and Bartram here are the only survivors. Beastmen rule in the capital. Damion and I have recaptured Negardien and the Drynnath holds it with the remainder of the Kramm garrison. The Marshal of Vavaun escaped from Grymaur with the nightwatch.' She dabbed the arm with a fragrant lotion and the duke couldn't stop a sigh of relief.

Damion took over the story. 'Marshal DeKramm has joined Prince Rhydd. Duke Venric was captured by the Dar'khamorth. Uwella and I took over.'

'Uwella and you? What do you mean?' The old man flushed darkly. 'With Venric out of the way, it is I...'

'Grandfather,' Damion said, his tone harsh. 'That nonsense between you and DeGry must stop before the people rise up and hang you on the nearest tree. We can no longer accept the country being ruined through the silly bickering of two stubborn old men. Uwella is Gry and I am Asharte – together we are Vavaun. And if the throne isn't large enough for both of us, then we'll make it wider.'

The old man wanted to move, but with Uwella holding his painful arm, he was forced to stand still, and that infuriated him even more. 'Silly bickering!' he shouted. 'Old men? I am the Duke of Asharte, not some bumpkin!'

Damion didn't budge. 'Listen, Grandfather. Uwella and I spent the last six months traveling all over the continent. We have visited all our countrymen abroad we could find. Over three-quarters of them have fled the fighting between both of you in the past forty years. Altogether, we spoke with six hundred compatriots. That is about half the population of Grymaur, Grandfather. One of the main complaints was about the hardships your stupid fight caused. This has to change. This will change. With or without your help, Grandfather.'

The old duke looked at his grandson and stayed silent so long Damion wondered if he had ruined his relationship with him. But then the old man roared with laughter. Tears ran from his eyes as he banged his leg with his good hand. 'What a fire-eater!' he bellowed. 'He's like his mother. "With or without your help," he said, as if something could be changed in Vavaun without me.' Then he became serious. 'But you forget that I rule here, boy. Not you, not... that DeGry. I was hoping you would help me, but instead you sold out to the enemy. You are my prisoner while I take over the reign.'

Damion's face was tight and pale. 'And I was hoping you would be reasonable,' he said. 'Unfortunately, you don't want to listen.' He turned to Grisa and Uwella. 'Take him to Negardien. Treat him well; he is my mother's father, but he will not disrupt our plans. I'm sorry, Grandfather.'

Before the old man could say something, a wildly grinning Grisa had ported him and Uwella away.

Damion sighed. He looked at Bartram. 'Now you've met Asharte. I had been afraid it would come to this. Luckily, your sister has a quick understanding.'

'She's too clever for words,' Bartram said with a sigh. Then he scratched where the rope had bitten into his arm. 'When those men stopped us, why didn't you show them your letter?'

'For the same reason I didn't go tiger. I wanted to see what they'd do. They are my men, but I've never met any of them. If that fool Marl had gotten his way with his killing, it would've been different. Ordinary ropes won't hold a beastmaster; had they wanted to harm us, Uwella and I would have been at their throats before they could have done anything foolish. But the old guy was honorable and the others deferred to him. That's good to know.' Damion grinned. 'Sorry about the rope burns.'

'As if that mattered,' Bartram said. He grinned. 'I was just curious.'

Damion stuck his head around the corner of the tent. 'Tell our people to gather,' he said to the guard.

Then he spied the gray soldier who had brought him here and beckoned him over. The man came in and looked around.

'Where is the duke?' he snapped.

'My grandfather is under house arrest,' Damion said coldly. 'He wanted to harm the person of the Valvodjara-regent. That is treason. My porter took him to Grymaur, and I will keep him there until we have defeated the true enemies of Vavaun.'

The warrior's face twisted into a wild grimace as he drew his sword. Damion went tiger and softly knocked the man to the ground. He stood over him and stared at him motionlessly with his yellow eyes. After a few seconds, he growled and returned to being Damion.

'Pick up your blade,' he said shortly. 'You are a soldier of Vavaun, you need to be armed.'

With trembling hands the old warrior picked up his sword and stared at Damion. 'What... are you?'

'I didn't hear the last word?' Damion said. 'That word after "you"?'

'Highness,' the man said quickly.

'I am the Valvodjar of Asharte,' Damion said, and this time he produced the letter that declared his identity. 'And I'm a beastmaster. From now on, I command here. Who are you?'

The man stared at the seal and swallowed. 'I'm Kedraun, Highness,' he said with fragile dignity. 'Knight and Constable of Asharte.'

'How many men have you here, Constable Kedraun?'

'Forty men of Asharte, Highness; nine of them are walking wounded. And there are another ten soldiers from a visiting lord.'

Less than I'd hoped, Damion thought. 'And how many enemies are there in Asharte?'

'At least twice that number, Highness. Most of them are monsters; men with the heads of beasts!'

'We know them,' Damion said. 'They're all over the country.'

Then Uwella and Grisa returned and Kedraun gasped when they so abruptly appeared.

'Constable,' Damion said formally. 'May I introduce you to Her Highness the Valvodjara-regent? Highness, this is the Knight Kedraun, Constable of Asharte.'

Kedraun's eyes nearly bulged from his head, but he saluted.

'I thank you for your loyalty to Vavaun, Knight,' Uwella said stately.

Damion looked at Grisa. 'Do you still feel big and strong?' he said with a smile.

The girl sniffed. 'I'm just warming up. Who should I take away next?'

'Not taken away, brought here. Rhydd's gardians.'

'Sure, no problem. And my father?'

'Give my compliments to the marshal. Tell him I want to recapture Asharte first. I'm holding his troops in reserve for the retaking of Grymaur. Got that?'

Grisa nodded. 'See you.' Then she was gone.

'And she's such a little girl,' Kedraun surprised. 'I have a granddaughter her age.'

'She's small, but a very strong porter, Constable. Sublieutenant Bartram DeKramm is her brother. He is aide to the Valvodjara and I. Both he and his sister are fire warriors of Fantus.' Damion looked at the knight. 'We're going to retake Asharte, but first I must know where you stand. Do you follow me, Knight Kedraun?'

'I...' The old warrior swallowed. 'You are the heir, I heard the duke acknowledge you. I... served him all my life, but this attack, these beastmen – it was too much for him. For us both. We need a younger head to lead us. I will follow, Highness.'

Damion stared a moment. The admission was very honest and more than he expected. He felt relieved; with Kedraun accepting him, the men would follow. 'Thank you, Constable,' he said gratefully. 'Together, we will succeed.' He squared his shoulders. 'Come with me, we'll tell the men there've been some changes.'

Asharte's soldiers were a rougher lot than the men of Kramm. A mixed lot of warriors, rangers, and trappers; bearded, in leather uniforms, and armed to the teeth. Damion saw curiosity and suspicion battling for supremacy as he walked forward, Kedraun a step behind him.

'Men,' he said, holding up his grandfather's letter. 'I'm Damion, son of Caerch, grandson of Cymric, and Valvodjar of Asharte.'

The men muttered at that, but no one protested.

'With me is Her Highness Uwella, the Valvodjara-regent of Vavaun. You will give her the respect due to her position, for you are all true Vavauners, as are the valvodjara and I.'

The muttering got louder, but still more in surprise than in anger.

'My grandfather is a Vavauner, as are all of us,' Damion continued. 'But he will not yet admit it.'

It became very quiet. He saw the waiting men tense, ready for whatever.

Damion folded his arms. 'My grandfather is a great man; a noble warrior. But he is old and wounded. He thinks slower than you and me. To allow him more time, I asked him to withdraw for the moment to the Gray kerran Negardien and leave the recapture of Asharte to me. He agreed and our porter Grisa has brought him there.' Now Damion stepped forward, with Kedraun following. 'Is there anyone here who wants to dispute my right to command Asharte's troops?' he demanded.

For a moment, all was silent.

'I do!' a rough voice said.

'Damnation,' the constable muttered. 'Old Harthenkraz. He doesn't listen to anyone but the duke.'

'Who is he?' Damion said, watching the owner of the voice approach. He was a tall, elderly man with a heavy chin and a curtain of hair circling the back of an otherwise bald head. He had only one leg; the other ended in a wooden stump, and he leaned on the shoulder of a massive young warrior.

'Lord Harthenkraz. He's a minor vassal with an ego far surpassing the size of his holdings,' Kedraun said. 'He's always bluffing about his prowess in war, though we all know he lost his blasted leg in a logging accident when he was a teen. He was at the duke's court when the attack came.'

The man moved to the center and faced Damion, leaning on a stout stick. His eyes reminded Damion of a pigman, just as small and bloodshot as he stared at him.

'Even if you're Asharte's grandson – *if* I say, for the duke didna seem fit to tell me in person – even if you're the heir, you're nothin' but a beardless wonder. And besides, you're a traitor, bringing *her* to where no livin' Gry bastard has ever come.' His finger shot out and pointed to Uwella. 'Her, that wretched chit of Venric's.'

'You are Harthenkraz?' Damion said frostily. 'I expect some respect from our vassals, *Lord* Harthenkraz. Respect for me as valvodjar and respect for our ruler, the Valvodjara-regent.'

'Respect?' the man said. 'Respect for a *boy*? You havna earned that yet, kid. But as yer so full of yerself, you will prove to us you can command anything bigger than a pram.'

He snapped his fingers and the warrior at his side stepped forward. He was half a head taller than Damion, a superbly muscled youth of some eighteen years with dark hair and insolent eyes.

'I am Madyc, my lord Harthenkraz's squire and champion. As his health doesn't permit him to fight, *I* do so for him.' He pulled a leather glove from his belt and threw it at Damion's feet. 'I challenge you. If you can defeat me, my lord will accept your command. If you lose, you will leave here, never to return.'

'You cannot!' Uwella said sharply. 'You can't challenge the heir of your liege lord.'

'Let the woman shut her mouth,' the young warrior said snidely. 'Or are you afraid to speak for yourself?'

'You're a fool,' Damion said and looked at the glove. *A challenge?* he thought, disgusted. *I'll go tiger; it will be over in seconds.* But before he could pick up the glove, Bartram had done so already.

'If Lord Harthenkraz has a champion to fight for him, so does His Highness,' he said in a clear voice. 'I am Bartram DeKramm, and I accept your challenge.'

'Bartram, no!' Damion said.

'Too late,' Kedraun whispered. 'The boy spoke all the right words; he can't back down now.'

The warrior Madyc blinked for a moment, but then his smile returned. 'You?' he said. 'A child championing a child? What will you prove, kid?'

'I will have your hide, braggart,' Bartram said calmly. 'Choose your weapons.'

Madyc looked him up and down. 'No weapons. We will fight, kid.' He pulled his tunic over his head and flexed his biceps.

'Fine by me,' Bartram said nonchalantly. He handed his blades to Grisa and unbuttoned his jacket. Naked to the waist, he walked forward.

'Damn,' Damion muttered. Bartram was well built and looked strong for his fifteen years, but he wasn't an ox like Madyc, who topped him by nearly a hand.

'Don't worry,' Grisa said brightly. 'He's done this before. My brother trained with the fire knights, remember.'

'But those are knights, not wrestlers.'

'Of course they are! A lot of them are jugglers; cloak-and-dagger knights. They're not paladins!'

The two boys eyed each other, balancing on their feet and making small feinting moves. All the while, Madyc talked, an endless stream of little slights meant perhaps to infuriate his opponent. But not Bartram; stoically, he watched the other and waited.

Then, swift as a striking cobra, Madyc closed the few feet between them and grabbed Bartram around the waist. But he held nothing and Bartram danced a few paces aside.

'Misdirection,' Grisa muttered. 'Oh, lovely!'

Madyc grunted and slammed a fist at Bartram's head. The boy ducked and planted his knuckles in Madyc's abdomen. The other boy absorbed the blow, but the hit clearly angered him. Glowering, he hit out and got Bartram on the shoulder. The boy twisted around, crying out. Madyc grinned, but then Bartram moved out of his twist and planted his elbow on the other's nose. Blood flowed freely, but Bartram didn't pause. He added a few swift blows on Madyc's face and shoulders. The young warrior roared and for a moment went berserk. He slapped Bartram six, seven times and every time the boy went with the blow, reeling as if dazed.

Then Madyc overbalanced slightly and in a flash, Bartram moved. He gripped the young warrior's arm and twisted. Madyc screamed. Then Bartram hooked his foot behind Madyc's legs and pushed. The warrior went down with Bartram on top, raining blows on the other's head.

So fast Damion couldn't see how he did it, Bartram got Madyc's arm between his legs and, gripping the warrior's wrist, bent the arm backward. Madyc screamed again. 'Enough!'

'You concede?' Bartram said, feigning surprise. 'Already?'

'Yes!' the young warrior said, clenching his teeth. 'I concede.'

Bartram let go of his opponent's arm and rose. Stiffly, he walked over to Damion and bowed. 'Your champion won, Highness,' he said.

'Thank you, Bartram DeKramm,' Damion said. 'You do us proud; it was an admirable win.' Then he turned to the old lord, who stood glaring at his champion, unable or unwilling to help him.

'It is decided, Lord Harthenkraz. Your champion lost, mine won. Now, to take away any lingering doubt about my own fighting ability, I will show you how I go to war.'

He changed into his tiger form and as he heard the cries of shock and fear from the waiting men, he lifted his massive head and roared his challenge. Then he padded over to where Madyc sat. Eyes bulging, the terrified warrior scrambled back and back, till he ended up against the first row of watching soldiers. Damion didn't want to humiliate him further, so he changed back.

'I am a beastmaster,' he said in a loud voice. 'I have no need of a sword – I carry far mightier weapons. Nor do I duel; I kill.' Then he held out his hands to Madyc and pulled the boy to his feet.

'You couldn't know this,' Damion said, 'so I don't blame you. I do suggest you first learn your opponent's strengths and weaknesses before you challenge him.' Still holding the young warrior's arm, he steered him back to his lord. 'And for the record, Her Highness the Valvodjara-regent is a beastmaster as well. So mind how you address her if you value your skin.'

Harthenkraz's face had turned gray and he bowed awkwardly. 'A beastmaster – you use the magic of your forebears; the power we thought lost to your House. The gods have blessed you, so I must accept your command, Highness.'

Damion gave a curt nod. 'Thank you; the gods are on the side of the righteous. With their help, the valvodjara and I will smite our enemies.'

The old lord shuffled back to his men, Madyc following him like a beaten dog.

Damion rejoined Uwella and the others. 'I should be angry at you, young man,' he said softly to Bartram. 'Did you think I couldn't best that fellow?'

'Of course you could,' Bartram said indignantly. 'Your tiger would've made mincemeat of the guy. But it wouldn't be fitting. Our rulers don't duel every two-bit lordling and his *champion*.' He snorted derisively. 'Fine champion; the guy had as much finesse as a pigman.'

'I agree with Bartram,' Uwella said. 'This was a much better way. You were an impressive fighter, Bartram. Those fire knights did a good job on you.'

Damion clapped the boy's shoulder. 'That's the gods' truth. Now let's continue.' He turned to the troops.

'Anyone else thinking of challenging my command?' he said, watching the men closely.

Nobody spoke; all soldiers stared at him with something approaching awe. 'Right, then prepare yourselves, for tomorrow we will take Asharte back.'

'We don't have enough people,' a hoarse voice said.

'I know. We will be joined by Prince Rhydd and forty gardians.'

'Rhydd is DeGry!' the same hoarse voice sounded indignant. 'No DeGrys in Asharte!' Some other voices joined in.

'Silence!' Damion roared. 'Rhydd is a Vavauner, like you, me, and the valvodjara.' Then he gave them the same speech he'd given the people in Erpenstaun. The men listened and Damion saw the idea of fighting for Vavaun take root and sprout in the minds of his listeners. Here and there someone nodded, and when Damion finally raised his clenched fist to the heavens and shouted the new battle cry, forty throats echoed. 'For our homeland! For Vavaun!'

'Tomorrow morning, we march,' Damion called. 'Tomorrow night, you sleep in your own barracks!'

A loud cheer greeted his words and when the men dispersed, there was a totally different mood in the camp. Confusion had been replaced by hope and expectation.

'You sound like your grandfather when he was younger,' Kedraun said. He ran a hand through his gray hair. 'The last year, the duke was but a shadow of his old self. The death eighteen months ago of his last son Reginaul, still unmarried and childless, was a heavy blow to him. He feared for the survival of House Asharte and it made him fretful and insecure. Then last year a rumor went round about a grandson living in Rhidauna. One who was son to the Princess Caerch, the duke's daughter, who had run away twenty years before. His Highness tried to discover the truth, but the princess did not reply to his letters and no one else could tell him anything. That frustrated him terribly. But after his visit to King Ghyllander's coronation, he behaved strangely. On the one hand, he was excited, and on the other, very depressed. Nobody knew exactly what was troubling him.'

Damion grunted. 'Me, probably. My grandfather and I met. He wanted me to come home, but even then we disagreed on that endless feud between Asharte and Gry and I refused to be part of it.'

Kedraun sighed. 'That must have hurt him. To take the throne away from DeGry was the purpose of his life and now you, the unexpected successor, denied him the meaning of that victory.'

Damion looked at him. 'I know. But I couldn't do anything else. That feud slowly destroyed our country. I was raised in Rhidauna. I know how far ahead of Vavaun the other countries are. Our peasants deserve better than those miserable hovels. Grymaur, with its open sewers and gloomy streets, is a source of disease and misery, not a proud nation's capital city. And there are plenty more examples. That has to change. That *will* change. But for change, we need peace.'

The knight clapped his hand to his sword hilt and squared his shoulders. 'I understand, Highness.' He hesitated. 'The men will accept the changed situation. They are used to obeying, and it's been a long time since Asharte and Gry met on the field of battle. To most of them, their dislike of Gry is out of habit rather than animosity. I'm less sure of our vassal lords. For them, it will be vital that the duke accepts the situation. If he openly makes peace with Gry, the vassals will have no choice but to follow.' Then he smiled. 'At least you silenced the loudest of them. Harthenkraz is with you now. That was well done; you have a rare youngster there, Highness.'

'I know; he and his sister both. We will convince Grandfather. Retaking Asharte together with Prince Rhydd will help, I think.' Damion smiled. 'Thank you for your candor, Constable.' Then he thought of something. 'I see only soldiers here. Where is the civilian population?'

Kedraun grimaced. 'They're still at Asharte.' He rubbed a hand over his big red face. 'When the attack began, the servants followed instructions and retired to the old tower that used to be the original Asharte keep. It may be ancient, but it is very solidly built, and well supplied for emergencies; the monsters won't get inside in a hurry. We were trying to reach them, but our forces were scattered and we couldn't get past the enemy. In the end, we had to... retire. But it's constantly in my thoughts, Highness.'

Damion laid his hand on the man's arm. 'You did what you could.'

Kedraun looked at him. 'I hope my wife will understand, Highness. She is one of them.'

Damion swallowed. 'I'm sorry.'

'You couldn't know.' The constable turned around. 'She'll understand,' he said softly.

Damion thought of all the servants hiding in an old tower. *Solidly built, but not for a Dar'khamorth sorcerer,* he thought. *They're surely going to blow up the whole burg. We must get them out before it is too late.*

CHAPTER 7 – BATTLE FOR ASHARTE

That afternoon, Grisa returned with the gardians. Dirty and unshaven, clad in battleworn leather and still bitterly angry over the treachery at Adalien, they looked as tough as the men of Asharte lined up to receive them.

Damion and Kedraun received Rhydd officially, and they all shook hands solemnly.

'Men of Asharte,' Damion cried. 'A welcome for Prince Rhydd DeGry, General of Vavaun, and his men!'

Knight Kedraun banged his sword on his shield. 'For the homeland! Together for Vavaun!'

When the shouting had died down, the men returned to their duties.

'General of Vavaun?' Rhydd said, as he and Damion watched his gardians set up camp. 'I don't know if Archodea will agree.'

'She did,' Damion said. 'Not readily or willingly, but she agreed. The country comes first.'

'You twisted her arm,' Rhydd said.

'I almost wrung her neck,' Damion said, keeping his voice low. 'Confound it! She's to blame for this mess! I told her I would expel her whole bliddy Order if she was stubborn. She didn't want to lose Negardien as well, so she gave in.'

'You didn't ask what I wanted?' Rhydd said coolly.

'You're a member of the ruling family. Doesn't your loyalty lie there, Prince of Gry?'

'Of course,' Rhydd grumbled.

'Will you go and tell Uwella you choose Archodea instead of her?' Damion said.

'You're mad; she'd rip out my guts with a crooked finger.' Rhydd suddenly laughed. 'No, it's all right. To be honest, it'll be a relief to leave the Order. Gardian Commander sounds nice, but it's a sergeant's job, no more. I'd rather serve Vavaun, and my gardians will follow me. I recruited them myself and they're all Grys, there's not a wikke among them.' He grinned. 'Neither am I; all the magic went to my sisters. I'm just a soldier.' Then he looked around. 'Where is Asharte?'

'My grandfather retired to Negardien, leaving me in command,' Damion said impassively.

Rhydd blinked. 'More arm-twisting? And you seemed such a meek little guy.'

'That was my Luyon-side,' Damion said. 'I've almost forgotten him.' He looked at the sky and the disk of the sun visible through the clouds. 'Let your people settle in. As long as it's still light, I'm going to scout around a bit. I'm not familiar with the castle, so I want to see it first. Tell Uwella I'll be back before dark.'

Damion turned into a hawk and flew quickly away over the tents. Kedraun had given him directions. "Follow the river; it runs straight to the Loden Morr, that's the lake beside the castle. You can't miss it." Well, the river was below him; a rushing stream that cut through the pine woods, easily seen from the air.

The land around here was rugged, a bleak stretch of forests and rocks. Only once he saw a village with fields and pastures, looking strangely deserted.

Then, almost without warning, the woods ended and he got his first look of Asharte. His crow-form croaked in surprise; that single image in the book hadn't prepared him for the sheer size of the castle. It was a giant mass of walls rising up from the dark waters of the Loden Mor as if they grew there. They were slanted, like the sides of an inverted bucket, with round towers protruding from them, and crowned with crenellated battlements.

Central was a massive, square keep. The back of the castle was a steep mountainside, whose snowy peaks disappeared into the clouds, and the front with the gates was only accessible via a narrow dam in the lake.

Dear gods, Damion thought, as he studied the gates and the massive towers flanking them. *How did those beastmen get inside? How in Greos' Hells will we?'*

'They used deceit, Highness,' Kedraun said when Damion had returned to the camp and called his commanders together. 'Asharte is well known for its hospitality to Arikal's followers. So when two Gray wikken asked for admittance, we opened the gate, though it was in the middle of the night.'

A little muscle in his face worked as he spoke of that moment. 'It was a trap! The traitors burned down the guards with their magic and before we knew it, their monsters were inside the walls. It happened so fast, they were at the hall doors before we could close the inner gates. Twenty minutes, that's all it took. The duke didn't want to flee, but he had no choice. We only got out because the tunnel was safe.'

'A tunnel?' Damion said quickly. 'An escape tunnel? Where is it and where does it lead?'

'The exit is a cave in the forest. From there, a corridor runs under the Loden Morr and comes out into the dungeons. Through them one passes the storage cellars and the kitchens to the rest of the hall.'

Damion's face turned dark as he listened. *A tunnel! And none here thought fit to inform me! What a pack of fools.* His thoughts must have shown, for Kedraun looked embarrassed.

'I should have told you,' he said. 'Your pardon; I keep forgetting the things that are well known to us, will be strange to you.'

'Yes.' Damion took five quick paces up and down the tent, letting his anger evaporate. 'No matter; now I know. Point is, will the enemy?'

Kedraun coughed. 'They won't find it easily, Highness. It's closed off with a sliding wall. No one who doesn't know it's there will discover it.'

Damion knew he had no choice but to risk it. A frontal attack on the burg was out and what other way was there?

'We'll use the tunnel,' he said. 'Assemble the troops, gentlemen; the Hamorth's beasts are waiting for us.'

In a long column, they left the camp, following a narrow trail through the trees. Everyone went along; even the wounded refused to stay behind. 'For the homeland,' a fellow said, with his arm in a sling. His friend, blinded by a sword wound, assented.

By ten o'clock, they reached the cave. The tunnel was closed off by two heavy doors, but Kedraun carried the keys. Once opened, the corridor before them was pitch dark, and seemed wide enough for two men side by side.

'We'll go first,' Damion said. 'Then Kedraun's men and after them, Prince Rhydd's troops. Twins, can you prepare some lights up and down the line?'

'Of course.' Bartram's face broke into a smile. 'Every tenth man, raise your sword!' he shouted and waited till the order was passed down the line. He knotted his brow and turned slowly red in the face as one after another, the lifted blades began to glow, producing enough light to walk without stumbling.

'Clever!' Grisa said admiringly.

'They can't fight with it,' Bartram said finally. 'That will break the spell.'

'Nicely done,' Damion said, as they walked down the tunnel. 'Doesn't it cost a lot of mana?'

The boy stared at him. 'And? There is plenty where that came from. I won't exhaust it in a million-million years.'

'You haven't got that much mana reserve,' Damion said, lifting an eyebrow.

'I haven't got any reserve,' Bartram said. 'I know mana-users must store some of the stuff in their heads before they can use it, but Grisa and I take ours directly from the Intermedium.'

'You what!' Damion nearly stumbled but quickly recovered. *Mages collect bits of wild magic from the world around them,* he thought. *To take it from the Intermedium, where there's as much mana as we have air, would make those kids unbeatable.* 'That's...' He shook his head. 'Sorry; it obviously is possible. But how?' Then he frowned. 'What are your limitations?'

Bartram grinned. 'The invocations and me. Spells are fragile things, written to use only tiny bits of mana. Giving them more of the stuff doesn't make them stronger, they blow up. That's definitely not funny when it is your spell. And me, I can handle only so much mana. It's like...' He sought for words to describe it. 'Like a river. I can scoop up some water with my hands, but all the rest of it flows past. With m'sister, it's the same; we can both do little things forever, but no big things at all. We're not gods.'

'You have thought it all out,' Damion said. He cast a quick look at the column of men walking behind them. All was still well.

'We had to,' Grisa said, walking behind them with Uwella. 'It's a matter of life or death for us to understand our limits. We're just as fragile as those spells, and we don't wanna blow up.'

She suddenly grinned. 'It's nice to have someone who wants to know about us. We haven't been home much, the last five years, and when we were, our parents hardly had any time for more than a quick kiss. Father had the army and politics; Mother was the Marshal's Wife with all her charity and societies, playing the Leading Lady of Vavaun.'

'She won't be that any longer,' Uwella said haughtily. 'I applaud her charity and her societies, but I am the Lady of Vavaun and I'm quite able to lead my own court.'

For a moment, they walked in silence. Then Grisa began to laugh, and sudden tears ran down her cheeks. 'Oh dear, Mother's been... she's been demoted! You will have your own court ladies and such? Say yes, say yes!'

'Of course I will,' Uwella said. 'I've spent too many years with all those old and earnest wikken to exchange them for old and earnest ladies-in-waiting.'

'Thank you.' Grisa hugged her. 'Perhaps Mother will stay home more and give me a chance to talk with her once in a while.'

'I think she will,' Uwella said. 'Once she sees what an important part you two play, she will make time for you. And your father always was very proud of you both. He said so often enough. He admired you for your strength and your independence. Perhaps he thought you were content with each other's company and didn't need him. You twins are very close, you know. My siblings and I were the same, but then we *didn't* want our father's attention. We are not a good example.'

Grisa made a strange noise in her throat. 'If you're right, it's stupid,' she said and she looked at Bartram. 'Of course, the two of us are close. But there are things I can't tell my brother, girl-things. And I'm sure he has boy-things he won't want to tell me. That's what parents are for.'

'But your parents didn't know that.' Damion nearly bumped into a stack of crates. 'Careful here,' he called softly to the men behind them. 'Pass the word.'

'Uwella, how did you do it with those girl-things?' Grisa said.

'By the time I got those, I was already a wikke and there were one or two others I could ask. And Rhydd...' Uwella looked around, but her brother was far enough away. 'He had his own ways. He, ah, experimented.'

Bartram choked and Uwella gave him a stern glance. 'You won't imitate him. Rhydd is a good soldier, but in several ways, he is not a suitable role model. Better ask Damion. He didn't do too badly.'

'Not now,' Damion said hurriedly. 'I think we're nearing the end of the tunnel. Pay attention, folks.'

Uwella laughed. 'Coward.'

The long walk underneath the lake ended at a blank wall. To the right was a heavy bolt of the type used on castle gates fastened with a large padlock.

Damion stared at it. 'What's that for?'

'A moment, Highness,' Kedraun said. He was patting his pockets with a worried frown. Then his face cleared. 'Here is the key. Pardon, dear.' He leaned over Grisa's shoulder to reach the bolt. 'I had locked it behind us when we, ah, left.'

The key was old and turned only with difficulty. Kedraun pocketed the padlock and the bolt slid aside with a soul-shredding screech of rusty metal.

'Damn,' the knight muttered. 'It probably won't penetrate the wall.' He pressed his hands flat against the wall and shoved sideways. With a grinding of stone on stone, the whole wall inched to the left.

Damion and Grisa helped, while the others had to wait as there wasn't enough space for more people. It took almost five minutes, but finally the whole opening was free.

'Follow closely,' Damion said. He went tiger and slipped inside.

Inaudible on his white paws, he walked through the unlit corridors past rows of small empty cells. *Cages*, he thought grimly. At an open door, he paused. The air beyond was rank with ancient suffering and never-forgotten pain. He growled in disgust when he saw the torture chamber. Behind him, Kedraun said something, but he couldn't understand the words and didn't listen. Past the last row of cells, five worn steps led to a half-opened door. The hinges squeaked when the tiger pushed it open, but still no one came.

Storage rooms, Damion thought. *They're bare and musty; probably unused for years.*

At the fourth cellar, Kedraun hurried forward and waved his arms.

Damion stopped and changed into his human form.

'Behind that door are the kitchens,' Kedraun said softly.

Damion nodded and looked at the soldiers following him. 'Let's wait till we're all here.'

The cellar wasn't large enough to admit the whole force, so when it was full, Damion gave the old constable a sign. He went back to his tiger body and crouched, waiting for Kedraun to open the door. The dizzying smell of fresh blood assailed his nose and he growled softly. Then he sprang inside.

Three beastmen were cutting up the carcass of a cow. No pigs or dogs, but leopards, and Damion was overcome by a feeling of pure hatred for these travesties of cats. With a snarl, he jumped, easily clearing the table and the dead cow, and smashed into the nearest catman. In his wake, old Kedraun and an unknown soldier ran past to attack the second one.

With his front paws on the chest of the fallen catman, Damion watched an archer loose an arrow at the third beastman, but the monster pulled it out and went for the man. Before Damion could react, Bartram sprang forward, his sword and dagger burning. The catman meowed, grabbed a stool and swung it as a club. A fiery arrow sped past Bartram's head and got the monster in the shoulder. The beast yowled and dropped the stool. Bartram's sword flashed and a burning line appeared, running down the catman's furry body. The beast turned to flee, but Bartram's dagger found its back and it died.

With the three catmen out of the way, the troops split up into smaller groups and spread out through the castle.

In the main hall, they found several more catmen. Kedraun's warriors howled and all their frustrations exploded as they hacked the beasts to bits.

'On, men,' Kedraun shouted, and they ran deeper into the building.

Damion was about to follow when he saw a catman on the first floor gallery. He roared and ran for the stairs. The beast retired into a room and Damion followed. Too late he saw the room hadn't been empty. Five of the spotted beastmen waited for him, swords at the ready.

Fool! Damion thought. *Now what?* He crouched, tail swinging, while his brain sought the best way to get them all.

The catmen circled him, growling softly, as they followed his moves intently.

Then he sprang. His heavy body crashed into two of the beasts, sending them sprawling. The others jumped aside, hissing furiously before they joined the fray.

Biting and clawing, Damion fought, yet five catmen were too much, even for him, and they managed to pin him to the floor. He snarled, snapping at their throats, but they stayed just out of reach.

Then feet pounded in the corridor, and Bartram's voice sounded close by. A flaming sword flashed overhead and a catman screamed in agony. With renewed energy, Damion used the confusion to get from under the clawing bodies. He got his teeth around a striped catman's neck and shook him like a kitten. Then he slammed the beast hard against the wall and heard its bones crack. He turned around to see another beast die, riddled by burning arrows, while Bartram skewered the last one.

Damion returned to his own form. Panting, he stared at the carnage around him.

'Damn!' he said. 'I was trying to be clever. Didn't work out well. Thanks, you two.'

'Pleasure,' Bartram said. 'Luckily we had seen you go in. We were a bit delayed on the way, but not too much.'

His sister grinned. 'Don't tell Uwella; she'll have your hide. In very thin slices.'

'Yes,' Damion said ruefully. 'And she'd be right.'

Like demons of vengeance, the warriors ran through the corridors tearing open all doors and killing every Dar'khamorth they found. The beastmen fought, but the few sorcerers they discovered appeared confused and panicky.

Clueless, Damion thought. *Without orders, they don't know what to do. Are these the former wikken? They look like a bunch of acolytes; low-level fodder. Yet somebody must be in charge here.* With the twins, he went through every room, stable, and barracks in the castle, searching for any higher-ups, but without success.

Hours later, Kedraun met him halfway in the courtyard. The old knight panted and his sweat dripped through the blood on his face, but he raised his sword in triumph.

'Caught them by their frippin' tails, beg your pardon. The castle's ours again.'

By that time, Damion had almost convinced himself that any leading Hamorths had either been away or managed to escape somehow. But he couldn't shake off a nagging feeling of unease.

He walked to the hall of the castle, the place where his grandfather held court. His mind had slowed down to a crawl and his whole body felt heavy and sluggish. Suddenly, a yawn beside him startled Damion. He looked to see Bartram at his side.

'Tired?' he said.

The boy nodded.

'Where's your sister?'

'Doing some fetching and carrying for the constable. Picking up wounded, mostly.'

Damion grinned. 'Great work.'

They entered the great hall, where soldiers were carrying the fallen away.

Damion stopped one of them. 'Any news of the servants?'

The soldier blinked through his weariness. 'They're safe and sound. The valvodjara is with them; she's as good as any healer, our highness is!'

'I know,' Damion said. 'She would make a great field nurse.'

The soldier saluted and hurried away with his dead load.

Damion surveyed the hall. It was big; a high, vaulted space of light stone, with many bright, colorful banners on the walls. Across from him on a dais stood his grandfather's high seat, crowned with the bear's head of Asharte.

He shook his head. *I'm not going to use that; would give the wrong signal. I'm Vavaun, not the Duke of Asharte.* He still felt uneasy.

'All seems well,' he muttered. 'I must be imagining things.'

'Eh?' Bartram said.

At that moment, Grisa popped out of thin air, agitated and scared as she gripped his arm.

'Come quickly! There's that undead guy from the cave! It has a bomb!'

Before Damion knew it, she'd ported them away.

The next breath, he found himself in a large storage room piled high with crates, barrels, and cloth bags. The old sorcerer with the beard lay folded over a barrel, dripping blood. His eyes were open, staring unblinking at Damion, and his mouth was working, as if he tried to speak.

Beside him stood the undead in his luxurious robe. He'd been a tall man in life, noble of face, with long graying hair. The cave had mummified him, leaving his face leathery but recognizable. His one hand held the crooked staff; in his other, he held something small. His eyes glittered, sending chills down Damion's backside.

'You!' he said, and his voice was like Neferestan's, a hollow, spell-made sound, clear and inflectionless. 'Bow to the will of Her. I command now, I am Her instrument, as I was in life.'

'Who are you?' Damion said, and his voice sounded steady enough.

'I am Ozandyas, High Ordealmaster of the Hamorth, archpriest of the second rank. Bow to your death, worm.'

'My death?' Damion said politely. 'Explain, please.'

At that, the undead's mandible shook in laughter. 'This thing,' he said, holding up a bony hand. 'This trifling gadget will be the instrument of your doom. It is...'

A plain arrow whizzed over Damion's shoulder and buried itself in the undead's chest. Ozandyas swayed, for a moment out of control, still clutching the bomb, or whatever it was. Grisa gasped and dove forward. She grabbed the undead around the waist and disappeared.

'No!' Damion shouted, his eyes wide with horror.

With a yell, Bartram sprang over a stack of chests and buried his sword deep into the bearded sorcerer's chest. 'Die, you fricking bastard!' he shouted in a paroxysm of rage.

Then, screaming and cursing hysterically, Grisa returned and threw herself into Damion's arms.

'Girl, girl,' Damion said, holding her close. 'What did you do?' Around him, people were crying and shouting, but he only saw the sobbing girl.

It took some time before she'd calmed down far enough to answer him, but then she lifted a tear-streaked face and gave a grin. 'Took it to that field outside Grymaur. The rabbits won't be hurt by it.' She wiped her nose on her sleeve. 'The corpse... I felt it crumble the moment I came out. Bits and pieces, no more. I saw the bomb fall down on the grass and I ported back immediately, before it exploded. Damn!' she said shakily. 'Was I fast!'

'Oiled lightning, girl,' Damion said. 'When you flashed away, Bartram killed that sorcerer who had brought it here. That must've sent Ozandyas' spirit back to the Underworld when you came out of the Intermedium!'

Grisa's tears dried quickly under the sun of everyone's admiration.

'I knew what that old beard had done,' she said. 'He'd overloaded a manatap; turned it into a grenade. Had it gone off, the mana overdose would have burned our brains out.' A salty droplet trickled past her nose and she angrily wiped her face with her sleeve. 'When a soldier clobbered the sorcerer, the undead took over. Then I went to fetch you.'

'You're amazing,' Damion said and he put her down gently. 'That took a lot of guts, girl.' He rubbed his face and straightened his shoulders. 'What place is this?'

'The armory,' one of the soldiers said. He stared at Grisa as if she were Tilia Luckgoddess herself. 'I work here. Many of our explosives are triggered by mana. Had that thing gone off like miss said, the waters of the Loden Morr would now be filling the hole where the castle had stood.'

Damion hugged Grisa. 'She's the bravest porter of all Vavaun.'

'That's not so difficult, as I'm the only one here,' she said tremulously.

'In the whole world,' Damion said with a smile.

'That's better.' She chuckled. 'And now? Back to the hall?'

Damion nodded.

The great hall was crowded. Not only were all the soldiers of Asharte inside, they had been joined by the castle servants.

Knight Kedraun came forward with his arm around a portly matron and saluted, grinning broadly. 'My wife, Highness,' he said. And proudly, 'She is Mistress of the Household.'

The woman made a quick curtsy, without letting go of the arm of her husband. 'Thank you for liberating us, Highness. And welcome to Asharte. Princess Caerch's son; who would have thought it would be you come to free us, after all these years!'

'The pleasure is mine, Mistress,' Damion said. 'You knew my mother?'

'Oh yes, Highness. I was seventeen and the nursery maid when your mother was an infant. It was my first post in the ducal service. I have watched your mother and her two brothers grow up. Ah, you are very like her, Highness.'

'I think I must be,' Damion said. 'I'm not at all like my father.'

Then he heard Rhydd call him and he apologized.

'What a handsome boy,' he heard Mistress Kedraun say as he walked away. Rhydd had heard it too and there was a small smile on his lips.

'Don't let my sister hear it,' he said. 'Wella can be quite jealous.'

'She won't,' Damion said. 'Not of a woman old enough to be my grandmother. What do you have to report?'

'Victory; we've cleaned out every last corner of the castle. I, Rhydd DeGry, have helped with the recapture of Asharte. Generations of ancestors are turning in their graves.'

'Generations of commoners are rejoicing in their graves because that nonsense finally ceases,' Damion said bitterly.

'I know.' Rhydd put his hand on Damion's shoulder. 'It was just a joke. Old habits die hard.'

'Be careful,' Damion said with a grim smile. 'I am quite willing to help them die. Under my heel.'

'It's really bothering you, isn't it?'

'More than I can say. When I think how my own family is the cause of my country living in poverty, I'm ashamed.' Damion lowered his voice. 'Asharte doesn't mean anything special to me. I'm a Vavauner and all my compatriots are equally dear.'

Rhydd nodded. 'I suppose you're right, but it will take some getting used to. I've been brought up believing us Grys are superior. So I thought our people's misery is you treacherous Ashartes' fault, not ours.' He lifted his hand as Damion opened his mouth. 'Hear me out. I have been thinking about all those fine speeches of yours, and I was wrong. Our side was as much to blame as yours; we're both guilty. There; I admit it. Now you and my sister are going to make things better. I tell you honestly, I'm glad it's Uwella's responsibility. She is much better at these things than me. She always was, bless her bitchy ways.'

Damion nodded. 'Besides, I would never have married you, Not even for Vavaun.'

Rhydd blinked. 'You're not at all my type.' Then he chuckled. 'It would have created a sensation, wouldn't it?'

Damion was spared an answer as his love came in and he waved. Over his shoulder he shouted, 'Constable!'

The old knight left his wife and joined him.

'Kedraun, the castle is back in our hands,' Damion said. 'I leave matters to you. Rhydd, pull your men back to the camp in the woods. Uwella and I will join you there; we'll be leaving for Gry tomorrow morning.'

'You're not staying here, Highness?' Kedraun said.

Damion shook his head. 'This is my grandfather's house. My place is in Grymaur, where the throne is.'

'Is that Grymaur or Kronmaur?' the knight asked carefully.

'What do you mean? The throne is in Burg Grymaur, I thought?'

'Until fifty years ago, we called town and burg Kronmaur. Duke Venric's father found it necessary to push his rulership down our throats by changing the names.'

'Oh.' Damion paused. 'Kronmaur, I'd say. The capital is from all of us.'

Kedraun saluted. 'Thank you, Highness.'

CHAPTER 8 – REUNION

'Kronmaur?' Uwella's eyes widened. 'I never knew that; we've always called the city Grymaur.'

'The older generations must know,' Damion said. 'It's not that long ago.'

'My grandfather would have renamed it? I don't remember him; he died when I was very small. Our old nurse was about the only one who dared tell us of him, even years after his death.' She snorted in disgust. 'Old Uwelric was the guy for it. He was a tyrant, within and outside of the family. When he was young, the usurper Kaspraun DeAsharte had taken the throne; your great-grandfather. Uwelric had him assassinated and established what my father always likes to call the Third Grysan Dynasty. Everyone was afraid of Uwelric. I don't think I've ever heard Father call him by name, it was always The Duke. Boy, compared to my grandfather, yours is a sweet, compassionate old man.'

They had returned to the forest camp with Rhydd's gardians for a night's sleep before Grisa would port them back to Andauz. During the fighting in Asharte, they had barely seen each other and they had some catching up to do. The sky was clear and full of stars while the only sounds were the snores of the soldiers.

Uwella lay in Damion's arms, with a warm, furry bear pelt pulled up to her breasts, and she sighed in contentment. 'Tomorrow we're for Gry. It's been years since I have been there,' she said sleepily.

Damion didn't want to think about tomorrow; he was nice and comfortable, and the now was a good place.

Then, out of the darkness, a snatch of evil shocked him from his lethargy.

'Beastmen!' Uwella snapped. 'They must've surprised the sentinels.'

Damion was already on his way to the soldiers' tents, running barefoot over the wet forest floor.

'To arms!' he cried. 'Alarm! Alarm!'

A sleepy trumpeter in pants and nightgown took up his call and the men tumbled out of their beds, half dressed, but each with his weapons.

Rhydd came rushing from his tent in his padded undertunic, with his helmet and sword in hand. 'Where is the enemy?'

Damion opened his mouth, but at that moment, a score of howling pigmen broke through the bushes and jumped the soldiers. A fierce battle ensued under the starlight. Damion went tiger and threw himself onto two monsters ripping up an archer. As the man fell, a massive paw sent the first beastman to join him in death and the second one followed rapidly.

'Damion!' He saw Uwella fall with an arrow through her arm, blood staining her underdress. With two, three jumps, he stood straddling her. His animal roar made the forest tremble and the pigmen hesitated. The gardians redoubled their efforts and slowly they pushed the enemy back. A pigman fell, his skull split, anther burned to death on one of Grisa's arrows, and suddenly it was over.

Panting, bewildered by the unexpected battle, the gardians lowered their weapons and stared at the ravages of their camp.

The field nurse came and gently shoved Damion aside, taking Uwella's arm.

'Darn,' she whispered, trying to focus her eyes on Damion's anxious face.

'Neat wound,' the nurse said after carefully inspecting the arrow. 'Passed clear through the limb. Bite your teeth, Highness.' With a practiced flick of his wrist, he snapped off the arrow's head and pulled the shaft out of the wound.

'Good,' he muttered as he dropped the remains of the arrow on the ground.

'Leave the rest to me,' Damion said as he dropped down beside Uwella.

The man hesitated, but then nodded and gave him a clean bandage roll before he hurried on to the next casualty.

Damion placed the five fingers of his left hand like a tent over the wound and buried his right hand in the forest soil. He closed his eyes and thought back to that first time in the Gisterwoud, when Uwella had taught him this technique. Since then, he hadn't used kiya, but he hadn't forgotten. He noted absently it was no longer necessary to restrict the influence of nature; he could manage it through his power. Slowly, the restorative effects of the forest flowed through him and with a slight push from his consciousness, into Uwella's arm. He became aware of someone watching him, but he paid no attention. The edges of the wound crept toward each other, merged, and faded. Gossamer veins regrew and the pale blue color of the arm returned to its normal pink. Then he sighed and laid Uwella's arm gently across her chest. He shook the earth from his other hand and opened his eyes to find the field nurse staring at him.

'I had heard of it, Highness,' he said. 'And I believed only half of it. But now I saw it happen with my own eyes. Impressive.' He hesitated. 'Can you... I mean, I have a man with a stomach wound. I can't do anything. I don't know how even if I had the gear for a major operation. Would that what-is-it technique work with him?'

'Kiya,' Damion said. 'I don't know. I'm willing to try, but I promise nothing. And should it prove too much for me, I'll stop.' He stood up and told two nearby gardians to bring Uwella to their tent before he followed the nurse.

The wounded man lay on a rough blanket between the tents with a silent circle of friends around him. They moved aside as Damion knelt beside the man.

The cut was long and narrow; a dangerous wound. Someone had provisionally sewn him up to prevent the intestines from falling out. Damion put his fingers over the wound. Then he buried his other hand in the dirt and closed his eyes. *Iodraune, please give me the strength to save this man,* he prayed. All around him was a rustling world of leaf and blade and twig and root, and their spicy life coursed through him like an irresistible earth flow. He heard nothing, knew nothing, became a willing tool of nature, without will or wit, sending wave after wave of healing into the limp body under his hand. When it was done, he fell over and slept.

Hours later, he woke up in their tent, still fully dressed. He felt stiff and there was a strange noise in his ears, but otherwise he felt fine.

He stretched and became aware of Uwella's eyes. She lay on her side watching him.

'What have you done?' she asked.

'Kiya,' he said, and he told of his healing efforts.

'You're mad,' she said. 'You can't *do* that with kiya. An abdominal wound? And my arm? I remember that arrow... and the pain. There isn't even a scar to show for it. With kiya?' She leaned over him and stared into his eyes. 'How do you feel?'

'A bit stiff,' he said. 'And I hear the wind in my ears. That's all.'

'That's all?' She pounded her fists on his chest. 'I told you not to turn the forest loose inside you. That way Nature will possess you and turn you into a tree or shrub yourself. Never do this again, Damion. Promise me you won't!'

'Your life is important,' Damion said stubbornly. 'And we have too few soldiers.'

'No!' Uwella said, livid with anger. 'I believed I could unify the country. But now I realize I can't – not alone. I'm too much a Gry, too much a part of the quarrel. We, Vavaun and I, need you! And I cannot fight the Dar'khamorth. I'm not a general; I wouldn't know where to begin. DeKramm cannot, either. He's a good officer, but for all his talk, he never fought a battle in his life. You can do it, but not when you're dead. Promise me you will not do again, Damion.'

'But...'

'Promise!'

He heard the edge of hysteria in her voice and it scared him. 'I promise,' he said. 'At least, where the troops are concerned.' His voice was harsh. 'When it comes to your life, I promise nothing. I love you, you know.' He kissed her gently on the forehead and sat with her until she fell asleep again. Then he lowered her to the mattress and stepped out of the tent. It was early dawn, and most gardians were up and readying themselves for duty.

There was a strange silence wherever he went. Nobody said anything, but their eyes followed him as he crossed the camp. At the command tent, he found Rhydd watching him approach with raised eyebrows.

'Good morning, Rhydd,' Damion said.

'What should I answer?' Rhydd asked, his face drawn and tired. 'Good morning, God?'

Damion blinked. 'What do you mean?'

'Only gods can do what you did with that soldier last night. The man had been given up. His friends were with him to ease his dying. And then you come, you put your fingers in the ground, and half an hour later, his wound was healed.'

'It wasn't I,' Damion said quickly. 'Iodraune did it. I prayed for help and she did the rest. I can't do it a second time.'

'And Uwella?' Rhydd watched him incredulously. 'Did the goddess heal her too?'

'No.' Damion smiled wryly. 'That was me. And after that, I was exhausted. Uwella wasn't half mad at me. I must never do it again, she said. I'm a beastmaster, not a priest.'

'Well, the men are convinced you are a god. They just don't know yet which one.'

Damion looked unhappy. 'What nonsense. I...' Suddenly he thought of Ghyll, and how the godlights in Rhidaun-Lorn burned brighter when he became king. A great awe filled him. 'You know, I think this is the gods' answer to my promise – I said I would bring their temples to Vavaun. Maybe they made me the new focus.'

Rhydd stared at him. 'The focus of the gods? Like they say your friend Ghyll is for Rhidauna?'

Damion hesitated. 'Not wholly. Ghyll is more than that. The gods call him their champion. We believed they meant for Rhidauna, but I think it applies to the whole continent at least. But something like that, yes. Focus for Vavaun, because I want us to be more than a one-god country.'

Rhydd nodded slowly. 'Focus for Vavaun... Well, Father never was that. I always thought he was afraid of the Orders siding with Asharte and threatening his throne.' He shrugged and smiled. 'It makes sense. Much more sense than your being a god. I will tell the men.'

'Good. Maybe then they won't be afraid to greet me. I don't need them scared; that's bad for discipline.'

'Let me be the first, then. Greetings, Damion DeAsharte, Valvodjar and focus of the gods in Vavaun.'

Damion held up one finger. 'Make it Damion DeVavaun.'

'A new dynasty?'

Yes, and a new title. Neither Gry nor Asharte will get precedence; Vavaun will be a grand duchy.'

Rhydd gasped. 'Just like that?'

'Why not?' Damion sighed. 'Look, the common folks don't give a hoot who rules them, as long as they're free from oppression and safe from enemies. Besides, they're fed up with all our quarreling anyhow. Our vassals – I guess most of them think the same. All those little skirmishes, the war taxes, and the lack of progress have been a burden to the lords as well. We're offering them peace, trade, and a lot of other things that will make life easier for them.' He walked a few quick paces up and down, slamming his fist in his hand in his enthusiasm.

'Sounds good,' Rhydd said. 'But what about the dukes? I don't know about your grandfather, but my father won't just step down.'

'He won't have any choice,' Damion said softly. 'Uwella and I are agreed we will not let him return to the throne.

We'll offer both dukes honorable retirement – if they behave, here in Vavaun; if not, we'll find some suitably secure mansion in Rhidauna.'

Rhydd stared at him. 'You won't harm Father,' he said flatly.

'Of course we won't.' Damion found even the idea repugnant and it must've shown in his face, for he saw Rhydd relax slightly. 'We will not start our reign through harming our elders,' he went on. 'They're our family, darn it!'

'Good. And how do you plan not to make us the world's laughing-stock by proclaiming yourselves grand dukes?'

'That's what we have friends for,' Damion said, giving Rhydd a bland smile. 'Neither King Ghyll nor Mo of Opit will mind and when they acknowledge our new title, the other nations will follow their lead.'

Rhydd's eyebrows rose into his hairline. 'Why not a king's crown then? With friends such as yours...'

'Nah,' Damion smiled. 'I want to leave something to do for our children and grandchildren.'

'Your... grandchildren.' Rhydd looked at him and laughed. 'That's for Uwella to say. She decides if she'll become pregnant and when.'

'I know,' Damion said. 'But her ideas about a dynasty are even more exalted than mine, so that's all right.'

Rhydd sighed. 'True. Well, what are the plans for today, oh great leader?'

The whole discussion bothered him. Damion didn't think of himself as someone special. He did what he could to get his country back on its feet and if the gods helped him, so much the better. That his people saw it as something miraculous only showed how isolated they were.

'When the men are ready, Grisa can port us back to Andauz. Next stop will be Gry.'

Some hours later, his hawk-form winged away from Andauz southward. The sky was clear, it was quiet and stirless in the forest, and the greenery showed the first, faint traces of the approaching spring. *Nice flying weather,* Damion thought. Next to his tiger-form, he loved being a bird. It gave a sense of freedom and security, high above all the enemies on the ground.

From the lodge at Andauz, Castle Gry was to the southwest. It was built on a high plateau with the high mountains that enclosed all of Vavaun at its back, and beyond them, the Endless Ocean.

After a while, Castle Gry came into view and Damion couldn't help but grin. Uwella's childhood home was almost a copy of Asharte, built with a lighter stone. It was equally gloomy, threatening, and designed to impress, as was his grandfather's place.

Below him, he saw the towers of the main gate, each with a human guard. The courtyard, the buildings, he had seen it all before. On the steps to the hall, two sorcerers were talking. He landed behind the stables and changed into his own form. Keeping to the shadows, he crept toward the hall in the hope to pick up some spoken information. He...

A flash of movement behind him caught his attention, but before he could react, a huge blow slammed his consciousness to shreds.

When he came to, he was lying on a stone floor in a dark, stinking cell.

Even the dungeons are the same, he thought groggily, and then he groaned as he became aware of a maddening pain in the back of his head. He had to bite down a cry as he moved and automatically he called on his kiya. Nothing happened. Painfully, he sat up. Chains rattled on his wrists. Silver chains, blocking access to his mana, making him helpless.

Damn! His head seemed about to burst and it cost him the greatest difficulty to concentrate. He had been knocked down, so much he understood. Someone had used a bludgeon or something, so they had wanted him alive. But for how long?

Slowly, the dangers of his situation dawned on him. He was alone and helpless, his forces miles to the north and unaware of his plight. If his captors knew who he was, they'd torture every ounce of information out of him. *Gods, help me,* he thought, but of course there was no answer. Not here among Her followers.

He looked about him and shivered. The cell was cold, damp, and small. The heap of rotting straw protecting his body against the hard floor stank of excrement, and the only light was the torch in the hallway. He moved his head and the world around him blurred. A wave of nausea overwhelmed him and helplessly he puked in the foul straw.

A sound of a door opening alerted him. Footsteps approached with military precision and he turned his face to the door. A key grated in the lock and reluctantly the grilled door opened. Damion saw a pair of well-polished boots come into his cell. With some difficulty, he glanced upwards; neat pants, a familiar blue-and-silver tunic, and then the shock almost made him lose consciousness again.

The man was tall, with a thin, pale face radiating disdain and a habitual displeasure. His hair was gray-streaked and cut with military severity, his uniform immaculate and his eyes filled with unholy anger. It was the face he knew from his worst nightmares.

'Father?' he muttered, unable to comprehend.

Sergeant Luyon, the most rigid disciplinarian in the Guard. Ironbiter, the men called him, with fear in their voices. His father, who had made his childhood a hell. Damion wanted to scream, but he couldn't. Gone was the beastmaster, gone was the valvodjar; he was back to being Damion Luyon, the scared boy he'd been all his life.

'Well, you little twerp,' Luyon said, and there vibrated a world of contempt in his deep voice. 'Still the same gutless ninny, I see.'

'Father! What...'

Luyon hit him full in the face and lights as from a major spell exploded in Damion's head.

'Shut up, changeling!' his father roared, and his eyes sparked in the light of the flickering torch in his hand. 'You have embarrassed me enough! I curse you and that filthy she-dog who has thrown you!'

'Mother is not a dog!' Damion said. Helpless rage welled up in him and he heard his own voice break. A second blow set his mind reeling.

'Your mother was a whoring she-dog and so is that painted slut with whom you soil yourself.' Sergeant Luyon's face was contorted with anger and Damion shuddered. He thought of the tiger who had protected him as a child, but the jingling chains prevented the image from coming.

His father grabbed him by the throat and dragged him up till they were face to face. The pain was like knives in Damion's head and he screamed.

'Where is she?' His father's voice was dripping with venom. 'Where is the she-dog hiding?'

'Mother?' Damion asked with difficulty, but his father slammed him against the wall.

'No, you little wimp! That one on whom you indulge your desires. Where is she?'

Uwella! All his nerves twitched. He looked at his father and said nothing.

'Tell, you spineless rat!' Luyon screamed. 'Tell me!' His father's hand still gripped his throat and shook him like a cat does a mouse. Then, for a moment, Damion saw the sergeant's badge his father bore so proudly on his tunic. There was something about that badge. Dizzily, he tried to think, while Luyon kept on shaking him.

Suddenly, he knew! His father wasn't a sergeant anymore; Ghyll had promoted him to lieutenant. That badge was false. This was a sorcerer's trick, not his father! He sobbed with relief.

All at once he felt very calm. 'Go away,' he croaked. 'You are not my father. You're a shadow, a mimic with an outdated image. False – your illusion is false.'

Before his eyes, Luyon's furious grimace faded. The hand that held him unclenched and Damion collapsed backward to the ground.

'You will talk, boy,' the stranger in a sergeant's uniform said coolly. 'We have other ways of making you speak. You will tell us all about the valvodjara, her plans, and her unexpected military acumen. Believe me, you will.' Then, as abruptly as he had come, the man turned and strode out of the cell. With a clatter, the door closed, and then the lock squeaked. The man hung the key on a nail opposite the door and without another glance, walked away.

As the sorcerer's footsteps died in the distance, Damion sagged against the wall. He felt strange, almost lightheaded. The confrontation had been terrifying, a reawakening of his worst fears. But it turned out to be a lie; a bad dream. His father had been harsh, sometimes angry, and then he would say things that hurt his son. But his anger came from frustration that Damion didn't meet his expectations. This maniacal image hadn't been his father. It had been his imagination; he had created his own boogeyman. The realization brought a flood of relief and for the first time in years, he wept.

CHAPTER 9 – RATS

'He what?' Uwella bit off her screech of rage and lowered her voice to a soft growl. 'He's gone off again and you let him?' Her eyes spat fire and her finger pointed at Rhydd's throat.

The gardian swallowed. 'How could I stop him?' he said weakly.

'How! Knock him down, tie him up; gods, there are plenty of ways.' She jabbed his flesh with a sharp nail and a little droplet of blood trickled down to the collar of his armor. With a shrug, she wiped it away with a knuckle. 'You and Damion are a pack of idiots!' she snarled. 'How long has he been gone?'

'Wella...' he stammered, but she slapped his face with two fingers.

'Don't call me that; you know I hate it! How long?'

'Six hours,' he said.

Uwella opened her mouth, but no sound came. Six hours! Damion should've been back long ago. In her mind, she saw him shot from the air, his body riddled with arrows, and she barely suppressed a shudder. She whirled around and walked a few furious steps up and down.

'Too long; something must have happened.' She glared at her brother, still standing at attention. 'Send for Grisa.'

Rhydd relayed the order, while Uwella paced through the wet grass, thinking furiously. He must be at Gry. Somehow, something had gone wrong, and it could only have been at Gry. That's where the enemy was. That's where she had to go. But not alone. Oh no, she wouldn't be stupid like that idiot Damion. She... 'Grisa!' she shouted.

'I'm here,' the girl said. 'I said so, but you didn't listen.'

'No matter. Go to Burg Asharte. Tell Kedraun I need half his force immediately, ready for battle. Then bring them here. Now!'

'Right,' Grisa said. 'I'll fetch them; don't worry.' Then she disappeared.

'We march?' Rhydd said and he sounded surprised. 'But...?'

Uwella suppressed an urge to hit her sibling. 'Of course we march! The fool's in trouble and I want him back. Go prepare the men. And when the Ashartes arrive, I want all commanders here. Now move!'

Her mood was their father at his worst and her brother knew her too well to protest. Without a word, he ran off to do her bidding.

It took another hour before Grisa returned with Knight Kedraun and his men.

Without prompting, Rhydd collected the commanders and joined his sister.

Uwella nodded to Kedraun and the various captains. 'I fear the kjavode met with some difficulty at his last scouting flight,' she said without preamble. 'We march for Gry immediately.'

'That will take several days,' an elderly captain said doubtfully.

'I know that,' Uwella snapped. Then she took a deep breath. *Relax!*

'I can take you inside,' Grisa said.

Beside her, Bartram frowned. 'Too dangerous. We won't know who or what is inside.'

Uwella swallowed a retort. *He's right,* she thought. 'Remember the Grazzly Mines?'

The twins both grinned at the memory of a youthful expedition.

'Of course,' Grisa said. 'We never got inside, did we?'

'The field in front of the entrance is large enough to hold the troops,' Uwella said. 'From there, it's a three-mile march to Gry.'

'And when we're there?' Kedraun said carefully. 'How will we get in?'

'We will decide that when we're there,' Uwella said and the tone of her voice betrayed the rage inside her. Rage at Damion, at the enemy occupying her ancestral home, at the gods and the whole bliddy mess.

Kedraun must have heard it, for he bowed his head and kept silent.

'Questions?' Uwella said. 'If not, prepare your troops for teleporting.'

Without a word, the commanders went to collect their men.

Uwella watched them go and fought against the desperation that threatened to overcome her.

Grisa hugged her for a moment. 'We'll find him,' she said.

'Of course,' Uwella said and she clenched her teeth. '*I* am going to kill him, not those Dar'khamorth bastards!'

Damion closed his eyes and let his mind wander around the castle. He needed help. What could he do? He sought for a beast within reach of the thimble-full of mana he had left. He found countless spiders and flies, but they were too small. Then he saw them. In the storerooms, of course; a dozen black rats. He sought out the one with the strongest aura; the ducal rat.

Come, he thought, and the animal rose on his hind legs, looking around. *Come to me!*

He felt the animal's curiosity and marveled at the beast's intelligence. As the rat scurried off to the dungeons, Damion kept contact as well as he could. Other little minds interfered and then he noticed the ducal rat wasn't alone; a swarm of black rodents followed him as befitted loyal retainers.

They entered the cell, milling about and squealing. The ducal rat sat on its hind legs and looked up expectantly at Damion. *Here we are. Now what?*

In his mind, Damion built a picture of himself, his chains, and the lock that kept them closed. The ducal rat squeaked.

He understood the idea *trapped*. Then Damion showed him an image of the key to his cell dangling on a nail. He imagined a rat, a big strong rat with the key in his mouth who came to him, and then of his chains dropping to the ground. It was quiet while the ducal rat thought about it, and the others waited patiently for his response. Then the ducal rat whistled and his followers screeched excitedly. Several rats ran outside and tried to climb the wall. Most dropped back to the ground, but two of them made a race of it. Damion watched their progress, his head ringing and his hands wet with sweat. Finally, it was the smaller of the two who tipped the key with his snout. Tinkling, it fell down and now the ducal rat shot forward. He carefully picked up the key between his teeth and ran over to Damion.

My thanks! With some difficulty, Damion turned the key around in his hand and tried to force his fingers to do what they weren't used to and fit a key into a lock dangling from his wrists.

It took a dozen heartbreaking attempts before the mechanism clicked and he could shake off the shackles. He looked at the rats and changed, shrank. The cell and all around him looked different, a landscape full of looming obstacles. His admiration for the two rodents' agility grew and he thanked them warmly. The ducal rat laughed and Damion heard amusement in his voice. But just like that time with the crows at Derivall, the rats simply accepted his transformation. They even found it rather comical.

What now? the ducal rat thought quizzically.

Damion thought of a garden, with soil and humus.

Follow, the ducal rat said and ran off through the dungeons. The rats waited every time he fell behind till they came out of a dark drainpipe into a large vegetable garden.

This? the ducal rat thought. *We must go. Little ones hungry.*

I'm grateful, Damion said. *May your eats be many!*

Will be; we smart, two-legs not! The ducal rat grinned and they all scurried off.

Quickly, Damion took his own form and with a sigh of relief, put his fingers into the soft earth. With Uwella's urgent warning in mind, he let nature enter him slowly. This time he heard no noise in his ears; everything stayed calm and the pain in his head faded slowly.

He didn't know how long he'd been sitting there in the dark between the carrots and the onions. The moon was high overhead, so it must be several hours past midnight. Again he transformed himself into a rat and began a room-by-room search of the castle. He noted the usual beastmen providing the muscle. Besides them were some forty humans, of whom only a handful were sorcerers and the rest soldiers and servants, on guard or at work.

They are human, he thought, watching a servant woodenly sweeping the floor. *But they seem drugged, or something. What's with those cursed crystals in their heads? They're not golems.*

When he had searched the whole castle, he knew enough; time to go back to Andauz. He hurried to the top of the outer walkway. After making sure he was unobserved, he turned into a hawk and with all his senses alert, shot off into the darkness.

He hadn't flown a mile when he saw below him a line of warriors making their way through the dark forest. He drifted down silently and then he recognized faces. These were Rhydd's troops and – damn, there were the bear tabards of Asharte! He flew to the head of the column and saw Uwella with Rhydd, Grisa, and Bartram, all looking dark and determined. He gave a whistling hawk's call and they stared up in surprise. Uwella's mouth opened in a shout he couldn't understand and Rhydd raised his hand. Behind them, the whole column came to a halt.

Damion landed on the muddy path and quickly took his own form.

Uwella rushed forward. 'It is you!' she shouted, her face contorted with fear and anger as she gripped his arms. 'It's really you. Curse you, boy! What happened? What kept you?'

'I'm all right,' he said quickly. 'I had an accident, but I escaped.' He covered her hands with his. 'I am sorry, love. I truly am.' He told her and the others what had happened, and Uwella's face tightened as he spoke.

'Your father?' she said, interrupting him. 'Has he...?'

Damion shook his head. 'He didn't turn traitor. It was someone else impersonating him. A mimicker or something. But the bastard failed in the details, even if I was slow in recognizing it. The whole idea was all nonsense, of course. My father may be a first class bully sometimes, but he would never ally himself with the Dar'khamorth. Besides, he hates all magic, and their magic most of all. It was a nightmare; no more.'

'Did they know you're the kjavode?' Rhydd said urgently.

'I... don't think so,' Damion said. 'The guy must have picked the whole business with my father from my mind. It wasn't a true image, more like a distorted memory. He can't have been a proper mindreader, for he never spoke of my being Asharte. Instead, he wanted to know all about Uwella, her plans and her military acumen.'

Uwella gripped his shoulders and shook him. 'You are my acumen, boy! You are the one who leads the troops. Stop risking your life; we can't miss you.' She growled softly. 'When Rhydd told me you'd gone alone to Gry, I almost scratched his face open for not stopping you. And when you didn't come back, I collected our troops and came to fetch you. We would've gotten you out, somehow.'

Damion swallowed. 'Thank you,' he said meekly. Then he raised his head. 'And now we're going to get our own back.'

'You counted forty opponents?' Rhydd smiled eagerly.

'Yes; mostly civilians and soldiers. They carry a crystal in their head; I don't know what to make of that. Let's try to keep a few of them alive so we can investigate it.'

'We'll do our best,' Rhydd said grimly. He lifted his hand and the army moved forward.

Another hour saw them at the gates of Gry. Here was no lake; instead, the entrance to the castle was a bridge spanning a deep ravine.

'We'll not port straight in,' Damion said. 'We wouldn't know in what kind of mess we'd arrive. We'll open the gates like civilized folk.' He looked at Uwella. 'Remember that hookfeather Grisa killed at Adalien?'

Uwella's eyes lighted up. 'Course I do. I knew we'd want to try it.'

'It's perfect for the job. You take the left tower and I'll do the other. If the forecourt isn't empty, we'll make it so and then I'll open the gate.'

Although most of the army would have heard of the hookfeather, none of the men with them had ever seen one, and the sight brought a wave of instinctive fear.

'Stand!' Rhydd yelled, and his voice shook. Then the two birds jumped into the air and the force of the wind from under their wings caused the nearest men to stagger.

Damion's cry shattered the nightly silence as he shot to the clouds. This! This was Power – a primal force not even his tiger could equal. He wheeled and dove with Uwella in a giant dance that had the watching soldiers gaping. He had forgotten them, forgotten Gry and the Dar'khamorth as he exulted in his new powers.

After a while, he slowed down, letting the wind carry him as he watched the long row of mice that were Rhydd's people. Then he chuckled.

'Ready?'

'It's incredible fun!' Uwella opened her curved beak and screeched as she circled her mate. 'Yes, I'm ready.'

Together, they set course for the castle gates.

Far below him, Damion's sharp eyes saw a shadowy watchman standing motionless, and he swooped down. The hapless man let out a single cry before the hookfeather's beak and claws turned him into a bloody rag. As he dropped the bleeding carcass over the side, Damion looked down into the courtyard and saw a sorcerer staring up at him in blank-faced incomprehension. With a single wing-beat, the hookfeather cleared the battlements and dove down. Desperately, the man began a spell, but the time separating him from death was too short and his blood spread out over the stones. The forecourt was empty.

While Uwella flew up to watch for enemy actions, Damion landed at the gate and quickly took his own form. He ran to the winch that raised the portcullis and grasped the lever. With a barely audible squeak, the gate rose foot by foot as he turned the heavy handle. On the other side of the gate, Rhydd and the mass of vengeful warriors behind him watched how he sweated. Once the fence was up far enough, a burly sergeant of Kramm crept beneath the steel points.

'Let me, Highness,' the man said and his big hands gripped the handle.

Damion stepped back. The sergeant worked faster, and in no time, the portcullis was hoisted high enough.

'Done,' the man said and he grinned at Damion. As he came upright, a beam of energy from the battlements struck the sergeant full in the back. Even before his smoking body touched the ground, Damion was on the ladder to the wall walk. The sorcerer never had time for a second shot. The tiger smashed him against the battlements, digging his claws into the screaming man's body. Damion finished him off and spied a second blackrobe below him, with four soldiers in his wake. The man was about to cast his bolt, but Damion jumped the fifteen feet down and snapped the man's spine as he landed on top of him. The moment he died, the soldiers' faces twisted horribly. They dropped their blades and sank to their knees, clawing at the crystal in their foreheads. Then, one by one, they keeled over and lay still. Damion turned into his own shape and checked their heartbeat.

'They're still alive,' he said to himself. 'Funny how they went down when I killed that sorcerer. Very much like golems. And yet...'
He sat down and stared at the four unconscious bodies.

From her vantage point on the tower, Uwella saw a blackrobe with a squad of archers appear on the wall walk. She saw him kill the big soldier at the portcullis winch, and Damion going tiger as he ran. It made her giggle somehow – she had never seen him change while moving, and it looked strange. *Pay attention!* she scolded herself. *You should have killed that guy.* But she was tired; lack of sleep, the nightly march, and the strain of Damion's disappearance was taking its toll.
A sound from the courtyard made her look down and she saw a small troop of dogmen come running around the keep, yapping like hounds. Uwella let out a screech and plunged from the tower. Her tiredness gave way for a massive hate and she came down on the beastmen like a taloned fury. Tearing with claws and beak, snapping at eyes and throats, she went for them till the dogs' blood flowed freely.
Just when she ripped out the guts of the last one, soldiers from Asharte ran through the inner gate. As they saw their valvodjara dragging the innards from a dogman, they cheered her and banged their swords on their shields in approbation. Suddenly, Uwella realized they were Harthenkraz's men, led by the old lord's squire Madyc. She changed to her own form before their eyes and grinned. 'Well met,' she called. 'Get into the keep! I'll be with you.'
Madyc lifted his sword in salute as they ran past her.
Quickly, she changed into her mountain lion and followed them inside.
Entering the large hall, she felt an unexpected pang of familiarity. *I've come home,* she thought for the first time. *After six years, I'm home.* Then the sounds of fighting pulled her to the sitting room, her late mother's favorite place. Uwella blessed her cat's lack of emotion; she was sure she'd

have cried in her own body. The room hadn't changed; her mother's chair was still at the hearth, her old spinning wheel stood in the corner at the window, and the curtains were still the same tapestries she'd enjoyed looking at as a child. *Damn!* she thought. Then she saw the pigmen battling her soldiers in her mother's room! She screamed and sprang at them, and for a while she forgot everything but the need to kill. Finally, she looked around at the men, panting and sweaty, blood-spattered but triumphant. She growled deep inside her throat, and Madyc made a strange, jerky bow to her. Then she turned around and leapt outside.

Going through the keep was like a bad dream; the familiar rooms, the memories of her childhood overrun by beastmen and empty-faced humans. Most enemies ran as she met them; even the pigs feared the monumental rage visible in every fiber of her cat's body. They fled from her to meet the swords of Asharte and death. She found the children's rooms she had shared with Rhydd and Gemedda as unaltered as the sitting room; as if her father couldn't be bothered to change them. *Or perhaps he didn't want to?* she suddenly thought. *Would he have* cared *about us running away? Cared for us, not for his throne?* Suddenly, she wanted to see him, to ask him. Then another group of pigmen crossed her path and she forgot all as she fought.

At last, it was done. The fighting was over; the blackrobes and their beastmen dead, the now dazed-looking humans herded together, and soldiers were in the dungeons to free the servants.

Uwella walked down the hall in her own form. *Damion? Where the heck is he?* She went out into the rainy courtyard and ran into the twins.

Both DeKramms were battered and bleary-eyed, their armor bloody and smoke-stained, but they managed to look cheerful at the same time.

'Glad you're both safe,' Uwella said. 'Been amusing yourselves?'

'We've been running around mostly,' the girl said. 'Cleaning out all those hiding places we used when we were small.' She grinned. 'Amazing how these big beastmen fit into those same spots. We flushed out quite a few of them.'

Uwella tried to smile in response, but she was too tired. 'Have you seen Damion?'

'He's in that workplace next to the stables,' Bartram said. 'They gathered all those addlebrained captives there.' He looked critically at her. 'You seem dazy yourself. Done a bit much, have you?'

'Of course she has,' Grisa said indignantly. 'She's been showing those Ashartes their valvodjara is as much a warrior as them.'

'So I have,' Uwella said, brightening at the idea. 'And I am, too.'

She found her mate and Rhydd together, examining the captured archers. As Damion saw her come in, he turned and enfolded her in his arms. 'You look done in.'

Uwella nodded. 'I'm feeling it. All those days in a row. Running, fighting, running back again and more fighting. I'm exhausted.'

'But every time we freed another part of our country.'

Uwella smiled. 'You've really become a Vavauner, haven't you?'

'Yes. One way or another, I feel at home here. This is my country, not Rhidauna.'

Behind them, something moved, and when they turned around, one of the soldiers sat up with his head in his hands. 'It's... silent,' he said. 'No whispering voice. What... Where am I?' He stared around him with blank, uncomprehending eyes.

'You're in Vavaun,' Damion said. 'Who are you and where are you from?'

'I am... O Gods, I don't know... This is Vavaun?'

Damion thought the man's face seemed outlandish. His skin was pale, his face boney, with lank, black hair and curiously light eyes that seemed unable to focus properly.

'In whose service were you?' Damion said, looking closely at the man.

The soldier sweated and wrung his hands. 'I - don't - know!' He broke down sobbing.

'Those crystals,' Uwella said suddenly. 'Those golems we fought with Ghyll wore them, too, and they were controlled by a golemaster. Would that work on humans as well?'

Wordlessly, Damion pulled a gold neck chain from his pocket. At the bottom was a many-faceted black crystal.

'I took it from the first one I killed.'

'We found several more of them,' Rhydd said. 'They couldn't be plunder; not from our treasury. They're worth quite a lot, so I wondered why they wore them.'

'They're foul magic,' Damion said. 'We fought golems before; makemen baked from animated mud, which were controlled by just such white crystals in their heads. A sorcerer gave them their orders through a gold chain like this. If what I think is true, these men were mind-controlled slaves.'

The gardian made a sound of disgust. 'That's horrible! Is there no crime too vile for those murderous traitors?'

'They don't care; they want to wipe us all out anyhow,' Damion said. 'We'll send these men and the chains to the kerran. Maybe Archodea knows how to remove the crystals without killing anyone.'

Rhydd nodded. 'I hope we have any wikken left who know how. Mind magic was one of Negardien's specialties and most of them are now dead.'

'Wrath of Nature!' Damion slammed the flat of his hand against the wall. 'We must have temple portals. Then I would have had those men brought to Rhidauna for healing.'

Rhydd smiled wryly. 'Contact with the rest of the world wasn't necessary, my father said. It only gave people wrong ideas.'

'He was a bleepin' dictator.' Damion sighed. 'All that's for later. First we'll take Grymaur – Kronmaur, that is.'

'Now?' Rhydd said. 'Shouldn't you take a rest?'

Uwella looked at Damion. He looked desperately tired, but she knew he was right. They had the upper hand for now, and one delay could mean the Dar'khamorth taking the initiative back and do something dreadful.

'We can't afford to wait,' Damion said. 'I'm going on another reconnaissance.'

'This time I'm coming,' Uwella said. 'No more one-man parties.' The look on her face was deadly earnest and Damion nodded.

'You'll probably kill me if I should slip away again.'

'Be sure of that,' Uwella said grimly.

Damion turned around. 'Grisa, can you port? You're not too tired? Honestly?'

The girl lifted her chin in the air. 'I can port,' she said. 'Honest and truly I can.'

'Bring those poor fellows to Archodea. Then I want you to get your father and his men, and after that, Lord Erpenstaun. Can you do that?'

'Eight, nine, ten,' she said triumphantly. 'There, I counted first and did not run off without thinking.'

'You're the best,' Damion said. 'I hate asking this after a battle, but I feel we have to keep this thing moving.'

'It's all right,' Grisa said. 'I'll take Bartram to clobber me awake. And no, we're not going to clean up first. Straight from the battlefield we'll go.'

'You show them, fighting girl,' Damion said. 'Rhydd, have your gardians and the troops from Asharte prepare for the big event while we go scout the city and the burg.'

Rhydd's gesture was half wave, half salute as Damion hooked his arm in Uwella's and strode away.

CHAPTER 10 – CASTLE GRY

Outside in the courtyard, Damion looked up at the sky. 'It has stopped raining.'

'A good omen,' Uwella said. 'Let's go to the kerran first and warn them about those prisoners they're getting.'

Damion nodded.

A moment later, they winged away from the tower, while over their heads a pale sun broke through the clouds.

From the air, the kerran looked as it always had. Soldiers walked the walls and the wikken were busy with their daily routine.

As they entered the hallway, they nearly bumped into Archodea on her way out.

'Welcome,' the Drynnath said without a hint anything untoward had passed between them. 'You two have been busy since we last saw each other. Grisa just brought us a group of manipuuls. Highly interesting. It is unfortunate we have lost the people who could help those brain slaves.'

'Is that what they are called?' Damion said. 'Manipuuls; what a fitting word for something so immoral. Please take care of them as well as possible. As soon as I can, I'll send you some experts from Rhidauna.'

'Experts from Rhidauna...'

The Drynnath sounded like she tasted something unpalatable and Damion smiled grimly. 'Don't make the same mistake you accuse the Council of Temples of, Drynnath of the Gray Order. Only by working together can we improve.'

Archodea gave him a long stare and suddenly a smile appeared, transforming her whole, ugly face. 'You are blunt,' she said. 'We wikken are not used to that; we prefer to work with circumspection. Yet subtlety wouldn't have brought the point home and your sledgehammer does. Thank you, Damion DeAsharte, for this lesson in tactics. I will discuss it with the others in my next sermon. Of course you're right; the priests of Mibras can help those wretches better than we.'

Damion bowed. 'You're welcome.'

'May I ask...' Archodea hesitated for a moment. 'What are your plans with Vavaun?'

'When this is all over, you mean?' Damion said. 'We will modernize our country. We want Vavaun to be like Rhidauna and Opit, instead of a backwater from the first century.'

'And what will Duke Venric say when he returns to the throne?'

'My father won't return to the throne,' Uwella said firmly. 'I will gladly greet his liberation, but then it is time for both Gry and Asharte to retire.'

'With us are DeVavauns on the throne,' Damion added. 'The endless struggle is over; our country can no longer afford it.'

The Drynnath straightened her back and then, to the amazement of both, she bowed to them. 'A worthy goal.' She smiled ruefully. 'Even though the Gray Order will be the loser.'

'Not really,' Damion said. 'Having competition will be good for you. You really must come out of hiding and take your rightful place among your peers. They are not the enemy, and working with them will strengthen your position.'

'Applause,' a deep voice said. 'These children know what they want.'

Damion turned quickly. 'Grandfather!'

The duke of Asharte stepped over the threshold and stretched his arms out. 'Grandson,' he said and grabbed Damion in a bearlike hug.

'You're not mad?' Uwella said, surprised, but the old man took her hands and kissed her.

'No, Highness,' he said, and his eyes gleamed. 'I'm very proud of that boy. Just when I thought I had him, *poof,* it was over. Never has someone turned the tables on me in such a way. And him only a brat. Pah!'

Damion blinked as a wave of unexpected emotion swept through him. 'I'm sorry, Grandfather, but there was no other way.'

'I know.' The old man shook him lightly. 'After all, it was what I was planning to do with you. But clearly you expected that.'

'I had hoped my arguments would sway you.' Damion suddenly grinned. 'But I didn't count on it.'

'And my people follow you, apparently? No one protested?'

Damion grinned. 'Lord Harthenkraz didn't think I was worthy. He had his squire challenge me.'

'His squire! That no good whipster he tries to present as his heir. That's what he had come to see me for. I didn't fall for it. Harthenkraz wasted three wives and got nothing from them, the impotent fool. He can't just *adopt* somebody to inherit his tenancy and expect I agree.' The duke looked piercingly at his grandson. 'What did you do? Sic your tiger on the boy?'

'Bartram didn't think it fitting,' Damion said straight-faced. 'He picked up the fellow's glove and fought him into submission.'

The duke guffawed. 'Grand fellow, that Kramm boy. Gods. I would have loved to see old Harthenkraz's face. That smug pup beaten by one years his junior! Then what did you do?'

'We recaptured Asharte and Gry,' Damion said.

The duke's mouth sagged open. 'You did? You just went and took them back?'

'We did; Rhydd DeGry and his men helped take Asharte, and later Knight Kedraun did the same when we went to Gry. We showed the whole duchy what we Vavauners can do together. Soon Grymaur will follow, or rather Kronmaur, city and burg. Our troops are preparing for another battle. Uwella and I will scout the city and as soon as we know what the situation is, we'll attack.'

The old Asharte looked at him. 'Dammit, boy! You manage those things like you've done nothing else in your life. And yet your father is no nobleman.'

'My father,' Damion said stiffly, 'is an instructor at the military academy of Rhidauna. He trains officers in tactics and logistics. He never managed to teach me how to fight, but I know all about organizing an army.'

'That's good,' the duke said soberly. 'Rhidauna's army is probably the best in the world. If your father is part of that, you have it from the best source.' He paused. 'I don't know him; your mother married without my permission and blessing, and their marriage didn't stand. But when I look at you, something good came out of it after all.'

'My upbringing had its positive sides,' Damion said. 'I use them and I try to forget the negatives.'

'Like most of us,' his grandfather growled. 'But enough talk. I'm going back to my studies, and you have to recapture a city.'

When the old duke had left, Damion looked at the Drynnath, who had quietly been watching them from the shadows. 'Studies?'

'Your grandfather rereads the history of Vavaun from our archives,' she said. 'His own were somewhat colored. He finds it very enlightening.'

'I want to read those, too,' Damion said. 'But not now, we have other matters to attend to.'

'Go then, young ruler. May Arikal guard your path.' With that, the high wikke left them.

A little later, two hawks flew up from the kerran. For hours, they drifted in circles over the town and the burg, watching all that went on.

When finally the sun went down in a red haze behind the walls, and the moon appeared in the sky, two rats crossed the heavy stone castle bridge without being observed. Through the bars of the portcullis, they came to the courtyard of the city burg. In the shadow of a stone wolf, totem animal of the DeGry family, they stopped.

There had been little sign of an enemy occupation in the city. Occasionally, a sorcerer passed with a beastman guard, but that had been all. Here in the burg, it was different. The court was crawling with monsters, mainly pigmen, but a few dogmen and a catman hung around here as well, all seemingly waiting for something. In the outbuildings, stables, and workshops they saw more monsters, but once in the keep itself, there were only sorcerers and some manipuuls busy at household tasks. Here, too, most infiltrators had give up all pretense and replaced their treacherous gray by Dar'khamorth black.

'Seen enough?' Damion said finally.

'Too much.' Uwella trembled with a fury too great for a little rodent. 'It's Gry all over; monsters running around in our house, wrecking and despoiling – it's way, way too much.'

'I know,' Damion said. 'Let's go back and prepare our troops. We'll kick them out and make all well again.'

CHAPTER 11 – ENEMY PLANS

The two rats were almost at the gate when a mighty bell tone rang out, reverberating against the walls of the keep.

'Gods!' Damion nearly jumped into the moat at the sound. 'What in Greos' cellars is that?'

'The chapel bell,' Uwella said tersely. 'I don't remember it this loud, though. Perhaps rat ears are more sensitive.'

The sorcerers dropped what they were doing and hurried over to a pillared building with a large godlight on the roof. The glass globe was meant to radiate the gods' blessings, but now it was dead, a clear sign even Arikal had fled Vavaun.

'That's our Chapel of the Gods,' Uwella said. 'For all the gods, though it was mostly Archodea who led the services. Let's go see what the fuss is.'

Unobtrusively, the two rats slinked after the blackrobes, keeping to the shadows.

Inside, the chapel's sanctum was an octagon with seats for a few hundred faithful. At the back, where the icon of the Pantheon of Gods should have been, stood the tall black statue of a four-armed goddess.

The sight of Her image here in the capital stoked the rage burning in Uwella's heart. 'Arikal aid me,' she said, breathing deeply.

'I count twenty of the bastards,' Damion said. 'Twenty-one,' he added, as a stocky figure in a black cloak with the hood pulled over his face appeared from behind the statue.

All present bowed three times in absolute silence before the hooded man began to speak.

At the first words, Uwella squealed softly in surprise. 'It's Syvvan,' she said urgently. 'I can't understand human words, but I'd recognize his voice anywhere. Is he the one in charge?' She looked around quickly. They were in an alcove, hidden behind an antique armor.

'Stay,' she said, and silently took her own form. At her feet, Damion jumped, and she lifted him up to prevent trampling her mate. Without moving, she listened to Syvvan's words.

'...And the great master, brothers and sisters, demands our best efforts...'

He sounded like the wikke she'd known, yet different. That Syvvan had been self-important, an unctuous old bureaucrat, but ever polite. This blackrobe one sounded arrogant, the voice of a Dar'khamorth high priest who'd kill his followers as easily as his enemies.

'...the valvodjara's unexpected actions gave us a set-back...'

She nearly gasped. Her actions? They still didn't know about Damion?

'... but new beastmen are gathering and now we'll go on the offensive again. We will retake the castles, but first of all, the city. This wretched collection of hovels has endured long enough.'

Uwella balled her fists. *Just you wait, you honorless dolt; I'll hovel you, right up your behind.*

Syvvan went on, unaware the one he wanted most was within feet of where he stood.

'As of now, the town gates will be closed. People may come in, but nobody may leave. No reason will be given, of course. We will act at midnight and tomorrow at sundown, all of Grymaur will have ceased to exist. Tonight, your torches will cleanse the earth on which the city stands and the death cries of its people will caress your ears.'

Uwella froze, pressing her back into the chapel wall to steady herself. *Gods, those monsters are going to burn the city!*

'Blood must flow, brothers and sisters, because spilled blood is a blessing in the eyes of the One. Devastation, all-encompassing devastation, he demands of us. The new world shall come through your hands! Blessed be the master in his greater wisdom. Hallowed be the Revenaunt Emperor, whose coming we are preparing. Praise Her by whose will we are.'

Trembling with desperate fury, Uwella watched the Hamorth sorcerers leave the chapel. They talked and laughed as children promised a treat. *We'll stop you!* she thought. *You won't destroy my city!*

Damion squeaked questioningly, and she was about to change back into a rat, when something stirred in the back of the chapel.

'Syvvan!' a voice spoke from the shadows.

The traitor spun around. 'My lord M?'

Uwella saw a richly clad old man with curly white hair and a noble face walk from the recesses of the chapel.

I know him, she thought, surprised. *I've seen that face before, staring down at me. Affable as a spider watching a fly, he was. But where? Who?*

'You disappoint me, Syvvan,' the man called M said. His voice was suave, courtly, but his words made the haughty Dar'khamorth infiltrator cringe.

'You had won everything, and you lost it. This is not how you serve Her. I want to see results fast, else I will replace you. You know what that means, Syvvan.' The undertone of ruthlessness in the urbane speech sent shivers down Uwella's back. *The spider shows itself.*

The man crashed to his knees, his head touching the floor in abject servility. 'Yes, sire. The valvodjara ...'

The old man flicked a wrist. 'A child, Syvvan; playing at ruler. She should be no match for a practicus of the Dar'khamorth. Or is that rank too much for you, Syvvan?'

'No, sire; no! Tomorrow we'll destroy the city and after that, one by one, the castles. Beastmen will massacre the population and the land will lay barren. The child will be homeless before we kill her.'

'Beautiful promises, Syvvan. I want to see results, and fast. Understood?'

'Yes, sir; yes!' But the white-haired old man was gone.

Shaking, Uwella changed back into a rat.

'We must be quick,' she said. While they ran from the chapel and across the stone bridge into the city, she told her mate everything she had heard. Minutes later, two hawks flew back to Castle Gry.

'Sit down, gentlemen,' Uwella said to the army commanders. 'We just returned from our reconnaissance and the news we bring is dire. At midnight today, the Dar'khamorth will send their beastmen into the city, armed with torches and axes to burn all down.'

Lord Erpenstaun looked at his rulers in bewilderment. 'To destroy Grymaur? Why? What do they gain by that?'

'Nothing,' Damion said bluntly. 'The Dar'khamorth isn't out to gain anything. They don't want our homes or our land, nor do they want us as slaves. They plan the return of the Revenaunt Emperor and think to offer him a planet devoid of life. We don't know why, but that's what they are working toward.'

'I never knew this,' Marshal DeKramm said, looking grim. 'I thought they were out for conquest. Burn Grymaur! We'll kill them first, of course.'

Damion looked at him. 'We will, Marshall. One thing, the aims of the Dar'khamorth are not something the Convocation and the Council of Temples care to make public,' he said and gave everyone present a hard look. 'I want you all to keep this a secret. Only realize losing is not among our options.'

The commanders muttered their agreement, but their faces mirrored their unease. Only Rhydd sat back relaxed and looked as if he at least had never ever doubted his sister's mate.

Damion smiled briefly. 'Not so gloomy! Like the marshal said, we will kill the enemy first, before those rabid idiots can put their plan into motion. Gentlemen, you may prepare the troops. In an hour's time, we'll port to Grymaur.'

Grisa brought the army directly under the walls of the city. As Syvvan had said, the gates were closed and beastmen posted on both towers. Damion and Uwella walked to the head of the troops with the marshal and the twins.

'The left tower will present no problem,' Damion said after a moment's observation. 'Its top is only a platform; we'll clear it in minutes. The other one is tricky; that shelter or whatever they built upon it is too small for our hookfeather bodies.'

'Bartram and I will take that one,' Grisa said firmly. 'We have been up there often enough.'

Damion didn't like sending the twins in first, but he knew they could do it. 'All right. But if you come up against too many enemies, you port back here.'

'Promise,' Grisa said with a big grin. 'Come, Bartram. We've got us some fighting.'

'Finally,' the boy grunted and they flashed away.

'You're the general,' Uwella said with a wicked grin. 'You must stay here and lead the army while I'll take the other tower. Wait for the gates to open.'

Before Damion had time to protest, she had changed and sped away. He bit back a curse and forced a smile.

'Not to worry, Marshal,' he said. 'All three have done it before.'

DeKramm didn't answer. His eyes were fixed on the right tower. 'What's those flames?' he said thickly. 'Have those beasts torched the roof?'

'It's the twins,' Damion said. 'If you haven't seen them fight yet, they use a lot of fire. They are very dangerous opponents.'

'Look!' the marshal said loudly. 'Bartram's grappling a pigman! He can't do that! He... Oh gods!' he exclaimed, as the beastman tumbled down the side of the tower, burning from a chest wound. 'How did he...?'

A bright beam of energy shot from the walls to the top of the tower and splattered against the stones.

'A sorcerer!' the marshal cried in agony.

Then a volley of flames sped from the tower and the blackrobed figure disappeared from sight in a trail of smoke.

'That's Grisa,' Damion said. 'She's a very fast shot.'

The marshal stared at him, his face wet with sweat. 'They did that? My children?' He brought his fists to his temples. 'I should have checked their progress more. Asked questions. But there never was time.'

Before Damion could answer, the gates opened and the waiting troops cheered as Uwella appeared, waving.

The twins ported in and saluted. 'You can enter the city, Highness,' Grisa said. 'The valvodjara awaits you inside.'

'Dammit,' the marshal said. 'I don't know what to say. You two make me proud and ashamed.' For a moment, he embraced his children. 'When we're finished here, you must show me all you can do.'

'With pleasure, sir,' Bartram said, beaming.

'First secure the city, Marshal,' Damion said, smiling.

DeKramm straightened and shouted an order. Immediately, the troops surged forward, shouting and cheering. Rank after rank, they ran into Grymaur. Then they split up in mixed detachments and marched through the streets, calling out to the citizens who they were. Soon, their calls sounded everywhere. 'DeGry for Vavaun,' 'Kramm! Kramm!' and above all, 'For the Homeland, for Vavaun,' reverberated through the narrow streets. People left their houses and joined the troops, armed with pitchforks, brooms, and what weapons they possessed.

As they passed the house of Beredt, the retired valet and the horse trader came out.

'The valvodjars!' they cried. 'Long live the valvodjars!'

Others took the slogan over and shouted it all the way to the castle gates.

'Locked tight,' Damion said, as he inspected the burg. 'Those archers can be bothersome. This time we'll both fly, love. Let's take out the sorcerers managing those poor souls and perhaps we can silence their manipuuls all at once.'

'Hurry up, we want to get at those beasts,' Grisa said.

'You got yours already; you can't have two treats,' Damion said sternly. 'Don't be greedy.'

The girl sniffed. 'Just a few little ones,' she said. 'I want to fight, too.'

Damion grinned. 'A few, she said.' He kissed Uwella. 'Let's go, love.'

As at Gry, the appearance of two hookfeathers caused stunned surprise among the sorcerers. Damion saw his prey staring up at him, his face blankly uncomprehending and all of a sudden, he understood. They knew those birds! The one Grisa had killed must've been a Dar'khamorth creature. Now they saw the same birds attacking them!

Damion chuckled and dropped straight down. His huge, razor-sharp claws dragged the unfortunate blackrobe from the wall and let him fall among the waiting troops. A dozen swords flashed and turned the body into a bloody mess.

Damion got a crazy idea and landed on the wall. He resumed his own form and turned to the motionless archers. Many manipuuls had dropped, unconscious, but a few remained standing, looking into nothingness.

'Shoot the beastmen!' Damion shouted and the dead-eyed men turned their bows into the courtyard, adding to the Dar'khamorth's confusion.

Damion ran down the stairs and into the gatehouse. Inside, he found the winch of the iron portcullis and put his hands to the spoked wheel. With a grating noise, the huge gate inched up. Damion panted; he was tired and raising the heavy iron grating was a two-man job, so it went slowly. Too slowly.

He ground his teeth as he sweated, turning the spokes around. *Damn! The enemy will rally... Faster, idiot!* Then Uwella rushed in and without a word put her hands next to his. Together, the wheel turned faster and they heard the waiting men outside cheer. Several soldiers crept underneath the gate and came to their assistance.

'Take over!' Damion wheezed, trying to get his breath back. 'We'll watch for the enemy.'

The beastmasters went hookfeather and sprang into the air. They saw a door open and several pigmen making a dash for the gatehouse. With a screech and the beating of mighty wings, the two giant birds attacked.

As they tore apart the last of the pigs, the warriors of Vavaun came roaring into the burg and fanned out in groups. Once again the superiority of the well-armed and armored soldiers against the barbaric beastmen became clear and one monster after another bit the dust.

With the fight well underway, Damion and Uwella changed into cats. On swift paws, they ran through the corridors of the keep. Their attention was focused on the sorcerers, and particularly Syvvan with his cronies from Adalien. They met several blackrobes, some defiant and others desperately hiding. None of the Hamorths survived, but the ones they sought above all weren't among them.

Finally, they came to the chapel where the evil idol stood. A couple of soldiers were trying to break it up with their axes and Damion's heart froze at the sight. He resumed his own form and ran at them.

'Stop that, you bleedin' idiots!' he bellowed. 'Stop!'

Unwillingly, the men lowered their weapons.

'But Highness,' one said.

'That image is alive, fool!' Damion raged.

The men paled and stepped back.

Damion took a deep breath to calm himself. 'Never try to destroy a god's image in whatever temple anywhere,' he said harshly. 'They carry the soul of their deity and each one can destroy you in a single second. And of all the gods and goddesses, the false Dar'khamorth goddess is the last deity I'd want to meet. Get out of here; you're very lucky she didn't wake up. Uwella, fly to the kerran and fetch the Drynnath. By the scruff of her neck if she tarries!'

Alone with the ominous presence, Damion dropped to the ground, turned his mind to the forest and the loose soil, and began to pray.

Half an hour later, the bone-thin figure of the Drynnath appeared in the chapel, with Grisa at her side. She glanced at the idol. 'Out, all of you,' she said.

Obediently, everybody left but Damion. Archodea raised her eyebrows. 'I said all, Damion DeAsharte.'

Damion stayed where he was. 'I think I should know, Drynnath,' he said calmly. His prayers had been answered, not by any words, but with a leaf green calm that offered shelter and strength.

'I can protect myself,' the high wikke said tersely. 'But not you as well.'

'Iodraune protects me. She is in me, Archodea. Do what you must, but I need to know this.'

The priestess studied him for a moment. 'Well, stay then. But remain where you are. Do not move and do not speak.'

Her face went blank and her eyes glazed over as she stretched her hands out to the idol. She began to sing and although the language was strange, Damion understood the words, though he couldn't ever repeat them.

The Drynnath sang with all the strength of her conviction and slowly the image began to crack. Black mist snaked down the feet of the false goddess across the floor and reached Archodea. The Drynnath sang faster and the cracks in the image grew. The dark fog became thicker and now the singing of the priestess sounded agitated. Damion's hand went almost of itself behind him and suddenly he touched a table, and on it something small and heavy. Archodea's singing faltered and the fog hung like a cloud of antimagical smoke around her, as if waiting.

Suddenly, the Drynnath fell silent and all lights in the chapel died. A cold wind blew in from the Intermedium and brought the smell of something awful and alien with it.

'Now, little brother,' a female voice in Damion's head whispered. With all the strength in his arm, he threw the heavy object in his hand at the idol. It struck the false goddess full on the cracked chest and with something like a sigh, the image collapsed into itself. Damion saw the pieces disappear as a deep hole in the heart of the image sucked them up. The blackness followed and when the last traces were gone, there was a flash, and it was done.

Without thought, Damion walked to the Drynnath and put his hand on her arm. 'Awaken, O daughter of my father's brother,' Iodraune's voice spoke from his mouth. 'The idol is destroyed.' Then she, too, departed, leaving Damion strangely empty.

Archodea moved slowly and lowered her arms. 'You were right,' she said, and her voice seemed to come from far away. 'Even my powers were insufficient. Thank you for your help, Damion.'

'It was Iodraune,' the young beastmaster said, feeling strangely lightheaded. 'I had prayed for assistance, and she told me what to do.' He walked forward and picked up the shiny object he had thrown. 'What's this? An egg?'

Archodea looked surprised. 'It's a cosmic egg. That is the symbol of the Creator, the very power that created the universes. They are extremely rare and not made by human hands. Sometimes a skystone crashes down from the All onto our world and brings one. They are indestructible.' Pensively, she looked at the golden egg in Damion's hand. 'Strange. I have often led the worship here and I've never seen that egg before. Where was it?'

'On the table behind me,' Damion said as he turned. 'I touched...' His voice trailed off. There was no table anywhere near them. 'I felt it, but how?'

'Iodraune,' the Drynnath smiled. 'The sense of humor of the younger gods is sometimes unpredictable. Although... giving you a cosmic egg against the idol of Her is very, uh... direct.'

'Why is that?' Damion looked curiously at the high wikke, but she shook her head.

'I'm sorry, ruler of Vavaun, but I cannot say more. The secrets of the Temples are for the archpriest to explain, not for us. Perhaps the Champion should ask that question, as soon as a new archpriest had been chosen.'

'Which won't be that soon,' Damion said with a hint of sarcasm in his voice. 'The position of archpriest has been vacant for eight months already.'

'It is not a decision to be made lightly,' Archodea said calmly. 'The archpriest is the guardian of our greatest mysteries. We cannot be too careful with this appointment.' She stretched her back and sighed. 'I'm feeling my years,' she said softly. With one of her radiant smiles for Damion, she walked to the door. 'I'm going back to the kerran, this old carcass needs sleep. And you probably have much to do. I wish you strength and wisdom, young prince.'

Absently, Damion rolled the egg back and forth in his hand, It felt strange. Not unlike the presence of Her, but different, too. She was darkness, a cosmic denial of life as they knew it. The egg felt... vibrant, like a living thing. They could be opposites... He shrugged and put the egg in his pocket.

Outside the chapel, a crowd was waiting for him.

'What happened?' Uwella asked urgently. 'Archodea didn't say anything... As usual.'

One way or another, Damion was reluctant to tell the truth about Iodraune and him. It needed a long thought first. 'Archodea sang the idol to pieces,' he said lamely. 'The spirit of the false goddess was driven out.' Applause followed his words, except from Uwella, who eyed him with suspicion. To his relief, she didn't ask any more, but he knew she'd come back to it when they were alone.

He looked around. 'Well?'

'The burg is ours again,' Marshal DeKramm said. He looked pale and from a makeshift bandage round his head, a thin stream of blood trickled down, soaking his long hair. Otherwise, he looked relieved and satisfied. *And a little more like the twins*, Damion noted.

'What are our losses?'

'Eight men,' DeKramm said. 'The number of prisoners is much higher.'

'Treat the manipuuls well. I hope we can save them from those damned crystals. They are innocent of what they did; the sorcerers were literally pulling all the strings.'

The marshal saluted, fist to the shoulder. 'I will make it clear to the men, Highness.'

Damion looked around the courtyard, at the bloodstains and the men carrying away the dead and wounded. He saw a group of servants huddling together, blinking against the sunlight. From their midst, an older man in a sober but expensive robe came forward. He looked hollow-eyed, and the dirty stains on his clothes indicated he had been one of the prisoners.

'Who are you?' Damion asked gently.

The man bowed. 'Costare, Highness. I am the seneschal of Burg Gry. I...' He couldn't go on and Damion saw his hands shook. 'We were locked in the dungeons, Highness. It was... horrible. The cells haven't been used for ages and in such bad condition; crawling with vermin, ground water forming pools on the floor, no light, and so cold. Every day, two or three of us were taken away. They never came back and I feared the worst. Some were still young, only fifteen, sixteen years old. Those monsters! Oh, those monsters.'

The tears trickled down his cheeks. Then he straightened his back and the mask of imperturbability returned to his face.

'I beg your pardon, Highness. How may I be of service?'

'Put everyone who can to work, Costare. If there are any among your people unable to work, care for them.'

A gardian marched from the keep and Damion saw in his face something was wrong. *Damn,* he thought. *Not another guy with a bomb...*

The man saluted. 'Prince Rhydd's compliments and would you please come to the kitchens, Highness.'

Damion looked at him and saw the sick expression in the man's eyes. *Not a bomb, but what else would upset a hardened gardian?*

'Lead on,' he said shortly. The kitchens were the one place he and Uwella hadn't visited on their reconnaissance, as there had been too many beastmen gathered.

In the doorway, he stopped and froze. This part of the keep was old, two dimly lit rooms overlooking a corner of the courtyard. The tables and the black and white tiled floor looked like a massacre had taken place.

Rhydd stood in the middle of it all and even his white face paint couldn't hide how ill he was. Wordlessly, he pointed to a large wooden washtub beneath the central table.

Damion looked and his stomach jumped into his throat. The tub was full of human limbs – hands, feet, and heads, glued together by a shimmering red mass of gore. Now he knew where the missing servants had ended up; processed into food for the beastmen. Damion let some of his tiger's personality take over and his feeling of horror faded.

'Rhydd,' he said, speaking clearly to penetrate the gardian's shock. 'Arrange for ten men from Asharte. Verify that none of the ten has family or friends in Burg Grymaur. They must first dig a deep pit in the forest. The bigger and deeper, the better. When they are finished, clear the courtyard. Then they will take this tub and bury it. Later we'll hold a last rite for the dead, but for now, we need to clean this mess up.'

Uwella's brother put his hand over his mouth and swallowed his bile down. He nodded and almost ran from the kitchens.

The men of Asharte were hardened warriors and hunters, and they'd all dealt with messy deaths often enough. But what they found in the kitchens shocked them. The thought of people being used as livestock sickened even the strongest fighters and filled them with a hatred for the Dar'khamorth they hadn't yet felt before. The men removed the tub with its grisly content and buried it as surreptitiously as they could.

When it was done, Damion sighed and walked back to the kitchens. The tiger was still strong in him. *Water*, he thought. Luckily, Gry at least had a water pump in the kitchen. He poured buckets full over the tables and began to scrub.

Many buckets later, the worst horror was gone.

'There,' he said aloud. 'The kitchen staff can do the rest.'

Outside it was dark. Unnoticed, the night had come, and the myriad of stars. All of a sudden, Damion felt exhausted and unspeakably filthy.

He hurried into the keep and as he passed through the great hall, he found Costare hovering as if waiting for him.

Damion gave him a curt nod. 'The kitchens are available again. Your people should do another round of scrubbing, with white sand and hot water.'

The old man bowed. 'I... I know what you did, Highness,' he said. 'I am sorry I could not help you. All those people. I am very, very grateful.'

'It was better this way.' Damion looked at Costare. 'Not that I was indifferent, but I can guard myself against these feelings. The servants don't have that luxury.' He forced a smile. 'But now I want only a few things – a drink, a bath, and a bed.'

The seneschal bowed again. 'Her Highness has had her father's rooms prepared. You have heard of the duke?'

Damion froze; he had completely forgotten Uwella's father was one of the prisoners here. 'No. What's wrong with Duke Venric?'

'He is dead, Highness. Prince Rhydd found him in the dungeons. He was not hurt or anything – his heart had given out. In recent months, the duke had complained of cramps in the chest, you see, and the stay in the dungeon was too much for him. He did not suffer.'

That sounded almost like an accusation, Damion thought, and fleetingly he wondered how popular the old duke had been among his retainers.

'Where is the valvodjara?' he said. She must have heard of her father's death by now and he wanted to be with her.

'In the ducal bedroom, Highness. But I would strongly recommend you first take a bath. The valvodjara has laid out some of Prince Rhydd's old costumes for you.'

'What! I hope no...'

The old seneschal smiled fleetingly. 'Nothing of the Gray Order, Her Highness did not find that appropriate. I think they will fit you fairly well. I will have you brought a carafe of wine, Highness.'

When he came into the bedroom, dressed uncomfortably in a black tunic and pants, with a silver wolf's head on the front, Uwella sat on the edge of the double bed and stared into space. Her hands were folded in her lap and she looked strangely lost.

'Hey,' Damion said and he held out his arms to her.

She looked at him and her face twisted for a moment. The next second, she was upon him with her arms around his neck. He hugged her while she buried her face in the wolf's head.

After a while, she looked at him. 'He's dead,' she said uncertainly. 'I always thought I hated him, yet I must cry.' She sniffed and her tearful eyes were surprised. 'He had a bad heart. I never knew that.'

'Are you sorry?'

Uwella slipped out of his embrace and sat back on the bed. 'Because we ran away? It was all inevitable, and that's what I'm sorry about. That there was no other way.'

Damion walked to the heavy sideboard along the wall and poured two glasses of wine. 'Here,' he said, and handed one to Uwella. 'Maybe it helps a little.'

Blindly, she downed half the wine and shivered, then began to shake uncontrollably. The glass in her hand dropped to the ground, spreading wine over the polished floor.

Damion dropped down beside her and enveloped her in his arms.

'He's... dead,' she said, and she sounded like a bewildered ten-year-old. 'Now I'll never... know... whether he loved us.'

She buried her head into his shoulder and cried. Damion thought of his own father, and even while he didn't give a damn about the sergeant's love, he couldn't stop his own tears. Physically exhausted and emotionally drained, they cried together and drank wine until they finally fell into a dreamless sleep.

CHAPTER 12 – STATE VISIT

Servants had come and gone unheard. They had cleared away the empty carafe and glasses, removed the discarded clothes, and opened the curtains. Damion's leather armor waited, waxed to a shine, the bath water was kept hot, the cawah ready to be poured, and the cooks even had found time to bake fresh bread for their new highnesses.

When Damion awoke, the sun was shining right on their bed and he blinked. 'Where...' Then all of yesterday came crashing in and he swore under his breath.

'Good morning, Highness.' The soft voice of the servant tore his attention away from last night. 'Your bath is ready.'

Damion swung his legs over the edge of the bed and groaned. He wasn't used to wine, and what he had drunk last night now scratched with sharp nails on the inside of his skull. 'What's the hour?'

'It just struck ten, Highness.'

'Gods! I've lost so much time.' He walked to the door, but then stopped. 'How is everyone?'

'Under the circumstances, well, Highness, thank you.' The man bowed and Damion saw his face was full of bruises as if someone with a hard fist had worked him over. 'Everyone is grateful you have freed us before...' His voice faltered and Damion understood that the horrible discovery in the kitchen had remained no secret.

'We were glad, too,' he said. 'I'll skip the bath this morning; I haven't got time for it. Keep the water ready for the valvodjara. Cawah and something to eat, that's all I need.'

The valet left and Damion dressed quickly. Then he leaned over Uwella and kissed her forehead. She opened her eyes and said petulantly, 'I was already awake.'

'Good, my dear. The sun is shining, your bath is waiting, and if you're very sweet, I'll leave some cawah and bread for you.'

'You had better,' she said. 'I won't manage being sweet on an empty stomach.' She stretched and yawned. 'Any plans for today?'

'Nothing strenuous. Inspecting the burg, meeting some townspeople, and planning for our trip tomorrow.'

'Are we going somewhere?' She looked at him suspiciously over the edge of her bed sheets. 'I returned home for the first time in six years and you want to drag me away again?'

He plopped down beside her and stroked the wild hair from her face.

'We did plan to visit Ghyll, didn't we?' he said lightly. 'We need so much; healers and magi, weapons, food. Portal priests. Temple soldiers. Diplomatic recognition.'

'Enough!' she said, and she hopped out of bed. 'I'm convinced.' She put on a simple morning dress and tucked her feet into furry slippers.

'I'll start making a shopping list,' she said as she walked to their little sitting room.

It was a cozy place. The fire in the hearth burned lustily and there was a pleasant smell of freshly cut pine logs in the air.

Damion poured her a cup of cawah from an ornate copper urn on a side table. 'Are we able to pay for things? I haven't had time to ask Costare yet.'

'Of course,' Uwella said, smiling brightly. 'My father liked things to be simple. I found the key to his private treasury under his pillows and his gold in a chest under his bed, like any old merchant. I'll take some letters of credit, too. They're Bank of Rhidauna, so we can easily exchange them there.'

'We have no bank of our own?' Damion said. He sighed. 'Of course not; that's too modern. Anything else?'

Uwella tapped her lower lip with her pen. 'We must have some pomp and circumstance,' she said. 'We can't slink into Rhidaun-Lorn like a pair of nobodies. The twins need some sort of livery with Vavaun's coat of arms.' She grinned briefly. 'That will be father's Wolf of Gry; even if we had decided on a new blazon, no one would recognize it. I'm sure

Costare can come up with something suitably impressive for them. And we must inform the other rulers of the changes in rulership. Costare will take care of that as well.'

'I'll tell the twins.' Damion walked to the door and called a servant. 'Ask Miss Grisa and Master Bartram to join us, will you?'

The two appeared suspiciously quick. Damion raised an eyebrow at the twins, who looked back innocently. He was sure Grisa had disobeyed orders and ported them, but he didn't say anything.

'Are you two interested in a few days to Rhidaun-Lorn?' he asked.

'Yes!' Grisa's face lighted up. 'Rhidaun-Lorn? Suuure we're interested! Finally I'll get me some coordinates.'

'How will we get there?' Bartram said practically. 'Do we walk?'

'We'll fly,' Damion said. 'Tomorrow.'

Three pairs of eyes stared at him.

'We'll go hookfeather?' Uwella said, scratching her chin. 'I didn't think of that.' She thought for a moment. 'Can do.'

'You mean you will carry us?' Grisa said.

'You're not very heavy,' Uwella said.

'I'm bigger than her,' Bartram said, flexing his muscles.

'I think I can manage,' Damion said. 'You'll take only a little baggage – if you need anything later on, we'll buy it. Costare will find some uniforms for you. I'm sure there is plenty of Rhydd's stuff he won't be wearing again.'

Bartram snorted. 'I'm bigger 'n Rhydd, too.'

'You're a hulking bear, I know,' Damion said. 'Don't worry; we must have some needlewomen around who can make everything fit you. That and a cloak will be all you'll need; it's only a hundred miles from Adalien to the portals at Underdin.'

'No armor?' the boy said, shocked. 'I'll look silly! A... a civilian!'

'Nonsense,' Damion said. 'We're on a diplomatic mission, not going to invade them. Now go and see Costare. We'll leave tomorrow after breakfast.'

The next morning, Damion stood in front of the mirror in their sleeping room, dressed in one of Venric's tunics made of some silvery cloth with matching black pants, and a solid gold chain around his neck.

'I feel like I'm going to a fancy-dress party,' he grumbled. 'That guy is not me.'

'No,' Uwella said calmly. 'He is the Grand Duke of Vavaun, a very august personage, and he should look the part.'

'I know,' the august personage growled. 'I still feel like a dressed-up idiot.'

Uwella went to stand next to him. Her hands slid down the sides of her dark red dress. Her maid had altered it cleverly, and while she didn't appear slim, she wasn't stout either.

'Strange,' she mused, staring at her image. 'I haven't worn anything but gray for six years. I had forgotten how I looked in anything else.'

Damion stepped aside and bowed to her. 'You look ravishing. Where did you get it?'

Uwella sighed. 'Ghyll's court will think I'm a hick,' she said dolefully. 'It was my mother's dress, in the finest Rhidaunan style – fifteen years ago.'

'You'll set a fashion,' Damion said firmly.

'Actually, I never cared for that,' she said. 'I am the kjavoda of Vavaun.'

'Right,' Damion said and he offered her his arm. 'Shall we go down to breakfast, Serene Highness?'

'Serene? I? Somehow that sounds fishy.'

'Costare assured me it's the correct title for grand duchesses,' Damion said.

'That may be, but it still sounds out of character,' she said. 'And I am not going to act serenely.'

Chin in the air, she strode from the room, leaving Damion to scurry after her.

After breakfast, their finery packed away in their rucksacks, Grisa ported the four of them to the kerran Adalien.

'Wikken?' Damion said, blinking at two women in gray robes walking slowly past a ravaged cabin. 'What are they doing here?'

'Taking care of the dead,' Grisa said. 'I brought them over yesterday, at Archodea's request. The Drynnath didn't like the two of them going, but they insisted. There won't be any danger, will there?'

'Probably not,' Damion said. 'The enemy has their eyes on Vavaun now.'

Uwella hurried over and kissed both women. They spoke softly for a moment before she rejoined the others.

'I had to thank them,' she said absently.

In silence, they walked to the other side of the kerran.

'Remember, we'll not be able to talk once I've changed,' Damion said to the twins. 'I've added a saddle with a seatbelt to my beast form. You must use it. We'll be going pretty fast, and I'd rather not lose you somewhere along the way. Wrap your cloaks around you; it will be cold. If there is anything, pound my sides and we'll land. Got that?'

'Yep,' Bartram said, his face taut with anticipation.

Damion changed, carefully adding the saddle, with stirrups and protective sides covering his razor-sharp feathers. He heard the two exclaim; now they saw him up close, the hookfeather was way taller than a horse and must look immense to them. Then Bartram climbed into the saddle.

With a screech and a mighty wing clap, Uwella changed as well. Quickly, Grisa scrambled onto her back and fastened her belt. Almost immediately, Uwella launched herself into the air. Damion followed her, leaping high and spreading his wings. He heard Bartram yell, but his voice sounded excited rather than scared and there was no side-pounding, so he joined Uwella and together they set course for Underdin.

The ease with which the hookfeather had adapted to the load on its back surprised him. After that first time, at Derivall with Ghyll when he had tried to fly as a crow, he had learned to trust the instincts of the animal form he used. He had expected awkwardness or worse, but it was as if he'd done this all his life. He felt Bartram on his back, and the pressure of his legs, but the boy didn't weigh more than a small rucksack; he could easily have carried both of them. *I must learn more about those beasts,* he thought. *Have they ever been tamed? A pity they're extinct.*

Sooner than expected, he saw a break in the endless forests, and then they were at the bend in the river with the wooden tower of Underdin.

Let's keep away from the village, he thought to Uwella. *No need to scare them.*

You like being obvious? she snapped back and spiraled down at the edge of the clearing.

He grinned at her grouchiness and looked down for a discreet place to land. Then he decided to give Bartram a treat. He folded his wings and dropped straight down, to brake just in time. He landed a second before Uwella.

Bastard! she thought, chagrined.

Damion waited for the boy to clamber down and then changed.

'Damn,' Bartram said. 'What a landing! I nearly threw up.'

'Cold!' Grisa joined them, shivering. 'I haven't been so cold before.'

'But it was great!' Bartram added, trying to keep his teeth from chattering. 'No horse ever went that fast!'

'You two do look a little frozen,' Damion said. 'Slap your arms, that'll get your blood running.'

In the portal building, it was blessedly warm and quiet.

A stout priest in the white robes of Dragos' Order received them with barely masked surprise.

'How did you arrive here?' he said. 'By the river?' Then he lifted his hands. 'It is none of my business, of course. How may I serve you?'

'We'd like a port to the capital,' Damion said.

'Rhidaun-Lorn; excellent. That would be either Dragos Grand Temple at the market or Palace Road.'

'The temple would be fine.'

The priest bowed. 'Stand in the circle, please. I wish you a pleasant journey.'

'And that's the first two coordinates,' Grisa said, rubbing her hands. As they stepped from the portal into the nave of the White temple, the twins stopped abruptly.

'Dear gods,' Grisa whispered. 'It's huge!'

'It is,' Damion said. 'The biggest temple in the world. King Ghyll and Queen Kerianna were married here. We had quite a fight on our hands that day. I'll show you.'

He led them past the rows upon rows of wooden benches to the altar with the immense statue of Dragos Godsfather, Lord of Justice, Wisdom, and the State. The god's tall staff lighted up as they neared and Damion quickly made the sign of Dragos over his heart.

'Like this,' he said to the twins. 'Now do the same.'

'I've never seen any gods but Arikal,' Bartram said, staring up at the bearded deity. 'He's impressive.'

'Dragos is the Eldest; a wise and kindly god,' Damion said. 'When Ghyll was going to be crowned king, the Dar'khamorth barged in; a big knight and a squad of golems in armor. Dragos lent us his magic to beat the intruders. Imagine it; the whole temple was packed with nobles and dignitaries. It was a miracle nobody got hit by a stray beam or fireball; it was quite a battle.'

They walked back through the nave to the tall doors. Outside, a pale spring sun shone.

'By the Fire,' Bartram said, staring out over the busy square. 'It's huge.'

'Everything in Rhidaun-Lorn is bigger. All but the people.' Damion grinned. 'They are as small as anywhere else. This is the great market. Those fountain statues are true images of all the gods and goddesses. Arikal is second from the left, past Dragos. We'll be going that way to the inn. As a visiting ruler, I don't want to stay at the palace, and the *Crown of Rhidauna* is a suitable establishment.'

They walked past a beefy helmeted statue with a huge ax in his hands. 'Mainal, brother to Dragos and Arikal. His son Fantus is two fountains down the line; the bearded one with the hammer.'

The twins hurried over to the statue of their adoptive god. He wasn't as martial as his father, or as wise looking as his uncle Dragos. Instead, the Fire God was massively muscled, bald as a toad and nearly as ugly. Yet his face was good-humored and comfortable.

'What's his symbol?' Bartram said softly.

'Crossed thumbs on your heart,' Damion said after a second's frantic thought. 'But these are fountains, not temple images.'

'He'll notice us the same,' Bartram said, placing his thumbs over his breast.

Grisa followed his example, and after a moment, stepped back. 'He winked at me.'

'Imagination,' Damion said quizzically, but she shook her head.

'He really did. I was looking straight at him.'

'Why wouldn't he?' Bartram said. 'We're His warriors, after all.'

'It wouldn't surprise me,' Uwella said. 'Though Arikal never did anything like it. But then, he's not a chummy god like Fantus.'

Damion shook his head. He thought of Iodraune's aid in the chapel at Gry. 'With the gods, everything is possible. Are you done here?'

They walked on, weaving their way through the masses milling around the market stalls. Everything was for sale here, from apples to horses, tapestries to little caged songbirds; everything legal and probably some things not.

Then they entered a large bronze gate and up the steps to the *Crown*'s gleaming, polished front doors.

The inn was a former ducal town mansion and the landlord catered to only the very best clientele. The result was an establishment of suffocating grandiosity.

On the top of the steps, Uwella halted. 'Rulers don't negotiate with innkeepers; that's what they got aides for. Bartram, you'll book us the Royal Apartment. Here is the gold.'

The boy swallowed as he accepted the heavy pouch. 'But...'

Beside him, Grisa chuckled, and he closed his mouth firmly.

Then a servant opened the door and they stepped into a vaulted hall, the wooden walls painted with lush landscapes and a shiny, many-armed chandelier hanging down from the rafters. A soft-spoken attendant in gold livery came to inquire their wishes. His air was lofty enough for ten dukes and the condescension in his voice made Bartram stiffen.

'The Royal Apartment for Their Serene Highnesses the Kjavodes of Vavaun,' he said curtly.

'There is no such thing in Vavaun,' the attendant said haughtily.

'There is, and I am their aide,' Bartram said. 'Quickly now, man. We're expected at the palace.'

'I'm afraid I can't...' the man began.

'Are you the proprietor?' Bartram snapped. 'No? Go get him.' He turned to Damion. 'Apologies, Serene Highnesses,' he said loudly. 'I was given to understand the *Crown* was a quality inn. I'm not sure they live up to their reputation.'

As he said that, a tall man in a dark suit walked in. He didn't move a hair of his studiously urbane countenance as he bowed.

'Good day. There seems to be some confusion. Who are the Kjavodes of Vavaun?'

'Are you the host?' Bartram said.

The man's brows rose. 'Indeed I am.'

'Then know the Kjavodes are Uwella and Damion DeVavaun, Valvodes of Gry, Valvodjars of Asharte, co-rulers of Vavaun. The kjavodes are in Rhidaun-Lorn on a visit to King Ghyllander, who is a personal friend.'

The host hesitated. 'Their Highnesses' faces are familiar,' he said slowly. 'Yet I don't recall...'

Damion smiled. 'Your memory is good. Her Highness and I stayed here with King Ghyllander, before he was crowned.'

The man's face cleared. 'Now I remember. I didn't know you were from Vavaun, Highness.'

'Politics,' Damion said. 'In those days, it couldn't become known the valvodjars of Gry and Asharte were traveling together. With Duke Venric's recent death, the need for this secrecy ended.'

The host beamed. 'I am honored with your confidence, Serene Highness,' he said, bowing deeply. He turned around. 'The Royal Apartments for Their Serene Highnesses.'

To Bartram's barely concealed disgust, the servants lined the stairs and bowed for Uwella and Damion as they walked up the stairs.

Upstairs, liveried attendants led Damion inside the apartment's vestibule and bowed themselves out of the Presences.

When they were alone, Grisa turned to her brother. 'I'm speechless,' she said. 'Where did you learn to talk that way? You sounded like daddy at his most stuffy.'

Bartram snorted. 'Well, I am his son, after all. Seriously, those self-important popinjays got my blood up with their pooh-blah-blah.' He looked around him. 'This is all too much. The richness, that circus on the stairs, it's a lot of sham. No true nobleman would want to live like this.'

Damion laughed at his earnest face. 'I wouldn't bet on that, The *Crown* is famous. We're staying here because of politics; else we'd spare the expenses and have Ghyll's people put us up in the palace. But we've plans to see a lot of important people and this is the expected background for visiting royalty. Now, let's change our clothes and go see the king.'

'We'll need horses,' Uwella said. 'This serene highness is not going to walk to the king. Bartram, be a dear and order four mounts for us.'

'Is that what an aide does?' Bartram said mournfully. 'Running errands?'

'Well, they don't run themselves,' Damion said. 'So I'd say, yes.'

The boy grinned. 'All right then.'

They rode slowly across the market, staying close together as they made their way through the throngs.

'Is it market day?' Grisa said, looking in wonder at the many stalls displaying their wares.

Damion laughed. 'If it were, we'd need half a line of horses to get through the masses. No, the great market is always like this. Remember, Rhidaun-Lorn is both the capital of the kingdom and the religious center of the world. All the temple Orders have their headquarters here and they draw people from far away to these market stalls.'

Past Dragos' fountain, they entered a broad lane, lined with tall silver-leaved poplars. In the distance, at least another mile away, the white towers of the royal palace caught the rays of the sun.

'It looks unreal,' Grisa said wonderingly. 'Like something you read about in a book.'

'It sure is very unlike Burg Grymaur,' Damion said. 'Much more comfortable, too.'

Halfway up Palace Road, the four of them came to a tall bronze gate guarded by two knights in blue-and-silver armor. As the men recognized Uwella and Damion, they saluted.

'Highness, Baron Damion,' the eldest said, smiling. 'Welcome back; it's been some time we saw you last at court.'

'Too long,' Damion said. 'Is the king at home?'

'His Royal Highness is at the palace,' the knight said. 'With the Big Event so near, he doesn't want to go anywhere.'

'I can imagine,' Uwella said. 'He's worried for so long over the queen's pregnancy.' Then she nodded at a colonnaded building beside the road. 'I've never seen that before.'

'It is the new portal,' the youngest knight said and there was a hint of disapproval in his voice.

'That gives a lot of extra work, does it?' Damion said, sympathetically.

The eldest knight kept his mouth shut, but the youngest nodded. 'I'd say it does. Somehow, with that portal, we get many more visitors than before. And they all have to be checked and registered. We're going to get assistance, but well, you know how such things go.'

'Slowly,' Damion said. 'There is a portal acolyte? Then we'd like to use their services. Transport officer DeKramm needs the coordinates.'

The knight looked at the twins and their smart uniforms as if he noticed them for the first time. 'You're from Vavaun?' he said, puzzled.

'We are,' Bartram said solemnly. 'Aides to their Serene Highnesses Uwella and Damion DeVavaun. The Kjavodes rule our country since Duke Venric's death.'

Damion grinned at the knights' evident confusion. 'He speaks truth. No need for the whole royal reception; it is a private visit and we much prefer to slip inside like we used to do.'

The eldest knight saluted again. Damion saw a change come over the two men and that saddened him. As a court baron, he had always enjoyed a friendly relationship with all palace officials, but his new status as a foreign ruler created a distance he didn't like.

'May we wish Your Serene Highnesses joy and a long reign?' the knight said, stiffly at attention.

Damion inclined his head. 'Thank you. Now, about the portal?'

'Of course, Highness. You will find the acolyte inside.' The knight lifted a hand and a boy came running to take their horses.

Inside, the portal building proved large and sober, with a separate living space for the portal servants. A young lad in a White tunic to his skinny knees came forward.

'You want a port?' he said, chewing on a bite from the small loaf of bread in his hand.

'Only to the dungeon,' Damion said. 'The gentlemen at the gate will vouch for our respectability.'

'The dungeon's *her* portal,' the boy said distastefully. 'She's a little dragon, that one, so beware.' He tore off another bit of bread while he ported them away.

'These coordinates are easy,' Grisa said, satisfied, as they arrived in the king's palace.

Bartram looked about him with a slight frown. 'This place is really a dungeon?'

Damion grinned. 'Oh yes. The king wanted a secure spot for his portal and what's safer than the royal gaol?'

He greeted the portal acolyte, a wisp of a girl with a gap-toothed grin – the little dragon.

'Baron Damion,' the girl cried. 'Thought you were dead!'

'I am, and I come back to haunt you!' Damion said in a sepulchral tone.

'Ta, get ya hence, ghost!' she said in mock terror.

'I demand a price, fair maiden,' Damion said. 'Would you help my porter Grisa with your wisdom and experience? She knows the ropes but no coordinates outside of Vavaun.'

'She is a portaller?' the little acolyte said, giving Grisa a suspicious glance. 'Is she coming to stay here?'

'She is not,' Damion said. 'No competition for your Royal Acolyteness. She's Army, not Temple; transport officer to the rulers of Vavaun.'

'Then she's a poor, starving soul. Vavaun is a blank wall, a nowhere place without portals.' The girl dug inside her oversized tunic and produced a crumpled sheet of paper.

'Here y'are; the collection of a lifetime. And don't you send me those who have no business here. They go to number two on the list, that stupid boy at Palace Road. This portal is for royalty and their likes.'

'Thank you, I will remember that,' Grisa said. 'Palace Road, for salesmen and shady customers.'

'But you can send *him* my way whenever you want to,' the acolyte said, giving Bartram a good look-over. 'Is he yours, portaller?'

Grisa grinned. 'My brother.'

'Ooh, my lucky day!' She patted Bartram's biceps with a grubby paw.

Damion saw the boy's face grow red with embarrassment and came to his aid. 'I'm afraid I must take him away from you,' he said. 'We're for the king.'

The acolyte chuckled. 'Ain't he a sweet lad? I got him blushing! The king; go cheer him up, Baron. Poor man mopes and frets over the queen's near birthing so much he forgets how to laugh.'

'Strange girl,' Grisa said matter-of-factly, when they walked up the flight of steps leading to the palace proper. 'Got strange tastes, too.'

Bartram growled something Damion couldn't hear and both his sister and Uwella laughed.

'She may be a silly chit, but she'll be twelve years at most. She was playing; no more – I hope,' Uwella said.

Then they emerged in a long, marble corridor and the twins stopped in their tracks.

'Oh,' Grisa said, staring at the slender columns in pale rose and the rows of candelabras burning brightly, at the priceless statues and the many-colored tapestries.

'The king must be very rich,' Bartram said faintly. 'This is class, which that inn isn't.'

Damion grinned at their reactions. 'King Ghyll rules over a wealthy nation. Don't forget Rhidauna is twenty times as large as Vavaun. In Rhidaun-Lorn alone live about as many people as in our whole country.'

Some minutes later, they came to a hallway.

Damion nodded at the priest seated behind a desk next to an immense pair of doors.

'Serene Highnesses!' the priest said, and Damion heard a surprised intake of breath from one of the twins. 'You'll find the king in the royal sitting-room.'

'Thank you, Father. The Lord Steward?'

'Baron DeGrathain is in the throne room.'

As they walked to the double doors, Grisa pulled Damion's sleeve. 'How did he know about the Highness bit?' she said.

Damion put a finger to his lips. 'That's a secret,' he said mysteriously. Then he laughed. 'It's a trick. Like the men of Asharte, they use trained pigeons. While we spoke with the noble knights, their messenger wrote a quick note of my new title to one of the stewards. These things are meant to flatter the visitor and prevent social mishaps.'

A guard in ceremonial uniform stepped from the shadows and opened one of the doors.

'Drat,' Bartram muttered. 'I hadn't even seen the guy.'

'They're the Hardingrauds,' Damion said. 'The elite corps guarding the king and the palace. You passed quite a lot of them along the way. Their uniforms blend with the shadows.'

The sight of the immense room with the silver and blue throne on the other side brought another sigh from Grisa.

'It's like a fairy tale,' she said. 'I never knew people lived like this.'

'Only kings do,' Uwella said haughtily. 'We grand dukes don't need all this to rule.'

'That man near the throne,' Bartram said softly. 'Is he the king?'

'That is the Lord Steward,' Damion said. 'He is the gentleman who keeps this whole palace up and running. Even the mice in the pantry need his permission to steal the cheese.'

The man turned and smiled. He was a small, elderly noble in court dress, carrying a massive staff.

'Serene Highnesses,' he said, and bowed. 'It is too long since we saw you last. How are you, if I may ask?'

'We are both well, though we have been sorely beset. Duke Venric died unexpectedly. Uwella and I succeeded him jointly, to end all clan troubles.'

'Both my felicitations and condolences,' the lord steward said solemnly. 'Duke Venric will be missed by all.'

Uwella bowed her head. 'Yes, he will.'

'Is the king available?' Damion said.

DeGrathain smiled. 'You come at the right moment, Highness. The king needs something to take his mind off the coming birthing. We all expect the royal baby any moment now, and the queen's pain makes the king feel very helpless.'

Upstairs, at the door to the royal sitting room, DeGrathain knocked, waited three breaths, and opened the door.

'Their Serene Highnesses the Kjavodes of Vavaun.'

'Huh? What?' The king looked up, his haggard face showing vexation, but then he jumped to his feet. 'Damion! Uwella!' He embraced his friends, slapping shoulders and kissing them impartially. 'By the gods, welcome! Oh, welcome!'

'You were sleeping! You're getting a state visit from Vavaun and you are asleep!' Damion said indignantly. Then he grinned and for a moment they stood all three holding each other.

Finally, Ghyll shook his head, as if to clear his mind. 'What was that? Who is on a state visit? Vavaun? When?'

'The state visit is already here,' Damion said. 'Bartram, do your herald-thing, mate.'

The boy stepped forward and bowed to the king. 'I am Sublieutenant Bartram DeKramm, herald for Their Serene Highnesses the Kjavodes of Vavaun. My master and mistress sent me here with a letter to Your Royal Highness of Rhidauna. May it please you, Sire.' He bowed again as he handed Ghyll the letter Costare had written the day before.

'Rhidauna is always pleased to hear from their friends in Vavaun,' Ghyll said stately. 'I thank you for this letter; you have executed your office with honor, Sublieutenant DeKramm.' Then he opened the letter and scanned the lines.

'What the heck is a kjavode?' he said.

'Grand duke,' Damion said with a straight face.

Ghyll looked up. 'You promoted yourselves?'

'Now the two of us outrank both Gry and Asharte. DeVavaun is boss, not one of the smaller Houses.'

Ghyll pursed his lips. 'I remember Venric and his tricks at our coronation. Old Asharte was polite enough, but Uwella's father tried my patience sorely. Smaller Houses indeed.' He smiled. 'Rhidauna acknowledges his brother and sister the Kjavodes of Vavaun. May their reign be long and glorious.'

'Phew,' Grisa said softly, and the king laughed.

'You were afraid I wouldn't?' he said.

'Damion was sure you would Sire,' she said. 'But I worried a little.'

'Not I,' Damion said. 'Ghyll is too good a friend to let us down. Grisa DeKramm is our porter. Bartram here is her twin and our aide; their father is the Marshal of Vavaun. And they are fire warriors of Fantus.'

'They're what?' the king said. 'Fire warriors? Since when has Fantus any?'

'Our god claimed us recently, Sire,' Bartram said. 'He said he didn't want Mainal to be the only one. Whatever that means.'

'Mainal's Prophet!' the king said. 'Last week Bo Lusindral was here. He and some other friends are on a quest to recover a bunch of Hamorth grimoires. He had this youngster with him, Fedar Garumgav, who was a duke from Rockath. Mainal had claimed the lad as his Prophet.'

'Are there dukes in Rockath?' Damion said. 'I thought they were all robbers and slaves.'

Ghyll shook his head. 'That's what we all thought. Apparently, there are many traveling nomad clans, much like Anliin's Yinno tribe. That boy Fedar is duke over them all. When they came here, Mainal claimed the boy as his agent in Rockath and made him the most unbeatable fighter in the world. Battling him is battling Mainal, and no one in his right mind fights the God of War.' The king looked at Bartram. 'What can you do?'

'My sister and I fight with fire. Not like a mage does,' he added hastily. 'We can make any weapon burn. With it, we make our enemy burn as well, from the inside. Grisa is ranged; arrows, knives, spears, and things like that. I'm swords, axes, and lances.'

'But we probably could do it with our fingernails,' Grisa added. 'Kill them by scratching.'

'I still don't understand why Fantus gave them such powers,' Damion said.

'Well, you could ask him.' Ghyll laughed. 'Whether he'd tell you is something else. It's clear the gods are making their own plans these days.'

Damion's face tightened. 'We could use some godly help. Times have been troubled lately.'

Before he could continue, the lord steward himself entered with a large tray of cawah and little cakes, and Damion waited until he was done pouring.

'Things haven't been going well in Vavaun,' he said when DeGrathain had left. 'Treason in the Gray Order and open war with the Dar'khamorth. Venric is dead, so Uwella and I mounted the throne together. My grandfather approves and the feud between Gry and Asharte is more or less over. Everyone is fighting the monsters.'

'You, too?' Ghyll stared at him. 'Tell me all.'

Damion sat up straight and told of everything that had happened from the moment Uwella got that traitorous call.

As he spoke of Adalien's destruction, Ghyll shocked upright in his chair. His face turned a furious red and he slapped his armrests.

'I didn't know that!' he shouted. 'Damn them!'

'I didn't think you would,' Damion said with a terse smile. 'Adalien is one place even your Herald spies wouldn't know about. It must have been that awful sorceress who betrayed the location to her masters.'

'DeMannau.' Ghyll shuddered at the memory. 'I'll never forget her pigman.'

Grisa nearly jumped from her chair. 'Those beasts!' she spat.

'Hush,' Uwella said. 'It was pigmen that butchered Adalien. Grisa killed five of them.'

Ghyll stared at the girl. 'You did?'

She lifted her chin. 'I burned them, Sire.'

'Good for you,' Ghyll said. 'No remorse?'

Grisa's eyes flashed. 'I *hate* those beasts. I could easily burn them again and again. They're not human.'

Uwella nodded. 'And that's a fact. Damion and I can hear their thoughts, so they're more beasts than men. They have done so many awful things; no Vavauner will show them any mercy.'

'And the bird!' Grisa said. 'Don't forget the bird.'

Uwella smiled. 'I won't.' She looked at Ghyll. 'A bird as large as an ox-and-wagon, with a slashing beak and hooked feathers. She killed that one, too.'

Ghyll leaned forward. 'When was that?'

'I'll not forget that date,' Uwella said. 'It was the fifth of this month.'

'So one escaped Mo's mages.' Ghyll said slowly. He grimaced. 'A flight of such birds had been terrorizing my province of Malend for weeks, together with wolves the size of warhorses. Somehow, Olle's countship of Orodaun was at the center of all sightings, so he and Kaati went to see what was going on. On the fourth of Gramatte, the beasts attacked their town. Their portal malfunctioned and instead of coming here for help, the messenger ended up in King Mojalman's palace. Opit's king is a true friend, and he came with a skyboat full of soldiers to relieve Orodaun. One of those birds must've gotten away then. Olle will be glad to know you killed it, Grisa.'

'My pleasure, Sire,' the girl said. 'It tried to eat Damion; we couldn't have that, of course.'

'Of course not,' Uwella said. 'Else I'd eat him myself.' She coughed. 'So they came from Orodaun. I wonder where those Dar'khamorth got the beasts. They used to live in Vavaun. There are several paintings of Grys hunting them in the recesses of Castle Gry. Hookfeathers, we called them, and we thought them extinct.'

Thoughtfully, she sipped her cawah. 'Darned blackrobes. After the bird was dead, Grisa ported us to Vavaun. Then we found the bastards had taken over most of my country.'

Ghyll listened silently as she told of Kramm and Erpenstaun. He had to chuckle at the way his friend had checkmated the old Duke and his eyebrows rose higher and higher when Damion took over and recounted the recapture of Asharte, Gry, and Grymaur.

'Darn it,' he said when the tale was told. 'You really went all out, didn't you? You had it worse than we in Rhidauna, with far fewer hands to fight them.'

'We did,' Damion said. 'But fighting side by side helped unite our people. Now we need your help, oh mighty king of Rhidauna.'

'Tell me,' Ghyll said, leaning back in his chair.

'First of all, we want the Orders to bring their temples to Vavaun. We urgently need priests, schools, portals; everything they have to offer. But before we can ask for anything, we need to convince them of our reign's legitimacy. A word from you would go a long way.'

'Can do,' Ghyll said. 'I'll invite them all to the palace. Then you two can tell them what you told me and they'll fall over their feet in their hurry to be first in.'

Grisa blinked at that. 'Would they? Why?'

'Influence,' the king said. 'The Whites want to bring schools and healers, the Blues want to extend their skyboat service, the Orange Order wants your mining concessions, which you would be wise not to give them, and they all want a piece of your life and your soul. It will ask for great wisdom to satisfy the lot of them without signing yourself out of a country.'

Damion nodded. 'I know. That's why I want something else from you as well. I need a few people who can help us set up a government. Uwella's father did it all on his own, and the result is nothing happened. We're centuries behind Rhidauna and Opit. We plan to change all that, but we're not going to make Venric's mistake. We have a chancellor, but that's about it. No mint, no bank, no trade nor functioning guilds.'

'Talk it over with Duke Kyssander,' Ghyll said. 'I'll tell him to help you in every way he can. As chancellor of Rhidauna, he knows the ropes of government better than anyone else, certainly including me.' Then he laughed. 'You know what? I'll send heralds into the city to proclaim your accession to the throne of Vavaun and tell the good folks we are honored to have you visiting us. No faster way to assure the world you're stuffy and legitimate. How's that?'

'It would certainly silence that popinjay innkeeper,' Bartram said. 'I suspect him of counting the table silver when we're out.'

Ghyll grinned. 'You're at the *Crown*? Keep a window open, before you suffocate from pretension.'

Then a servant came to announce the evening meal was awaiting the king's pleasure.

'Now you'll see how royalty dines,' Damion said to the twins. 'Don't expect us to feed you the same way; we cannot afford it.'

Bartram rubbed his stomach. 'Perhaps the temples would help in exchange for a minor concession?' he said hopefully.

'Forget it,' Damion said sternly. 'All that rich food would only make you fat.'

'I'm not fat!' Bartram said indignantly, slapping his midriff. 'It's all muscle.'

Beside him, Grisa sniggered.

At nine o'clock the next morning, the highest priests and magi of Zolastyr assembled in the throne room. Some were surprised at their unexpected summons, others irritated, but all came. The two green thrones beside the king's blue and silver seat drew some comments. What visiting royalty came in pairs? Several names went round, but soon they gave up and everyone sat down to wait.

When all were present, Ghyll entered with Uwella and Damion, their squires and aides in attendance.

The robes Master Costare had selected for formal wear, with the golden coronets of long-dead dukes on their foreheads, made a proper regal impression.

'His Royal Highness Ghyllander of Rhidauna,' the lord steward cried. 'Their Serene Highnesses Uwella and Damion DeVavaun, Kjavodes of Vavaun.'

All present bowed, but there was a sudden tension in the room. The frowns and scowls showed many were suspicious of the unexpected changes in Vavaun's rulership.

Dennator Leviss, the High Priest of Dragos, who spoke for the temples while there was no archpriest, voiced everyone's thoughts.

'We just received the announcement of your succession and Vavaun's new status. Both were highly unexpected, Highnesses.' The White high priest's face was bland, but his eyes were critical as they studied the two rulers.

'Vavaun has gone through a brief but bloody period of this unexpectedness, Eminence,' Damion said. 'And no, there wasn't any rebellion or fratricidal war. Our opponent was the Dar'khamorth.'

Leviss froze, and several of those present muttered.

Damion's voice sounded unusually hard and he had everyone's attention. 'Not only we of Vavaun were the victims; the Gray Order has suffered major losses. The kerran in the Gisterwoud was completely destroyed and the wikken of the kerran in Grymaur have been assassinated. The Drynnath lives; she is in Vavaun, hence you do not find her here.'

Priests and magi looked at each other in shock. Although the Gray Order enjoyed little popularity among her brothers and sisters, any attack on a temple order was an unprecedented and dramatic event.

'Are there many casualties?' Leviss asked.

Uwella sat straight, her face sad. 'In Adalien, ten; all the elders Archodea had left behind. In Negardien, most of the kerran was poisoned. At least a third of the Order died.'

It was quiet in the throne room as the enormity of her words sank in. The Grays were a small Order and all members were specialists. Their deaths meant an enormous loss in knowledge and experience.

Softly, Damion told the same story he had given Ghyll. As he spoke, he saw Leviss was making notes. His counterpart, Archmage Karmandros of the Convocation, sat with closed eyes motionless in his chair and Damion was sure every word was etched into his memory.

When Damion was finished, the archmage opened his eyes. 'Manipuuls.' The bitter disgust in his voice made all present stare at him.

A few seats behind him, the high priest of Mibras joined him. 'I thought we had eradicated that infamy. For this alone, the Hamorths deserve a special place in Greos' cellars.'

'They are slaves?' Uwella asked.

'Worse,' Karmandros said. 'A slave is at least master of his own mind. A manipuul has a master who forces him to do the most horrible things, fully conscious, without the slightest possibility of refusing. A manipuul-master can make his victim rape his own children, eat his wife alive, burn down his home and his village, with his full awareness, unable to resist.' He looked at them with eyes half closed. 'Where did you leave them?'

Damion thought of the vacant-looking archers. It was as he had feared. Golems had been brainless creations, but to use those crystals on humans was sickening.

'In Grymaur, in the kerran under Archodea's care,' he said. 'It's a bitter thought the very wikken who perhaps could have helped them were murdered.'

The high priest of Mibras lifted a hand. 'Please send them to our main temple. With our god's help, we should be able to save most of them.'

'Disaster struck the Grays,' Ghyll said and he looked sternly around the room. 'Infiltrators burrowed their way into their Order and brought them to the brink of destruction. Are you sure that your Orders are free from such scum?'

Pandemonium broke out as every priest and mage shouted their denial.

Ghyll raised his hand. The noise died away and High Priest Leviss said hesitantly, 'Our gods would never allow that.'

'A week ago, the Drynnath would have said the same. Yet Arikal did not warn her. Why not? Could it be that the gods can't see members of the Dar'khamorth? After all, they don't tell us who the Exhumyst is and where we can find him.'

The learned members looked at each other.

'You scare us, Sire,' Taindragon said heavily. The head of the Red mages smiled wryly. 'Another example of how we all stopped thinking. I speak the gods of our order regularly. If they had information about the Dar'khamorth, they wouldn't withhold it. Perhaps they are counting on us. The gods are subject to different rules than we humans. We knew they see things we don't. But I never thought this could work two ways. I'm not a priest, of course.' He looked at Leviss but the high priest only shook his head.

'That means every one of you can unknowingly harbor infiltrators among your people.' Ghyll sighed. 'How will we find out?'

'Couldn't they pray?' Bartram said hesitantly and then colored hotly.

'Pray?' Damion stared at his aide. 'What do you mean?' Then he thought of the times he'd prayed lately and how the gods had helped him, and he nodded slowly.

'Pray!' Father Leviss echoed. 'The young man is right, but that creates other problems.'

Most attendees looked doubtful at the idea.

'Perhaps the gods may not recognize a Dar'khamorth man,' Bartram said more firmly. 'But they do know their loyal followers. If you should all pray sincerely for a sign, the gods won't hear the traitors and those get nothing. Then you could do, ah, whatever you do with traitors.'

Leviss pulled a long face, but Damion saw he took the suggestion seriously. 'I'm afraid not all clerics are strong on sincerity, young man. Too often, priests see the temple as a way to acquire a comfortable position, not as a vocation.'

'Wouldn't the gods hear the indifferent ones too?' Bartram said. 'I mean, those priests may not care much, but they don't deny their god, do they? Those who worship Her do; they want to destroy everything.' He suddenly grinned. 'Besides, the fear of being seen a traitor should stimulate most indifferent ones, I'd say.'

'Good point,' Leviss said, giving Bartram an intent stare. 'I'd say it would.'

'Hogwash! Why doesn't a so-called *infiltrator* betray themselves already, young man?' Druull, the bearded high priest of Mainal gave Bartram a haughty look. 'They would attend the divine services too, I'd say? No one can simulate every prayer; certainly not the ones we speak aloud.'

Bartram looked unafraid at the burly priest. 'A traitor who has denied their god can mouth the prayers whenever he needs to. His former god won't listen and his Dar'khamorth goddess will be pleased at the mockery, while he seems as devout as ever. Would you hear the difference, Eminence?'

Druull reddened. 'You're insolent! There is no idolatry in my house!' he cried. 'That's impossible.'

'Don't talk nonsense,' Leviss said sharply. 'It's what the whole discussion is about. The boy speaks wisdom; it can happen in your temple, Druull. Or in mine, without us ever noticing.' The high priest turned to his colleagues. 'I suppose each of you has regular contact with your deity.' An affirmative murmur was his answer. 'Then I would think no one here is an infiltrator.'

The hall exploded.

'I? An infiltrator for the Dar'khamorth?' Druull spluttered with rage. 'You go too far, Leviss! The idea!'

'Not in the least, Druull.' The high priest of Dragos gave him a cold look. 'Anyone can be an infiltrator.'

Damion nodded. 'Father Leviss is right. Some of the traitors in the Gray Order had been there for ten years or more. One of them was a department head at the main kerran; one of Archodea's right-hand men. I'm sorry to say this, but no member of either Temples or Convocation is above suspicion.'

'I agree.' King Ghyll stared around the room with a look that made several attendees shiver. 'There is only one way to permanently clear yourself,' he said in a merciless voice. 'Let every one of you beseech your deity to manifest themselves.'

'Now?' a female voice said shakily.

'Now.' Ghyll clapped his hands. A row of archers marched in to stand beside the throne. With the living sword Childegard in his hand, the young king gestured to the hall. 'Go ahead, ladies and gentlemen. Beg your god to show up. And you, magi, pray as if your life depends on it. You wouldn't be very wrong, either. Do it aloud, so the kjavodes and I can hear you.'

Slowly, the shocked attendees knelt down on the floor, and their supplications flowed through the throne room. One by one, the earthly forms of the gods of Zolastyr appeared beside their supreme representatives and the total of their presence was overwhelming. Damion felt breathless, and he had to call on all his tiger's relentless will to stay aware.

An old man with a white beard and an antique toga appeared beside Father Leviss. He smiled at Ghyll and the warmth of his personality shone on everyone.

'A family gathering,' he said. 'How nice.'

'That was unintentional, Dragos,' the young King said apologetically. 'We need your help.'

'I know, Champion.' The face of the eldest god darkened. 'It frustrates us all we cannot recognize apostate followers. My brother Arikal is prostrate with shock at the betrayal. That young man's suggestion was much to the point. We realize not all of our followers bear the same love for their god and we forgive them; that is how it works. But we cannot see or hear those who pretend their devotion and follow Her wicked way instead. Thus they will not be blessed as I now bless my beloved son Leviss.'

A bright light shone from Dragos to the high priest, and on Leviss' forehead appeared a luminous symbol, a letter from an alphabet Ghyll didn't recognize.

'Each of my followers will receive this glyph at their ordination,' the god said. 'But beware! Who strays from my path and stops praying will lose it. And no one without the

Mark of Dragos can be a member of my order. This solves the problem, Champion?'

Ghyll looked at Leviss and the shining mark on his forehead. 'Impressive,' he said. 'Exactly what we need.'

'I am glad,' the god said 'Then my family will follow this system.'

At once, the room was full of light and they heard the high priestess of Kathauna whisper, 'Oh, how elegant!'

The ensuing laughter was quickly aborted when Dragos turned to the room. 'I don't see my nephew Eresto!'

All eyes turned to Tennail Sarn, the bald high priest of the Orange Order, who stood there livid, fists clenched at his sides.

'Where is your god, Sarn?' Leviss said sternly.

'I curse you all' Sarn shouted. 'Be damned, laughable godlings! For a while longer you can play at having meaning, but you've already lost. The Dar'khamorth shall rule all! Blessed be the Revenaunt Emperor; praised be Her name!'

The other priests backed away from him in horror.

'Traitor!' Father Leviss said, hitting out with his staff. 'May your soul rot in the deepest crevasses of the Underworld.'

Sarn cried out as the staff hit him full in the face.

A goddess with a scarred face and a thin, sinewy body stepped forward and automatically everyone present made way for her.

'He is mine,' she said, in a voice that must have been beautiful once, but now sounded hoarse and painful.

Millibaune, Goddess of Revenge, Lady of the Underworld at Greos' side, had been a battle goddess and wife of Mainal. Captured by the Revenaunt Emperor, she had survived while her two sisters were killed, and returned to the Pantheon altered beyond recognition. She left her husband and went to live in the Underworld, where she kept guard over the souls of the most wicked dead, the ones who would never be allowed to resurrect. She was rarely seen among gods or men, leaving her business among the living to her Venger assassins. Now she walked up to the dazed Orange priest and stretched out her hands, pushing them all the way into Sarn's body. The bald man screamed, a high-pitched sound that racketed every ear and harrowed their senses as the goddess tore his soul from his body. Then she dropped the lifeless husk and without another word, rejoined her high priestess.

'He will suffer to the end of time,' Millibaune's prelatess said coldly. 'Proceed, please. My goddess wants to return to her realm.'

'Thank you,' the king said, and he swallowed. 'Does this answer your objection, Father Druull?'

Mainal's priest only gaped at him, too shocked to react.

Ghyll turned around to his senior squire. 'Torril, take a half-line of Guards and occupy the temple of Eresto. None may leave. I want to see the temple leadership here immediately and the rest should keep themselves available. Oh, and not a word on why.'

Torril saluted and hurried away.

'I can't believe it,' Leviss said softly. 'Sarn. I've known him for twenty years. High Priest of the Orange Order... What made him sell out?'

'My son, Her followers promise power.' Dragos looked immeasurably sad. 'Godly power and wealth. Those promises are false, because the Dar'khamorth desires only the destruction of all life. But those blinded by the false promises do not see that. Not every manipuul has a crystal in his head; for some, their own greed suffices.' He sighed and his hands made a gesture of resignation. 'So be it.' With a wave of his hand, he disappeared.

A tall, wiry goddess in green hunting garb strode up to Uwella and Damion. 'Well met, young rulers of Vavaun. The gods are pleased with both your accessions. Build the temples we need and your people shall prosper. For now, go with the blessing of Iodraune.'

A light, green as the sun on the leaves in spring, engulfed rulers and thrones, and the two kjavodes shone. Then the

Goddess of Beasts winked away, and one after another, the other gods followed.

'You've got a sign,' Uwella said, touching Damion's forehead.

'So do you,' Damion said. 'It's not Arikal, either. You really are no longer a wikke, love; Iodraune claimed us both.'

For a moment, Uwella sat in silence.

'It is fitting, I suppose,' she said and shrugged. 'I never was a very good follower; the Gray Order was a refuge, not a vocation. I hope Iodraune knows I serve my country, not any temple.'

'I'm sure she does,' Damion said. 'She accepted us in spite of that, because we're beastmasters and we needed a glyph.'

Grisa stood staring at Uwella. 'It's... strange,' she said. 'Like a warning sign, "Watch out, I'm dangerous".' She chuckled. 'Well, so you are.' Then she turned to her brother and gasped, her eyes large. 'You...' She brushed the curls from his forehead. 'You've got one, too.'

'So do you,' Bartram said and there was dismay in his voice. 'My God, we're not mages!'

'Battlemages perhaps?' Ghyll said, as he studied the twins' glyphs.

'But we're army, not temple!' the boy said despairingly.

'Don't worry,' Damion said. 'We four all got a glyph. It's just a legitimalization of our magic, to show we're not the enemy.'

He sat back in the throne and watched the high priests and magi whispering among themselves while they all waited for Torril to return.

It seemed an age before Ghyll's squire came back with a small group of orange-clad clerics under guard. Their leader, a stout senior priest Damion vaguely remembered as Father Verell, protested vehemently.

'What is all this? Guards barging into the temple! Why are we dragged here like common criminals?'

Only then the expressionless faces of the entire temple authority watching him must have penetrated his anger, for his mouth sagged open. Then his eyes found the discarded body of his superior and before anyone could catch him, he swooned.

The king stared bleakly at the priest and his colleagues. 'For this once, we shall overlook his lack of manners,' he said, his voice cold. 'Their Highnesses and I will wait while you care for him.'

Damion folded his arms, watching the other Orange priests frantically trying to revive their senseless colleague.

Finally, the cleric staggered to his feet, bowing and stammering excuses until Ghyll cut him short.

'Your high priest was a traitor, Verell,' he said harshly. 'He had sold his soul to the Dar'khamorth.'

The Orange priest looked as if his world collapsed around him. 'Sarn? The... Dar'khamorth? How... Impossible.'

'He confessed, Father Verell. Here, with all of us and the gods as witnesses. What about your beliefs and those of your fellow priests? Are you devout or apostate? Pray to your god, Father Verell, and you, priests of Eresto. Do it here and now, out loud, so that we can all hear the sincerity of your words. Kneel and beg your god to appear. Millibaune herself took Sarn, so pray you will be heard, priest.' The flames licked along Childegard's sword blade to the ground and Verell trembled.

With the terrible sword on their retina, the Orange priests sank down as one and their most heartfelt prayers rose up like so many cries for help.

Suddenly, the figure of Eresto, God of Trade and Wealth, appeared in the hall. He looked more like a prosperous tradesman than a deity, with a round, normally cheerful face and tufts of graying hair over his ears. Now his countenance was somber as he gazed down at Sarn's remains.

'For some years, I missed the contact with him who once called himself my son,' he said immediately. 'It troubled me, but not enough.' He turned to Ghyll. 'I blame myself for this, Champion. When the apostate stopped honoring me, I should have questioned. Nevertheless, even though I could no longer hear him, his works kept the flow of wealth coming in and I rejoiced. Therefore, I left it so and that was my fault.' He made a quick gesture. 'Verell, my priest, your prayers were sincere enough. I bless you and yours with the Mark of Eresto. Clean my house, my priests. Remove all stains of Her from our temples.' Then he moved his hands and a shining symbol appeared on the foreheads of the kneeling clerics. 'Thank you for your intervention, Champion,' he said. 'And you, too, Rulers of Vavaun.' Then the divine presence was gone, and Sarn's remains with him.

'Your god recognizes you,' Ghyll said sternly. 'That's your luck. However, you are not yet done with me. You can expect a visit from the Royal Treasurer informing you of my demands. All Sarn's works will be reviewed and what was to the detriment of our country will be canceled. The Mint goes back to the Crown, and the Bank of Rhidauna. These are not toys for priests. All estates acquired by guild members through usurious loans are the property of the Crown and I want them returned. You will hear the other measures soon.'

Then he turned to the collected priests and magi. 'Ladies and gentlemen, you know what to do. Let your people pray as they haven't done in a long time and they will be blessed. And remember, this blessing lasts as long as you lead a righteous life. Father Verell, once the cleansing of your temple has been completed, I will withdraw the Guard. I wish you all strength and wisdom. Know that I will follow your endeavors with interest.'

It was dead quiet in the throne room. Everyone was still struggling to understand the enormity of the events and Ghyll's last words didn't make it easier.

'Let us end our first state visit to Rhidauna on a pleasant note,' Damion said with a smile. 'Vavaun has decided to open its borders to all Orders. We have land available for a

Garth as in Rhidaun-Lorn, although on a less lavish scale. Plots will be distributed on the basis of first come-first build. Priests and magi are welcome, as well as units of the temple guards. Who first signs up, gets the right to maintain the ducal portal in Burg Kronmaur. This portal should be operational before the end of the week.'

A hand shot into the air and Damion bowed. 'The temple of Iodraune offers their services. Thank you, Reverend Mother.'

'Crua, you're too fast for us old men,' Leviss said while he lowered his arm.

The high priestess made an apologetic gesture, but with a triumphant gleam in her eyes. 'It is but fitting,' she said, 'seeing our goddess blessed their Highnesses.'

'Vavaun will eagerly await your delegations,' Damion said. With that, he gave Uwella his hand and after a glance at Ghyll, the three of them left the throne room.

Once in his office, Ghyll exploded. 'That cursed Sarn! So all those malpractices weren't greed! He deliberately tried to destabilize the country.'

'Would he have financed the Dar'khamorth with that money?' Damion said as he plopped down in a chair.

Ghyll wheeled around, his face red. 'With our money? The Treasury will turn their temples inside out and every stolen penny will be returned.'

'Poor Eresto.' Uwella's grin belied her words. 'His chief priest a traitor, all the hard-won possessions forfeited, and now he loses the gold as well.'

'He should've paid more attention to his temples,' Ghyll growled.

'But Bartram has earned his pay today.' Damion looked at his aide. 'A brilliant suggestion about that prayer. How did you come to think of it?'

Bartram looked unhappy at the question.

'I've been praying to Fantus a lot, lately,' he said stiffly. 'I never had a god before, you see, until he chose us for his service. I asked him things and a few times he even answered, so I knew he'd recognize me. I assumed it would work the same for priests. If they prayed, their gods should know them and bless them with a sign. The ones who couldn't pray would remain unblessed.' He shrugged. 'If the priests hadn't been so shocked, they would have thought of it themselves.'

'Maybe,' Damion said. 'But the idea to betray the god who gives you your strength and existence is so alien it didn't occur to them.' He stood up. 'I will never understand those renegades. Highly placed people let themselves be dazzled by a bunch of promises?' He looked at Uwella. 'We have earned a treat,' he said. 'Shall we go plunder the riches of Rhidaun-Lorn?'

'Back to the *Crown* and change first,' she said practically.

'Yes, love,' he said, kissing her hand.

'You're henpecked, boy,' Ghyll teased. 'Admit it.'

The next morning after breakfast in the *Crown*, a servant knocked and announced a visitor.

Damion looked at Uwella, who was busy fixing her hair. 'Do we receive?'

'Let him come in,' she said, quickly pushing the last pins in place.

A man in a dark green robe entered. 'Your Highnesses,' he said, and bowed deeply.

Damion rose. 'Do I know you?' he asked, but the man shook his head.

'No, Highness. However, I got word of Duke Venric's death and then this morning the heralds announced your visit to Rhidaun-Lorn. As a man of Vavaun, I want to offer you both my condolences and my heartfelt congratulations. I am Baron DeLamon. My family owns an estate in eastern Vavaun. I was an Asharte supporter and a bit too emphatic to the late valvode's taste. There came a moment it seemed prudent to leave my homeland and now I run a trading company here in Rhidaun-Lorn.'

'Welcome, Baron,' Uwella said, smiling. 'I do not recall seeing you at my father's court, but I am pleased to meet you.'

'DeLamon,' Damion said thoughtfully. The name was familiar and suddenly he remembered. The fire spirit in the temple of Fantus in Leudra City. The priest superior who had died there was also called DeLamon.

'Indeed,' the baron said when Damion brought it up. 'Lessaun was my cousin. He was a vain man, I fear, but his death was brave in defense of his temple.'

Damion had his own opinions of the senior's bravery, but he nodded. 'And what can we do for you, Baron?'

Their visitor coughed softly. 'I am well aware of Your Highness's opposition to your father's rule,' he said with another bow to Uwella. 'I was hoping we could come to a mutually satisfactory arrangement.'

'About a safe return to Vavaun?' Damion asked.

'Actually, it is about my son. He's waiting outside.'

Damion raised an eyebrow. 'Then call him in.'

'Thank you.' DeLamon opened the door and a boy stepped into the room. He was a thin, red-haired lad of about the twins' age, with a pale, pointed face. He didn't seem scared or nervous, and he had the greenest eyes Damion had ever seen. He bowed, all the time grinning as if it were a huge joke.

'Hello,' Damion said. 'What's your name?'

The boy's smile widened and he gestured with his hands.

'Bryaun has no voice, Highness,' DeLamon said. 'He used to speak normally, like any child, but when he was seven years old, he caught a cold and from that moment, he never uttered another word.'

The boy beamed. For him, the loss of his voice didn't seem much of a problem.

'Nobody knows what happened?'

'We went from temple to temple, but no one could help us. His hearing is good, he can read and write, and his hands are faster than lightning. He could earn gold as a pickpocket, but that is not an appropriate position for a DeLamon.' The baron paused and suddenly seemed embarrassed by the situation.

'What do you want from me, Baron?' Damion said.

'I wondered if you had a page. Bryaun is deft and quick-witted, so I was hoping you could use him in your retinue.'

Damion frowned. 'You must have heard Vavaun is not the safest place in the world right now. Are you sure you want to risk your son?'

DeLamon sighed. 'A little risk for a greater gain. I cannot use him in the trade. Being dumb, he could never become a priest or a mage, even if he had the mana for it. Nor does he have the physique for the Guard. I had him instructed in the art of knife fighting, which he does well, being quick and fearless, but of course, there is no future in that. A place at court would be ideal and then, with all due respect to King Ghyllander, preferably in our own country.'

Damion saw Grisa frown as she inspected the boy. Unabashed, Bryaun looked back at her. He gestured and a little writing tablet appeared in his hand. Quickly, he wrote something and showed it to the twins. The boy had very clear handwriting, and Damion had mastered the trick of reading upside down. *Any adventures?* Bryaun had written. *Treasures?*

Grisa grinned. 'Fighting.'

The boy nodded, his eyes gleaming. *Nice.*

Damion chuckled inside and he knew he'd take the boy on. 'We're not taking pages or squires,' he said, 'but we do have need of a clerk. A boy with a quick mind and a ready pen would do excellently.'

'It's an honorable profession,' DeLamon said slowly. 'It would certainly fit his capabilities. He will accept, Highness.'

Damion looked at the boy. 'Will you?'

Bryaun bowed. Then he nodded, gave a thumbs-up, and clapped his hands.

'I take it that means yes?' Damion laughed at the boy's face. 'All right; you're in.' He turned to DeLamon. 'You can return to Vavaun, you know. That foolish feud between Gry and Asharte is over.'

The baron bowed. 'Thank you, Highness.' He spread his hands apologetically. 'But I have built a new life here. My trading company employs thirty people. As a foreigner, I am exempt from the requirement to join a guild. I'm paying more taxes, but I have much more freedom as well and that is lucrative. I mediate between Rhidaunan guild merchants and nobles in Terekander, where I have many contacts. Besides, my brother has the family castle, so for me, there is not much to return to. It is different for Bryaun.'

Damion looked at the man thoughtfully. 'I do want something in return, Baron DeLamon.'

'Anything within my power, Highness,' DeLamon said cautiously.

'It will profit both of us. We want to modernize our country. Trade is going to be important, so we are looking for people with vision willing to trade with Vavaun. I expect you to use your connections in making our country prosperous.'

'An interesting challenge, Highness,' DeLamon said, and Damion thought he seemed relieved. 'I can agree to that.'

'Good,' Damion said. 'It's settled then. Immediately after my return to Grymaur, I will have someone contact you.'

'Excellent, Highness. May I ask when you want Bryaun to join you? His mother will want to take her leave of him first, you see.'

Damion saw the boy lower his eyes and all animation drain from his face. *He isn't scared, is he?* 'I understand,' he said cautiously. 'We will be staying a few days more, as we have a long list of appointments. Bring him at the inn tomorrow morning; that gives all of us time to see how it goes before we return home.'

'I will deliver him here at six tomorrow morning, Highness.'

As if you're talking about a trade good, Damion thought as they shook hands. But the boy looked up and the big smile had returned as he nodded and laughed.

CHAPTER 13 – SHOT

Bryaun's father brought him to the inn exactly at six o'clock, with two large traveler cases.

Damion stared at them. 'What's all that?'

The boy grimaced and produced his slate. *Clothes, mother's idea. All nothing.* He seemed nervous, but whether it was the thought of his mother or the clothes wasn't clear.

'We'll store them for you,' Damion said. 'At the court, you'll wear an aide's uniform like the twins and when we're going into the country, there's leather armor.'

Bryaun clapped his hands and bowed.

While servants took care of the luggage, Damion brought the boy to their apartment. He made his bow to Uwella and then waited, brightly at attention.

'Relax,' Damion said. 'Among ourselves, we're informal. Now to work. Uwella and I have a long list of appointments. Bryaun will come with us. I warn you it may be dull, mate; we're going to talk about governing a country like they do Rhidauna. You will keep your eyes and ears open, make notes, and ask if you don't understand something.'

Bryaun nodded earnestly. *Need a bigger tablet,* he wrote.

Damion grinned. 'That's the spirit.'

'And us?' Grisa said.

'I've a special treat for you,' Damion said. 'I expect him any moment.'

Grisa cocked her head. 'A him? What are we planning?'

'You wanted coordinates? Iodraune's temple promised us a portal instructor to take you and Bartram on a crash course around the hotspots of the continent. You will memorize the coordinates and I want Bartram to see those places; get a feeling of the world. Would that suit you two?'

'Yes!' Grisa said. 'Yes, yes, yes!'

The next days, Damion and Uwella met with a great many people.

Rhidauna's chancellor was first; Duke Kyssander, by now in his eighties, but a canny and experienced administrator whom they knew well.

'My condolences on Duke Venric's death,' he said when they met in his office. 'I have met your seneschal Costare several times and I know a little of his troubles. He is a good man, and willing to listen; that will help. Have you any idea how you want to run things?'

'I've seen Rhidauna's organization at work,' Damion said. 'We want something like that, but adapted to our size. I am afraid we don't have enough people to run it, though.'

The chancellor pursed his lips. 'I would suggest I send you one or two of our most experienced men, who together with Master Costare will examine the possibilities. They can list your needs and see what candidates are available to fill the necessary positions. It would be wise to find a healthy balance between the two major Houses and their vassals. To cement their loyalty to your thrones, you could employ younger sons and daughters from the nobility.'

'That'll keep them from going abroad,' Uwella said. 'We're losing too many people as it is.'

'Sometimes they come back spontaneously,' Damion said and he winked at Bryaun.

After the duke, they spoke with the commander of the Skyboat service about air transport, with the temples about health and education, and many other arrangements. Bryaun went with them, silent and always listening. After a while, Damion started dictating notes the boy wrote down in his careful handwriting and later into neat paper reports.

After nearly a week and hoarse with talking, the kjavodes were ready to go home. The twins had returned, filled to the brim with new impressions and all the wonders of the Western Continent.

'You haven't forgotten Burg Grymaur's coordinates?' Damion teased Grisa. 'You collected so many grander places, like Mo's palace.'

'Sterrevank,' she said seriously. 'That was the grandest.'

'You've been there?' Damion said. 'But they're all ruins. Did you meet Archmage Neferestan?'

She nodded. 'He is... powerful,' she said. 'Very powerful. I'm glad he's on our side.'

Damion stared at her. 'You didn't mind his being undead?'

'I barely noticed,' she said. 'He's all light, blue light.' She sighed. 'He knows so much.' Then she grinned. 'But never enough, he said. Shall we go?'

They arrived in the courtyard of Burg Grymaur, gray and wet in the drizzle.

'There we are,' Damion said. 'Welcome in your new home, Bryaun.'

The boy looked around, his eyes brimming with wonder. *Different,* he wrote.

Damion grinned. 'It certainly is; we have none of the conveniences of Rhidauna. But we're going to change all that.'

'It's quiet,' Bartram said. 'No guards on the wall?'

'Yes.' Damion said quietly. 'I noticed.'

They walked briskly to the great hall without meeting anyone. The stables and workshops lining the courtyard were all as empty of people as the battlements.

As they hurried up the stairs to the keep, the big door swung open and Costare came out to meet them.

One look at his drawn face told Damion something was wrong indeed.

'Welcome back, Highnesses,' the seneschal said tremulously. 'It is not...' His voice faltered for a moment.

'Trouble?' Uwella said.

The old man took a deep breath. 'I'm afraid so, Highness. The city is still safe, but everywhere else is chaos. Beastmen!

Hundreds and hundreds of them. They swarm through the land like a plague and where they go, everything dies. For now, they avoid the city and the castles, but the countryside is lost. They are everywhere!'

'Let's go inside,' Damion said. 'Cawah to the library,' he told a servant. 'A large pot. And bring us something to eat.'

To his surprise, he found his grandfather in the library, studying a map spread out over a side table.

Before he could say anything, Asharte banged the map with his fist. 'Damned beasts!' he shouted. He lowered his voice to a growl. 'You left it late, grandson. Another day, and you would've found only smoking ruins.' He glared at the servant tending the hearth. 'Stop fumbling with those logs, man, before you burn down the house. You behave like a scared child; we're not done yet. Bring me a chair.'

Damion looked around for the seneschal, but Costare had discreetly vanished, leaving it to the duke to explain things. 'Grandfather, what's the situation?'

'It's bad,' the old man said simply. 'Very bad.'

The servant dropped the chair with an unseemly bang and Asharte gave him a furious look.

'Act a man! You are a Vavauner, not a chicken. Things aren't going well, but that doesn't mean we are going to lose. At most, we need a greater effort to win.' Impatiently, he waved the man away and sank into the chair. 'Fool!' he grumbled. Then he looked at Bryaun. 'Who's that kid?'

Bryaun wrote quickly. *Kjavode's clerk, Sire.*

'Why don't you speak up, lad?'

Unabashed by the duke's piercing eyes, the boy wrote an answer. *Lost my voice, Sire.*

The duke laughed grimly. 'Good; can't stand tattlers.'

Bryaun laughed silently. *Won't, I promise.*

'Ha, you've got a rare one there, grandson. What's his name?'

'Bryaun DeLamon,' Damion said, cocking an eye at his grandfather. 'We engaged him in Rhidaun-Lorn. His uncle is a vassal of yours.'

'Lamon Castle; you're Baron Aiwan's son?'

Bryaun nodded.

'Why isn't he coming back himself, eh?'

My father is getting rich in Rhidauna, Sire.

The duke guffawed. 'Is he now? He won't do that here, that's a fact.' He watched a maid pour the cawah. 'Filthy habit. What's wrong with beer? Or wine? All that foreign stuff ruins your stomach.' But he accepted the offered cup and sniffed its aroma. 'Things aren't going well. There are more beastmen loose in the country than we have men to catch them.'

Damion stared at the dusty bookcases, while his brain worked feverishly. 'Where do those beasts come from? Where is their headquarters?'

'We don't know.' Asharte bent over the map of Vavaun he had been studying. He tapped a spot with his dagger. 'The first report came from Hargen Keep. A large band of pigmen burned the local farms, but they left the stronghold alone. The same story here, to the north, and here, westward. In both cases it was roving gangs of twenty or more beastmen. Pigs, dogs, cats, the lot. Went for the easy targets, but left the castles and bigger towns alone. When the first reports came in, Costare was clever enough to inform me, so I moved my headquarters here.' He glared at Uwella, but she only smiled.

'You know you're welcome,' she said.

The duke grunted and slurped his cawah. 'Kedraun's holed up in Asharte, DeKramm in Gry. Young Rhydd is somewhere out there; the gods know where. Mannar is away, too. A messenger came some hours ago, to report an attack on the Brena Bridge at Kastelmaur. A handful of beastmen, he said, but too strong for the locals, who were holding them off by the skin of their teeth. Seeing Kastelmaur is Kramm's jurisdiction, the captain went with his men to help them.'

Asharte shook his head. 'I was havin' a nap, or I would've kicked him back to his barracks. The man's a fool, running around like that. We need troops here in the capital; that bridge isn't worth a cat's life, let alone his troops.'

Bartram growled his assent. 'We should fetch him back!' the boy said. 'Shall I?'

'Of course not,' Uwella said round the sausage roll she was eating. 'I'll go.' She downed the bite with her cawah and rose.

Damion glanced at her and nodded. *She can fly, pigs don't; she'll be safe.*

Uwella stuffed the remainder of the sausage roll into her mouth and hurried out.

The duke watched her go, but he didn't say anything.

'How many men have we left here?' Damion said.

'Fifteen,' his grandfather said. 'They're mostly those newbies the city sent as replacements for the daywatch. Woodsmen and hunters, so they can at least hold an ax or a bow.'

There was a knock on the door and a servant entered, looking distraught.

'A skyboat arrived from Rhidauna, Highness. Their captain wants to see you. She is rather upset; it seems they were shot at when entering the country.'

Damion's heart skipped a beat. 'Show her in, will you.' He slapped his thigh. 'Damn, what more?'

The captain was a tall woman with a ruddy countenance and grizzled curls. She strode in and bowed. 'The kjavode?' she said, looking from one face to another.

Damion stepped forward. 'I heard you were shot at? I am truly sorry. It seems our mutual enemy got some reinforcements.'

'*Shot at* is a small word for the gaping hole in my *Cloud Lady*'s side, Highness,' the sky skipper said, full of suppressed rage. 'We can thank our elemental we arrived here at all.'

'That bad?' Damion frowned. 'What could cause such damage?'

'A very strong mage,' the skipper said. 'A master elementalist might do it.'

Damion tapped the map on the table. 'Could you give me the location?'

The captain stared down at the map and traced a line with her finger. 'We came in here, over the Platten Pass. The shot came from around here, about a mile below us. There wasn't any warning. No flash, no light, only a massive blow that caught even the air elemental by surprise, for *Cloud Lady* shot away sideways and it was some seconds before his hands stabilized us. Thanks to the elemental's quick thinking in covering up the hole, we didn't lose our cargo.' She grunted. 'The damage is extensive, and I don't know whether our insurance covers this.'

'If not, Vavaun will,' Damion said tersely.

The sky skipper bowed. 'Thank you, Highness.' She gave a grim smile. 'Luckily our passengers weren't hurt. Shocked, but safe.'

'Oh?' Damion said.

'A delegation of Iodraune's temple. I sailed the last miles on a cloud of prayers.'

Damion took a deep breath. 'I'm glad everyone is safe. Captain, if there is anything you need, ask my seneschal.'

When the sky captain had gone, Damion slammed the table. 'Damnation! We can't have this! I am going to the Platten Pass; I must see for myself what is going on there.'

He turned to the twins, who stood aside with Bryaun. 'You two go back to Rhidaun-Lorn. Explain the situation to Ghyll and ask him for support. We need troops to hunt down those filthy beastmen.'

'Of course,' Bartram said. 'Port us to the dungeons, Grisa.'

'To the little dragon,' his sister said. 'Don't worry; I'll protect you.'

Damion saw them flash away and beckoned to Bryaun. 'You write out a copy of your reports for Master Costare, will you? Beastmen or not, that part must go on as well. Tell him those Green priests will build us a portal in the courtyard.' He glanced at his grandfather. 'Should Uwella be back first, please explain what I'm doing; I'll be as fast as I can.' Then he walked from the room.

Outside, he went hookfeather and launched himself into the air. Again, the sense of enormous power took possession of him. With only a few wing beats, he reached the clouds and set course to the east. Even from that height, his eyes could see a rabbit in the fields. He opened his mind to the world and left it to his subconscious to filter out the common beasts.

The area around the city appeared free of beasts, and it wasn't until the next valley that he caught the cruel thoughts of a troop of pigmen. Their minds were exultant, dripping with anticipated gore, and he knew he had to go and see what evil they were doing.

He dove down and saw a large field where a pitched battle raged. A single armored man on horseback with a handful of soldiers and some farmers were engaging a band of at least twenty pigmen. It was an unequal fight, with pitchforks against those monsters. Without a second's hesitation, Damion dropped down. His claws and beak made short shrift of the first beast and, wheeling around in the air, he turned to another. The pigman roared and whirled his ax, only to have it bounce harmlessly off Damion's armored feathers. Then the hookfeather's claws tore at the pig's head, and the beast went down squealing in terror.

I'm not a warrior, Damion thought as he tore and slashed at another beast. *I never use what father tried to teach me. I'm a beastmaster, Sergeant Luyon; a beastmaster!* Suddenly, the field was empty of enemies, and the locals stood panting, eying him uneasily. Damion landed and changed into his own form.

'Well met,' he said. 'Any casualties?'

'Hell's Damnation! Who are you?' the mounted man said, lowering his sword. 'And what are you?'

'Damion DeVavaun. I'm the kjavode. And a beastmaster.'

The man stared at him. 'Kjavode...'

'You are the local lord?'

'Arnstaun, knight. These are my lands.' The man shook his head. 'Duke Venric...'

'He is dead; his heart gave out. Valvodjara Uwella and I took over, unified the Great Houses, and upped the country to a grand duchy.'

'I heard,' Arnstaun said. 'But I couldn't believe. I've been a man of Gry all my life, brought up badmouthing Asharte. Now what must I do?'

Damion grinned. 'I was born Asharte. We just fought side by side. That's what you must do, Knight Arnstaun. We are both Vavauners, nothing else.'

The knight bowed. 'I admit those endless feuds were bad for us small men. So I'll not complain – Highness.' He hesitated. 'Those pigheads... They aren't... I mean, who do they serve?'

'Ever heard of the Hamorth?' Damion said.

The knight stiffened. 'I have,' he said. 'But they're gone.'

'They're not. A nest of them wants to take over our country, but we're not about to let them. See to your defenses, Arnstaun. There are many of those beastly bands on the loose. We're hunting them, but it will take time.'

'Many bands – that's mighty bad news, Highness,' the lord said. 'I lost three men just now; I can't afford any more killed.'

'None of us can. If you cannot fight, hole up. If you cannot hole up, retire to Grymaur. We're doing everything we can, Arnstaun,' Damion said gravely. 'I must be going; my business was elsewhere today. Good luck to you and your people and remember we're all Vavauners.'

The man sighed and lifted his blade in salute. 'I will, Highness. Good luck to you and the val... the kjavoda.'

'We'll meet again.' Damion went hookfeather and sprang into the air.

Skirting the clouds, he listened closely but no other beastmen were near, so he continued eastward.

Below him, the land rose slowly. All of Vavaun was a like a giant bowl, a series of interconnecting valleys and mountain ranges with the highest peaks circling the country's borders. The Platten Pass was like the spout of the bowl, making outside travel on foot into Opit difficult, but at least possible. The pass was flanked by two dead volcanoes, terraced like giant steps on the Vavaun side, while their backs were smooth walls of stone. Most terraces were wooded, but near the tree line grew only grass and low shrubs.

Suddenly Damion's keen eyes spied movement below him. On the highest plateau, a snowy field with a lake, was an old stone tower. On the ramparts stood a group of people in black robes. One of them pointed at him and the others raised their hands in a threatening spell.

Damion thought of the hole in the side of the skyboat and with a mighty beat of his wings, he shot sideways away from the tower and the blackrobes. Something like fireworks exploded in the air over his head. A mighty fist hit him, slammed him out of control. His heavy hookfeather body tumbled around like a wind-blown leaf, stunned and fighting for breath. Then he crashed into the treetops and fell.

'Uwella...' he thought, and then no more.

CHAPTER 14 – BRIDGE

Munching her bread, Uwella strode outside. The courtyard was still deserted and she quickly changed. Launching herself into the air, she set course for Kronmaur.

It wasn't far to the little town; ten miles and a bit more and she reached it in five minutes. Even from the air, it was clear things were amiss. Several buildings burned fiercely and there were a lot more than a handful of beastmen milling around the bridge watchtower. From its roof, a handful of soldiers fired an incidental arrow at the beasts below, but that was all. Apparently, Mannar had encountered more opposition than he'd expected and pulled back into the dubious protection of the tower.

Circling high over Kronmaur, Uwella spied a mass of beastmen carrying a large tree trunk with ropes over their shoulders. *A battering ram?* They were slowly walking down the steep road toward the watchtower, with some manlengths below them the swift Brena River running past.

Oh, no! she thought. *That trick won't work.* She gathered speed and dove straight at the laboring pigmen. Hampered by the heavy trunk, the beasts panicked as the monster bird, easily as large as a horse-and-cart, came down among them. Some stumbled and fell, dragging down others, and in seconds, the whole mass tumbled squealing and yelling down the high road into the water. As Uwella flew up, she saw the struggling beasts being swept away and she screeched mockingly.

Then she hovered over the top of the tower and the soldiers scrambled below to make room for her. She landed and changed into her human form.

'Gods love me, Highness,' a young soldier cried out, his chest a mass of blood, but with no visible wounds. 'I never...' Then he couldn't go on and cried.

'Where's the captain?' Uwella said.

The youngster wiped his nose on his sleeve and gestured to the town. 'Out there with most of us. Corp'ral's below. He... he... got us here.'

'Ask him to come up here,' Uwella said firmly. 'Is that your blood?'

The soldier shook his head. 'Me mate's,' he said. 'He died.'

'I'm sorry,' she said. 'Be strong awhile longer, soldier. Now go get the corporal.'

The young man gave a hasty salute and went down.

Moments later, a tall man with a squint and a long chin came up the ladder. He was the soldier who had greeted them that first time at Andauz.

'Corporal Lobarth,' Uwella said. 'I heard you could use a hand.'

The soldier saluted, his face tired but calm. 'So we could, Highness,' he said. 'We won't fight off another wave of those bastards. Not with ten exhausted men we will, orders or no.' He looked at Uwella, his eyes expressionless.

'What are your orders?' Uwella said. 'Where's Mannar? And the locals?'

'The townsfolk fled while we fought our first skirmish; they'll probably be in Grymaur already. Don't blame the buggers, I don't. A small band of pigs, the captain said. He didn't mention the hundred-and-more hiding among the trees. When we were down to a single squad, captain ordered us into the tower. Keep the bridge at all costs.' The corporal stared at the scene below and the beastmen, who had withdrawn to the town's edge. 'Captain's last command before they brained him.'

'Forget it,' Uwella said. 'Time to get out. Can your men run?'

'Back home? For a short while, but not the whole bloody ten miles.'

'Run as far as you can, then walk. I will cover your rear from the air.'

Lobarth's eyes searched her face and then he nodded. 'Thank you, Highness.' He went to the top of the stairs and yelled down. 'Put on your shoes, comb your hair, and pay the ladies. We're making a run for it.'

'About time; as a whorehouse, this ain't scoring, Corp,' a voice grumbled.

'Shaddup, the Highness can hear you,' another said.

Uwella grinned. 'You won't catch me blushing, gents,' she shouted. 'Now you run, while I keep the pimps down.' She nodded to Lobarth. 'Good luck; I'll go clear the way.'

The man went down the ladder and closed the hatch behind him. Alone again, Uwella went hookfeather and hopped onto the tower's battlements. She saw the beastmen stop and stare at her. Some shook their axes and their mouths opened in a roar she couldn't hear over the distance. But she could answer and her hoarse cry of defiance made the beasts jump.

Below her, the tower door opened and some of the bravest beastmen came running.

Immediately, Uwella swooped down and raked the first pig with her claws. Even before the beastman was down, she opened her beak and slashed at four of the pigs at once. The others turned tail and fled back to the protection of the burning houses.

Meanwhile, behind her, Corporal Lobarth led his men up the road back to Grymaur. For about a mile they ran, driven on by anger and fear. Then exhaustion made them slow down to a walk.

The pigs followed, but time and again, Uwella dove and harried the beasts, whittling down their numbers and keeping them at a distance.

It was a long and wearying road to Grymaur, but at last the city came in sight. Finally, the pigmen gave up and slunk away.

As the gates opened to let the men enter, Lobarth turned his head. 'Holiday's over; straighten up, Kramms!' His soldiers righted their shoulders, took up position, and marched into town as if they were on parade.

Uwella watched them go, feeling both sad and very angry, and then returned to the burg.

Back in the courtyard, she changed and hurried into the keep. She marched through the great hall, muttering and cursing, and the servants blanched as she passed.

'She's the spit of Uwelric,' an ancient, deaf maid said to another. 'A proper terror, our Highness!'

Uwella heard the loud whisper. *I'm not Uwelric,* she fumed. *He was an incompetent fool who ruined his son and his country. I just hate our soldiers dying through stupidity!*

She strode into the library and found the old duke making some notes on the tabled map.

'You took your time,' he said, as she slammed the door closed behind her. 'I began to think we'd lost you.'

'Not me,' she said, wrestling with her rage. 'But that idiot Mannar is dead with forty of his men. It must've been a trap; there were at least a hundred of the pigs.'

'Then what happened?' Asharte looked at her from under bristling eyebrows. 'Any survivors?'

In clipped, angry words, she told what happened. When she was done, the duke gripped her shoulders.

'You fought those beasts? I never thought I'd say it,' he said gruffly, 'but I'm proud of you, granddaughter.'

Uwella blinked, suddenly at a loss for words. 'Why... Thank you. Grandfather?'

CHAPTER 15 – GETTING HELP

Grisa and Bartram arrived in the dungeon portal of Ghyll's palace, to be met by the little acolyte.

'Back again?' the girl said, surprised. Then she scowled at Grisa. 'You cheated. You didn't use the portal at all.'

'I'm used to porting myself,' Grisa said curtly. 'We're in a hurry.'

They almost ran to the stairs, leaving the portal acolyte staring after them.

At the door to the throne room, they halted at the priest's desk.

'Master Bartram,' the man said. 'I thought the kjavodes had returned to Vavaun?'

Bartram nodded. 'So we did. I come back with an urgent message for King Ghyllander.'

The priest spread his hands. 'His Royal Highness is not at home, I am afraid.' He studied Bartram and seemed to come to a decision. He signaled and a small messenger appeared almost out of nowhere.

'Go and advise the lord steward the herald from Vavaun has arrived.'

Without a word, the boy sped away. Minutes later, he was back.

'Lord steward would see the herald in his office,' he said, without even panting.

The priest smiled. 'Excellent. Show him the way, will you?'

The boy bowed. 'Follow me, Herald,' he said importantly. He led them past the throne room to the administrative wing, a long corridor lined with doors. At the first door he halted and knocked. Without waiting, he gestured for the twins to enter.

Baron DeGrathain rose from behind his desk. 'Master Bartram, Miss Grisa,' he said, smiling. 'I am afraid you find the king away. You have a message from the kjavodes?'

'A vocal message, Excellence,' Bartram said. 'His Highness told me to explain the situation to King Ghyll myself. It is very urgent, you see.'

'Perhaps you could tell me?' the lord steward said. 'It may be something I can help you with.'

'We need support,' Bartram said, and he told of the many beastmen despoiling the countryside. 'We haven't got enough men to fight them all,' he said finally. 'Without help, we... We will lose.'

The lord steward studied his hands for a moment. 'This is beyond my powers,' he said finally. 'Only the king can issue orders to the army. Or the queen might...' he added. 'Come with me.'

DeGrathain managed to walk fast while appearing to stroll. They mounted a broad staircase and Bartram had to take two steps at a time to keep up with the old man.

'Upstairs are the royal apartments,' DeGrathain said. 'You will know Queen Kerianna is expecting, and the Event is very near. She has been ill with it for months. Still, she's a determined lady and if her attendants permit it, she might hear your plea.'

At a door, he nodded to the guard on duty and scratched softly on the wood. It opened a crack and a female voice said something Bartram couldn't hear.

'Herald from Vavaun for the king,' DeGrathain said. 'It is a matter of great urgency; would the queen be well enough to hear him?'

The door opened wider and now Bartram found himself inspected by a handsome brown lady who wore a sword with her court dress.

'You're the herald?' she said, and there was a hint of surprise in her voice. 'Both of you?'

'I am Bartram DeKramm, aide to the kjavodes of Vavaun. M'sister Grisa is our porter.'

The lady smiled. 'I'm Cianabetta Querfero, the queen's first attendant. You may come in for a moment, but keep your voices down; the queen has a terrible headache.'

'You're expecting trouble?' Grisa blurted, eying the lady's incongruous blade.

Cianabetta paused and stared at her. 'Always,' she said. 'We're here to serve and to protect the queen. If you'd prove a threat, we would kill you before your brother had drawn that sword.'

Bartram nodded. He didn't think it prudent to boast of their magic right now.

They entered a dim bedroom, where a small, very pregnant young woman lay, propped up by several pillows. Her face was gray with pain, but her eyes were alert as she watched them.

'Royal Highness, the herald from Vavaun,' Cianabetta said and retired to the shadows beside the queen's four-poster.

Kerianna patted the side of the bed. 'Sit with me,' she said, her voice soft but strong. 'I'm glad to see some new faces; the last months have been awfully lonely. You're younger than I expected. Friends of Damion and Uwella?'

'Uwella and I grew up together,' Grisa said. 'She's older than me, but there weren't all that many children at Burg Grymaur. Besides, we were both a bit wild in those days.'

'A bit?' Bartram said. 'Crazy monkeys, you were.'

His sister sniffed. 'You had your swords and spears to play with, and no one was trying to make a proper young lady out of you.'

The queen laughed a little. 'I was fortunate; my sister and I were trained by temple assassins.'

'You were?' Grisa said. 'Oh, I would have liked that.'

'Are you a soldier?' the queen said. 'With your sublieutenant's knots?'

'We both are, Ma'am,' Bartram said. 'We're army, like our father. He's the Marshal of Vavaun, you see.'

'And now you're here with an urgent message. Ghyll is from home. Someone murdered the Landscommander of Stiphet, and his son asked Rhidauna's assistance to prevent a war.'

'More war,' Bartram said, and suddenly he felt awfully tired. 'Then he won't have time to help us.'

'There is war in Vavaun as well?' Kerianna said, and she visibly tensed. 'Tell me all.'

Once more, Bartram recounted the whole story and when he was done, it stayed silent in the bedroom.

Finally, the queen stirred. 'We must help,' she said. 'I won't abandon Damion and Uwella in a time of need. Cianabetta, fetch me pen and paper, will you?'

Bartram started as the lady with the sword moved just behind his shoulder. He was sure she'd been on the other side of the bed.

A moment later, she returned and the queen quickly wrote a few lines. She signed it with a flourish and waited for the ink to dry. Then she handed the note to Bartram.

'There you are. I've directed our marshal to give you what aid he has available. I'm sure one of my girls will guide you to him.' The queen lifted her hand. 'We'll meet again later, when I'm up and about again. I'm happy to know Damion and Uwella have such stout friends!'

Bartram bowed. 'Thank you for seeing us, Ma'am.'

'Come,' Cianabetta said. 'I'll let you out. One of us will bring you to the Marshal's office.'

Duke Gard-Galleth, Marshal of Rhidauna, was a tall, thin man of an age at which less energetic people would be long retired.

He inspected the twins from head to toe, frowning at their officer's knots. 'Bit young for it, aren't ye?'

'Three years' fire knight training, sir,' Bartram said. 'We're both well-schooled and battle-blooded. The kjavode said we had earned our ranks.'

'Did he now? Well, for a young whipper... I mean Luyon-Asharte knows how to judge a soldier. What's your name, Sublieutenant?'

'Bartram DeKramm, sir. Aide to the Kjavodes of Vavaun. My sister Grisa is our transport officer.'

'And undoubtedly able to speak for herself. You're Radon DeKramm's offspring?'

'Yes, sir,' Bartram said.

'So the army is bred into you. What can I do for you, Sublieutenant?'

Bartram handed over the queen's note. 'We need urgent assistance, sir,' he said.

The marshal frowned at the note. 'Most unusual,' he said. 'I'm not sure if even the queen...' He harrumphed. 'What's going on in Vavaun?'

Once more, Bartram told all, skipping over the non-essential details. As he spoke, the marshal sat staring at him, slapping his armored gloves softly against his palm. Bartram's fists clenched, but he wasn't about to be discomfited, and he kept his voice even and emotionless.

When he was done, the marshal threw his gloves on the table. 'Well told,' he said, grimly. 'A darnably bad situation.' He rose and walked up and down the room. 'The problem is I'm not sure the queen has the legal right to command the army. But I know my king. If I disobey her, he'll have my head on a platter at the next evening meal.' He stopped walking. 'I can give you one line. That's a hundred guards; mounted infantry and archers.'

'That would be a help, sir,' Bartram said. In his heart, he'd hoped for a full kolonne of twelve hundred strong, but he knew all too well the limitations of even a commander-in-chief and to Vavaun's standards, a line was a sizable force.

The marshal shouted for a messenger and wrote a quick note.

'Right,' he said. 'Here are the orders. Messenger will guide you to the barracks. You have transport?'

'That's my job, sir,' Grisa said. 'I'm used to porting armies around.'

Gard-Galleth stared at her. 'You are, aren't you?' Then he shook his head. 'All those youngsters nowadays, with their strange abilities.' Then he grinned. 'Your parents may be proud; they produced some stout offspring.'

Bartram felt his cheeks grow hot. 'Thank you, sir,' he said, before following the messenger out.

The young lieutenant in command of the line was visibly pleased with his new assignment.

'After a year of guard duty, action will be welcome,' he said. 'One doesn't earn promotion standing watch over Rhidaun-Lorn's northern approaches. Nothing ever happens there.'

'Well, around Grymaur's approaches, plenty happens,' Bartram said. 'We're plagued by beastmen, so you'll have lots of fighting awaiting you.'

'Good,' the lieutenant said, rubbing his hands. 'Let's make some plans. You can house us and what's more important, our mounts?'

Bartram quickly thought. 'There are barracks and stables at the back of the keep,' he said. "I don't know in what state they are; probably haven't been used for ages.'

'No matter,' the lieutenant said. 'We can make do with little. It does mean we won't come in with the whole line at once.' He looked at Grisa. 'You mind porting me with half a line without horses, and go back to fetch the rest of them later with the mounts? Then we can see to proper accommodation for the horses first.'

'Sure,' Grisa said. 'Perhaps I'd better not port the horses all at once anyhow. Grymaur is a city burg. I'm not sure we have a plot large enough receive them. Twenty-five at a time would be neat.'

'I'm fine with that,' the lieutenant said. 'Arrange it with my senior sergeant.'

When all was arranged, Grisa ported them home, into the courtyard in front of the keep. The rain had turned to sleet, and in spite of himself, Bartram shivered after the sun in Rhidauna.

Almost immediately, the door to the keep opened and a small figure slipped out. A large cloak flapped around running legs, a soldier's helmet bobbed and showed wisps of red hair as he hurried to intercept them.

'Bryaun?' Bartram said, surprised, as the other boy stopped before him. 'Where's Damion?'

The boy whipped out his tablet. *Watch out!* he wrote. *Pigmen!*

'Inside the walls?' Bartram said sharply.

A yell from the keep's battlements made him spin around. 'Beastmen!' he snarled, as he saw three bulky shapes running toward the keep. 'Blast, there's a whole horde of them.'

A mass of howling pigs ran through the gates. From the battlements, castle bowmen fired into them, but the frenzied pigmen didn't let the arrows stop them.

'Get under cover, Bryaun, before they swamp you,' Bartram said. He turned to the lieutenant. 'You wanted action?'

The soldier grinned. 'Alert! First section, Bows. Second section, Out Swords!'

Without any fuss, the men obeyed his orders. Bartram's blade burst into flames as he joined them.

Then Grisa's burning arrow passed his ear and caught a pigman in the chest. As the beast died howling, the guards attacked.

Bartram was in his element. Yelling at the top of his voice, he hacked and slashed his way through the pigmen, an exuberant, flaming warrior who put the fear of death into the beasts' hearts.

Grisa had jumped to the roof of the portal and shot burning shafts at every pig she could reach, commenting loudly with each shot.

'Take that, ugly!' she shouted, and a pigman ran away, its hairy bristles aflame. It didn't get far, for one of the garrison's archers finished it off from the wall.

The guards were fresh and fought with a will, stimulated by the twins' fiery efforts, and finally the last pigman died.

Bartram lowered his sword. 'Nice,' he said. 'That'll teach the bastards.'

Bryaun skipped by several dead beastmen and joined the twins. There was blood on his cloak and on the woodman's hatchet in his hands. He grinned hugely, giving them a thumbs-up, and patted his little ax.

'You been fighting?' Bartram said, staring at the redhead.

'He did.' Grisa jumped down from the roof and joined them. 'I saw him. You're crazy, mate. Absolutely stark raving bonkers. You should have been dead several times, dancing round them beasts like that.'

Bryaun shrugged. *Am not, am I?*

She laughed. 'Are you sure?'

Bartram sheathed his sword and the flames died on his fingers. 'Now, what's going on here? Where's Damion and Uwella?'

Gone, Bryaun wrote. *Old duke's inside.*

'Trouble,' Bartram said to the lieutenant. 'Come inside and I'll present you to the duke of Asharte.'

In the hall of the keep, they found the duke, leaning heavily on a servant's shoulder. His right leg was bound up and he both looked and sounded a hundred years old.

'Well done, you two,' he grunted, as if every word hurt. 'In the darn'd nick of time, you arrived. Who are those men?'

The lieutenant saluted. 'Guards of Rhidauna, Highness,' he said. 'The first half, fifty men; compliments of Marshal Gard-Galleth.'

'How did those beasts get inside?' Bartram said.

The duke's face twisted. 'Some bastard ported them past the walls. We fought them at the forecourt and managed to rout them. That's where I got this.' He patted his wounded leg. 'We didn't have the men to defend the whole burg, so I pulled back to the keep.' He sounded querulous, without the customary bark to his voice.

Grisa listened impatiently. Finally, she burst out. 'Highness, where are the kjavodes?'

'Those idiots,' Asharte said grimly. 'You heard my grandson say he'd go have a look at that blasted mountain. When he didn't return, Uwella went to search for him. Now both are missing.'

'We must get them back,' Bartram said. 'That skyboat overhead, is she airworthy?'

'No idea,' the duke growled. 'Ask the captain; she should be on board.'

Bartram nodded. 'We'll do that. Come,' he said to Grisa, and they ran from the room.

CHAPTER 16 – AN OLD FRIEND

Uwella walked up and down Grymaur's hall, fuming and fretting, wanting to kick and snarl at anything and anyone.

'He wouldn't be long,' she cried. 'A few hours. It's nearly half a day, and he isn't back yet. What the flippin' demons is keeping him?'

No one answered. The servants didn't dare; the old duke was having a much-needed nap and with the twins gone to Rhidauna, there wasn't anyone she could talk to.

'Damn!' She snatched a little stool from the ground and threw it against a pillar. The wood crashed and splintered. 'Curse you, Damion; I'm going to look for you!'

She stormed from the keep into the courtyard. 'Tell Duke Asharte I'm out on patrol,' she snapped to the guard at the door.

Then she went hawk and launched herself into the air.

Uwella's hawk-form was fast and both her anxiousness and the favored winds added to her speed, so it was a little over an hour and a half when she came to the Platten Pass.

She didn't see the strangeness of the volcano; her eyes scanned the ground for a sign of Damion. Almost immediately, she noticed a tall tree, its branches broken as if something heavy had crashed into them. The damage was fresh, she thought, and she circled down to the crushed underground.

No Damion. She bit her lip as she saw the large pieces of bark ripped off the tree trunk, and then she cried out. There, on the end of a branch, hung Damion's backpack.

In bird form, it was part of the saddlebags he'd added. It must've been torn off his side as he fell and turned into its true form. She flew up and, straddling the heavy branch, she went with one hand through the pack. It was empty, but unmistakably Damion's.

She sat there, twenty feet up in the air. Had they shot him down, like that skyboat? She could see no blood anywhere, which was something. But where was he now?

She went hawk again and flew toward the mountain. This time she noted the curious steps leading up almost to the cone of the volcano. The lower ones were wooded, and at least three hundred feet deep. She circled them, but each one seemed wild and undisturbed.

Going higher, the greenery became sparser, and the steps smaller.

Watch out, she thought as she came to the top tier. *That tower...* Her sharp eyes had spied movement on building's platform. Shapes in all too familiar black robes. *Dar'khamorth!* She suppressed a cry of anger. *Damn them.*

She skirted the tower and looked up at the volcano's top. Her wikke-trained senses yelled danger. She sniffed an overwhelming reek of falmagic, the Hamorth's dark anti-matter mana coming from the cone.

I must see what's there, she thought and carefully flew along the side of the volcano to its very mouth. The air was thinner here and her wings barely large enough to carry her hawk body. For a moment, she feared she wouldn't manage it. Then a lucky wind lifted her up and over the cone mouth.

To her surprise, she could see all the way down into the mountain. *It's hollow!* she thought. *Damn, a hollow mountain stinking of dark magic and we never knew it.*

Then she stopped thinking and with all her senses on high alert, she flew down into the mountain. There were more birds here, she saw. Crows, mostly, hoping for something edible. At the first available ridge, she landed and changed her form to blend in with the black birds.

As a crow, she descended into the impossible mountain. *Gods, it's enormous; how will I find him in here?* A feeling of helplessness threatened to overwhelm her.

Near ground level, she saw the multitudes of beastmen and the black dots of Dar'khamorth priests, the beast pens and stables, and she cursed hotly.

Then all thoughts were wiped from her mind. Damion! There burned some large fires on the ground and over them, in a cage hanging from a beam two manlengths in the air, was Damion. His mind was dark, unresponsive but alive, and she sighed softly. Winging down, she landed on the beam and peered down. To a crow, Damion's unconscious body was enormous; too large to see how he looked. Instinctively, she cawed her distress.

A movement on the ground below alerted her. Uwella spread her wings to fly away, but then something slammed into her wing and hot pain lanced through her body. Fighting against hurt and dizziness, she flapped away and managed to land behind a barn.

Back in her own form, she saw an enormous bruise spreading over her arm. *It must've been some projectile,* she thought. *A thrown stone. Damned lucky hit.* Her arm was numb and refused to obey her brain. There wasn't any pain – there was no feeling at all. With the other hand, she ripped a strip off the hem of her robe and fashioned it into a crude sling. Then she walked carefully around the corner of the barn, straight into the foul-smelling embrace of a large pigman. Its surprised snort was the last thing she heard.

When she came to, she found herself curled up inside a low cage. She felt battered, and her whole body screamed with pain. As she moved, the cage door rattled. She tried to change into a mouse, but her spell didn't work.

'Ah, your highness is back among us common folk,' a familiar voice said.

Uwella looked up at the pretty, blonde girl standing before her. 'Mauvine?'

'Yes, Highness?'

'Let me out of here, will you?'

'I'm afraid not, Highness,' the girl said and she smiled.

'Why?' Uwella said hoarsely. 'Why do you do this? You were my friend.'

'Oh, but I never was,' Mauvine said. 'I had to seem your friend, you fat cow. With my stupid father gambling away his money, being your friend was the only way to continue living as I wanted to.' She giggled. 'It was so easy. I only had to admire you loudly; you lapped it all up. "Oh, your hair is so beautiful! Oh, what fine eyes you have. Oh, that dress becomes you fabulously." Yes, like an army tent would.'

'You really are a nasty bitch,' Uwella said, shocked at the malice in the blonde girl's voice. 'So it was pretense.'

Mauvine smiled brightly. 'Yes, it was all false. I fibbed you and you fed me; kept me at court, which suited me. Then you ran away to join the Gray Order. I damned you for that, you bitch. For with you gone, that creep Venric dismissed all your girls. What was to become of me? Live in an empty family manor, breeding pigs? No way, you idiot. So I followed you and became a wikke. Then I met Syvvan and his handy gifts of money, and I joined the service of Her. A famous deal! Soon I will be rich and beautiful forever in the new world She will create. So take that, stupid fat girl. For by that time, you'll be dead. Dead, as a gift to Her. And Syvvan and I will rule Vavaun – to pieces.'

Uwella stared up at the girl she once called her friend and a feeling of utter hopelessness came over her. Why hadn't she seen through this shallow creature's wiles? Had she been so blind? So arrogant? She knew the answer was yes. And that arrogance would now be the death of her.

'Drop dead, you dung-headed piece of pigman shit,' she said calmly.

CHAPTER 17 – MOUNTAIN

The skyboat was moored on the hill behind the castle. The crew had pulled up the scrambling net and only a rope ladder hung down, with an armed guard.

'Who're you?' the man said. 'I half 'n half expected a bunch of pigmen, not three youngsters.'

'Three?' Bartram said and he looked around. 'Bryaun!'

The boy nodded, his helm bobbing up and down.

'Sneaky dog! I hadn't even noticed you following us. You...' *can't come,* he wanted to say, but somehow he couldn't. The guy looked so cheerfully eager. Bartram shrugged and turned back to the sky sailor. 'I'm the kjavode's aide. The beastmen are dead. I'd like to see the captain.'

The man studied him. 'Kjavode's aide, boy?' he repeated slowly.

Bartram touched the knot on his shoulder. 'Try again, Skyman,' he said clearly.

The man sighed and saluted a bit clumsily. A skyboat crew was paramilitary at best, but an officer was an officer, even if he was a beardless stripling. 'You'll have to climb, sir,' he said. 'Captain won't lower the nets.'

'That's all right,' Bartram said. 'We can do it.' He'd never climbed a rope ladder before and the blasted thing swayed like he was boarding in a gale, but he reached the deck.

Here he was met by an officer in a dark blue uniform. Bartram knew nothing of Skysailor Corps ranks, so to be safe, he saluted first.

'Sublieutenant DeKramm, Kjavode's aide. I'd like to see the captain, please.'

The officer smiled. 'Welcome on board, Sublieutenant. Follow me.'

But Bartram had seen the wind elemental, a huge, translucent being who carried the whole ship in his hands, and he stared in awe.

'Impressive, isn't he?' the officer said with a proprietary air.

Bartram could only nod.

Inside, the great cabin was dimly lit. Only a single candle burned on the desk, where the captain sat writing.

She looked up as they entered, frowning slightly.

'Visitors?' she said. 'You came to tell me all is safe again?'

'That, too, ma'am,' Bartram said. 'We fought the intruders and they are all dead. But I fear they won't be the last.'

'No,' the captain said coolly. 'If I'd known Vavaun had gotten this dangerous, I wouldn't have sailed here.'

Bartram gave her a straight look. 'Captain, we are all part of this war. If we lose here, in the end, Rhidauna will go down as well.'

The captain stared at him. 'Possibly,' she said.

'It happened once before,' Bartram said. 'With the Revenaunt. We must prevent that from happening again.'

'True. What can I do for you, Sublieutenant?'

'It's about that mountain, ma'am. The one that holed your ship. We need to see it from the air, to provide coordinates for my sister, who is a porter.'

'Sublieutenant,' the captain said harshly. 'When I fly over the Platten Pass, it will be at great height. Very great height.'

'I understand your reluctance,' Bartram said earnestly. 'But we must destroy whatever danger lurks on that mountain, and the only way in is by porting. So we need those coordinates, to prevent further mishaps.'

The captain was silent. 'You youngsters are going down there,' she said suddenly, her eyes mustering the three of them.

'We have to,' Bartram said. 'We must know how and where to bring the army.' He didn't say a word about Damion and Uwella.

The captain rose. 'Come,' she said and went outside. The skyboat's bridge was at the stern and here was the officer who'd welcomed them on board.

'Mr. Weathersinger,' she said. 'You are to sing a strong song today. The kjavode's people need to see the Platten Pass from the air. Inform the elemental and set a course over the pass as low as can safely be done.'

The weathersinger was the officer responsible for the wind elemental and things like speed, altitude, and navigation, Bartram knew. After the captain, he was the most important officer on board. Now he stiffened as the captain spoke.

'Low over... But... Yes, Captain. What do you want to see?' he said, addressing Bartram.

'That's my sister's department; she's the porter.'

'I need several spots to port to,' Grisa said. 'That's all. It shouldn't take much time.'

The weathersinger took a deep breath. 'All right. Let's have a look at the map.'

They followed him to the map table in a corner of the afterdeck.

'This would be our course,' the man said, drawing an imaginary line over the map. 'You'll see the two mountains flanking the pass are rather strange. They're dead volcanoes. Their western flanks are a series of terraces leading up to the crater mouth. All but the highest ones are wooded; only the uppermost are bare. The eastern flank is a sheer drop of about two thousand feet to the pass. Platten Pass itself looks like it's been cut out with a square gouge; smooth walls, smooth floor. An unusual place.'

'You seem to know the place well,' Bartram said.

The weathersinger smiled. 'The *Cloud Lady* has been here before,' he said. 'We fetched the local dukes to Rhidaun-Lorn for the coronation. The late Valvode was curious about the mountain, too, and we flew over slowly. Charting landmarks is part of my duties, so I took a good look myself.' He looked up at the sky. 'Time to go. You have your own way of returning here? The captain wants to reach the dockyards at Yanthemonde soon as possible, so we'll not be back here for a while.'

'I'll port us out when we're done,' Grisa said.

'Then I must leave you for a moment. You can watch from the main deck if you want to.'

'There is the pass,' the captain said, gesturing in the distance. Bartram stared ahead. Then, vaguely through the thin snow, he saw the silhouettes of two strange mountains.

'They can't be real!' he said. 'It's all far too regular.'

'I know what you mean,' the captain said. 'But who could make something as big as that? No mage I ever met.'

'The gods?' Bartram suggested.

'The Dar'khamorth?' Grisa said softly.

The captain shut her telescope with a loud click, but didn't reply.

As they watched, more details became visible.

'The shot came from the left?' Bartram said. 'Seeing that's the damaged side.'

'Yes,' the captain said tersely. 'From farther up the mountain.'

'There's a tower,' Grisa said. 'Uppermost plateau, I can see it well enough to...'

A blinding beam shot upward and the elemental twisted the *Cloud Lady* out of its path. The whole skyboat rocked, but the misty hands that bore her absorbed the worst shocks.

'We're getting out!' the captain snapped. 'Get us away from here, Windsinger!'

Again the ship swerved, and a bright beam flashed past.

'They got us pinned!' a sky sailor cried, holding on to the railing as the boat lurched a third time.

'Grab my shoulders,' Grisa yelled to the boys. 'I'm porting down.'

Bartram obeyed instinctively, and seconds later, they were on the uppermost platform of a ruined tower. Three dark shadows were watching the skyboat.

'We got her,' a sorcerer said in a high-pitched voice. 'Hold your beams like this; let's see if we can shake her apart.'

'But the elemental?' a female voice said. 'If we destroy the boat, wouldn't it come for us?'

'We'll disassemble it,' a third voice said. 'Working together, we have enough binding energy to return that tempest to its original components.'

'Working together...' The woman sounded frustrated. 'How unnatural.'

'I know you'd rather try and disassemble us,' the first voice said sarcastically. 'But the masters said we're to cooperate, so shut up and obey.'

'If you two are done, let's kill that boat,' the third voice said peevishly.

Bartram glanced at the others, while he slowly and silently drew his sword. As he sprang at the nearest shape, his blade lit up. The high-voiced blackrobe screamed in terror as flames bit into his robe. Then the dagger found his shoulder and the fire reached his blood, searing its way through his body with every heartbeat. Bartram stepped back and nearly stumbled as something small dove past him.

It was Bryaun, crouching low, with that same little ax in his hand. He sprang like a frog in an overlarge cloak for the female blackrobe, who had turned and was mouthing some hasty spell. Bryaun chopped at her knee; the woman shrieked as her leg folded and her spell broke off in mid-cast. All the power she'd gathered ricocheted back into her mind. The sorceress blacked out from the force of it, never to rise again as Bryaun, soundlessly sobbing, broke her head open with his ax.

Meanwhile, Grisa pumped three flaming arrows into the third sorcerer, who slammed against the wall and went down burning like a Midwinter bonfire.

'Those will not ambush our boats again,' she said grimly as she watched the battered *Cloud Lady* rise in the clear sky and quickly disappear in the distance.

Bartram wheeled around and gripped Bryaun's shoulders. 'Guy, you're a bliddy maniac, you know that? You sure you're a merchant noble's son and not a Nhael barbarian? Where did you learn to fight like that?'

Bryaun smiled through his tears. *It's in my book.*

'What book?'

Fighting Almanac. Very clever book; pictures of all the moves.

Bartram grinned. 'I've never been bookish, but that one sounds handy.' He turned and leaned over the battlements. 'Great view!' He glanced around at the dark lake beside the tower, at what looked like a path beyond it and then he stilled.

'Hey, come and look,' he said. 'There's a door into the mountain.'

Grisa joined him and cursed. 'Darn, I'm too small. Can't see the ground over those parapets.'

Bryaun, who wasn't any taller, gestured at the stairwell in the center of the platform.

'Yeah, we'll go down and check that door,' Bartram said. 'Damion and Uwella must be here somewhere.'

'All right, but stay close by me,' Grisa said. 'In an emergency, I can port us out, but not when you're wandering all over the place.'

They went down the stairs, kicking up dust and dodging partly destroyed cobwebs. There wasn't any door to the tower, only bits of rotting wood strewn around the entrance. A vaguely visible path led them past the lake to the door Bartram had seen from above.

'The old Hamorth!' Grisa said disgusted. 'It has that same bird in the lintel as we saw in that nasty undead temple at Erpenstaun.'

Bartram looked at his sister. 'Would this be another one? A mountain-sized temple?' He thought of the four-armed statue and the aura of total despair it had exuded. Then he breathed in noisily, and put his hand to the door.

He jumped back as without a sound, it slit aside. Darkness and a smell of brimstone wafted out and for a second, Bartram hesitated.

Then he stepped across the threshold. A light on the wall awoke and he gasped as its reddish glow lit up the rough stone corridor.

'Darn,' he muttered. Then he grinned sheepishly. 'Magical lights.'

Grisa closed the door behind them, and the three walked into the mountain. 'We're going down,' she said softly. 'Would they've dug out this tunnel or is it natural?'

Bartram looked around. 'For all I know, they magicked it. This whole mountain doesn't look natural to me.'

Then Bryaun tackled him.

Bartram stumbled and fell into Grisa. Together, they went down at the same moment several arrows sped through the space they had just occupied.

'Daghuur!' Bartram snarled, as he came to his knees and fumbled for his sword. Then he stared as Bryaun, his face twisted in desperation, rolled on and bowled over several skeleton archers. With a shout, Bartram ran to his aid and the brittle daghuur became a sea of scorched bones.

Bryaun hacked around him, screaming wordlessly at the rolling skulls till Grisa pulled him away and held him close.

'It's all right,' she said. 'You got them. Darn it, mate, that was a brave thing!'

Gasping for breath, Bryaun cried into her shoulder.

Awkwardly, Bartram patted his back. 'Brilliant move! That can't have been in the book,' he said. 'You made it up yourself.'

Bryaun pulled away from the girl's grip and drew a dirty sleeve across his wet face. Then he spat in the dust. *Sorry; me darn nerves,* he wrote in a shaky hand. *Ever played village ball? Did once. Once. Much like this. Mother hysterics. Never again. Fight daghuur, great; Mother's tears, not so much.*

Bartram had heard of the game; some sort of free-for-all to get a ball from one spot to another several miles away. He shook his head; thin little Bryaun against hulking farm boys and apprentices out for blood? Those louts wouldn't play fair. The guy had guts for sure.

'Let's go,' he said.

Bryaun spat into his palms and grinned.

They followed the tunnel for some time without meeting anybody else.

Finally, they saw a bright light in the distance. They slowed to a tiptoed walk as they came to the end. Pressed flat against the walls of the corridor, they looked out.

'Gods,' Bartram said, and he felt his body grow cold with shock. 'The whole mountain is hollow.'

Before them was a cavern of immense proportions. A stone walkway about ten feet wide followed the walls to the left and the right, with stairs leading up and down to other walkways. The other side of the cavern was perhaps a mile away and the volcano's mouth was a tiny patch of sky over their heads.

Impossible, Bryaun wrote firmly. *This ain't natural.*

Bartram nodded. 'Those Hamorths must've been powerful to make a hollow mountain.'

Grisa touched his hand. 'Do you feel it?' she whispered, and Bartram saw she was deadly pale.

'Feel...?' Then he stiffened as his senses rebelled. Not only a feeling, but a smell, a sound, an off-color taste of something awful.

'Gods,' he said again, and he pressed his hands to his mouth.

Bryaun looked surprised at his reaction and he sniffed, then shrugged. *Sulfur,* he wrote. *Not nice, but not sickening.*

'It's not that,' Bartram said. 'You're no mana-user; this whole place is full of falmagic.'

They followed the walkway to the left, keeping close to the wall. There wasn't any railing and the bottom of the volcano was too far below them to see.

'Where the heck do we go?' Bartram said after a while.

'Down.' Grisa stared into the abyss. 'We can't possibly search the whole mountain; it'd take an army. I say let's try and see what's at the bottom and then go back to Grymaur.'

But Damion? Bryaun wrote. *Can't run away!*

'We're not,' Bartram said. 'We go back to fetch troops. With those hundred men, we're a lot stronger.'

Bryaun's face cleared. *Sorry, wasn't thinking.*

Bartram grinned. 'That's all right. I don't think a lot of the time.'

They walked on, cautiously creeping past every door opening they encountered. Every now and then they came to a crystal on a stone pedestal, emitting faint lines of shadow along the walls.

'That whole pattern looks like a cobweb,' Bartram said. 'I can't see it does anything.'

'Watch out!' Grisa said sharply. A party of blackrobes stepped from a doorway and pointed their staves at them.

Bryaun gestured over his shoulder and Bartram saw several more sorcerers behind them.

'A trap,' he said, strained. 'Do we fight?'

A purple beam just missed his ear and instinctively he ducked. 'Won't get the chance,' he shouted. 'Grisa!'

His sister drew an arm around his waist and grabbed Bryaun with the other. 'Hold me tight!' she said breathlessly and pulled them over the edge into the bottomless depths.

CHAPTER 18 – GRISA SHOWS HER MUSCLES

Grisa knew she could port anywhere. To Grymaur, even to that old tower outside; they were safe. Perfectly safe. So she screamed, but didn't panic as they fell. The air rushed past her, faster and faster. It tore at the bodies in her grip, but as Bartram had said, she was a strong girl and held them tight.

The walkways flashed past, but no beams followed them down. The blackrobes probably thought them dead already and wasted no more efforts on them. In her right grip, her brother hung quietly, arms around her waist, trusting his twin. On her other side, Bryaun suddenly moved, disrupting their balance.

Immediately, they began to spin. Round and round they went and Grisa lost all sense of up and down. *Don't pass out!* she thought and the thought brought a gush of ice-cold fear that cleared her mind. *Look around for a place to land! Any moment now...* She caught a glimpse of the bottom rushing up, and crowds of antlike figures milling around. *Not there!* Their speed was frightening; if she left it too late, they'd splatter. *A suitable spot...* She'd only one chance... *There!*

She ported.

The familiar strangeness of the Intermedium – cold, airless, a chaos of dimensions no human could understand. It wiped out all of them but their consciousnesses and that's what she had counted upon. Then they came back into their universe, bodies restored and motionless, on a small ledge a hundred feet over the floor.

Bump.

Then she fainted.

When she opened her eyes again, she saw the faces of the boys hovering over her, pale and something else... Awed.

'You're all right?' Bartram said, holding her. She could only nod and then he hugged her. 'Gods' Love, that was the craziest,' he said. 'How did you do that? It wasn't Fantus, was it? No, I'd have known that. It was you.'

Bryaun sat staring at her, his thin face drawn and strangely grownup. Then he got his tablet. *Saw my fear,* he wrote. *Always fought fear, always it came back. Now it's gone. Thank you.*

Impulsively, Grisa grabbed his arm. 'I wasn't sure,' she said, near to tears. 'I wasn't sure it would work. I thought my porting would break our speed; I always come out standing still, but I wasn't sure. If it hadn't...' She suddenly felt cold and small, and very stupid. 'I should've ported home; that would have been safe.'

'But now we're at the bottom,' Bartram said reasonably. 'If you'd brought us home, we wouldn't be.'

True, Bryaun wrote. *Lots going on below us. Not-looking-good things.*

Grisa stifled a sob and came to her knees. 'Let me see.' She crept to the edge and looked down. Rows and rows of barn-like structures made of unprepared wood, each with a stout fence and a tall gate. 'Beastmen!' she said, fighting against a wave of revulsion. 'Hundreds of them.'

'It's an army base,' Bartram said. 'We've been watching them. There's a portal where you can see them come and go. Those monsters crawling all over Vavaun must come from here.'

Bust it up! Bryaun wrote.

'How?' Bartram looked at Grisa, but she shook her head.

'We can't go near those portals. Too dangerous, all in the open. Besides, they must have spare taps on hand.'

Then bust up the mountain.

Both twins gaped at Bryaun.

'What do you mean?' Grisa said. 'It would be the solution, but it's a bleeping *mountain*, mate.'

What's holding it up? Bryaun gestured at the immense emptiness over their heads. *Too big, too much nothing. Something keeps it from falling down. Spell?*

'A spell?' Bartram said skeptically. 'Where are the ten thousand mages to keep it going?'

A spell to maintain spells? the boy wrote quickly.

'Does something like that exist?' Grisa said.

Her brother shrugged. 'I'm a fighter, not a mage.'

Those crystals? Bryaun persisted. *Like vaulted roof castle.*

Grisa looked at the dark cobwebby pattern running all over the walls. They did look like the curved beams carrying the high roof of Burg Grymaur's great hall.

'Would that be a spell?' She turned around. 'There's one of them here,' she said, gesturing at the crystal on its pedestal against the wall behind them.

It was big, about the length of her lower arm, of some pinkish translucency cut into a pattern that made her dizzy as she tried to make sense of it. Impulsively, she sent the tiniest bit of her mana into the crystal, as she would've done with a mana tap. The crystal jumped and sparked like mad, and for a moment, the lines it emitted on the wall wavered. Dust fell and little cracks appeared in the stone. Somewhere below them, an alarm went off, howling its urgency over the hubbub of voices below.

'Uh-oh,' Grisa said. 'We better get out, before someone comes looking.'

'There's an empty barn over there. Can you make that?' Bartram said.

Grisa looked past his pointing finger. 'Can do,' she said. Seconds later, they stood in the shadows of the wooden building.

'Now what?' Bartram said. 'We can't just walk out of here among the beastmen.'

'Yes, we can,' Grisa said triumphantly, pointing at a heap of discarded black robes. 'Old Hamorth smocks.' She wrinkled her nose. 'Probably used for mucking out those stables. Gods, those pigs smell.' Her skin crawled as she donned the long smock. Bryaun with the hood deep over his eyes seemed almost to disappear within the black folds. *I must look the same,* she thought. *Like those bliddy falmages outside. That's good.*

Bartram tried to pull the hem of his smock lower down, but it came to just below the knees, leaving his leather boots exposed. Then he shrugged and walked to the door.

Grisa followed him outside and looked around. Up close, the mountain's floor was covered with a thin layer of black dust that swirled around their ankles as they walked. The air was heavy with the smell of sweaty beastmen and their dung, worse than even the pigsty at Kramm. She pointed to the nearest wall. 'Let's follow that. See if there are more crystals.'

Hunched, imitating the slouching pace of the real Hamorthmen around them, they walked past several more barns, each housing some ten pigmen.

The nearness of so many beastmen was terrifying, and Grisa fought down the urge to run. She forced her mind to think of something else and began reciting the coordinates she had collected. The exercise soothed her and faster than she thought, they'd reached the mountain wall.

Bryaun inspected the nearest crystal. *Where would it get its power?* he wrote.

'If it works like a portal tap,' Grisa said, 'there must be a central point that sends out the antimana. This crystal would catch the power and send it on to the taps higher up the wall.'

Deep in thought, she followed the wall. Then, suddenly, a tall blackrobed figure barred their way.

'What are you doing?' a female voice said suspiciously.

'Inspecting,' Grisa said curtly. 'There's been a disturbance and now we must check every one of these.'

'You don't look like a mech,' the Hamorth said.

Grisa lifted a hand and let some flames leak from her fingers. 'I said inspecting. Are you doubting me?'

'No,' the woman said, suddenly nervous. 'I was just curious.'

'Do it on your own time; we're busy.' Grisa turned back to the crystal, while the woman walked away quickly.

'You sounded perfect,' Bartram said. 'Like one of those she-dog traitors at the kerran.'

Grisa made a face. 'Bitching is easy; it could become a habit.'

'Let's not stay here. Just in case, you know.'

'Nervous?' she said.

'Yes.'

'Me too.' Grisa grinned at the boys and pointed in the distance. 'Is that another four-armed statue?'

As they came near, Bartram sneezed. 'It gives off power,' he said. 'Don't touch it!'

Bryaun stepped back and hid his hands inside his sleeves. He shook his head emphatically and Bartram gripped his shoulder for a moment.

'Sorry, didn't want to snap at you. It's those idols, they give me the creeps.'

'This one is alive.' Grisa stared at the statue. It was life-size, made of some dark material that seemed to blot out the light around it. From its pedestal, a line of darkness ran across the floor to some place further away.

'Don't step on it,' she said, staring it. 'That must be antimana.'

Bartram shivered. 'I'm glad we don't have a mana pool in our heads, like mages do. I'd feel like a walking bomb.'

Why? Bryaun wrote.

'Mana and antimana can't exist together,' Grisa said. 'When they touch – boom!'

You use mana; can you boom! this mountain? Bryaun wrote.

Grisa blinked. 'Me?' she said. 'But...' Her conscious mind went blank as she thought. 'It would be very dangerous,' she said finally. 'But I think it could be done. As a porter, I channel mana all the time. This wouldn't be much different; I could overload the idol with mana – I'd only channel it, so I could handle quite a lot. The idol would blow up and if I'm right, kill that part of the cobweb connected to it. Would that be enough to collapse the mountain? It should leave us a little time to port away. Let's get inside that shack; I need to think.'

They hurried into a small wooden two-room hut filled with spare planks and building material.

'I'm not sure one small idol would be enough,' Grisa said. 'I...' She stopped at the sound of voices in the next room.

'Why?' a woman's voice said hoarsely. 'Why do you do all this? You were my friend.'

'I never was,' a second, girlish voice said. She sounded amused.

'That's Mauvine!' Bartram whispered. 'But who's the other?'

Grisa drew her daggers and fire ran from her fingers to the sharp blades. 'Uwella,' she said harshly. She listened for a moment to the false girl's boasting and then stepped into the next room. Inside was a blonde woman in a black robe, her hand playing with the key ring on her belt as she lounged against a cage just large enough for a medium-sized dog. Inside crouched Uwella.

Grisa was icy calm. 'Behold the Gray Order's wrath!' she said, lifting her crossed, burning daggers.

The tall blonde turned around, her pretty face blank. 'Who're you?' Then horror dawned with recognition. 'Grisa! Don't! I can make you rich! Powerful! I...'

Grisa raised her daggers. 'You're a traitor and a murderer.' With a cry of desperation, Mauvine jumped, hitting her on the shoulder. Grisa twisted around and fell, dropping her daggers.

'Stop her!' she cried, as Mauvine ran for the door. Bartram moved, but Bryaun was quicker. He sprang, hitting the girl in the small of the back. Mauvine screamed as she pitched forward and crashed to the rocky floor.

Grisa dove on top of her, slamming her fist into the side of Mauvine's face. Again, the blonde girl screamed and for a moment, the two wrestled.

'Knife,' Grisa panted, and Bartram kicked one of the blades her way. His sister grabbed it.

'You're finished, traitorous bitch!' she said and stuck the knife deep into Mauvine's throat. The blonde girl thrashed while the blood ran down her chest. Then her eyes glazed over and she went limp.

'What's going on here?' a harsh voice said from outside and a male Dar'khamorth stepped into the other room.

Grisa jumped to her feet and went to intercept him. 'A private matter,' she said and her voice was cold as a winter's blizzard. 'None of your business, so don't ask any more.'

The man looked from her bloodied knife to the still form of Mauvine and a slow smile spread over his face. 'I wouldn't dream of interfering, sister,' he said dryly. 'It seems the matter is settled anyway. May She be with you in your endeavors.' With a jerky bow, he turned and departed.

Grisa barely noticed him going. She stooped and unhooked the small key ring from the dead girl's belt and ran to the cage. There was only one key. It turned easily in the lock and opened the silver cage door. Grisa kneeled down and stretched out her hands.

'Uwella, what have they done to you?'

Uwella looked nothing like the trim grand duchess. Her hair was in a tangle, her robe in tatters, her face bruised and dirty as if she'd been in a brawl.

'A beastman,' she said painfully. 'Where by all Greos' Demons do you three spring from?'

'Through the front door,' Grisa said, and tears ran down her face as she helped Uwella to her feet. 'Like any good visitors. We came looking for you and Damion.'

Uwella's eyes flashed. 'Damion. Went for him. Flew inside as a crow. Some guy winged me, and I ended up here. Listen, they've got him! They've got Damion! In a cage. I can't reach him; can't fly with this arm.'

'Where is he?' Bartram said.

'In a cage,' Uwella repeated, trembling with rage. 'A cruel hanging cage. He's hurt; can't move!'

'Where is that cage?' Grisa said.

'Close by,' Uwella said. 'To the left, where the fires are. They're going to sacrifice him!'

'Not if we can help it,' Grisa said firmly. 'Can you walk?'

Uwella nodded. 'Of course; just give me a moment.' She closed her eyes and some of the worst bruises faded. Then she smiled grimly. 'Can't heal my arm; I'm as weak as a newborn foal. But I can walk.'

'Leave it all to us,' Grisa said. 'We have a plan.'

'*We* have?' Bartram said, but Grisa was already in the next room.

She remembered having seen fires; she'd not paid them much attention, but she knew where they were.

'Over there,' she said to the others. 'Let's act as a prisoner's escort. That should get us close to the fires.'

They formed up around Uwella and in the slow tempo characteristic of the Dar'khamorth, they marched to their goal.

The fires were a circle of large iron braziers, spreading light and heat to a chanting crowd of blackrobes. At the other end of the circle was a four-armed idol, much larger than the one against the wall. From its pedestal, many lines of darkness led into the distance. The statue was full of power; a malignance that was slumbering now, but could awaken any moment.

'That's the one,' Grisa whispered. 'She's alive; I'm sure it's her power that keeps the mountain up.'

A group of blackrobes was chanting, on their knees to the idol. A stocky man stood facing the goddess, with his arms wide. He seemed to be leading whatever ceremony they held.

'That's Syvvan,' Bartram grunted. 'Doing his foul work.'

Over their heads, just out of reach of the idol's two uppermost arms, hung a cage from a heavy beam. In it was a body, one arm hanging out between the bars.

'I know,' Grisa said, absently. As she looked up, she had never been more aware than now. Damion, Syvvan, Uwella's harsh breathing, the crackling of the fires, she knew it all and disregarded them. She studied the cage, the chain that held it, and finally nodded. 'Can be done. Let's go to the first walkway; I need a slightly more secure place than this.'

They hurried to the nearest stairs.

'That's far enough,' Grisa said. 'Now I'd like a bit of luck. Pray to Fantus for me, Bartram. Ask his aid, I won't have time for it.'

Her brother nodded.

What will you do? Bryaun wrote.

'A trick,' Grisa said, grinning tersely. 'Wait and see.' Then she ported away.

She landed on top of the cage, sending it swinging. Below, Syvvan broke off his singing and shouted something, but she didn't listen. She reached down and sought with her fingertips for Damion's body. She felt only air, and lowered herself till she hung over the side, head down, clinging with one hand to the rusty chain, while reaching with the other inside the cage. She felt a shoulder and got a good grip on the fabric of the tunic. Then she ported them both back to the walkway.

'There,' she said, panting. 'They didn't dare to shoot me for fear of killing Damion. They won't be so afraid now. Cover me, folks.' Several blackrobes had seen what happened and hurried to the stairs.

Uwella grunted. 'Damnation, I must leave it to you, mates.'

'Our pleasure,' Bartram said. He weighed one of the pebbles he carried since that cave at Erpenstaun and threw it. The first blackrobe exploded into fire and the others hesitated.

Grisa touched the statue with her mind. She felt the tiny bit of the goddess inside the stone, barely awake. She ignored it; that wasn't what she sought. There must be something else, something that channeled all the antimana, but what? Then she touched a small, many-legged thing in the heart of the idol. It squirmed and squiggled under her thought. Shadows streamed through it, useless to her, but full of foul power. She reached through the thin membrane between their universe and the Intermedium around it. Mana raced through her into the twisting thingy, that crackled and flashed as the incompatible powers met. She pulled all stops and the mana poured down in a torrent of blue. Everywhere, sirens began to scream, instantly creating panic on the mountain floor. Noiselessly, the thingy inside the idol blew, and now the bit of Her flashed into full awareness of the danger.

'NOOOO!'

The cry of godly rage hit Grisa like a pole-ax, and for a moment, the mana flow faltered. Then she felt Uwella's hand on her shoulder and a thin trickle of kiya helped her recover. Quickly, the mana flow resumed, more than even the false goddess' bit of personality could handle. The dark lines running from the idol's feet smoked and sparked, the cobweb across the mountain's inside curled and disappeared. Everywhere, stone creaked and shrieked as the rocky mountain walls sought for support that was no longer there. The wail of the sirens became deafening over the screaming voices.

With a hollow boom, the idol exploded. From high overhead, castle-sized chunks of rock came crashing down on the scurrying Hamorths below. As she watched the destruction, Grisa saw Syvvan standing at the foot of the stairs, looking around wildly as if he searched for a way out. Then a chunk of the wall, with a pedestaled crystal still attached, crunched him into the mountain floor. The walkway under Grisa's feet shuddered and moved like an awakening snake.

No more; she thought. *We're done here...* She wheeled around to the others. 'Hold me, we're getting out!' she screamed. Bartram and Bryaun obeyed blindly. Uwella clutched Damion in her good arm. Grisa grabbed the kjavoda's shoulder and as the mountain crashed down, ported them all home.

CHAPTER 19 – IT'S DONE

'You don't say,' Damion said for the umpteenth time. He lay propped up in bed, his upper torso swathed in bandages. The healer's art had reduced the damage done by the beam that shot him from the air, and now the muscles needed rest to heal properly. At his side lay Uwella, her arm in a sling, one eye swollen shut and purpling alarmingly, resting her head against her love's good side.

'The mountain's gone,' Bartram said. 'Rhydd confirmed it.' The boy grinned broadly. 'His gardians were holed up close by and they witnessed it coming down. Must have been spectacular.' He coughed. 'Not as spectacular as it was on the inside, of course.'

'You're all stark, raving mad.' Damion had said that before, but for once in his life, he was at a loss for words.

'I know,' Grisa said hoarsely. 'It all just happened.' She shook her head. 'I mustn't think too much. Remembering that jump makes me want to sit and bawl.'

Damion grabbed her hand. 'That's the reaction. You were incredibly brave and now comes the backlash. Bawl if you need to. Uwella and I owe you three our lives and we'll never forget that.'

'Tell our father,' Bartram said, embarrassed.

Damion nodded. 'Better still; you three write a report and I'll forward a copy to the marshal and to Bryaun's father, if he wants me to.'

Do, as long as I'm not home to hear my mother scream, Bryaun wrote. *Those sirens in the mountain were bad enough.* His big grin was back, but he looked relaxed. Before, he'd appeared strained when he mentioned his mother; now he just laughed.

'You got Syvvan,' Damion said. 'That's one traitor less in the world.'

'Deldor was with him,' Bartram said, rubbing his hands. 'The pieces from their own stupid idol ripped him to shreds as it exploded.'

'Don't forget Mauvine,' Uwella said. 'Grisa did her in so nicely.' Her battered face looked at once vengeful and unhappy. 'All those years she'd lied to me, laughed behind my back, and ridiculed me in secret. I never knew her.'

'She was a loser,' Grisa said. 'She needed you to be someone herself and she hated you for her own emptiness. Forget her. We all love you.'

'Madly,' Damion said. 'And you're beautiful, my love.'

Uwella rubbed her head against his shoulder. 'So are you.'

Damion couldn't turn; therefore he kissed his fingertips and pressed them to her face. 'Wait till I'm up and about again,' he promised.

'Not while we are here,' Grisa said firmly. 'Keep it discreet, stallion.'

Damion laughed. 'If I must.' Then he sighed and looked tired. 'So it is done?'

Uwella nodded. 'Rhydd was searching for the place those beastmen came from. He was close, too. Now, with both him and Ghyll's guards mopping up all beastmen in the country, we should see Vavaun free of the late Syvvan's creatures soon.'

She chuckled. 'And the fellow behind Syvvan, that white-haired old man we saw chewing out the traitor in the chapel? Well, he is also dead. The Rhidaunan lieutenant told me.' She frowned. 'When I saw him in the chapel, I was sure I had met him before, but I couldn't remember where. Then I heard Opit, and I knew. He was the Jaddar, the mightiest man in Opit after King Mo, head of the Jaddara clan and rich enough to buy Vavaun with his pocket money. Somehow he went over to the Dar'khamorth and became a big shot, going by the silly code name of M. We weren't his only victims; he was the one who bred the hookfeather Grisa killed and the ones that attacked Olle in Orodaun.' She grimaced. 'A double traitor he was, but he got his deserts. It seems he was the grandfather of one of Ghyll's other squires, and the lad killed him with his own hands. Opitian honor requires such things.'

'Hurray for Opit.' A spasm of pain shot through Damion's chest and he winced. 'Victory on all sides, then.'

'You should sleep,' Grisa said quickly. She rose from the bed. 'We'll leave you two alone, before those big nurses come to kick us out.'

'Let's go write that report,' Bartram said. 'The sooner that's done the better.'

Bryaun sighed. *Great*, he wrote. Then he grinned.

'You're worried,' Uwella said when the three youngsters had gone.

'Yes.' Damion tried to shrug, but he couldn't. 'I want to believe it's over, but I dare not.'

'Sleep,' Uwella said, touching his cheek with her fingers. 'Tomorrow you'll believe it. We got our country back. Now we can rebuild and make it a nation to be proud of.'

'For our homeland! For Vavaun!' Damion said softly.

LIST OF NAMES

AnMarevale, Kaati, grandmaster-battlebard; later Duchess Sillaine
Archodea, the Drynnath of the Gray Order, High Priestess of Arikal
Arnstaun, Knight; a Vavauner lord.
Beredt, a merchant of Grymaur; former Gry retainer
Costare, seneschal of Burg Grymaur
Curly, Gray wikke infiltrator; Dar'khamorth agent
DeAsharte, Caerch, Princess of Asharte; mother of Damion
DeAsharte, Cymrian, Duke of Asharte; grandfather Damion
DeAsharte, Reginaul (D); Valvodjar of Asharte; uncle Damion
DeAsharte-Luyon, Damion, hereditary prince of Asharte; beastmaster
DeGrathain, Gillem Baron; Lord Steward, Royal Palace Rhidauna
DeGry, Gewella, triplet sister Uwella
DeGry, Rhydd, triplet brother Uwella; Gardian in Kerran Adalien
DeGry, Uwella; Valvodjara of Vavaun
DeGry, Venric, Valvode of Vavaun, father of Uwella and her siblings
DeKramm, Bartram, aide to Damion, twin brother to Grisa
DeKramm, Grisa; portal wikke, twin sister to Bartram
DeKramm, Radon; Baron of Kramm, Marshal of Vavaun
DeLamon, Aiwan Baron, father of Bryaun
DeLamon, Bryaun; Damion's clerk
DeLamon, Lessaun (D), father superior of the temple of Fantus
Deldor, Gray wikke infiltrator; Dar'khamorth agent
DeMannau, Margha (D), senior neophyte Dar'khamorth
Druull, Isamber; High Priest of Mainal
Erpenstaun, Othaun, Lord of, an Asharte vassal
Exhumyst, the; leader of the Dar'khamorth
Gard-Galleth, Bryadd Duke, Marshal of Rhidauna
Garumgav, Fedar; Kasar of the Garumgav, Great Kasar; Rockath.
Hardingraud, Ghyllander III Halban (Ghyll); King of Rhidauna
Jupold; a horse coper from Grymaur; former Gry retainer
Karmandros, Archmage; Head of the Convocation of Magi
Kedraun, Knight and Constable of Asharte
Kedraun, Mistress, his wife; housekeeper of Asharte
Kyssander, Garender Duke; chancellor of Rhidauna
Levianne, a barmaid from Grymaur
Leviss, Dennator; High Priest of Dragos
Lobarth, a Kramm soldier
Lusindral, Bernabo, adept of Wimaun; firemage
Luyon, Sterman, 'Ironbiter', lieutenant of the Guard; father of Damion
Mannar, Captain, commander of the Kramm garrison
Mauvine, Gray wikke infiltrator; Dar'khamorth agent

Neferestan, Ambiaunt, undead Archmage of Sterrevank
Nikkelsen, Torril Nikkel, Crown Prince of the Nhael, Prince of Stit
Orsille, Gray wikke infiltrator; Dar'khamorth agent
Ozandyas (D), Archpriest of the Hamorth; High Ordealmaster; undead
Querfero, Cianabetta Marchesa, first attendant to Queen Kerianna
Salerde-Tamm, Crua, High Priestess of Iodraune
Sarn, Tennail; high priest of Eresto
She, the Anti-Goddess, ZA from the Intermedium
Sillaine, Olle, Duke; Count of Orodaun, King Ghyll's foster brother
Syvvan, Gray wikke infiltrator; Dar'khamorth agent
Taindragon, High Magus of the Red Order
Tinnurad, Olle (see: Maubyn)
Un-Balhamber, Kerianna; Queen of Rhidauna, Princess of Opit
Un-Balhamber, Mojalman VIII, King of Opit
Verell, Father; senior priest of Eresto's high temple

LIST OF GODS

White Order
Dragos, God of Justice, Wisdom and Government
Illiaune, Goddess of Knowledge and Education
Kathauna, Goddess of Healing
Tillia Fategoddess, Goddess of Fate and Charity

Red Order
Mainal, God of War
Wimaun, God of Elemental Fire
Fantus, God of Raw Fire and Smithing
Klinkilla, Goddess of the Underclass, Mother of Thieves

Blue Order
Tartraun, God of the Sky
Zoander, God of the Sea
Naulda, Goddess of Rivers and Springs

Green Order
Medesta, Goddess of Growth
Throm, God of Nature
Aphasta, Goddess of Agriculture
Iodraune, Goddess of Animals

Magenta Order
Uthelno, God of Music, Art and Architecture
Mibras, God of Illusion, Brain Arts and Dreams
Yathillia, Goddess of Love and Beauty

Purple Order
Greos, God of the Underworld
Millibaune, Goddess of Revenge
Odorn, Master of Demons

Orange Order
Eresto, God of Trade and Money
Bonthar, God of Crafts
Hathnorm, God of Travelers and Messengers
Tallas, God of Magimechnica

Gray Order
Arikal, God of True Chaos and Renewal

www.ingramcontent.com/pod-product-compliance
Lightning Source LLC
Chambersburg PA
CBHW071425260626
47170CB00008B/2598